D0383169

ARTEMIS FOWL

FOWL

THE ETERNITY CODE

THE GRAPHIC NOVEL

Adapted by **Michael Moreci**
Art by **Stephen Gilpin**

Los Angeles   New York

First Hardcover Edition, June 2022
First Paperback Edition, June 2022

10 9 8 7 6 5 4 3 2 1

FAC-038091-22112
Printed in the United States of America

This book is set in Colleen Doran/Fontspring; DIN Next LT Pro, ITC Novarese Pro,
Neutraface Condensed/Monotype

Designed by Stephen Gilpin and Tyler Nevins

Library of Congress Cataloging-in-Publication Data

Names: Moreci, Michael, adapter. • Gilpin, Stephen, artist. • Colfer, Eoin.
Artemis Fowl.
Title: Artemis Fowl, the eternity code: the graphic novel / adapted by
Michael Moreci ; art by Stephen Gilpin.
Other titles: Eternity code
Description: Los Angeles : Disney-Hyperion, 2022. • Series: Artemis Fowl ;
3 • Audience: Ages 8–12 • Audience: Grades 4–6 • Summary:
Twelve-year-old criminal mastermind Artemis Fowl's only hope of saving
his loyal bodyguard, Butler, is to employ fairy magic and contact his
old rival, Captain Holly Short, to help him pull off the most brilliant
criminal feat of his career.
Identifiers: LCCN 2020037500 (print) • LCCN 2020037501 (ebook)
ISBN 9781368065085 (hardcover) • ISBN 9781368065313 (paperback)
ISBN 9781368065368 (ebook)
Subjects: LCSH: Graphic novels. • CYAC: Graphic novels. • Fairies—Fiction.
• Magic—Fiction. • Criminals—Fiction.
Classification: LCC PZ7.7.M658 Art 2022 (print) • LCC PZ7.7.M658 (ebook)
• DDC 741.5/973—dc23
LC record available at https://lccn.loc.gov/2020037500
LC ebook record available at https://lccn.loc.gov/2020037501

Reinforced binding
Visit www.DisneyBooks.com

To my sons, little criminal geniuses
in their own right
—M.M.

For Geoff: thanks for always being
my steadfast friend
—S.G.

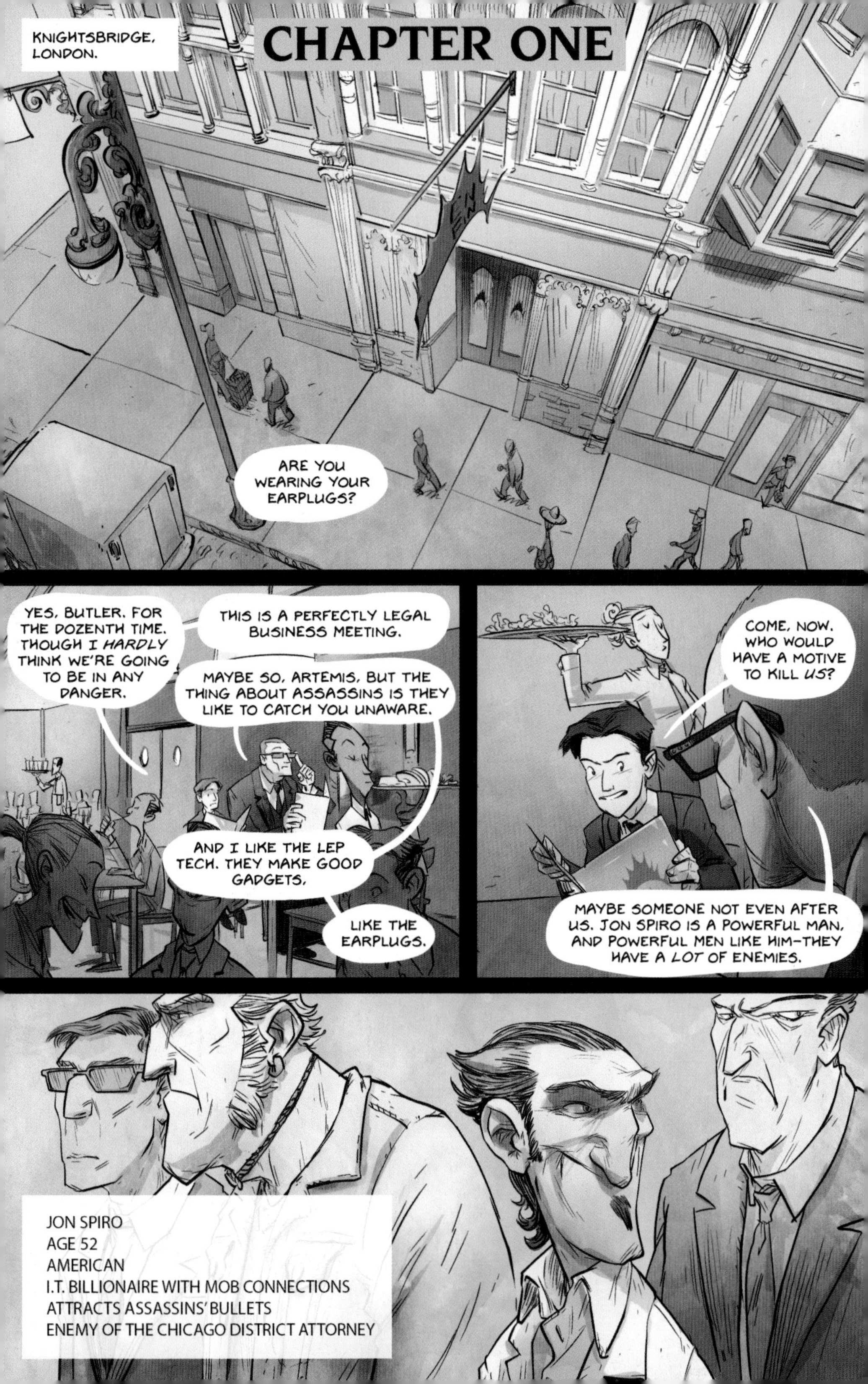
KNIGHTSBRIDGE, LONDON.
CHAPTER ONE
ARE YOU WEARING YOUR EARPLUGS?
YES, BUTLER. FOR THE DOZENTH TIME. THOUGH I HARDLY THINK WE'RE GOING TO BE IN ANY DANGER.
THIS IS A PERFECTLY LEGAL BUSINESS MEETING.
MAYBE SO, ARTEMIS, BUT THE THING ABOUT ASSASSINS IS THEY LIKE TO CATCH YOU UNAWARE.
AND I LIKE THE LEP TECH. THEY MAKE GOOD GADGETS.
LIKE THE EARPLUGS.
COME, NOW. WHO WOULD HAVE A MOTIVE TO KILL US?
MAYBE SOMEONE NOT EVEN AFTER US. JON SPIRO IS A POWERFUL MAN, AND POWERFUL MEN LIKE HIM—THEY HAVE A LOT OF ENEMIES.
JON SPIRO
AGE 52
AMERICAN
I.T. BILLIONAIRE WITH MOB CONNECTIONS
ATTRACTS ASSASSINS' BULLETS
ENEMY OF THE CHICAGO DISTRICT ATTORNEY

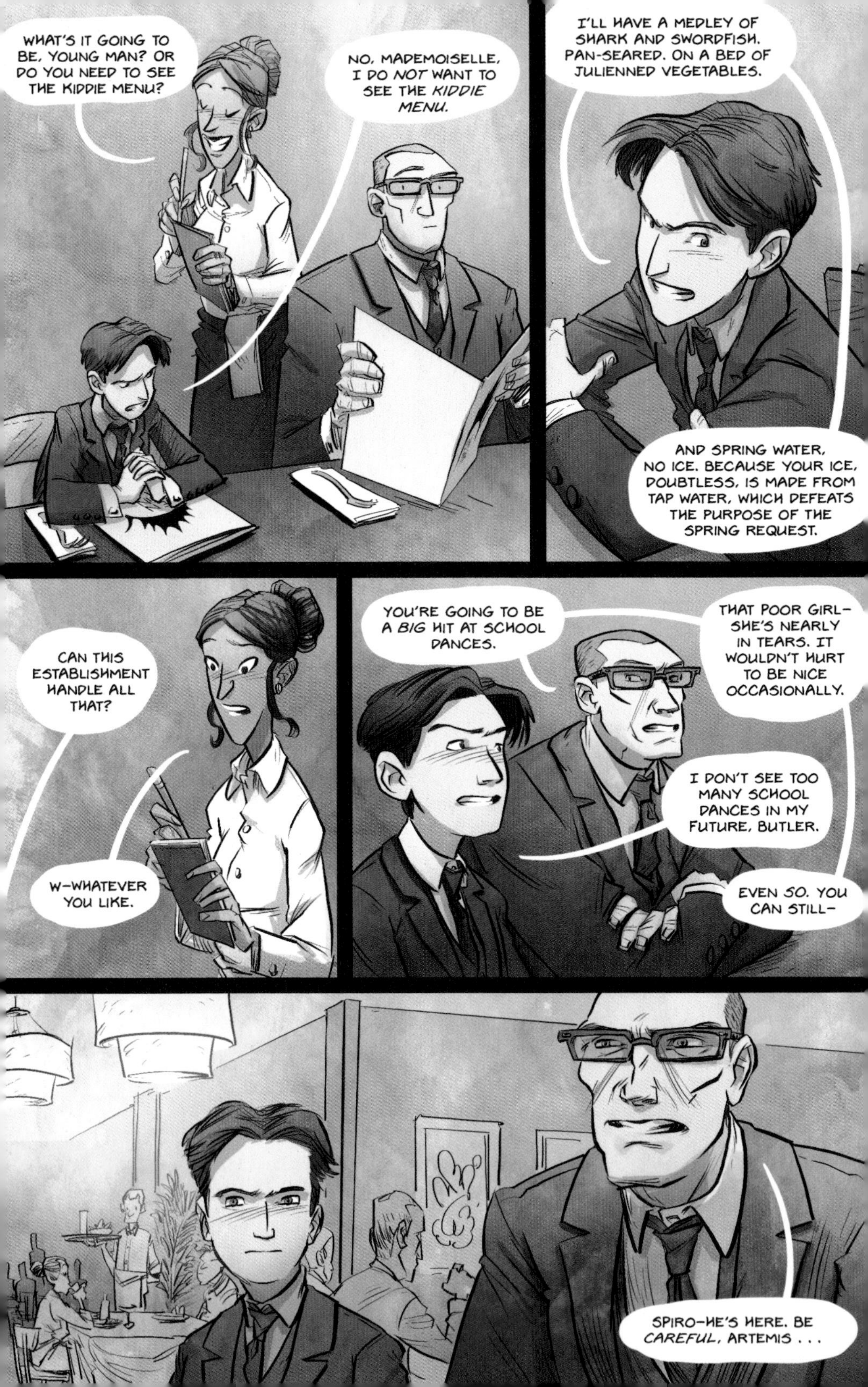
WHAT'S IT GOING TO BE, YOUNG MAN? OR DO YOU NEED TO SEE THE KIDDIE MENU?
NO, MADEMOISELLE, I DO *NOT* WANT TO SEE THE *KIDDIE MENU*.
I'LL HAVE A MEDLEY OF SHARK AND SWORDFISH. PAN-SEARED. ON A BED OF JULIENNED VEGETABLES.
AND SPRING WATER, NO ICE. BECAUSE YOUR ICE, DOUBTLESS, IS MADE FROM TAP WATER, WHICH DEFEATS THE PURPOSE OF THE SPRING REQUEST.
CAN THIS ESTABLISHMENT HANDLE ALL THAT?
W-WHATEVER YOU LIKE.
YOU'RE GOING TO BE A *BIG* HIT AT SCHOOL DANCES.
THAT POOR GIRL-SHE'S NEARLY IN TEARS. IT WOULDN'T HURT TO BE NICE OCCASIONALLY.
I DON'T SEE TOO MANY SCHOOL DANCES IN MY FUTURE, BUTLER.
EVEN SO. YOU CAN STILL-
SPIRO-HE'S HERE. BE *CAREFUL*, ARTEMIS . . .

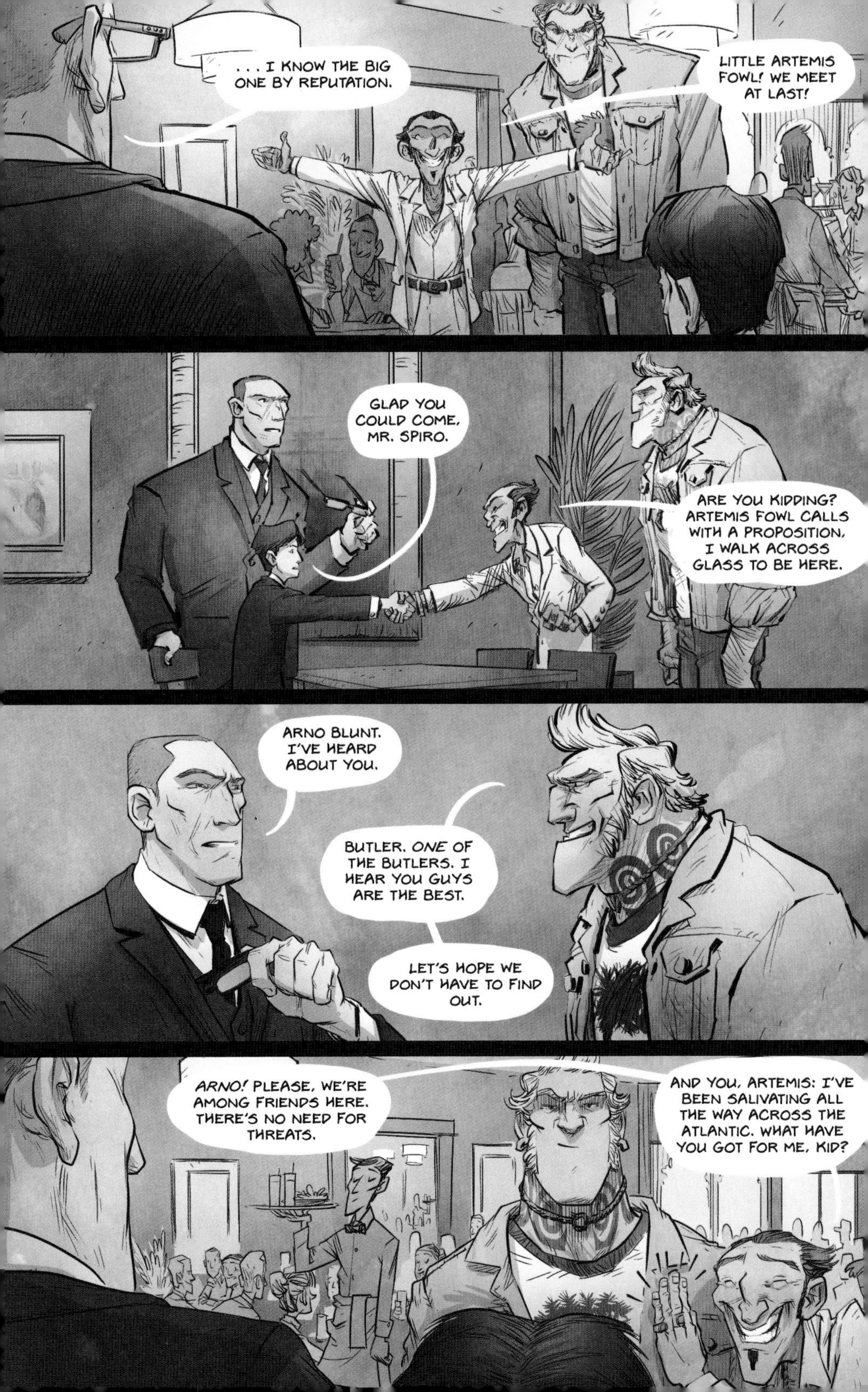
. . . I KNOW THE BIG ONE BY REPUTATION.
LITTLE ARTEMIS FOWL! WE MEET AT LAST!
GLAD YOU COULD COME, MR. SPIRO.
ARE YOU KIDDING? ARTEMIS FOWL CALLS WITH A PROPOSITION, I WALK ACROSS GLASS TO BE HERE.
ARNO BLUNT. I'VE HEARD ABOUT YOU.
BUTLER. *ONE* OF THE BUTLERS. I HEAR YOU GUYS ARE THE BEST.
LET'S HOPE WE DON'T HAVE TO FIND OUT.
ARNO! PLEASE, WE'RE AMONG FRIENDS HERE. THERE'S NO NEED FOR THREATS.
AND YOU, ARTEMIS: I'VE BEEN SALIVATING ALL THE WAY ACROSS THE ATLANTIC. WHAT HAVE YOU GOT FOR ME, KID?

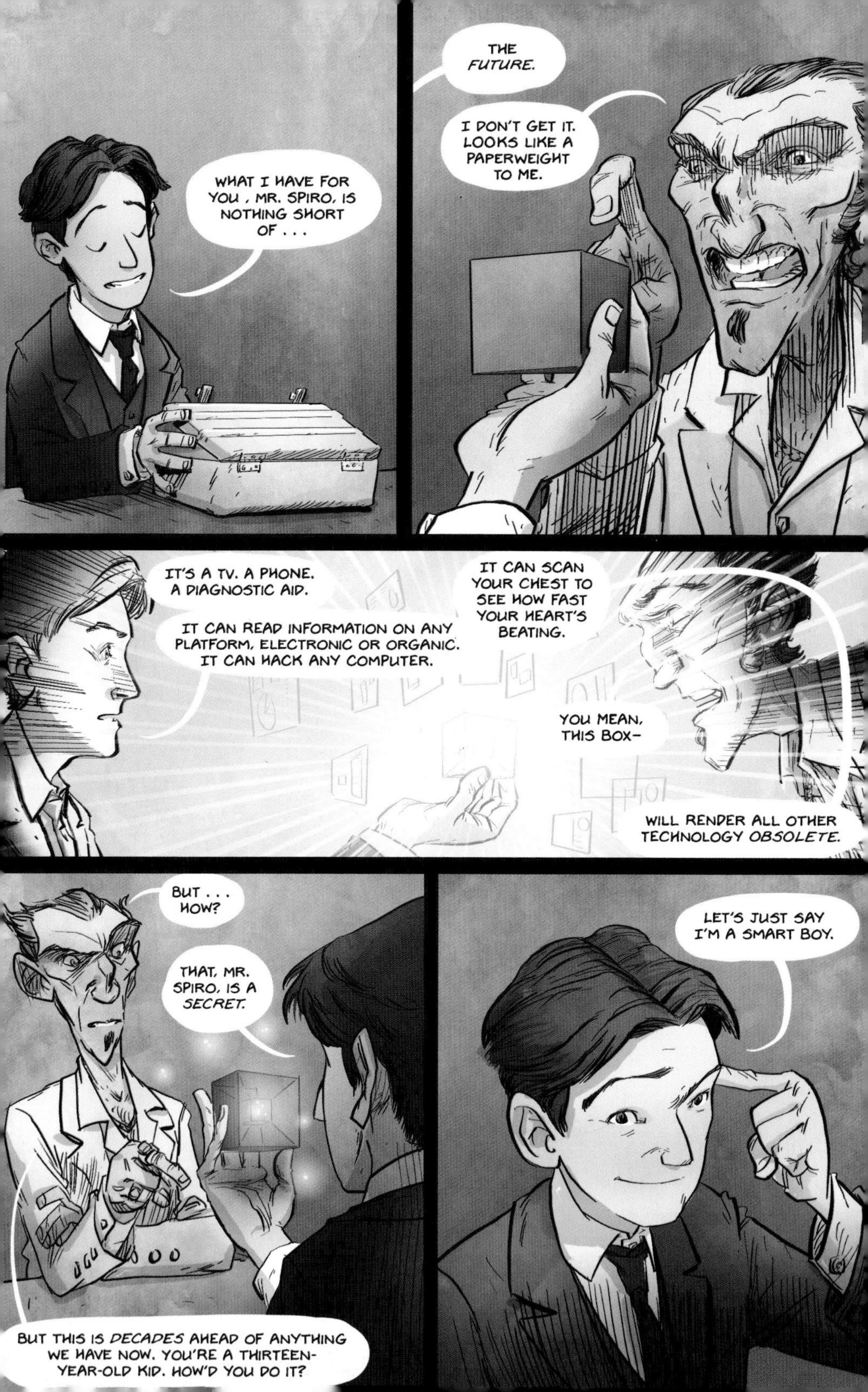
WHAT I HAVE FOR YOU , MR. SPIRO, IS NOTHING SHORT OF . . .
THE *FUTURE.*
I DON'T GET IT. LOOKS LIKE A PAPERWEIGHT TO ME.
IT'S A TV. A PHONE. A DIAGNOSTIC AID.
IT CAN READ INFORMATION ON ANY PLATFORM, ELECTRONIC OR ORGANIC. IT CAN HACK ANY COMPUTER.
IT CAN SCAN YOUR CHEST TO SEE HOW FAST YOUR HEART'S BEATING.
YOU MEAN, THIS BOX–
WILL RENDER ALL OTHER TECHNOLOGY *OBSOLETE.*
BUT . . . HOW?
THAT, MR. SPIRO, IS A *SECRET.*
BUT THIS IS *DECADES* AHEAD OF ANYTHING WE HAVE NOW. YOU'RE A THIRTEEN-YEAR-OLD KID. HOW'D YOU DO IT?
LET'S JUST SAY I'M A SMART BOY.

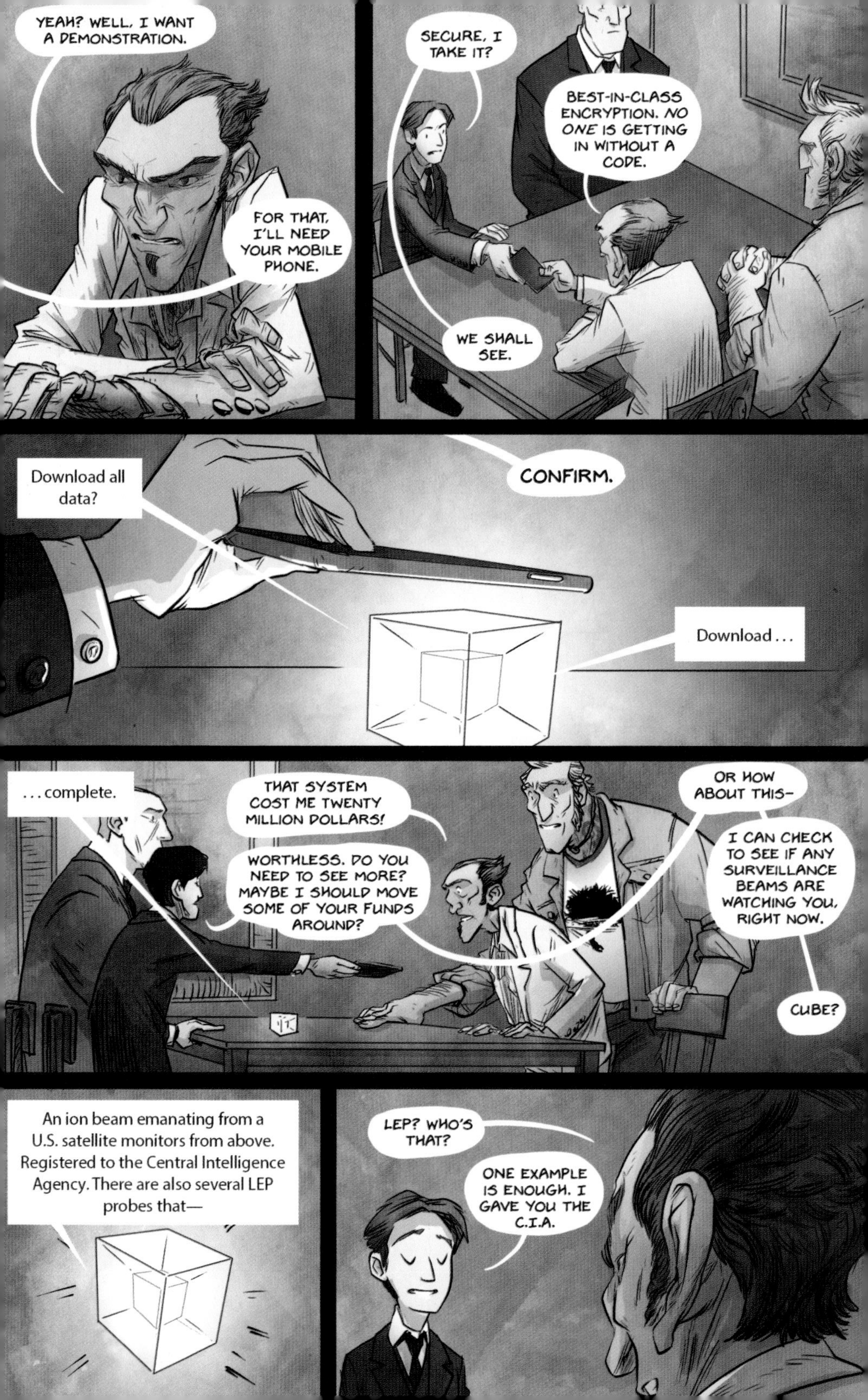
YEAH? WELL, I WANT A DEMONSTRATION.
FOR THAT, I'LL NEED YOUR MOBILE PHONE.
SECURE, I TAKE IT?
BEST-IN-CLASS ENCRYPTION. NO ONE IS GETTING IN WITHOUT A CODE.
WE SHALL SEE.
Download all data?
CONFIRM.
Download . . .
. . . complete.
THAT SYSTEM COST ME TWENTY MILLION DOLLARS!
WORTHLESS. DO YOU NEED TO SEE MORE? MAYBE I SHOULD MOVE SOME OF YOUR FUNDS AROUND?
OR HOW ABOUT THIS–
I CAN CHECK TO SEE IF ANY SURVEILLANCE BEAMS ARE WATCHING YOU, RIGHT NOW.
CUBE?
An ion beam emanating from a U.S. satellite monitors from above. Registered to the Central Intelligence Agency. There are also several LEP probes that—
LEP? WHO'S THAT?
ONE EXAMPLE IS ENOUGH. I GAVE YOU THE C.I.A.

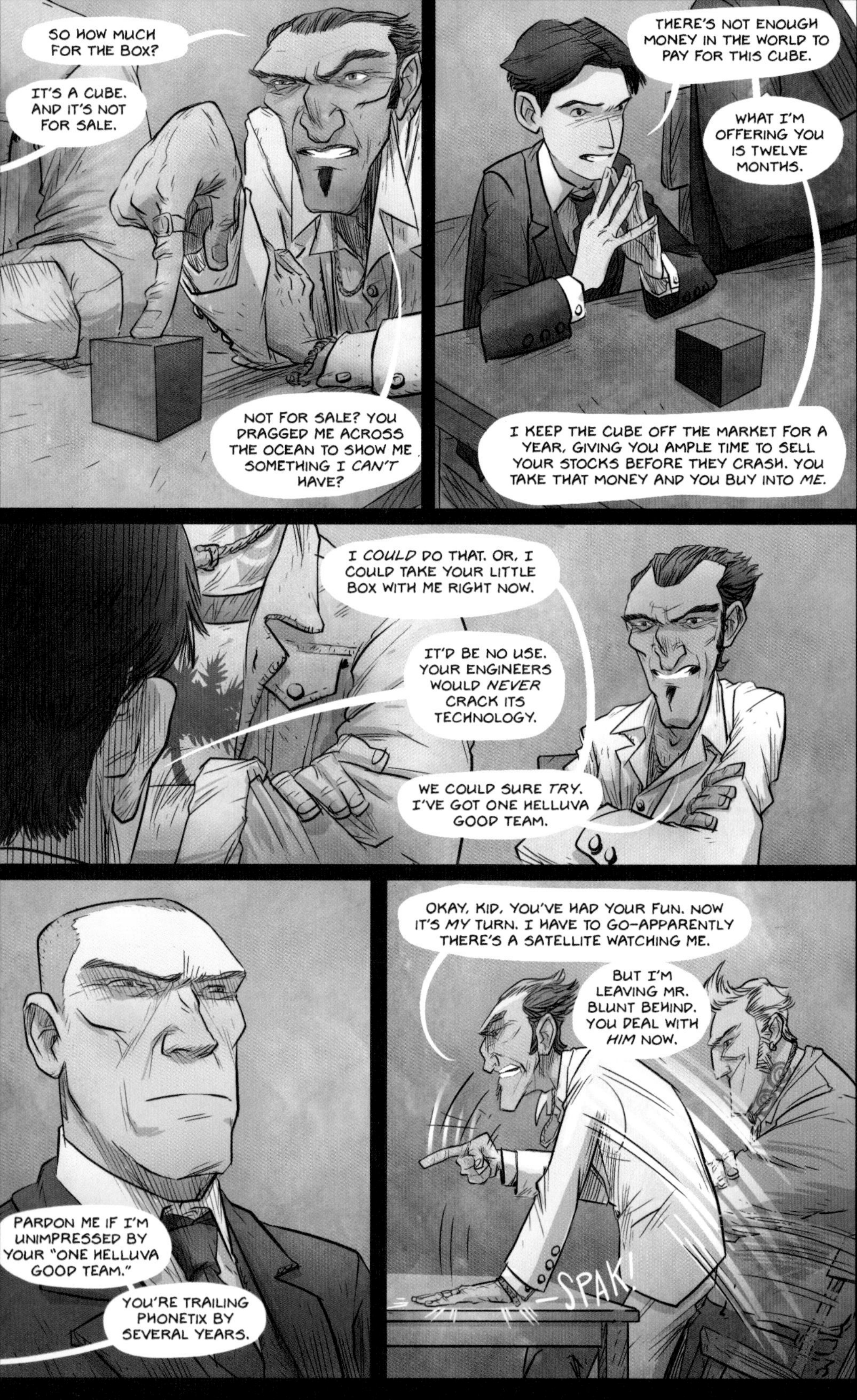
SO HOW MUCH FOR THE BOX?
IT'S A CUBE. AND IT'S NOT FOR SALE.
NOT FOR SALE? YOU DRAGGED ME ACROSS THE OCEAN TO SHOW ME SOMETHING I *CAN'T* HAVE?
THERE'S NOT ENOUGH MONEY IN THE WORLD TO PAY FOR THIS CUBE.
WHAT I'M OFFERING YOU IS TWELVE MONTHS.
I KEEP THE CUBE OFF THE MARKET FOR A YEAR, GIVING YOU AMPLE TIME TO SELL YOUR STOCKS BEFORE THEY CRASH. YOU TAKE THAT MONEY AND YOU BUY INTO *ME*.
I *COULD* DO THAT. OR, I COULD TAKE YOUR LITTLE BOX WITH ME RIGHT NOW.
IT'D BE NO USE. YOUR ENGINEERS WOULD *NEVER* CRACK ITS TECHNOLOGY.
WE COULD SURE *TRY*. I'VE GOT ONE HELLUVA GOOD TEAM.
PARDON ME IF I'M UNIMPRESSED BY YOUR "ONE HELLUVA GOOD TEAM."
YOU'RE TRAILING PHONETIX BY SEVERAL YEARS.
OKAY, KID, YOU'VE HAD YOUR FUN. NOW IT'S *MY* TURN. I HAVE TO GO—APPARENTLY THERE'S A SATELLITE WATCHING ME.
BUT I'M LEAVING MR. BLUNT BEHIND. YOU DEAL WITH *HIM* NOW.
SPAK!

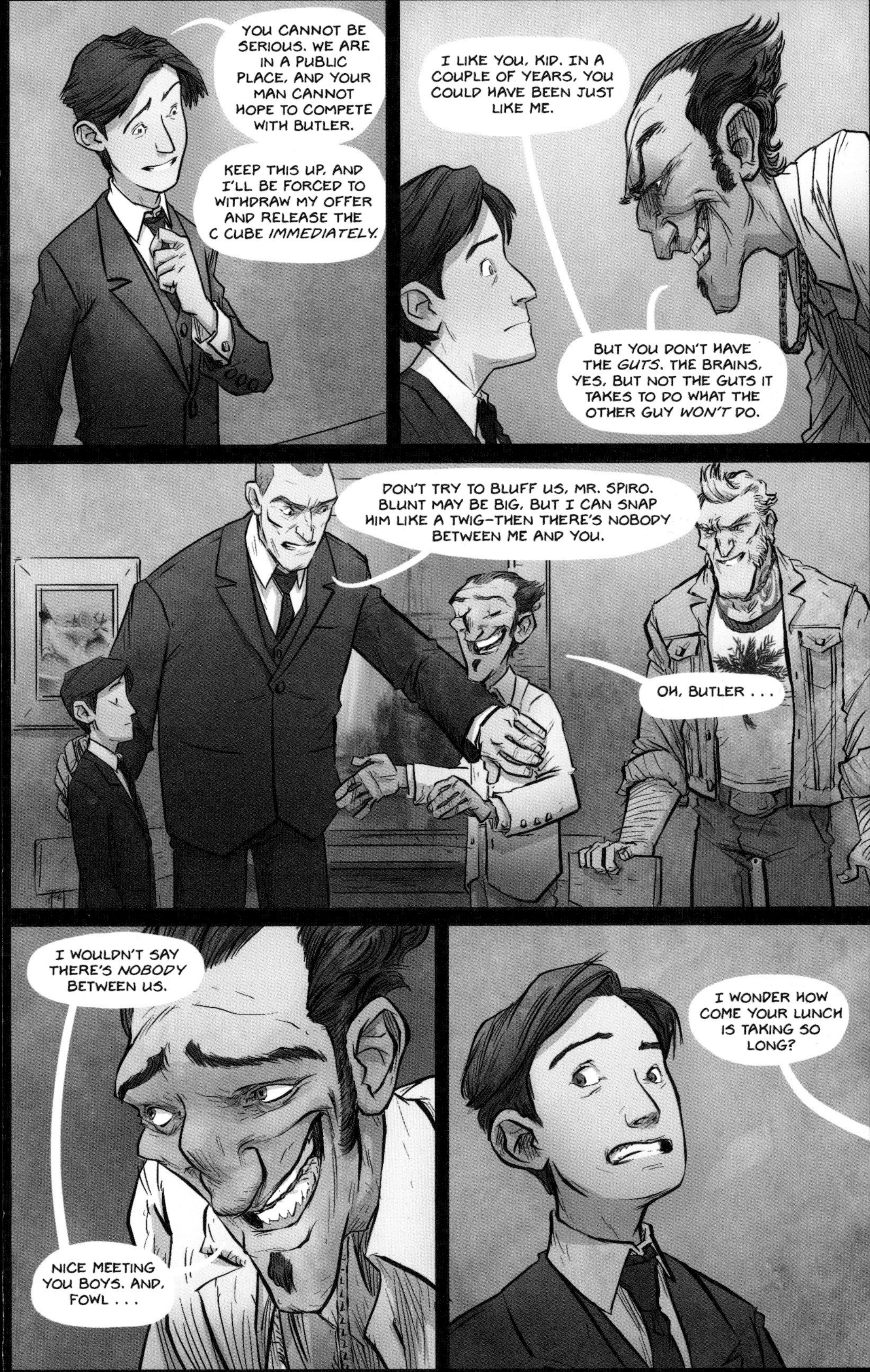
YOU CANNOT BE SERIOUS. WE ARE IN A PUBLIC PLACE, AND YOUR MAN CANNOT HOPE TO COMPETE WITH BUTLER.
KEEP THIS UP, AND I'LL BE FORCED TO WITHDRAW MY OFFER AND RELEASE THE C CUBE *IMMEDIATELY.*
I LIKE YOU, KID. IN A COUPLE OF YEARS, YOU COULD HAVE BEEN JUST LIKE ME.
BUT YOU DON'T HAVE THE *GUTS*. THE BRAINS, YES, BUT NOT THE GUTS IT TAKES TO DO WHAT THE OTHER GUY *WON'T* DO.
DON'T TRY TO BLUFF US, MR. SPIRO. BLUNT MAY BE BIG, BUT I CAN SNAP HIM LIKE A TWIG—THEN THERE'S NOBODY BETWEEN ME AND YOU.
OH, BUTLER . . .
I WOULDN'T SAY THERE'S *NOBODY* BETWEEN US.
NICE MEETING YOU BOYS. AND, FOWL . . .
I WONDER HOW COME YOUR LUNCH IS TAKING SO LONG?

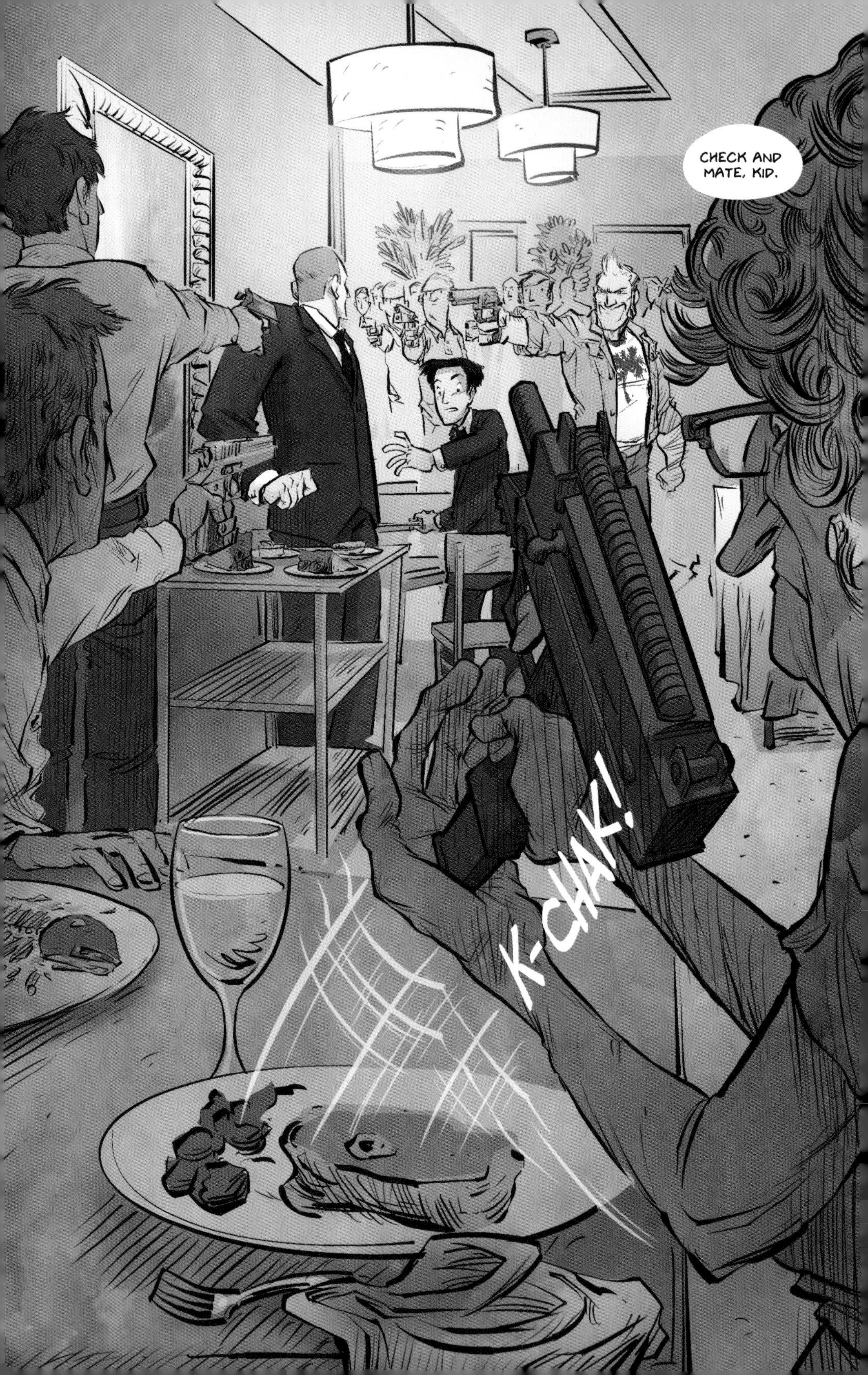
CHECK AND MATE, KID.
K-CHAK!

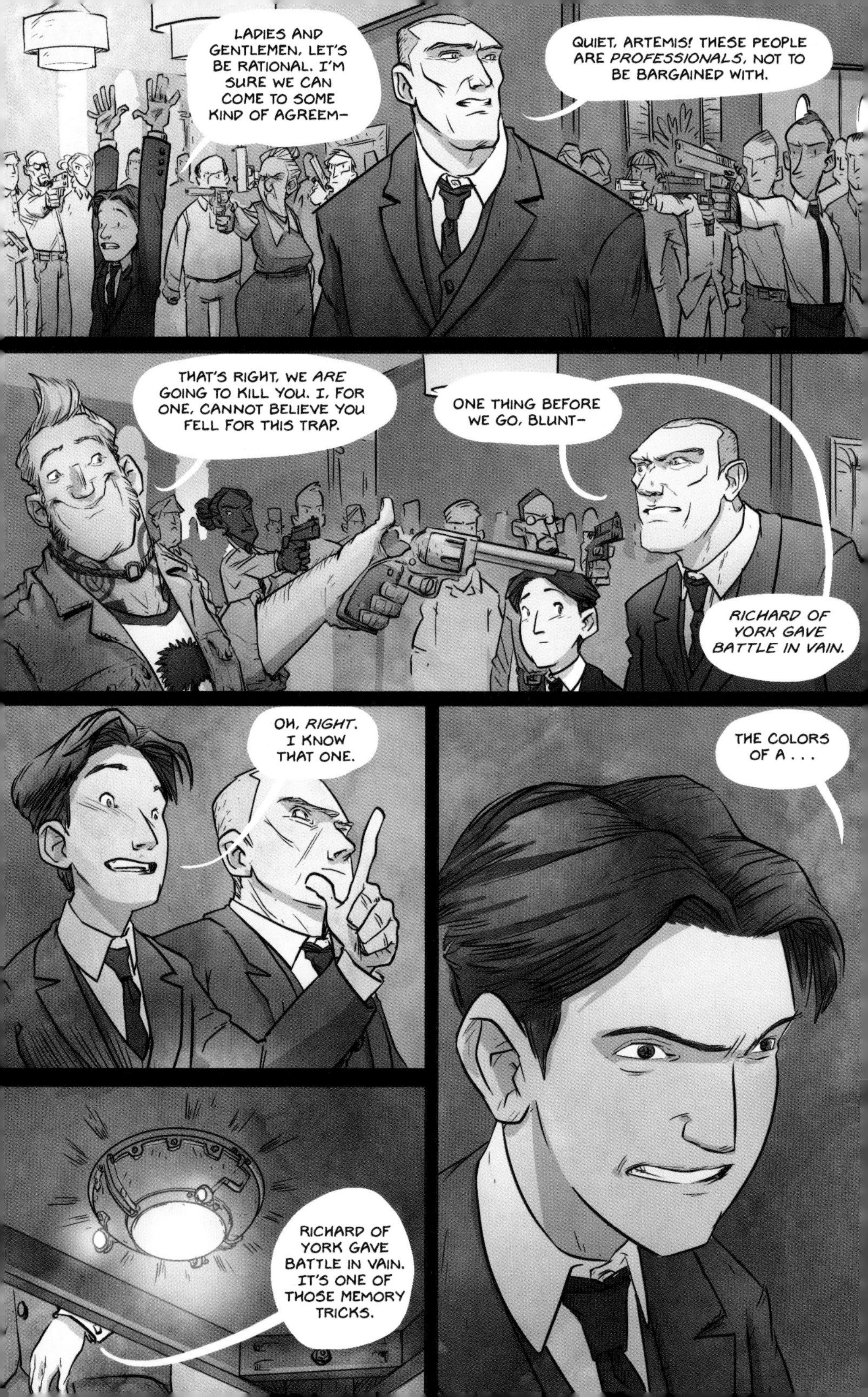
LADIES AND GENTLEMEN, LET'S BE RATIONAL. I'M SURE WE CAN COME TO SOME KIND OF AGREEM–
QUIET, ARTEMIS! THESE PEOPLE ARE *PROFESSIONALS*, NOT TO BE BARGAINED WITH.
THAT'S RIGHT, WE *ARE* GOING TO KILL YOU. I, FOR ONE, CANNOT BELIEVE YOU FELL FOR THIS TRAP.
ONE THING BEFORE WE GO, BLUNT–
RICHARD OF YORK GAVE BATTLE IN VAIN.
OH, *RIGHT*. I KNOW THAT ONE.
THE COLORS OF A . . .
RICHARD OF YORK GAVE BATTLE IN VAIN. IT'S ONE OF THOSE MEMORY TRICKS.

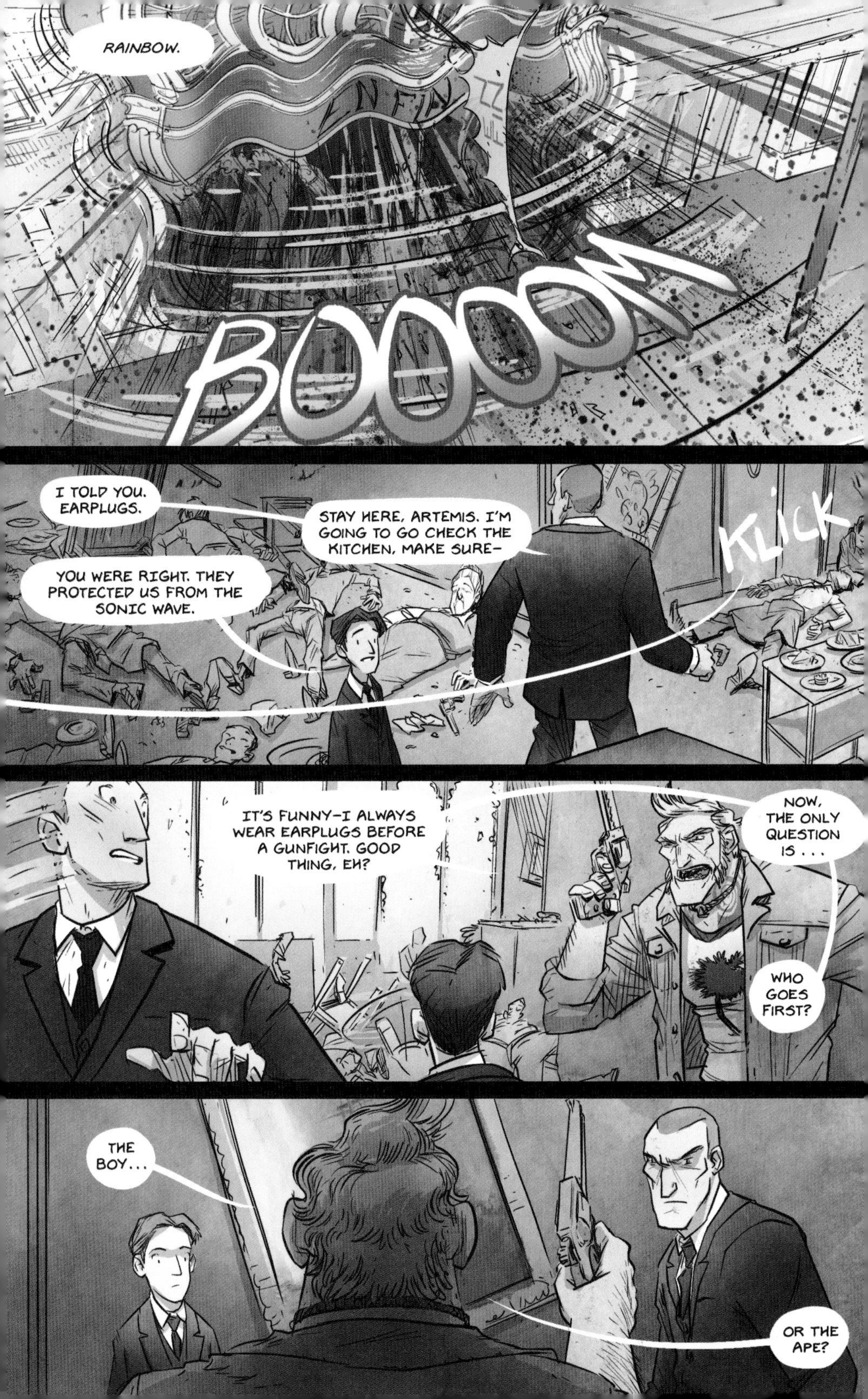
RAINBOW.
BOOOOM
I TOLD YOU. EARPLUGS.
STAY HERE, ARTEMIS. I'M GOING TO GO CHECK THE KITCHEN, MAKE SURE–
YOU WERE RIGHT. THEY PROTECTED US FROM THE SONIC WAVE.
KLICK
IT'S FUNNY–I ALWAYS WEAR EARPLUGS BEFORE A GUNFIGHT. GOOD THING, EH?
NOW, THE ONLY QUESTION IS . . .
WHO GOES FIRST?
THE BOY...
OR THE APE?

CHAPTER TWO

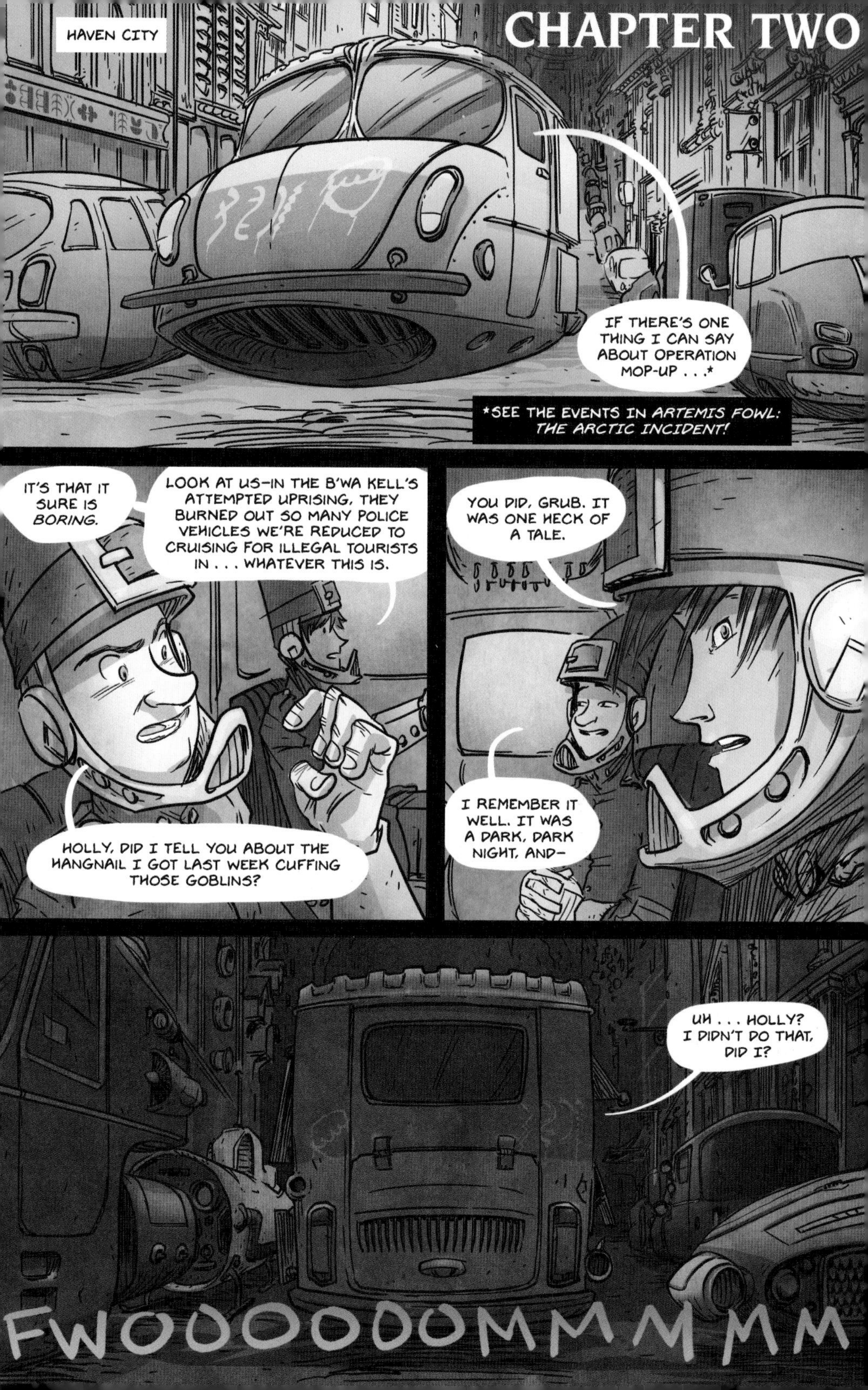
HAVEN CITY
IF THERE'S ONE THING I CAN SAY ABOUT OPERATION MOP-UP . . .*
*SEE THE EVENTS IN *ARTEMIS FOWL: THE ARCTIC INCIDENT!*
IT'S THAT IT SURE IS *BORING.*
LOOK AT US—IN THE B'WA KELL'S ATTEMPTED UPRISING, THEY BURNED OUT SO MANY POLICE VEHICLES WE'RE REDUCED TO CRUISING FOR ILLEGAL TOURISTS IN . . . WHATEVER THIS IS.
HOLLY, DID I TELL YOU ABOUT THE HANGNAIL I GOT LAST WEEK CUFFING THOSE GOBLINS?
YOU DID, GRUB. IT WAS ONE HECK OF A TALE.
I REMEMBER IT WELL. IT WAS A DARK, DARK NIGHT, AND—
UH . . . HOLLY? I DIDN'T DO THAT, DID I?
FWOOOOOOMMMMMM

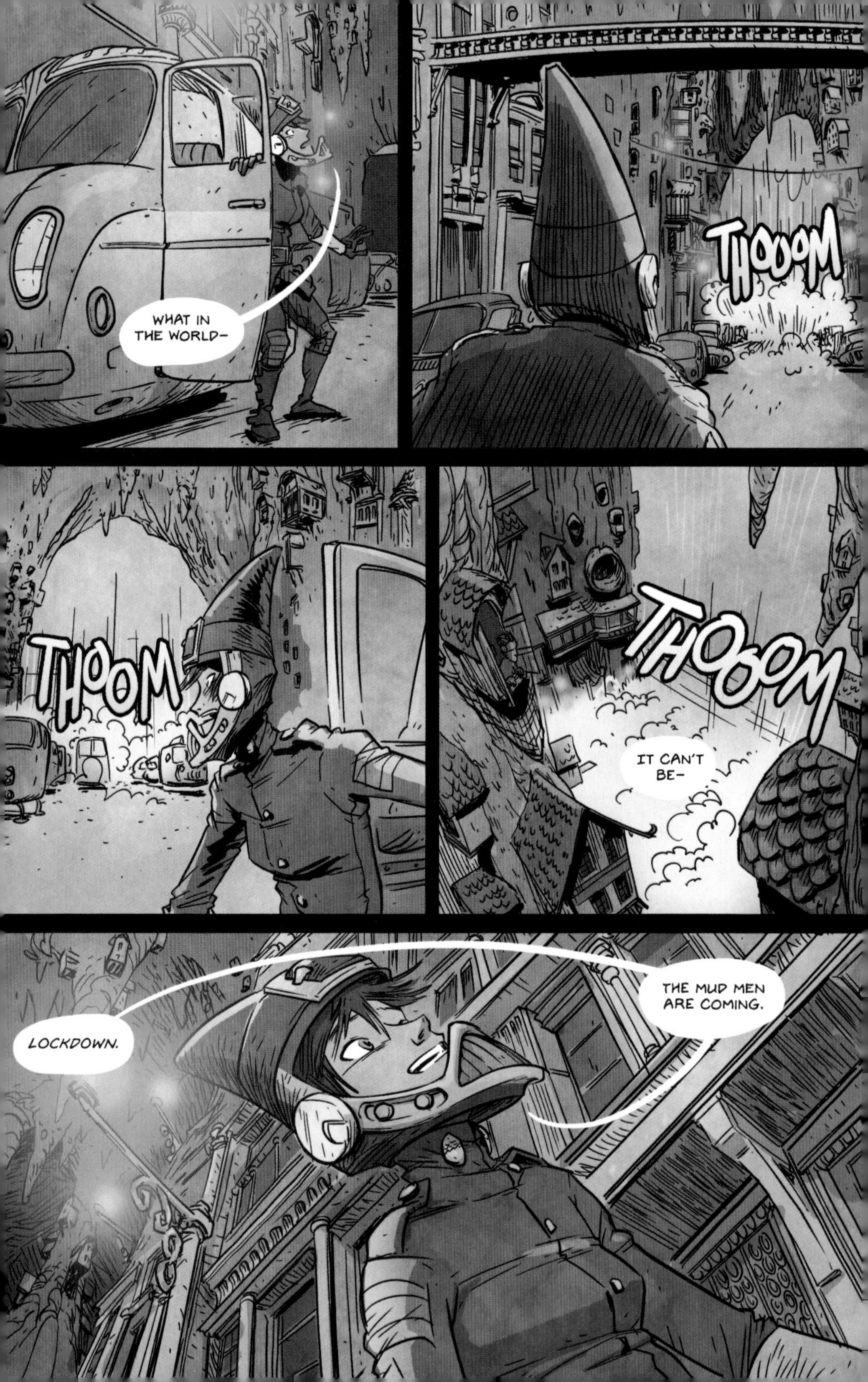
WHAT IN THE WORLD–
THOOOM
THOOM
THOOOM
IT CAN'T BE–
LOCKDOWN.
THE MUD MEN ARE COMING.

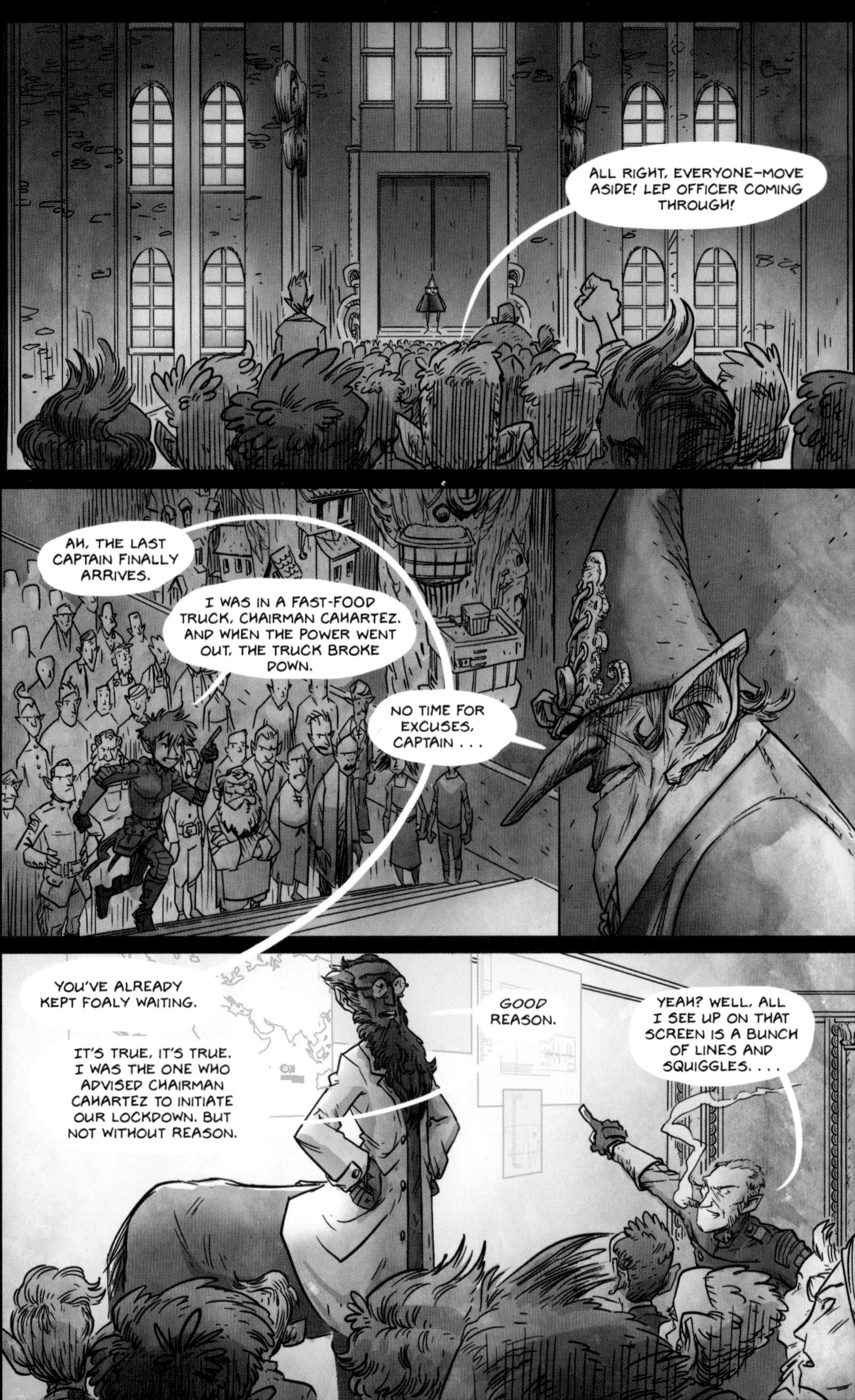
ALL RIGHT, EVERYONE—MOVE ASIDE! LEP OFFICER COMING THROUGH!
AH, THE LAST CAPTAIN FINALLY ARRIVES.
I WAS IN A FAST-FOOD TRUCK, CHAIRMAN CAHARTEZ, AND WHEN THE POWER WENT OUT, THE TRUCK BROKE DOWN.
NO TIME FOR EXCUSES, CAPTAIN . . .
YOU'VE ALREADY KEPT FOALY WAITING.
IT'S TRUE, IT'S TRUE. I WAS THE ONE WHO ADVISED CHAIRMAN CAHARTEZ TO INITIATE OUR LOCKDOWN. BUT NOT WITHOUT REASON.
GOOD REASON.
YEAH? WELL, ALL I SEE UP ON THAT SCREEN IS A BUNCH OF LINES AND SQUIGGLES. . . .

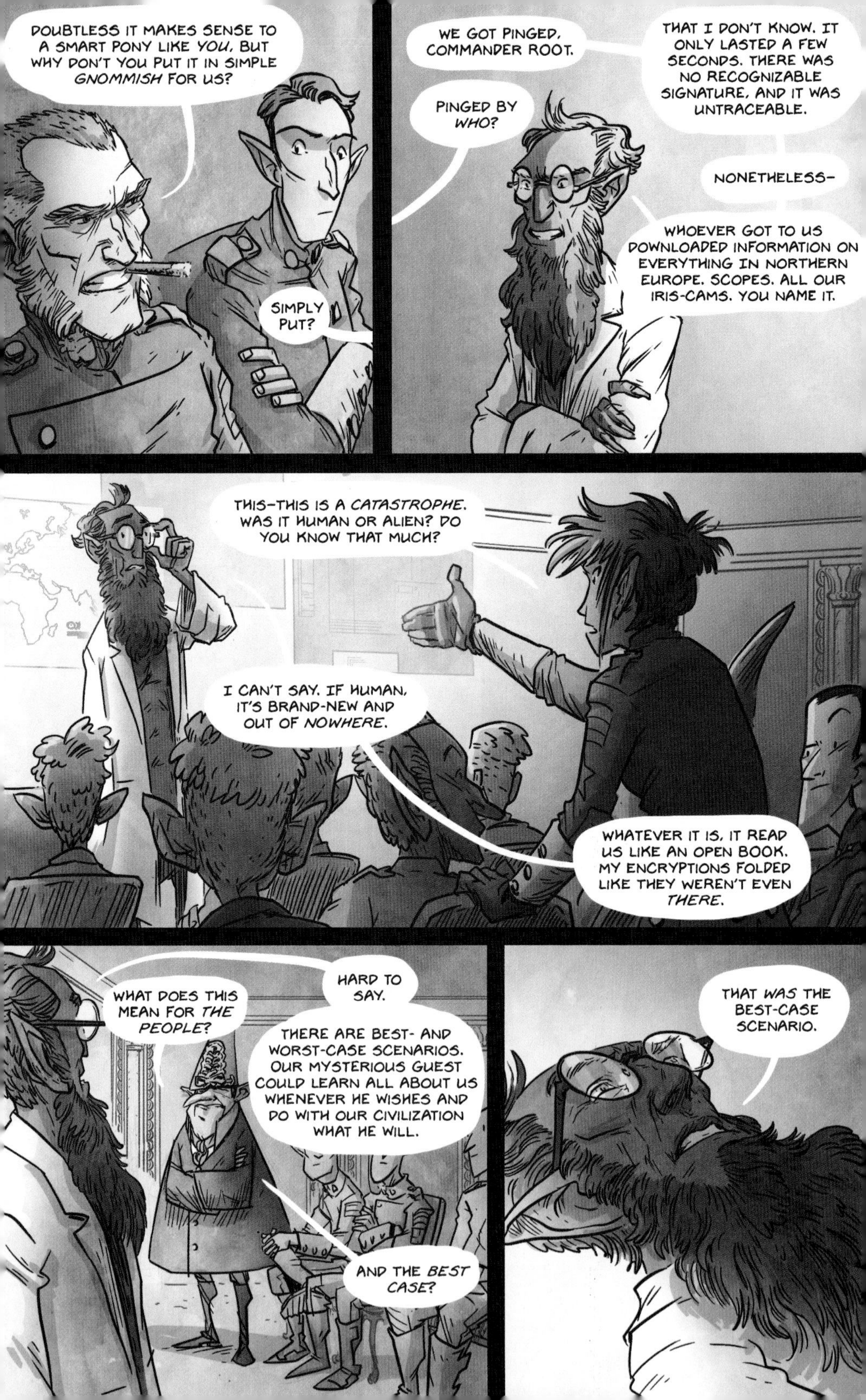
DOUBTLESS IT MAKES SENSE TO A SMART PONY LIKE *YOU*, BUT WHY DON'T YOU PUT IT IN SIMPLE *GNOMMISH* FOR US?
SIMPLY PUT?
WE GOT PINGED, COMMANDER ROOT.
PINGED BY *WHO*?
THAT I DON'T KNOW. IT ONLY LASTED A FEW SECONDS. THERE WAS NO RECOGNIZABLE SIGNATURE, AND IT WAS UNTRACEABLE.
NONETHELESS–
WHOEVER GOT TO US DOWNLOADED INFORMATION ON EVERYTHING IN NORTHERN EUROPE. SCOPES. ALL OUR IRIS-CAMS. YOU NAME IT.
THIS–THIS IS A *CATASTROPHE*. WAS IT HUMAN OR ALIEN? DO YOU KNOW THAT MUCH?
I CAN'T SAY. IF HUMAN, IT'S BRAND-NEW AND OUT OF *NOWHERE*.
WHATEVER IT IS, IT READ US LIKE AN OPEN BOOK. MY ENCRYPTIONS FOLDED LIKE THEY WEREN'T EVEN *THERE*.
WHAT DOES THIS MEAN FOR *THE PEOPLE*?
HARD TO SAY.
THERE ARE BEST- AND WORST-CASE SCENARIOS. OUR MYSTERIOUS GUEST COULD LEARN ALL ABOUT US WHENEVER HE WISHES AND DO WITH OUR CIVILIZATION WHAT HE WILL.
AND THE *BEST CASE*?
THAT *WAS* THE BEST-CASE SCENARIO.

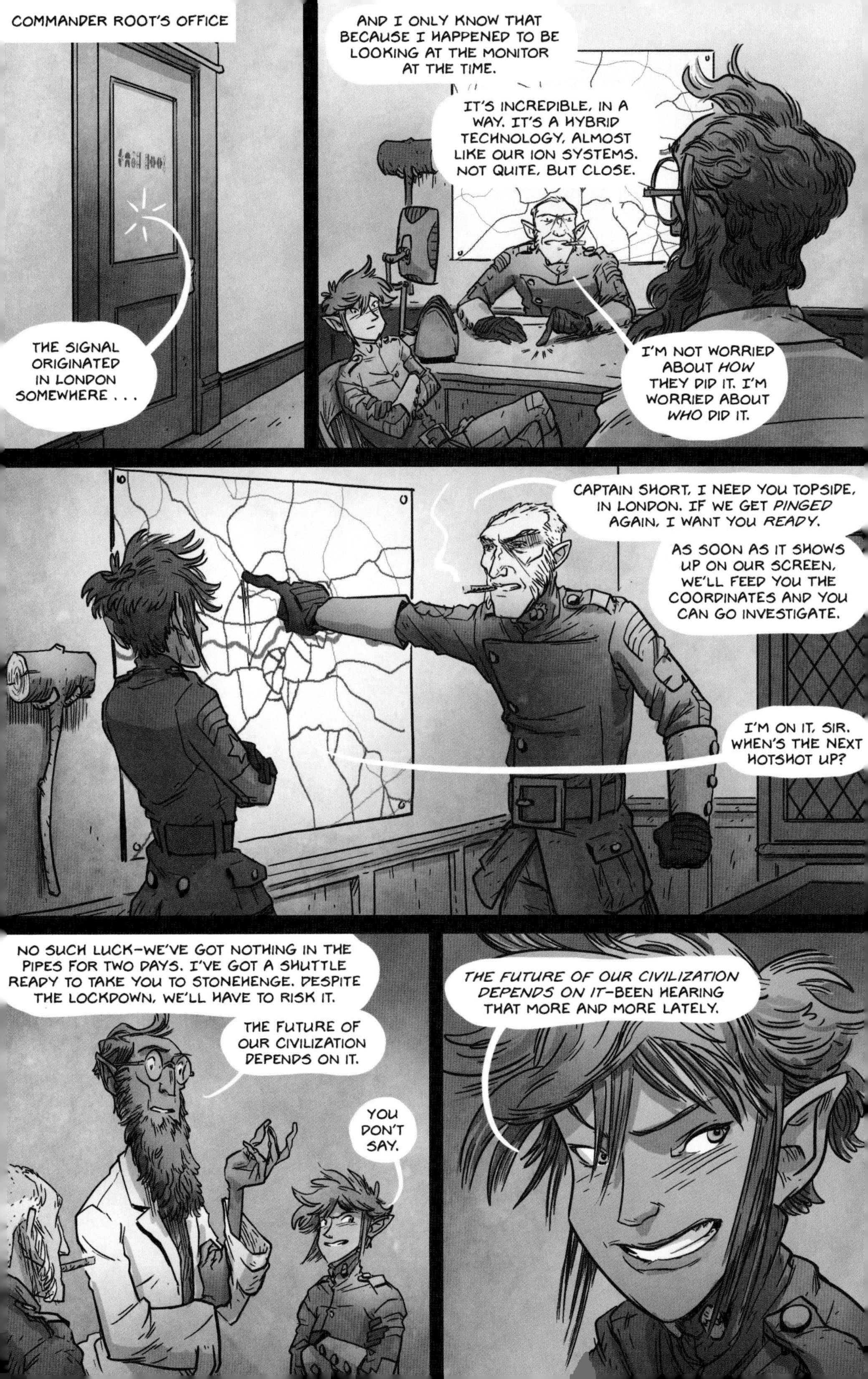
COMMANDER ROOT'S OFFICE
THE SIGNAL ORIGINATED IN LONDON SOMEWHERE . . .
AND I ONLY KNOW THAT BECAUSE I HAPPENED TO BE LOOKING AT THE MONITOR AT THE TIME.
IT'S INCREDIBLE, IN A WAY. IT'S A HYBRID TECHNOLOGY, ALMOST LIKE OUR ION SYSTEMS. NOT QUITE, BUT CLOSE.
I'M NOT WORRIED ABOUT *HOW* THEY DID IT. I'M WORRIED ABOUT *WHO* DID IT.
CAPTAIN SHORT, I NEED YOU TOPSIDE, IN LONDON. IF WE GET *PINGED* AGAIN, I WANT YOU *READY*.
AS SOON AS IT SHOWS UP ON OUR SCREEN, WE'LL FEED YOU THE COORDINATES AND YOU CAN GO INVESTIGATE.
I'M ON IT, SIR. WHEN'S THE NEXT HOTSHOT UP?
NO SUCH LUCK—WE'VE GOT NOTHING IN THE PIPES FOR TWO DAYS. I'VE GOT A SHUTTLE READY TO TAKE YOU TO STONEHENGE. DESPITE THE LOCKDOWN, WE'LL HAVE TO RISK IT.
THE FUTURE OF OUR CIVILIZATION DEPENDS ON IT.
YOU DON'T SAY.
THE FUTURE OF OUR CIVILIZATION DEPENDS ON IT—BEEN HEARING THAT MORE AND MORE LATELY.

CHAPTER THREE

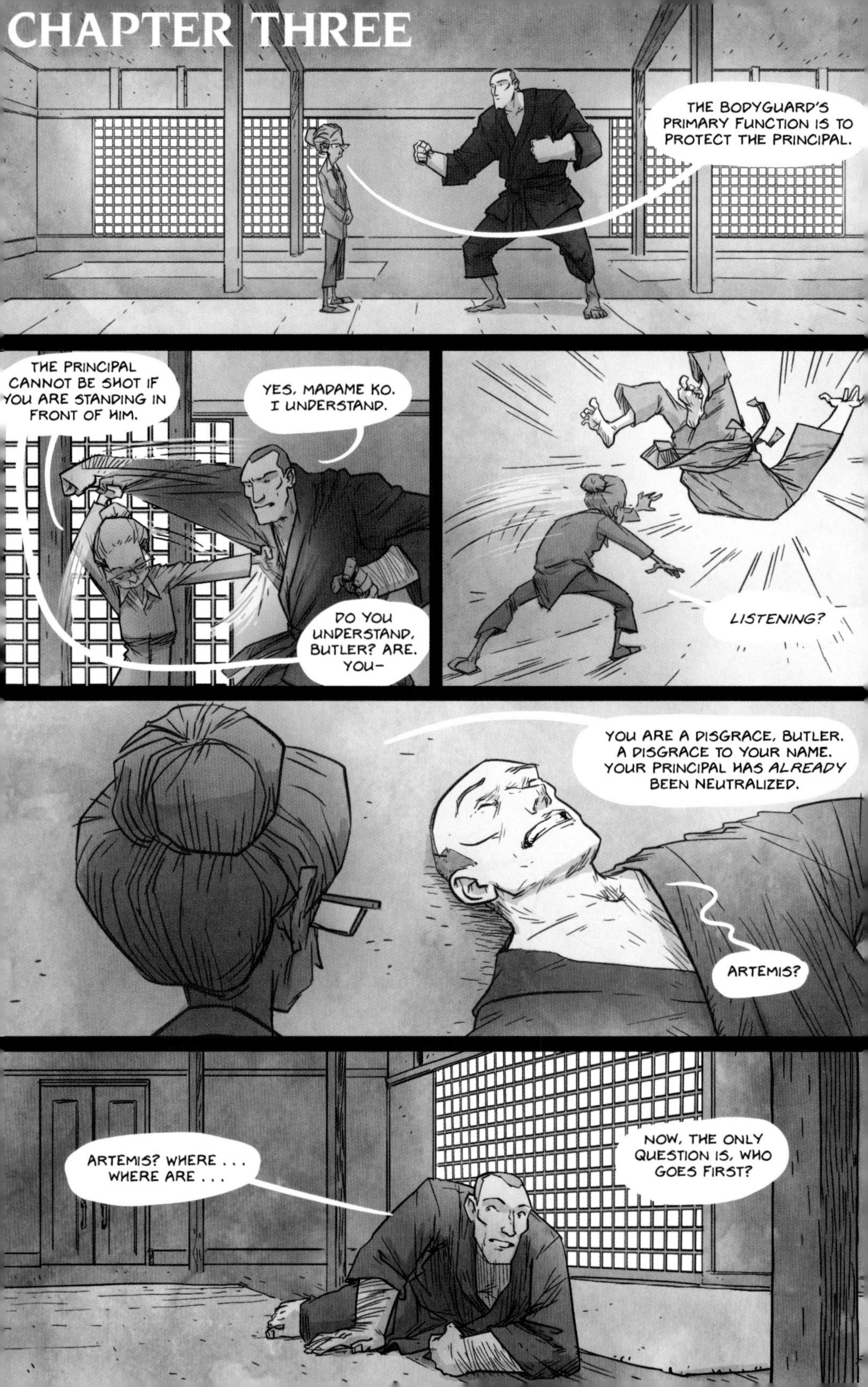

THE BODYGUARD'S PRIMARY FUNCTION IS TO PROTECT THE PRINCIPAL.
THE PRINCIPAL CANNOT BE SHOT IF YOU ARE STANDING IN FRONT OF HIM.
YES, MADAME KO. I UNDERSTAND.
DO YOU UNDERSTAND, BUTLER? ARE. YOU–
LISTENING?
YOU ARE A DISGRACE, BUTLER. A DISGRACE TO YOUR NAME. YOUR PRINCIPAL HAS ALREADY BEEN NEUTRALIZED.
ARTEMIS?
ARTEMIS? WHERE . . . WHERE ARE . . .
NOW, THE ONLY QUESTION IS, WHO GOES FIRST?

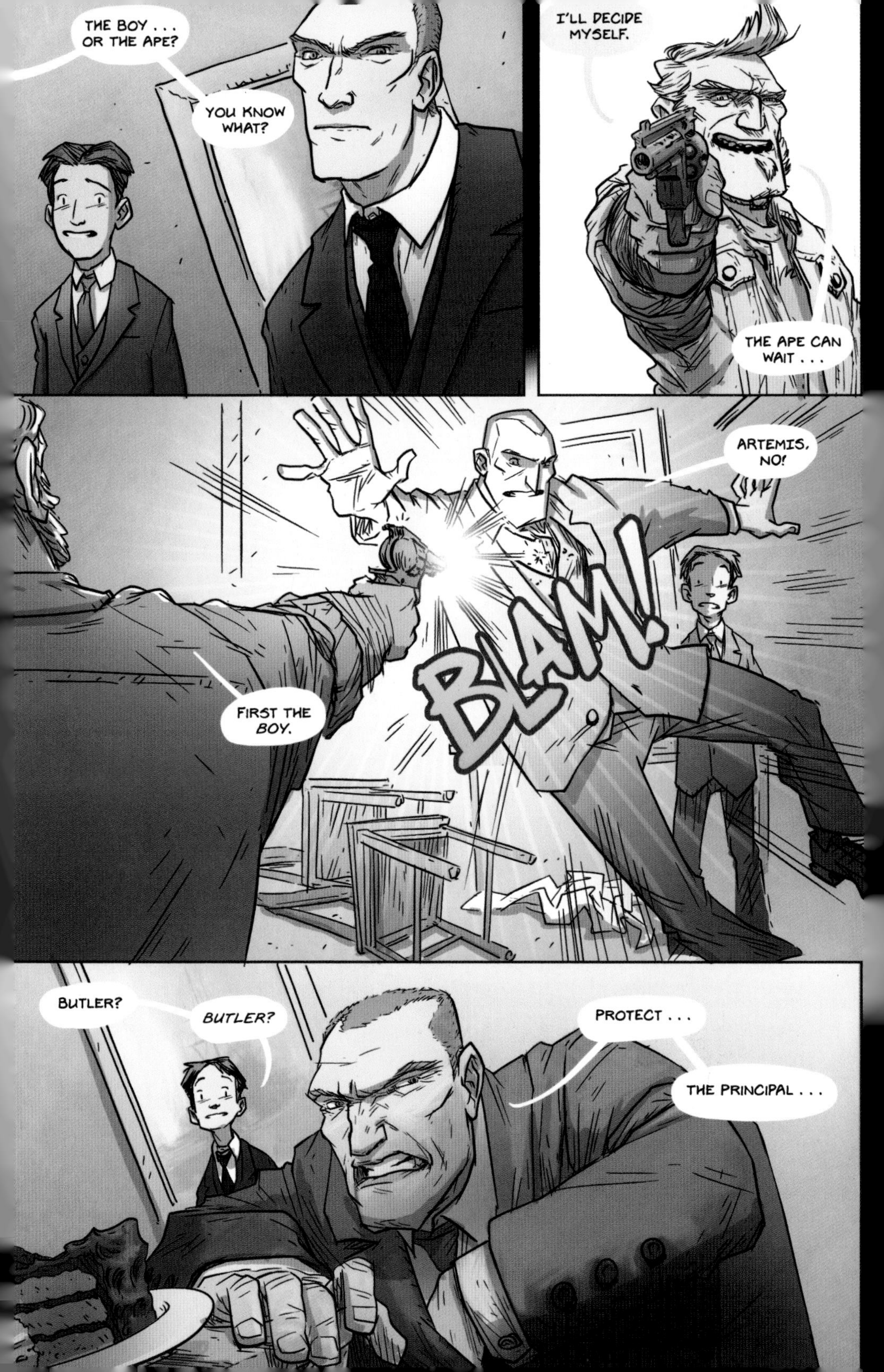
THE BOY . . .
OR THE APE?
YOU KNOW
WHAT?
I'LL DECIDE
MYSELF.
THE APE CAN
WAIT . . .
ARTEMIS,
NO!
FIRST THE
BOY.
BLAM!
BUTLER?
BUTLER?
PROTECT . . .
THE PRINCIPAL . . .

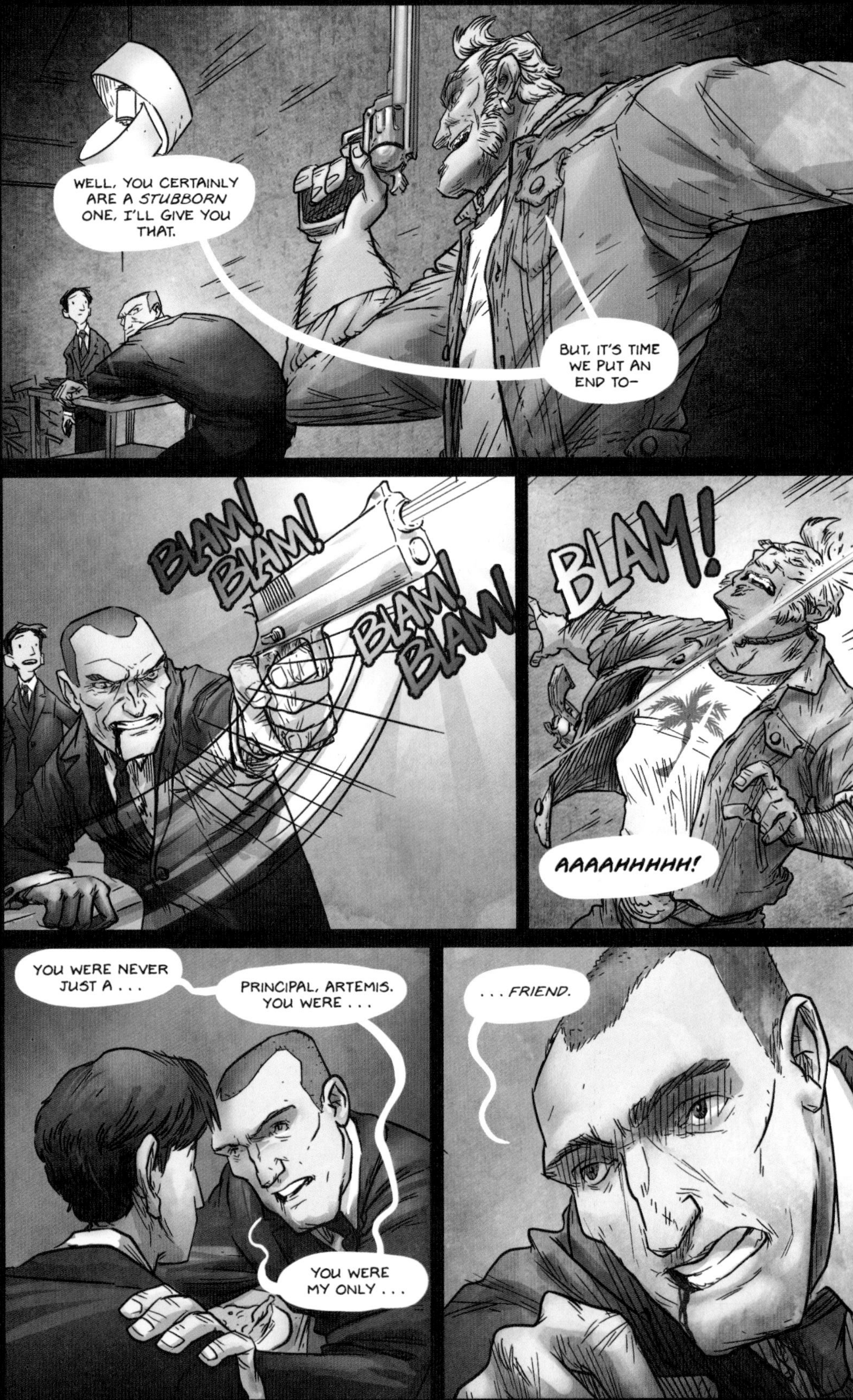
WELL, YOU CERTAINLY ARE A *STUBBORN* ONE, I'LL GIVE YOU THAT.
BUT, IT'S TIME WE PUT AN END TO–
BLAM! BLAM! BLAM! BLAM!
BLAM!
AAAAHHHHH!
YOU WERE NEVER JUST A . . .
PRINCIPAL, ARTEMIS. YOU WERE . . .
YOU WERE MY ONLY . . .
. . . *FRIEND*.

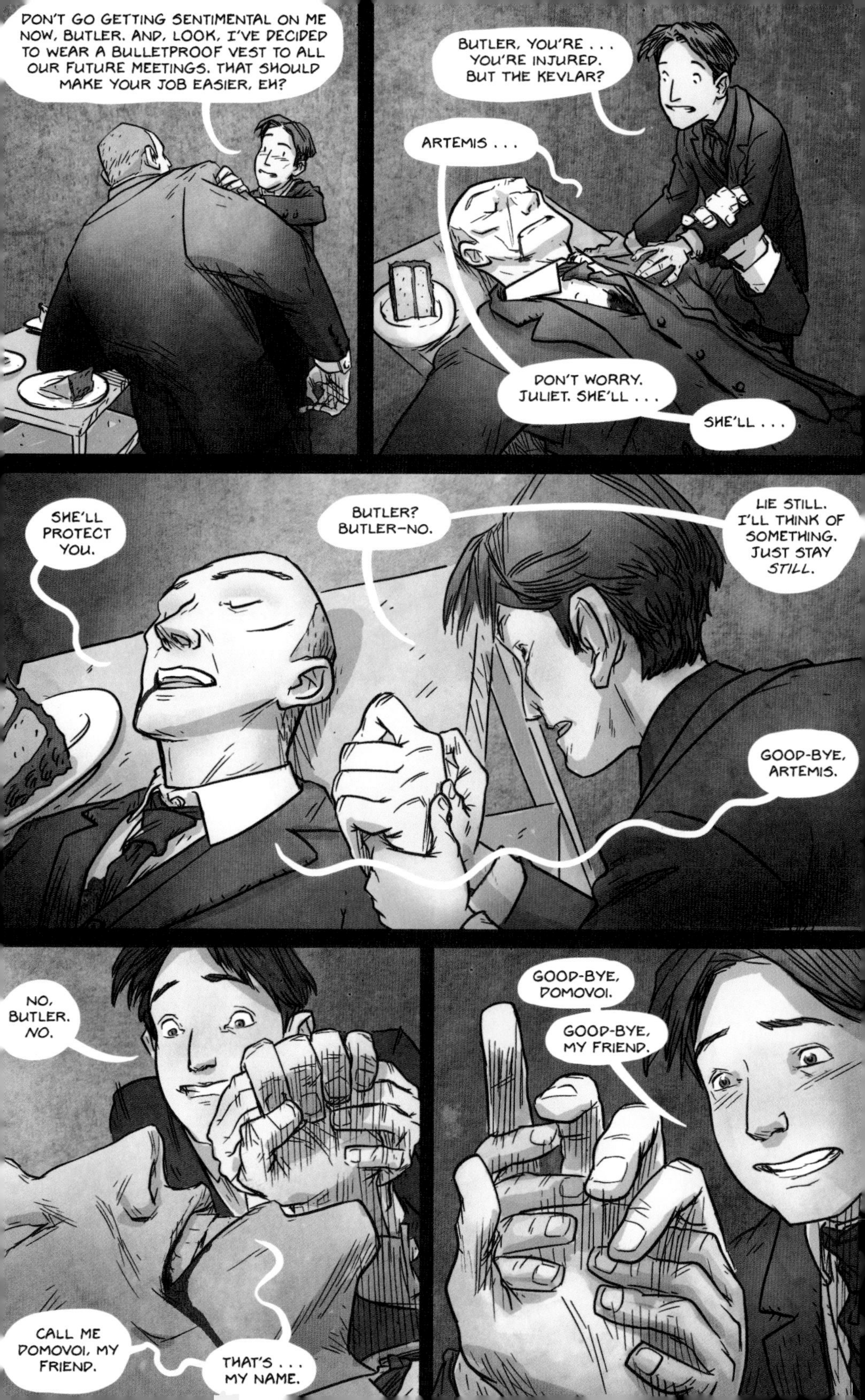
DON'T GO GETTING SENTIMENTAL ON ME NOW, BUTLER. AND, LOOK, I'VE DECIDED TO WEAR A BULLETPROOF VEST TO ALL OUR FUTURE MEETINGS. THAT SHOULD MAKE YOUR JOB EASIER, EH?
BUTLER, YOU'RE . . . YOU'RE INJURED. BUT THE KEVLAR?
ARTEMIS . . .
DON'T WORRY. JULIET. SHE'LL . . .
SHE'LL . . .
SHE'LL PROTECT YOU.
BUTLER? BUTLER—NO.
LIE STILL. I'LL THINK OF SOMETHING. JUST STAY *STILL*.
GOOD-BYE, ARTEMIS.
NO, BUTLER. *NO*.
CALL ME DOMOVOI, MY FRIEND.
THAT'S . . . MY NAME.
GOOD-BYE, DOMOVOI.
GOOD-BYE, MY FRIEND.

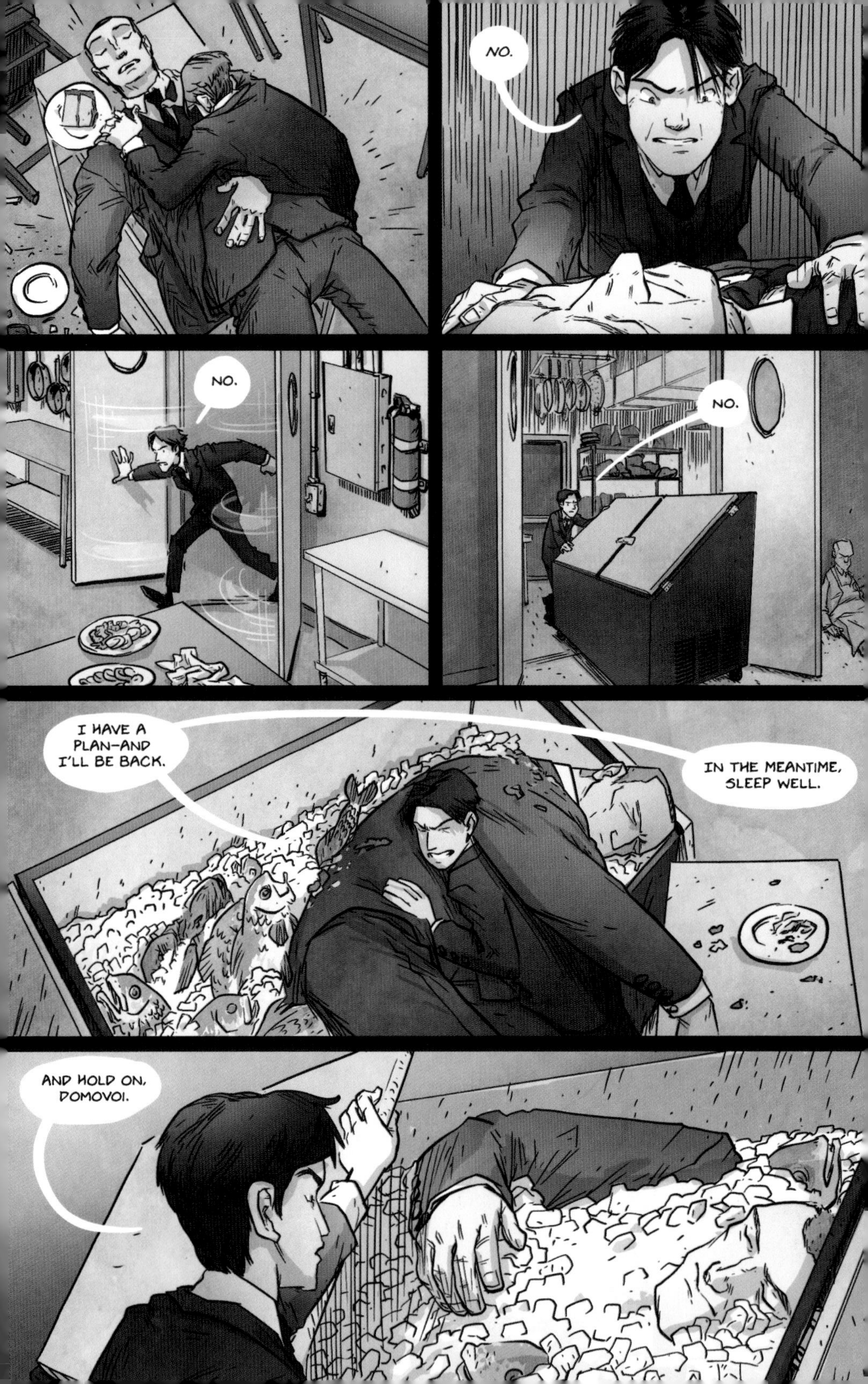
NO.
NO.
NO.
I HAVE A PLAN—AND I'LL BE BACK.
IN THE MEANTIME, SLEEP WELL.
AND HOLD ON, DOMOVOI.

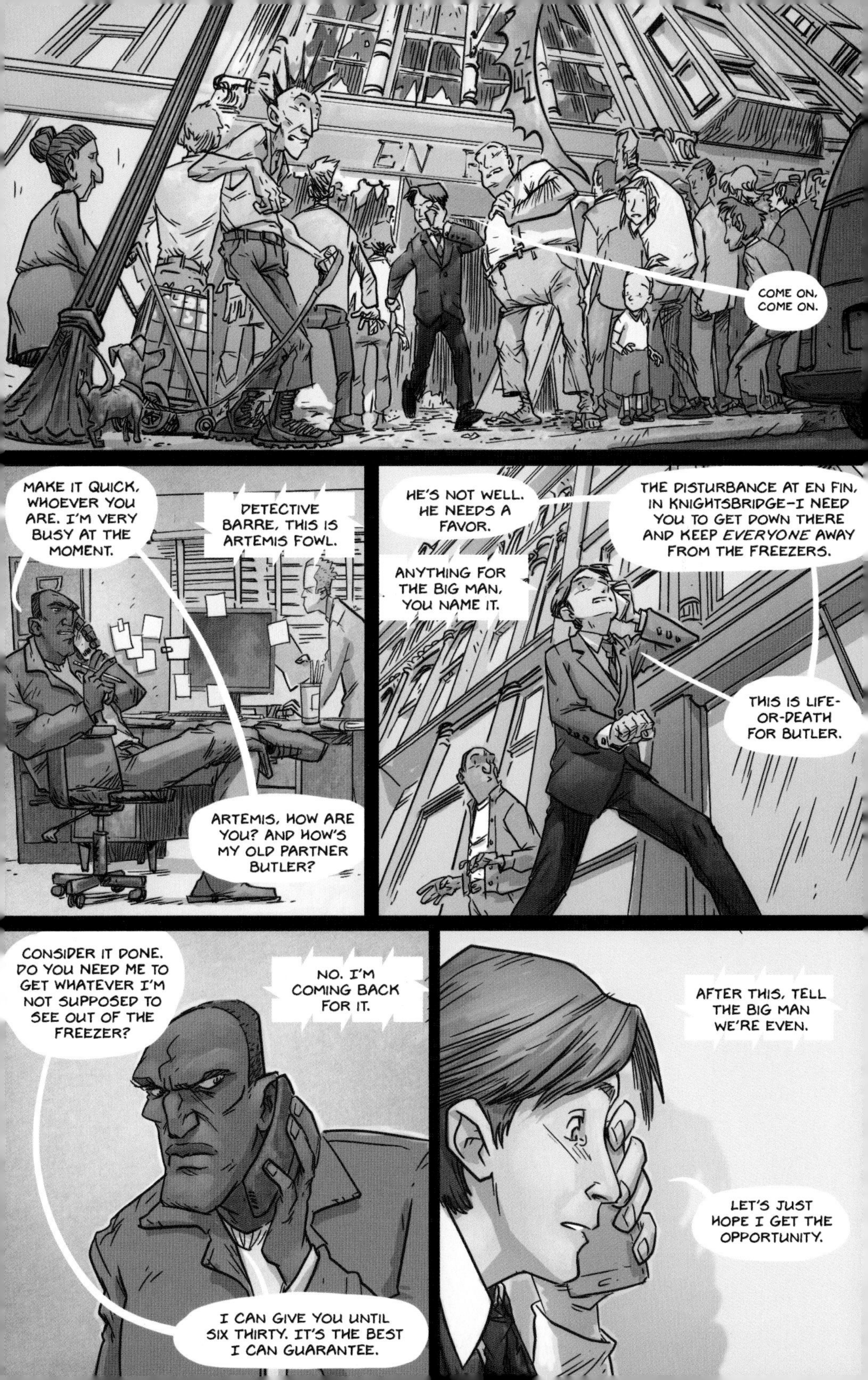
EN F
COME ON, COME ON.
MAKE IT QUICK, WHOEVER YOU ARE. I'M VERY BUSY AT THE MOMENT.
DETECTIVE BARRE, THIS IS ARTEMIS FOWL.
ARTEMIS, HOW ARE YOU? AND HOW'S MY OLD PARTNER BUTLER?
HE'S NOT WELL. HE NEEDS A FAVOR.
ANYTHING FOR THE BIG MAN, YOU NAME IT.
THE DISTURBANCE AT EN FIN, IN KNIGHTSBRIDGE–I NEED YOU TO GET DOWN THERE AND KEEP *EVERYONE* AWAY FROM THE FREEZERS.
THIS IS LIFE-OR-DEATH FOR BUTLER.
CONSIDER IT DONE. DO YOU NEED ME TO GET WHATEVER I'M NOT SUPPOSED TO SEE OUT OF THE FREEZER?
NO. I'M COMING BACK FOR IT.
I CAN GIVE YOU UNTIL SIX THIRTY. IT'S THE BEST I CAN GUARANTEE.
AFTER THIS, TELL THE BIG MAN WE'RE EVEN.
LET'S JUST HOPE I GET THE OPPORTUNITY.

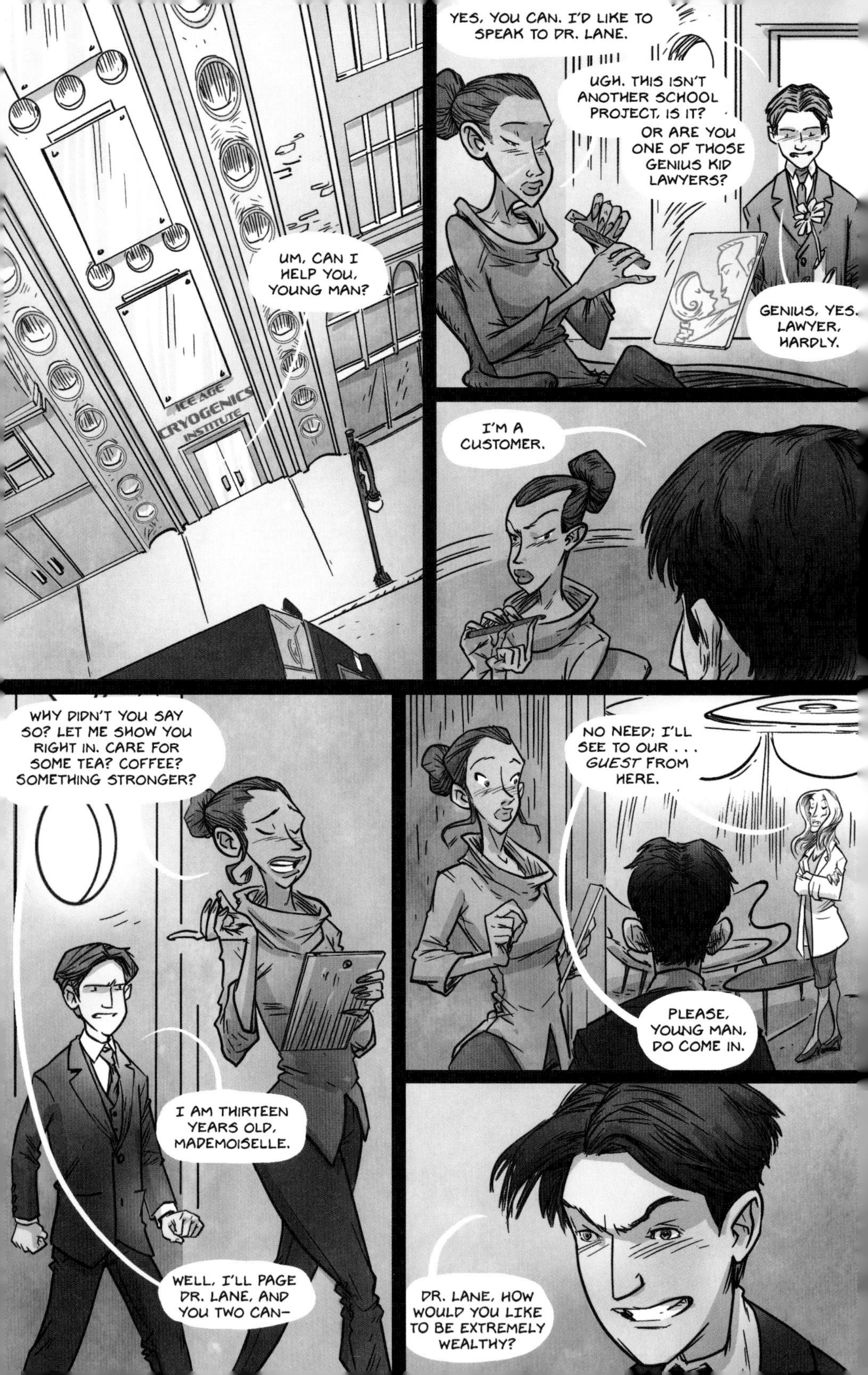
ICE AGE
CRYOGENICS
INSTITUTE
UM, CAN I HELP YOU, YOUNG MAN?
YES, YOU CAN. I'D LIKE TO SPEAK TO DR. LANE.
UGH. THIS ISN'T ANOTHER SCHOOL PROJECT, IS IT?
OR ARE YOU ONE OF THOSE GENIUS KID LAWYERS?
GENIUS, YES. LAWYER, HARDLY.
I'M A CUSTOMER.
WHY DIDN'T YOU SAY SO? LET ME SHOW YOU RIGHT IN. CARE FOR SOME TEA? COFFEE? SOMETHING STRONGER?
I AM THIRTEEN YEARS OLD, MADEMOISELLE.
WELL, I'LL PAGE DR. LANE, AND YOU TWO CAN–
NO NEED; I'LL SEE TO OUR . . . *GUEST* FROM HERE.
PLEASE, YOUNG MAN, DO COME IN.
DR. LANE, HOW WOULD YOU LIKE TO BE EXTREMELY WEALTHY?

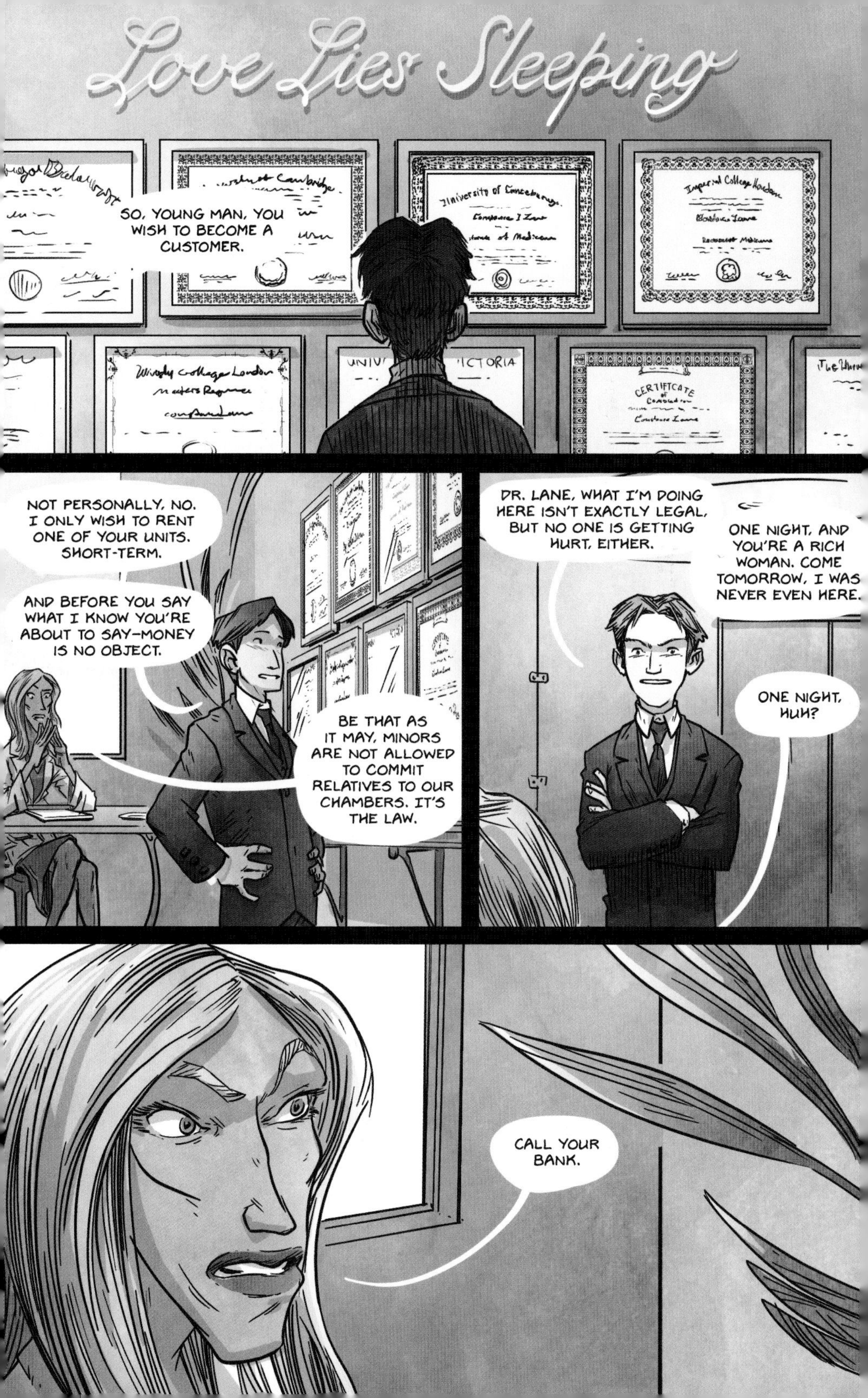
Love Lies Sleeping
SO, YOUNG MAN, YOU WISH TO BECOME A CUSTOMER.
NOT PERSONALLY, NO. I ONLY WISH TO RENT ONE OF YOUR UNITS. SHORT-TERM.
AND BEFORE YOU SAY WHAT I KNOW YOU'RE ABOUT TO SAY—MONEY IS NO OBJECT.
BE THAT AS IT MAY, MINORS ARE NOT ALLOWED TO COMMIT RELATIVES TO OUR CHAMBERS. IT'S THE LAW.
DR. LANE, WHAT I'M DOING HERE ISN'T EXACTLY LEGAL, BUT NO ONE IS GETTING HURT, EITHER.
ONE NIGHT, AND YOU'RE A RICH WOMAN. COME TOMORROW, I WAS NEVER EVEN HERE.
ONE NIGHT, HUH?
CALL YOUR BANK.

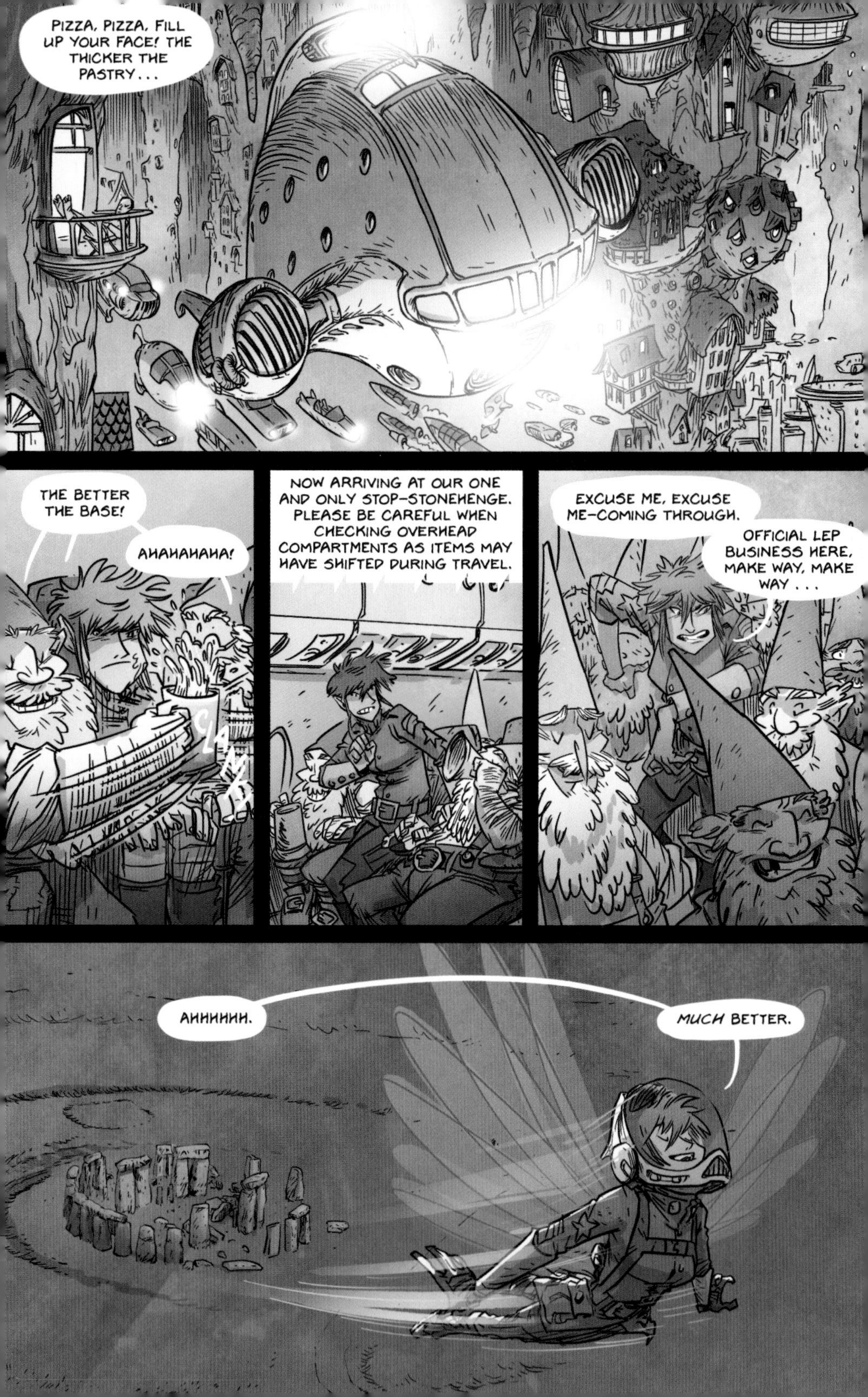
PIZZA, PIZZA, FILL UP YOUR FACE! THE THICKER THE PASTRY . . .
THE BETTER THE BASE!
AHAHAHAHA!
CLANK
NOW ARRIVING AT OUR ONE AND ONLY STOP—STONEHENGE. PLEASE BE CAREFUL WHEN CHECKING OVERHEAD COMPARTMENTS AS ITEMS MAY HAVE SHIFTED DURING TRAVEL.
EXCUSE ME, EXCUSE ME—COMING THROUGH.
OFFICIAL LEP BUSINESS HERE, MAKE WAY, MAKE WAY . . .
AHHHHHH.
MUCH BETTER.

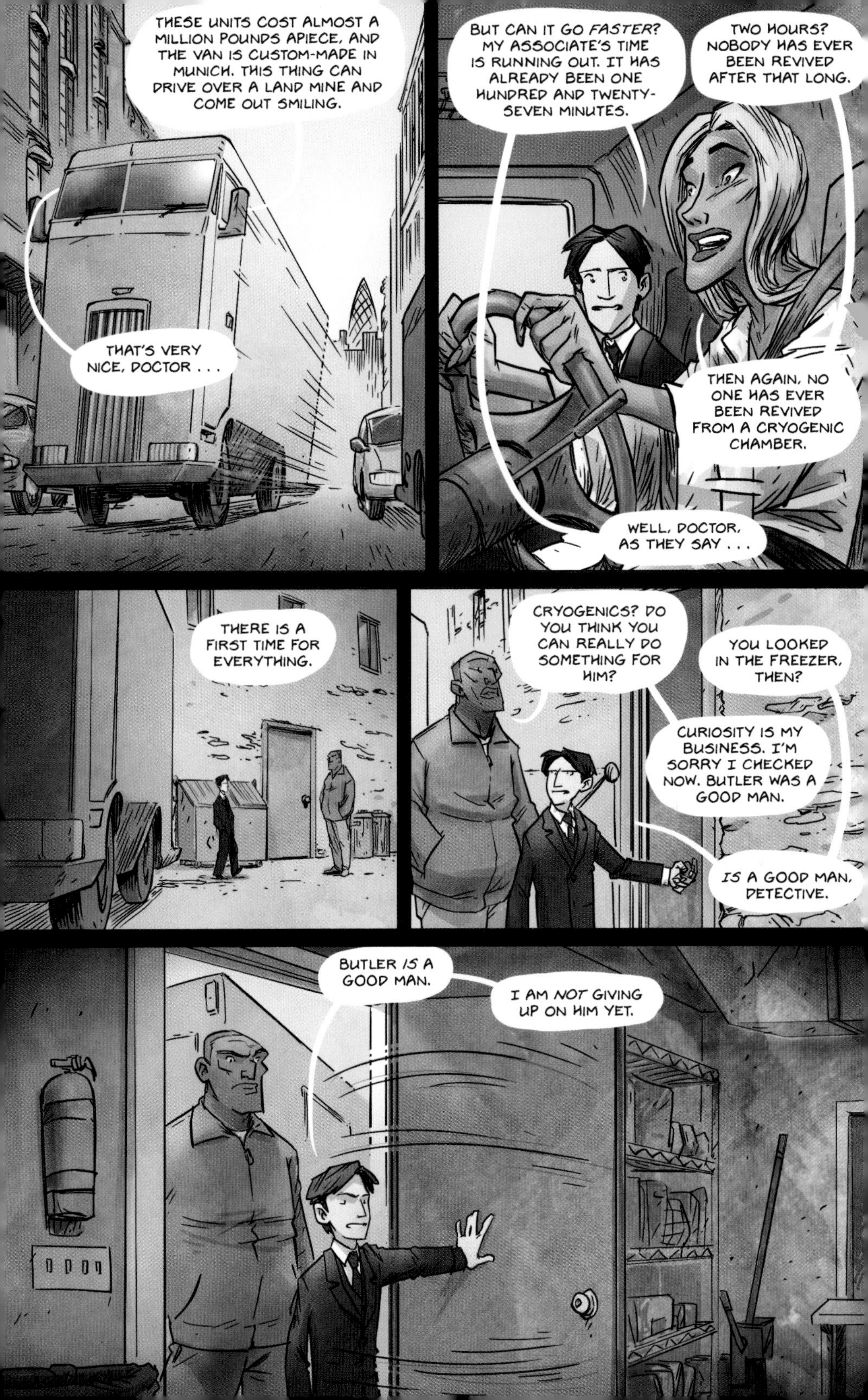
THESE UNITS COST ALMOST A MILLION POUNDS APIECE, AND THE VAN IS CUSTOM-MADE IN MUNICH. THIS THING CAN DRIVE OVER A LAND MINE AND COME OUT SMILING.
THAT'S VERY NICE, DOCTOR . . .
BUT CAN IT GO *FASTER*? MY ASSOCIATE'S TIME IS RUNNING OUT. IT HAS ALREADY BEEN ONE HUNDRED AND TWENTY-SEVEN MINUTES.
TWO HOURS? NOBODY HAS EVER BEEN REVIVED AFTER THAT LONG.
THEN AGAIN, NO ONE HAS EVER BEEN REVIVED FROM A CRYOGENIC CHAMBER.
WELL, DOCTOR, AS THEY SAY . . .
THERE IS A FIRST TIME FOR EVERYTHING.
CRYOGENICS? DO YOU THINK YOU CAN REALLY DO SOMETHING FOR HIM?
YOU LOOKED IN THE FREEZER, THEN?
CURIOSITY IS MY BUSINESS. I'M SORRY I CHECKED NOW. BUTLER WAS A GOOD MAN.
IS A GOOD MAN, DETECTIVE.
BUTLER *IS* A GOOD MAN.
I AM *NOT* GIVING UP ON HIM YET.

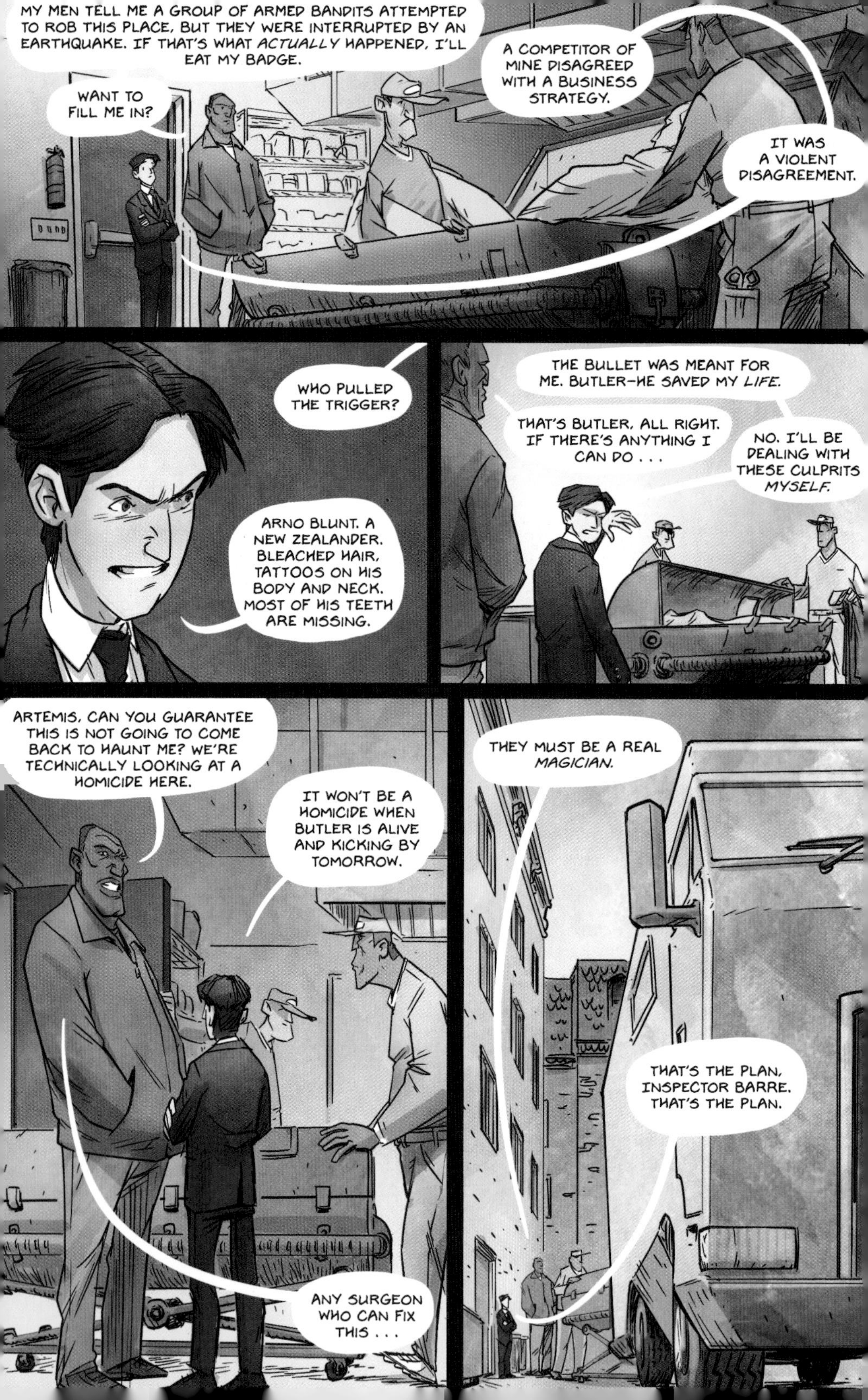
MY MEN TELL ME A GROUP OF ARMED BANDITS ATTEMPTED TO ROB THIS PLACE, BUT THEY WERE INTERRUPTED BY AN EARTHQUAKE. IF THAT'S WHAT *ACTUALLY* HAPPENED, I'LL EAT MY BADGE.
WANT TO FILL ME IN?
A COMPETITOR OF MINE DISAGREED WITH A BUSINESS STRATEGY.
IT WAS A VIOLENT DISAGREEMENT.
WHO PULLED THE TRIGGER?
ARNO BLUNT. A NEW ZEALANDER. BLEACHED HAIR, TATTOOS ON HIS BODY AND NECK. MOST OF HIS TEETH ARE MISSING.
THE BULLET WAS MEANT FOR ME. BUTLER—HE SAVED MY *LIFE*.
THAT'S BUTLER, ALL RIGHT. IF THERE'S ANYTHING I CAN DO . . .
NO. I'LL BE DEALING WITH THESE CULPRITS *MYSELF*.
ARTEMIS, CAN YOU GUARANTEE THIS IS NOT GOING TO COME BACK TO HAUNT ME? WE'RE TECHNICALLY LOOKING AT A HOMICIDE HERE.
IT WON'T BE A HOMICIDE WHEN BUTLER IS ALIVE AND KICKING BY TOMORROW.
ANY SURGEON WHO CAN FIX THIS . . .
THEY MUST BE A REAL *MAGICIAN*.
THAT'S THE PLAN, INSPECTOR BARRE. THAT'S THE PLAN.

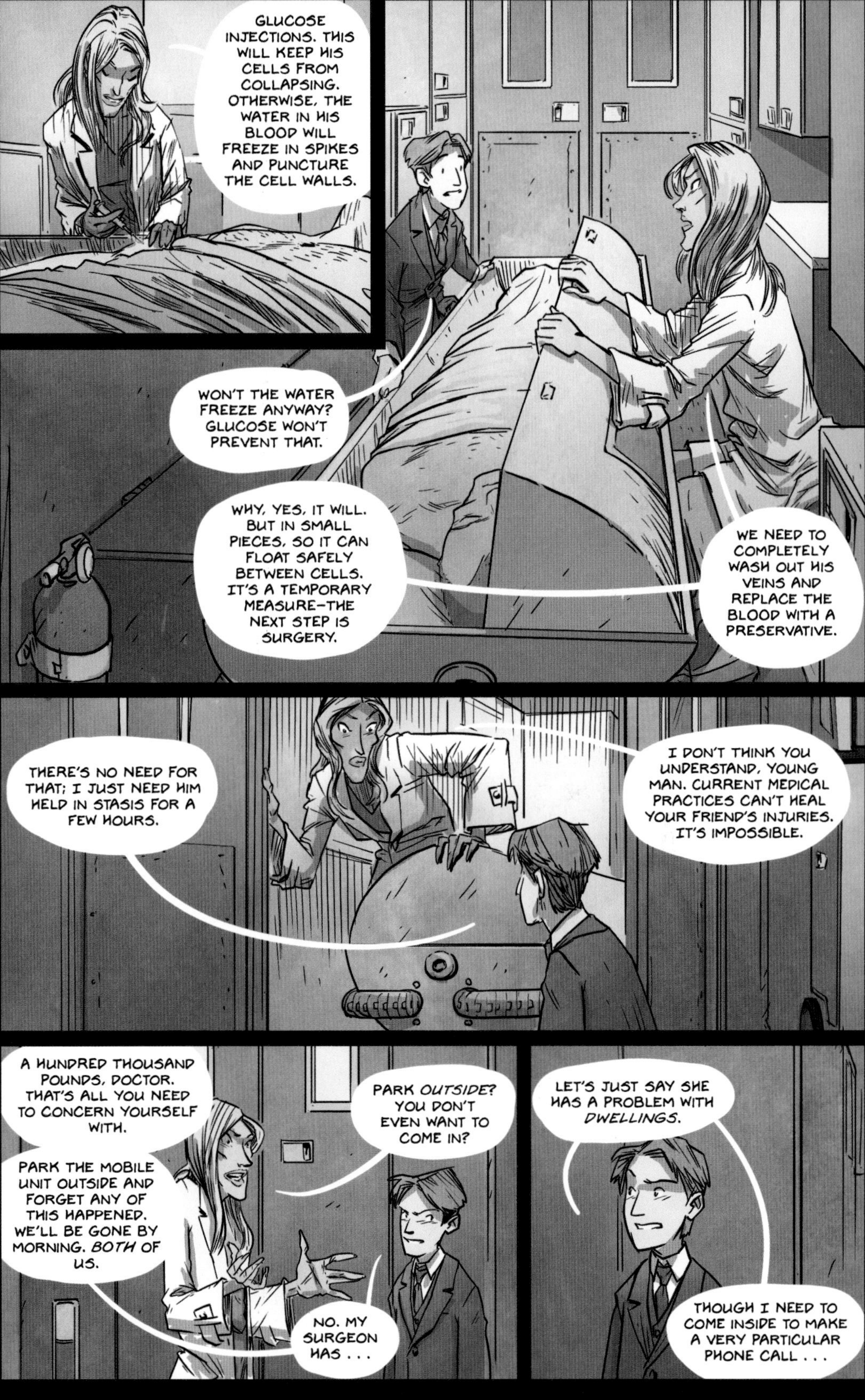
GLUCOSE INJECTIONS. THIS WILL KEEP HIS CELLS FROM COLLAPSING. OTHERWISE, THE WATER IN HIS BLOOD WILL FREEZE IN SPIKES AND PUNCTURE THE CELL WALLS.
WON'T THE WATER FREEZE ANYWAY? GLUCOSE WON'T PREVENT THAT.
WHY, YES, IT WILL. BUT IN SMALL PIECES, SO IT CAN FLOAT SAFELY BETWEEN CELLS. IT'S A TEMPORARY MEASURE—THE NEXT STEP IS SURGERY.
WE NEED TO COMPLETELY WASH OUT HIS VEINS AND REPLACE THE BLOOD WITH A PRESERVATIVE.
THERE'S NO NEED FOR THAT; I JUST NEED HIM HELD IN STASIS FOR A FEW HOURS.
I DON'T THINK YOU UNDERSTAND, YOUNG MAN. CURRENT MEDICAL PRACTICES CAN'T HEAL YOUR FRIEND'S INJURIES. IT'S IMPOSSIBLE.
A HUNDRED THOUSAND POUNDS, DOCTOR. THAT'S ALL YOU NEED TO CONCERN YOURSELF WITH.
PARK THE MOBILE UNIT OUTSIDE AND FORGET ANY OF THIS HAPPENED. WE'LL BE GONE BY MORNING. *BOTH* OF US.
PARK *OUTSIDE*? YOU DON'T EVEN WANT TO COME IN?
NO. MY SURGEON HAS . . .
LET'S JUST SAY SHE HAS A PROBLEM WITH *DWELLINGS*.
THOUGH I NEED TO COME INSIDE TO MAKE A VERY PARTICULAR PHONE CALL . . .

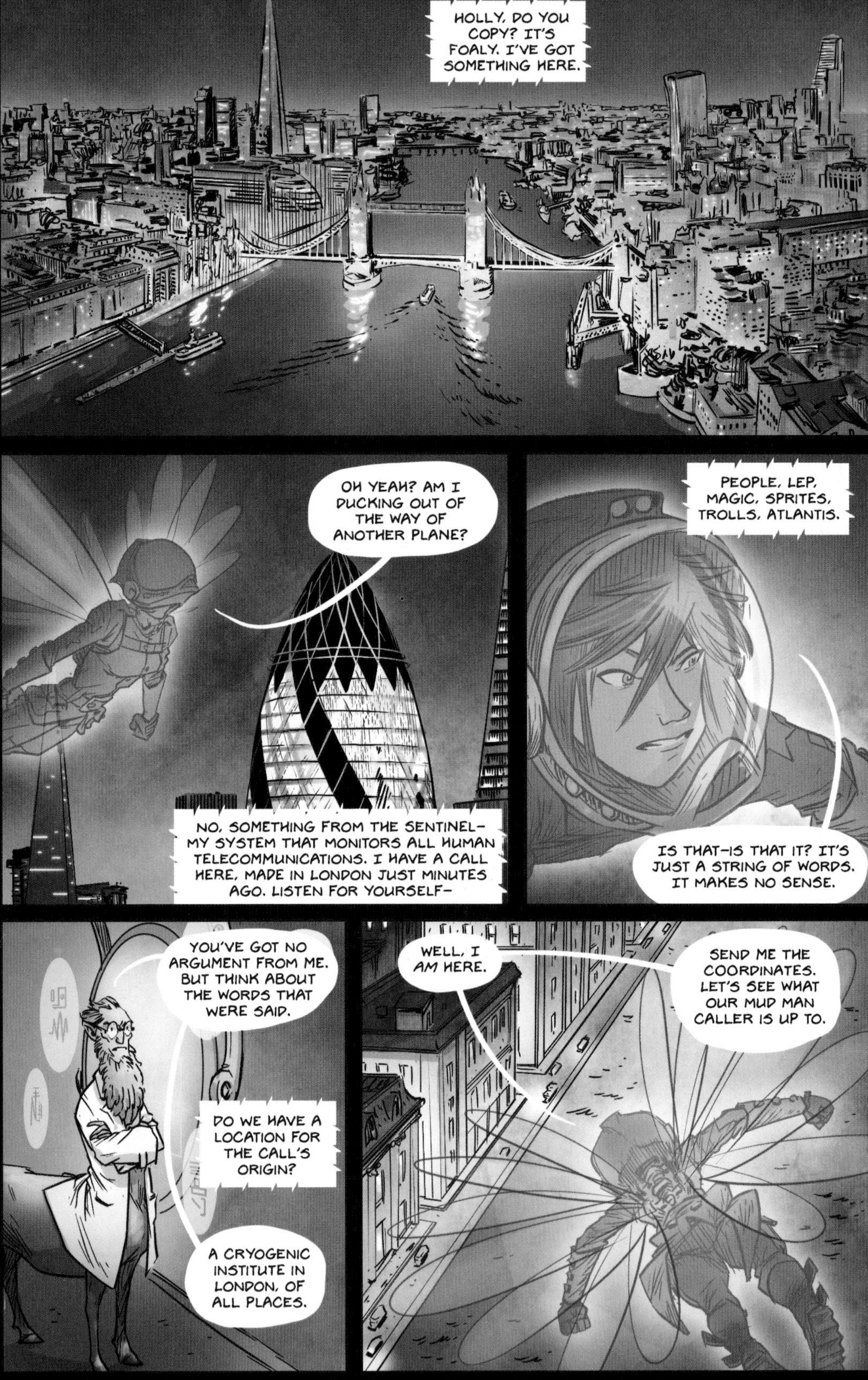
HOLLY, DO YOU COPY? IT'S FOALY. I'VE GOT SOMETHING HERE.
OH YEAH? AM I DUCKING OUT OF THE WAY OF ANOTHER PLANE?
NO, SOMETHING FROM THE SENTINEL— MY SYSTEM THAT MONITORS ALL HUMAN TELECOMMUNICATIONS. I HAVE A CALL HERE, MADE IN LONDON JUST MINUTES AGO. LISTEN FOR YOURSELF—
PEOPLE, LEP, MAGIC, SPRITES, TROLLS, ATLANTIS.
IS THAT—IS THAT IT? IT'S JUST A STRING OF WORDS. IT MAKES NO SENSE.
YOU'VE GOT NO ARGUMENT FROM ME. BUT THINK ABOUT THE WORDS THAT WERE SAID.
DO WE HAVE A LOCATION FOR THE CALL'S ORIGIN?
A CRYOGENIC INSTITUTE IN LONDON, OF ALL PLACES.
WELL, I AM HERE.
SEND ME THE COORDINATES. LET'S SEE WHAT OUR MUD MAN CALLER IS UP TO.

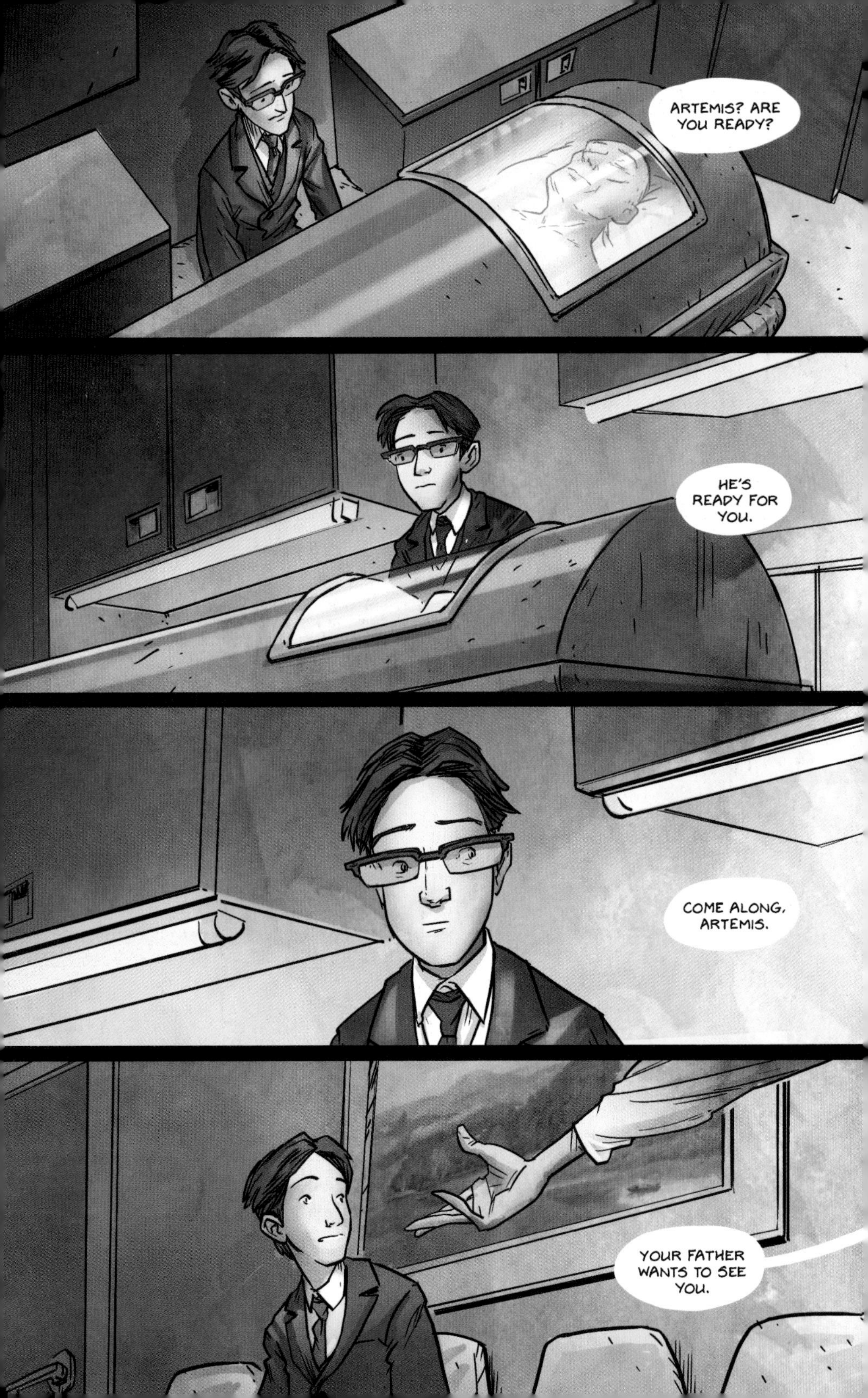
ARTEMIS? ARE YOU READY?
HE'S READY FOR YOU.
COME ALONG, ARTEMIS.
YOUR FATHER WANTS TO SEE YOU.

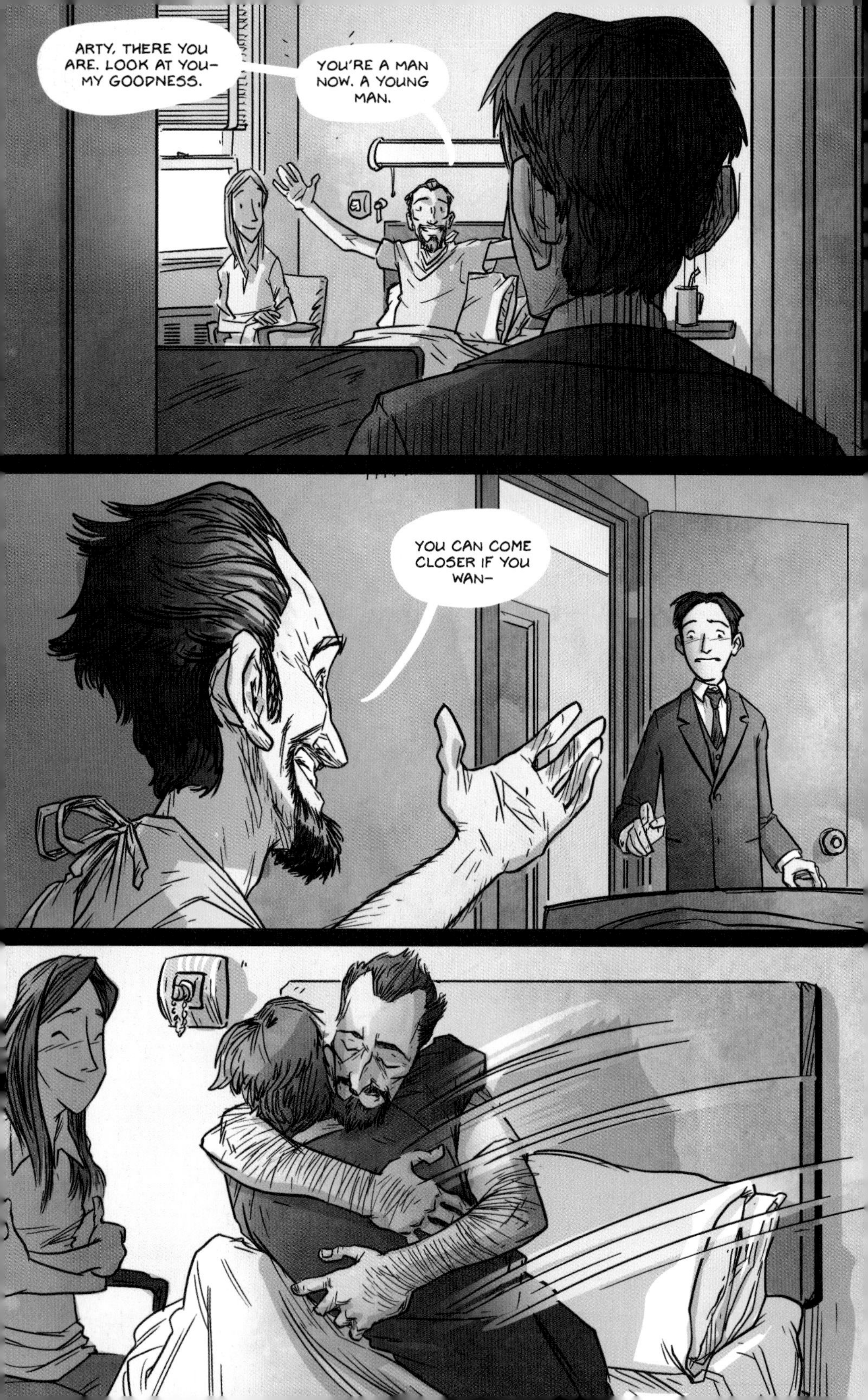
ARTY, THERE YOU ARE. LOOK AT YOU— MY GOODNESS.
YOU'RE A MAN NOW. A YOUNG MAN.
YOU CAN COME CLOSER IF YOU WAN—

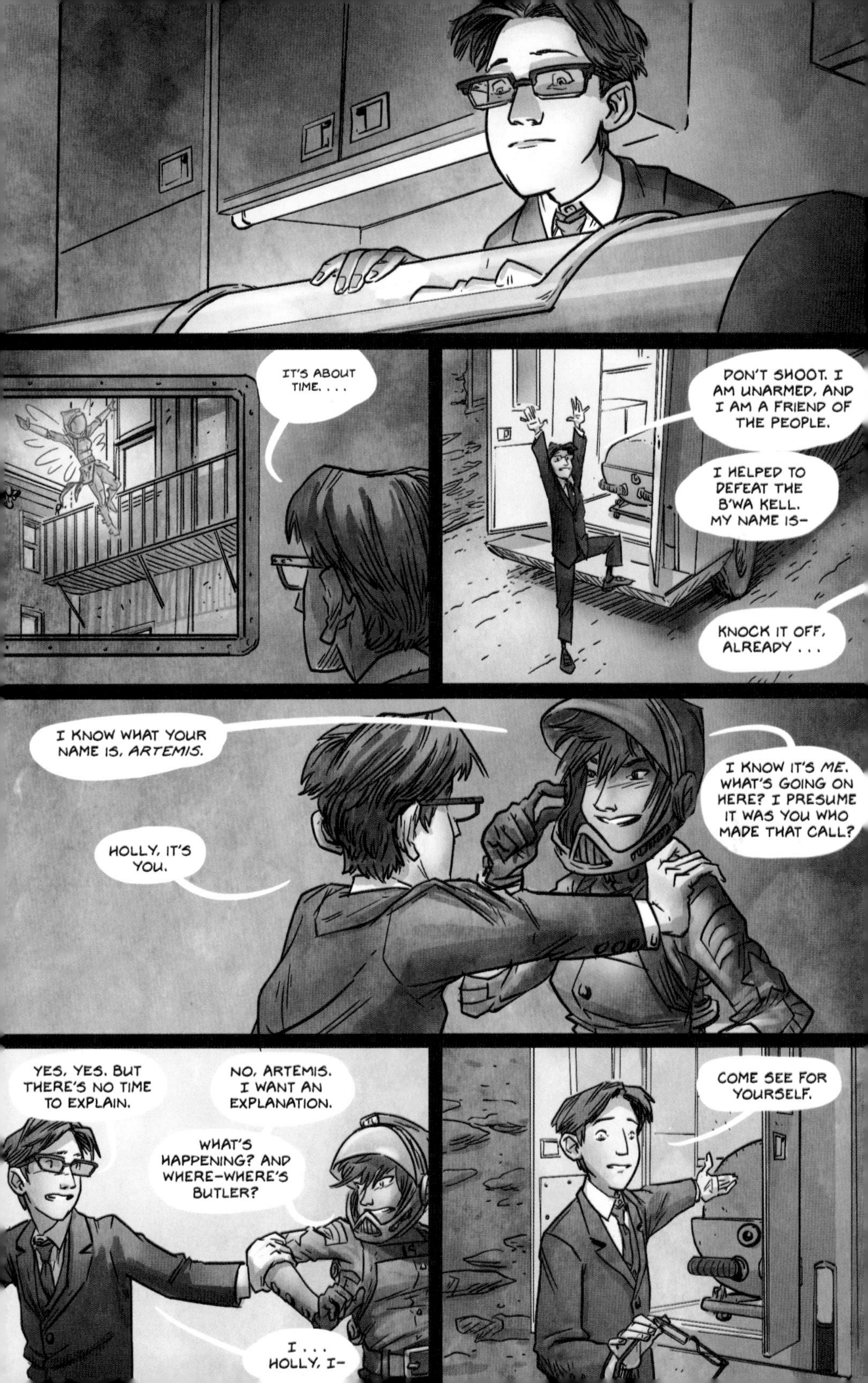
IT'S ABOUT TIME. . . .
DON'T SHOOT. I AM UNARMED, AND I AM A FRIEND OF THE PEOPLE.
I HELPED TO DEFEAT THE B'WA KELL. MY NAME IS–
KNOCK IT OFF, ALREADY . . .
I KNOW WHAT YOUR NAME IS, *ARTEMIS*.
HOLLY, IT'S YOU.
I KNOW IT'S *ME*. WHAT'S GOING ON HERE? I PRESUME IT WAS YOU WHO MADE THAT CALL?
YES, YES. BUT THERE'S NO TIME TO EXPLAIN.
NO, ARTEMIS. I WANT AN EXPLANATION.
WHAT'S HAPPENING? AND WHERE–WHERE'S BUTLER?
I . . . HOLLY, I–
COME SEE FOR YOURSELF.

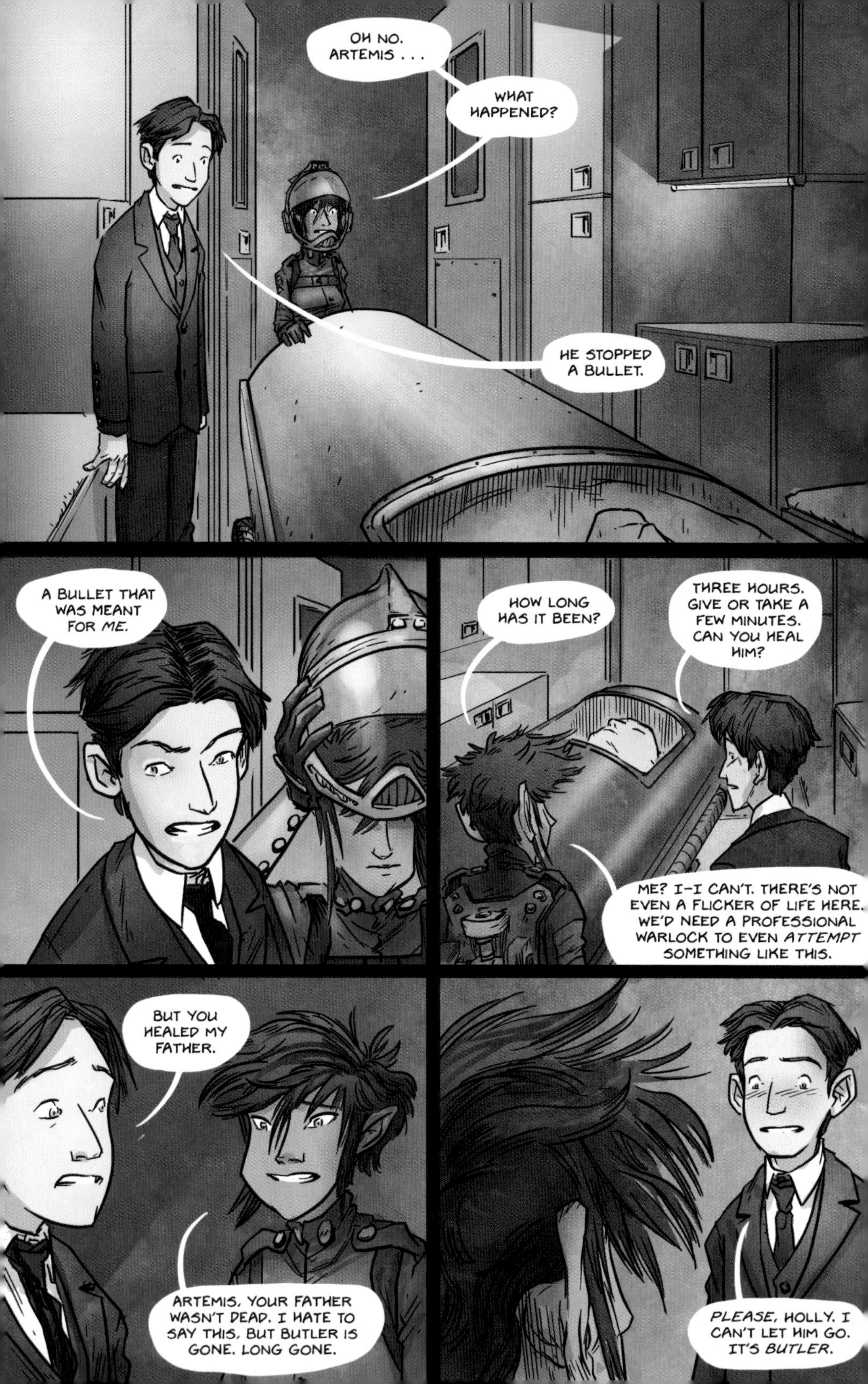
OH NO. ARTEMIS . . .
WHAT HAPPENED?
HE STOPPED A BULLET.
A BULLET THAT WAS MEANT FOR *ME*.
HOW LONG HAS IT BEEN?
THREE HOURS. GIVE OR TAKE A FEW MINUTES. CAN YOU HEAL HIM?
ME? I–I CAN'T. THERE'S NOT EVEN A FLICKER OF LIFE HERE. WE'D NEED A PROFESSIONAL WARLOCK TO EVEN *ATTEMPT* SOMETHING LIKE THIS.
BUT YOU HEALED MY FATHER.
ARTEMIS, YOUR FATHER WASN'T DEAD. I HATE TO SAY THIS, BUT BUTLER IS GONE. LONG GONE.
PLEASE, HOLLY. I CAN'T LET HIM GO. IT'S *BUTLER*.

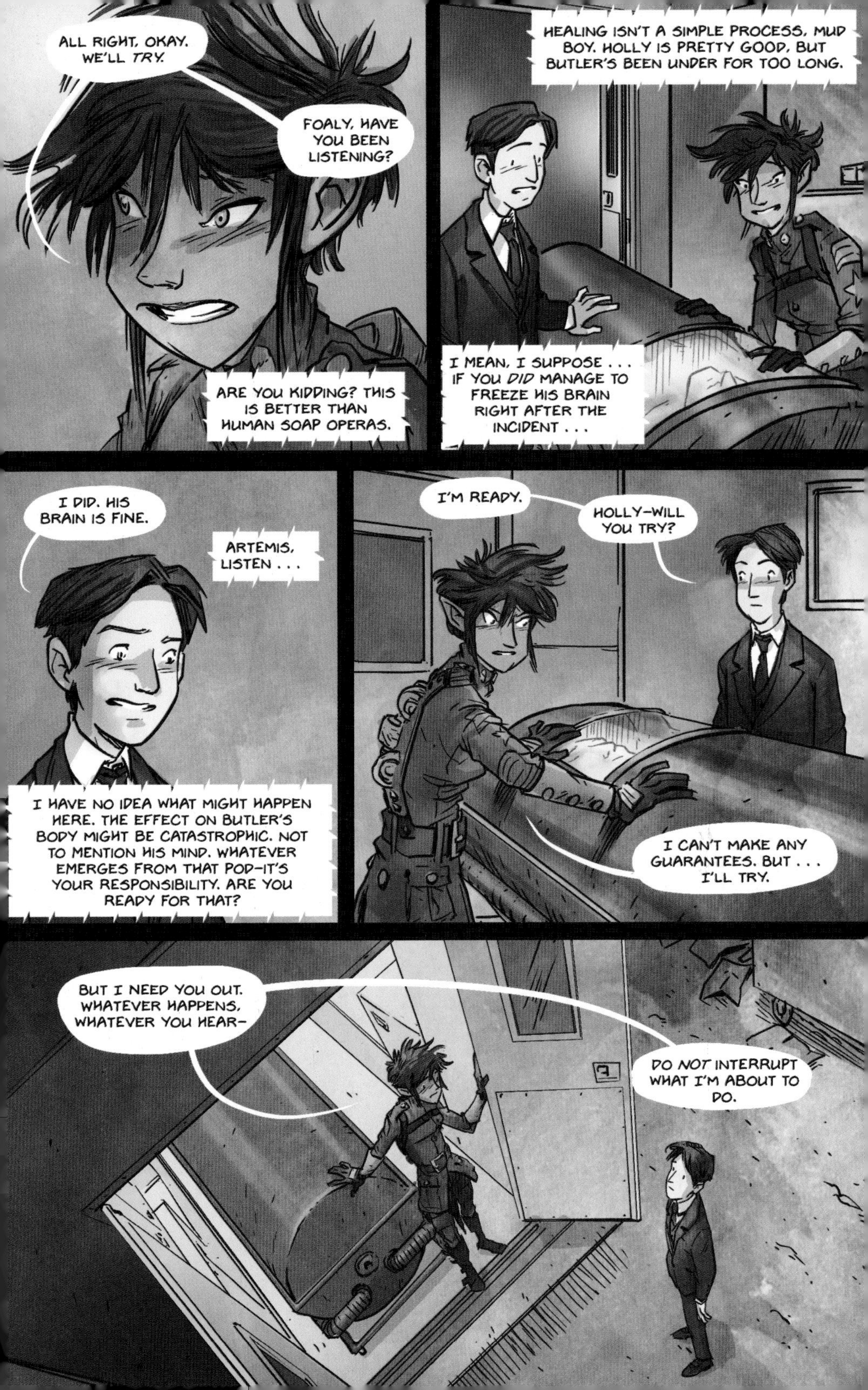
ALL RIGHT, OKAY. WE'LL *TRY*.
FOALY, HAVE YOU BEEN LISTENING?
ARE YOU KIDDING? THIS IS BETTER THAN HUMAN SOAP OPERAS.
HEALING ISN'T A SIMPLE PROCESS, MUD BOY. HOLLY IS PRETTY GOOD, BUT BUTLER'S BEEN UNDER FOR TOO LONG.
I MEAN, I SUPPOSE . . . IF YOU *DID* MANAGE TO FREEZE HIS BRAIN RIGHT AFTER THE INCIDENT . . .
I DID. HIS BRAIN IS FINE.
ARTEMIS, LISTEN . . .
I HAVE NO IDEA WHAT MIGHT HAPPEN HERE. THE EFFECT ON BUTLER'S BODY MIGHT BE CATASTROPHIC. NOT TO MENTION HIS MIND. WHATEVER EMERGES FROM THAT POD—IT'S YOUR RESPONSIBILITY. ARE YOU READY FOR THAT?
I'M READY.
HOLLY—WILL YOU TRY?
I CAN'T MAKE ANY GUARANTEES. BUT . . . I'LL TRY.
BUT I NEED YOU OUT. WHATEVER HAPPENS, WHATEVER YOU HEAR—
DO *NOT* INTERRUPT WHAT I'M ABOUT TO DO.

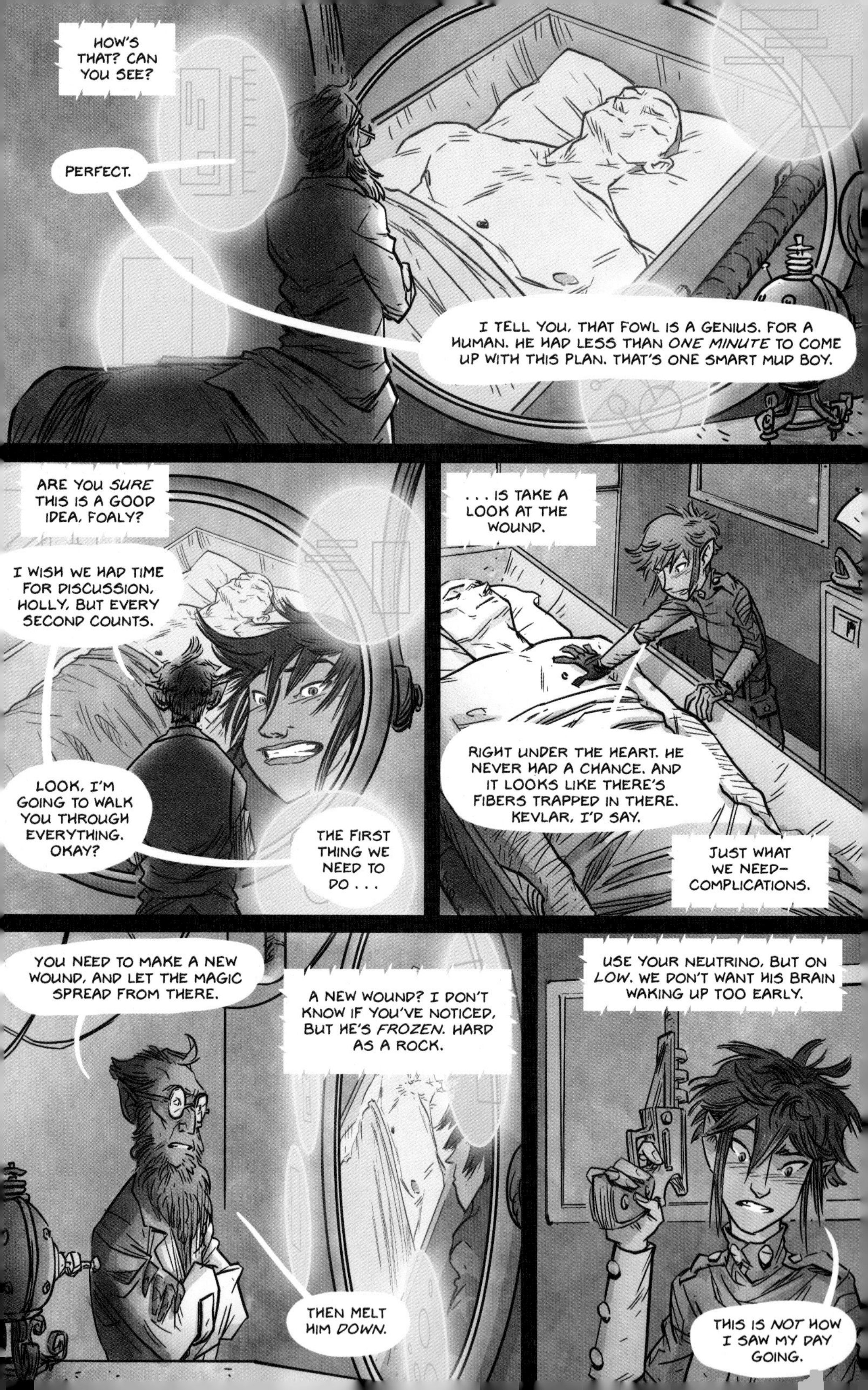
HOW'S THAT? CAN YOU SEE?
PERFECT.
I TELL YOU, THAT FOWL IS A GENIUS. FOR A HUMAN. HE HAD LESS THAN *ONE MINUTE* TO COME UP WITH THIS PLAN. THAT'S ONE SMART MUD BOY.
ARE YOU *SURE* THIS IS A GOOD IDEA, FOALY?
I WISH WE HAD TIME FOR DISCUSSION, HOLLY, BUT EVERY SECOND COUNTS.
LOOK, I'M GOING TO WALK YOU THROUGH EVERYTHING. OKAY?
THE FIRST THING WE NEED TO DO . . .
. . . IS TAKE A LOOK AT THE WOUND.
RIGHT UNDER THE HEART. HE NEVER HAD A CHANCE. AND IT LOOKS LIKE THERE'S FIBERS TRAPPED IN THERE. KEVLAR, I'D SAY.
JUST WHAT WE NEED— COMPLICATIONS.
YOU NEED TO MAKE A NEW WOUND, AND LET THE MAGIC SPREAD FROM THERE.
A NEW WOUND? I DON'T KNOW IF YOU'VE NOTICED, BUT HE'S *FROZEN*. HARD AS A ROCK.
THEN MELT HIM *DOWN*.
USE YOUR NEUTRINO, BUT ON *LOW*. WE DON'T WANT HIS BRAIN WAKING UP TOO EARLY.
THIS IS *NOT* HOW I SAW MY DAY GOING.

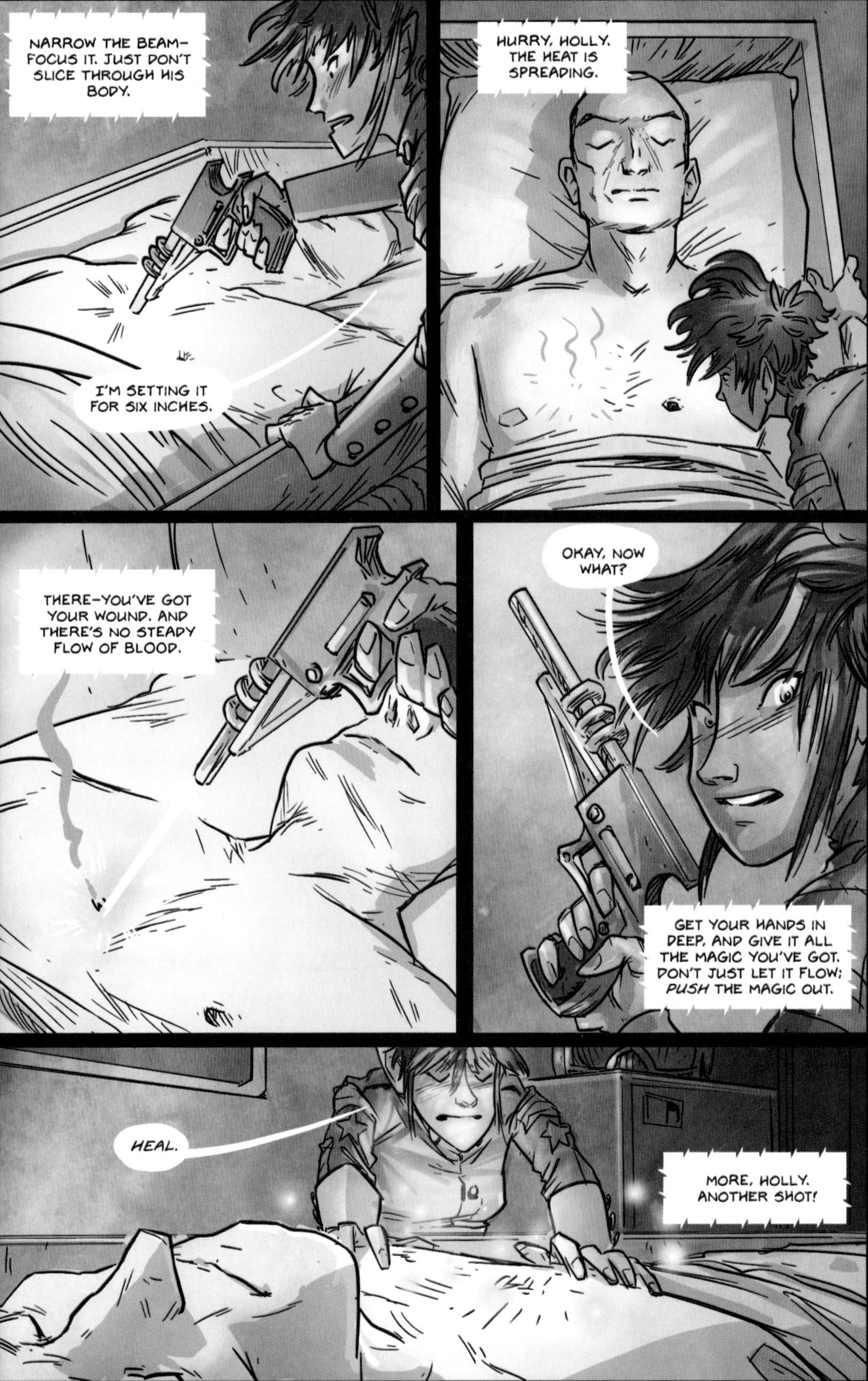
NARROW THE BEAM—FOCUS IT. JUST DON'T SLICE THROUGH HIS BODY.
I'M SETTING IT FOR SIX INCHES.
HURRY, HOLLY. THE HEAT IS SPREADING.
THERE—YOU'VE GOT YOUR WOUND. AND THERE'S NO STEADY FLOW OF BLOOD.
OKAY, NOW WHAT?
GET YOUR HANDS IN DEEP, AND GIVE IT ALL THE MAGIC YOU'VE GOT. DON'T JUST LET IT FLOW; *PUSH* THE MAGIC OUT.
HEAL.
MORE, HOLLY. ANOTHER SHOT!

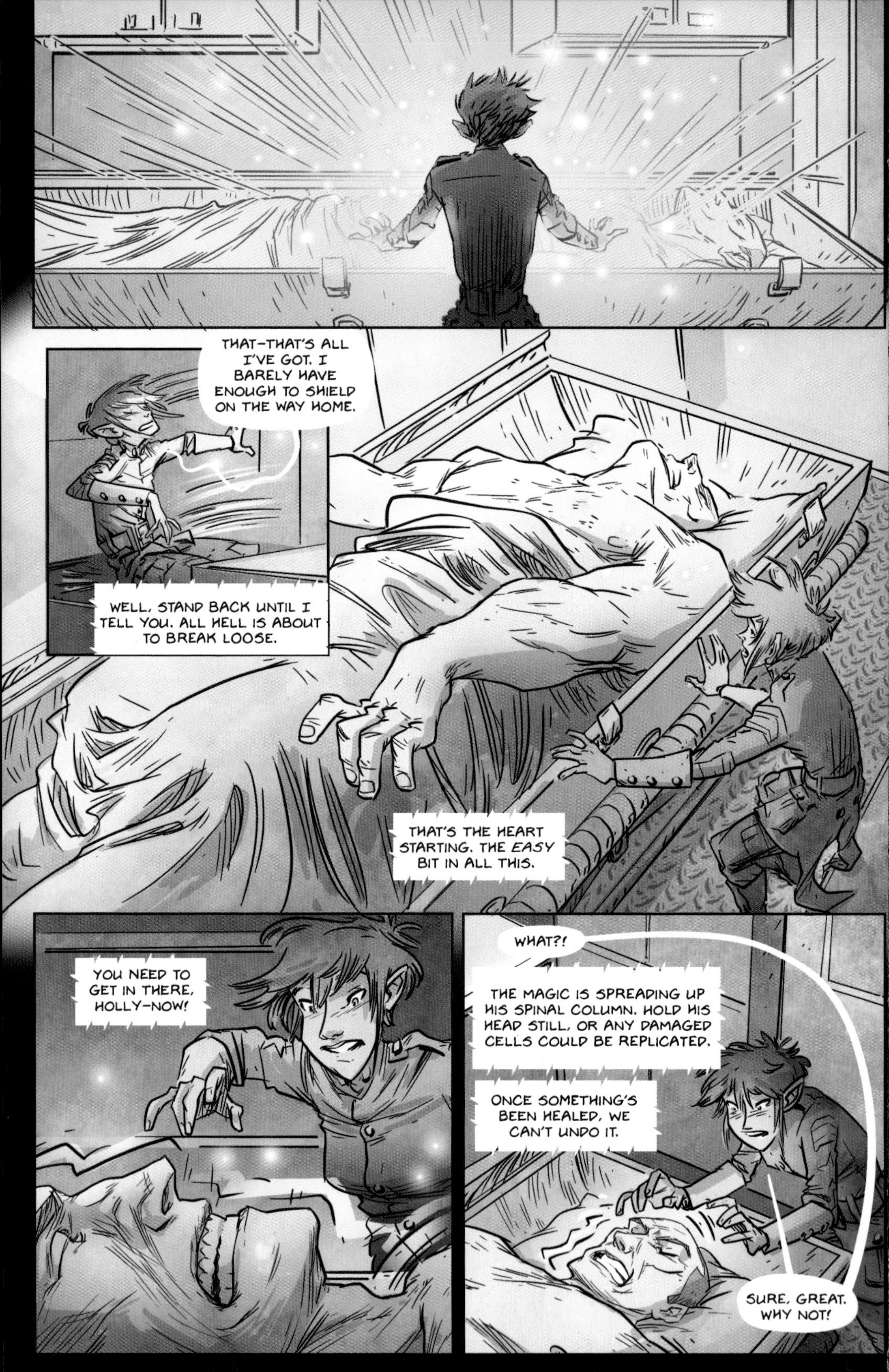
THAT—THAT'S ALL I'VE GOT. I BARELY HAVE ENOUGH TO SHIELD ON THE WAY HOME.
WELL, STAND BACK UNTIL I TELL YOU. ALL HELL IS ABOUT TO BREAK LOOSE.
THAT'S THE HEART STARTING. THE *EASY* BIT IN ALL THIS.
YOU NEED TO GET IN THERE, HOLLY—NOW!
WHAT?!
THE MAGIC IS SPREADING UP HIS SPINAL COLUMN. HOLD HIS HEAD STILL, OR ANY DAMAGED CELLS COULD BE REPLICATED.
ONCE SOMETHING'S BEEN HEALED, WE CAN'T UNDO IT.
SURE, GREAT. WHY NOT!

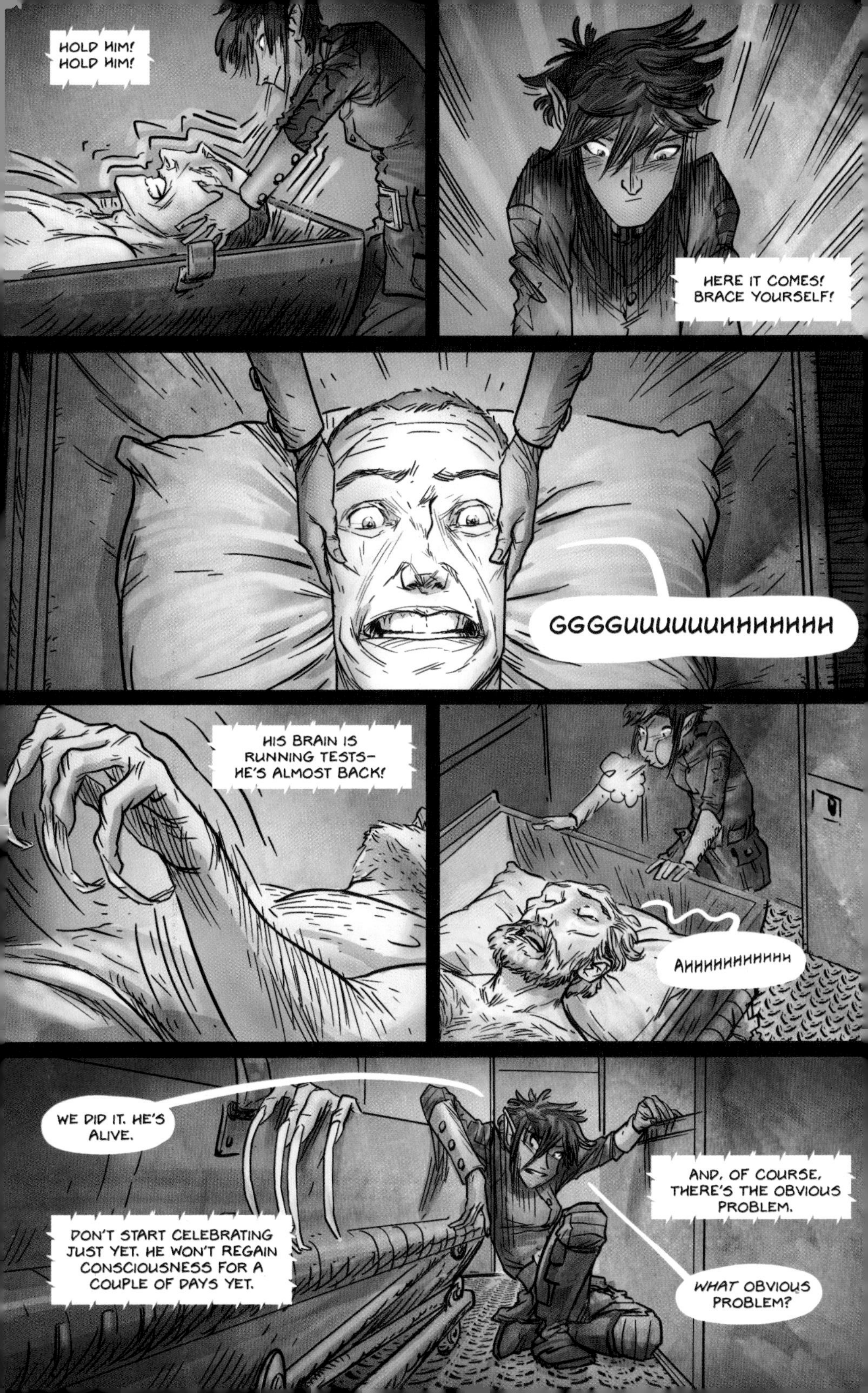
HOLD HIM! HOLD HIM!
HERE IT COMES! BRACE YOURSELF!
GGGGUUUUUUUHHHHHHH
HIS BRAIN IS RUNNING TESTS— HE'S ALMOST BACK!
AHHHHHHHHHHH
WE DID IT. HE'S ALIVE.
DON'T START CELEBRATING JUST YET. HE WON'T REGAIN CONSCIOUSNESS FOR A COUPLE OF DAYS YET.
AND, OF COURSE, THERE'S THE OBVIOUS PROBLEM.
WHAT OBVIOUS PROBLEM?

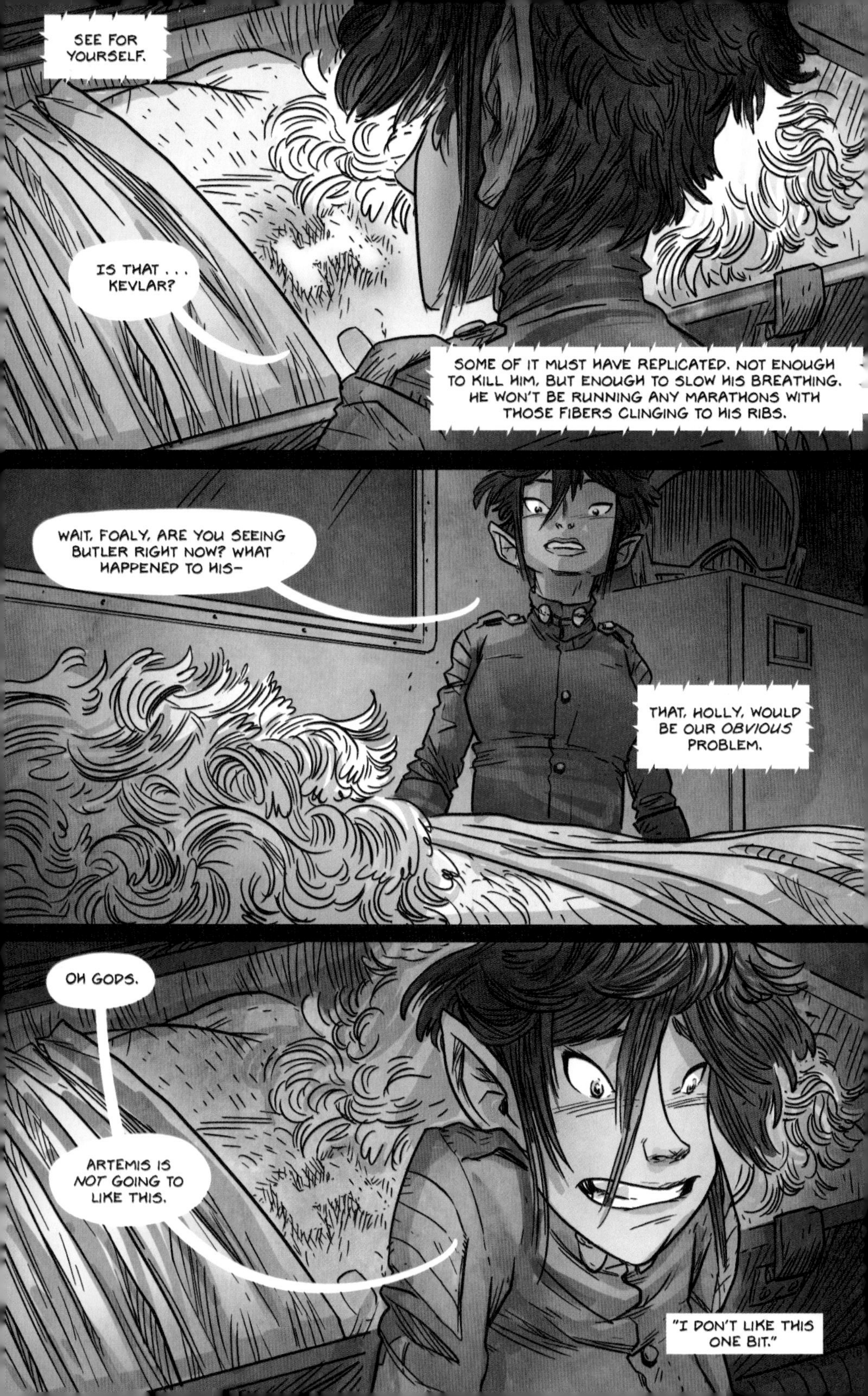
SEE FOR YOURSELF.
IS THAT . . . KEVLAR?
SOME OF IT MUST HAVE REPLICATED. NOT ENOUGH TO KILL HIM, BUT ENOUGH TO SLOW HIS BREATHING. HE WON'T BE RUNNING ANY MARATHONS WITH THOSE FIBERS CLINGING TO HIS RIBS.
WAIT. FOALY, ARE YOU SEEING BUTLER RIGHT NOW? WHAT HAPPENED TO HIS–
THAT, HOLLY, WOULD BE OUR *OBVIOUS* PROBLEM.
OH GODS.
ARTEMIS IS *NOT* GOING TO LIKE THIS.
"I DON'T LIKE THIS ONE BIT."

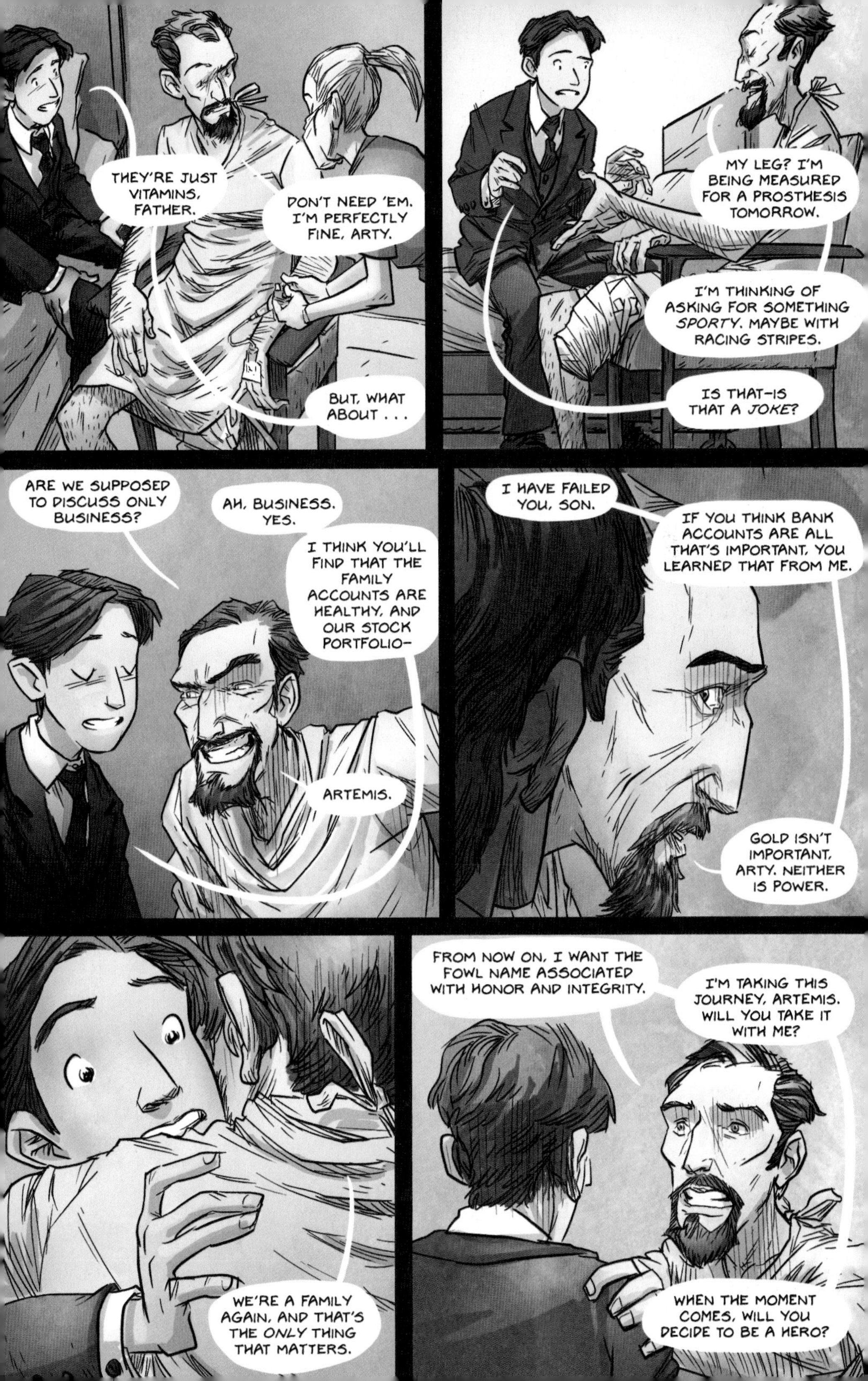
THEY'RE JUST VITAMINS, FATHER.
DON'T NEED 'EM. I'M PERFECTLY FINE, ARTY.
BUT, WHAT ABOUT . . .
MY LEG? I'M BEING MEASURED FOR A PROSTHESIS TOMORROW.
I'M THINKING OF ASKING FOR SOMETHING *SPORTY*. MAYBE WITH RACING STRIPES.
IS THAT—IS THAT A *JOKE*?
ARE WE SUPPOSED TO DISCUSS ONLY BUSINESS?
AH, BUSINESS. YES.
I THINK YOU'LL FIND THAT THE FAMILY ACCOUNTS ARE HEALTHY, AND OUR STOCK PORTFOLIO—
ARTEMIS.
I HAVE FAILED YOU, SON.
IF YOU THINK BANK ACCOUNTS ARE ALL THAT'S IMPORTANT, YOU LEARNED THAT FROM ME.
GOLD ISN'T IMPORTANT, ARTY. NEITHER IS POWER.
WE'RE A FAMILY AGAIN, AND THAT'S THE *ONLY* THING THAT MATTERS.
FROM NOW ON, I WANT THE FOWL NAME ASSOCIATED WITH HONOR AND INTEGRITY.
I'M TAKING THIS JOURNEY, ARTEMIS. WILL YOU TAKE IT WITH ME?
WHEN THE MOMENT COMES, WILL YOU DECIDE TO BE A HERO?

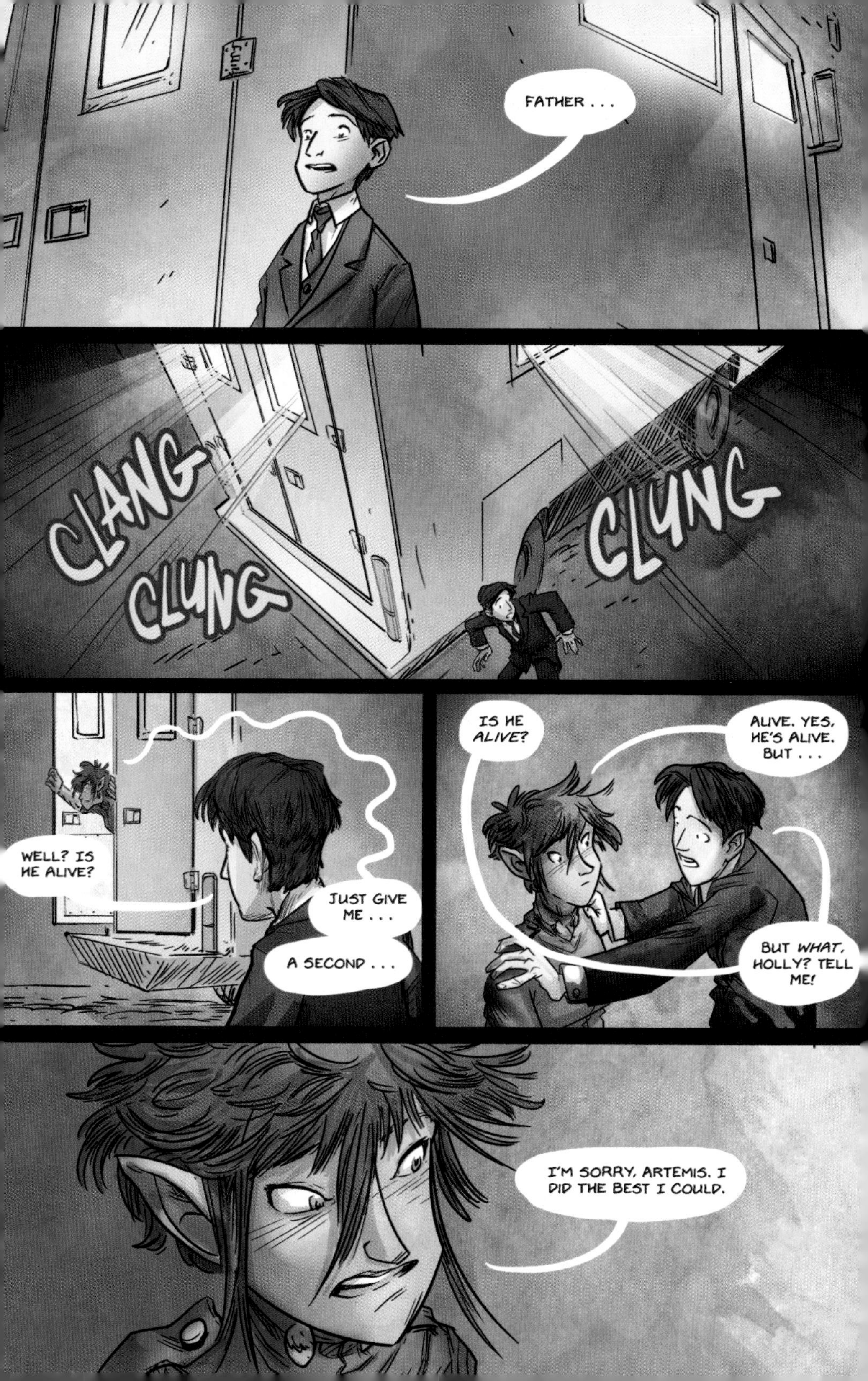
FATHER . . .
CLANG
CLUNG
CLUNG
WELL? IS HE ALIVE?
JUST GIVE ME . . .
A SECOND . . .
IS HE ALIVE?
ALIVE. YES, HE'S ALIVE. BUT . . .
BUT WHAT, HOLLY? TELL ME!
I'M SORRY, ARTEMIS. I DID THE BEST I COULD.

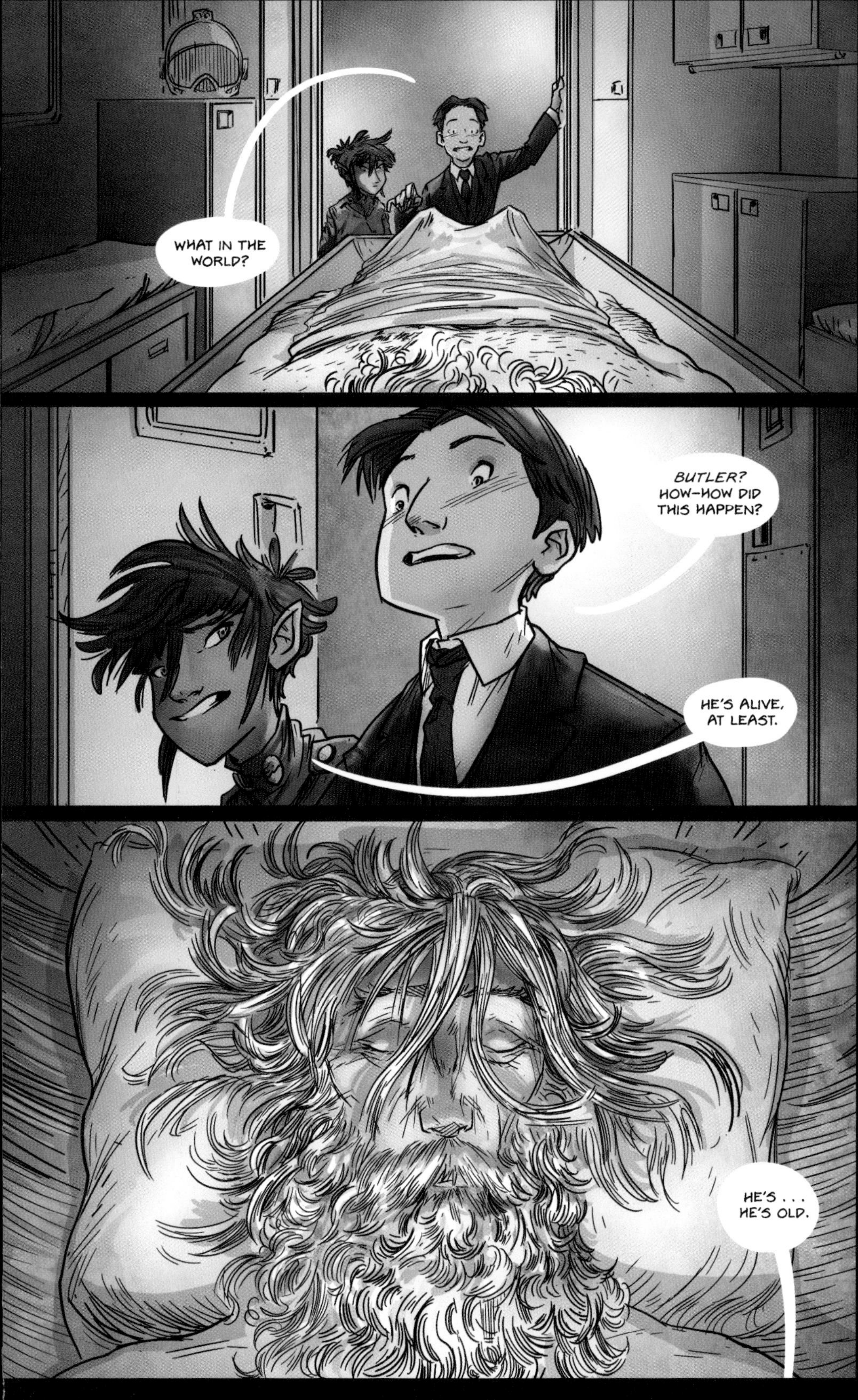
WHAT IN THE WORLD?
BUTLER? HOW—HOW DID THIS HAPPEN?
HE'S ALIVE, AT LEAST.
HE'S . . . HE'S OLD.

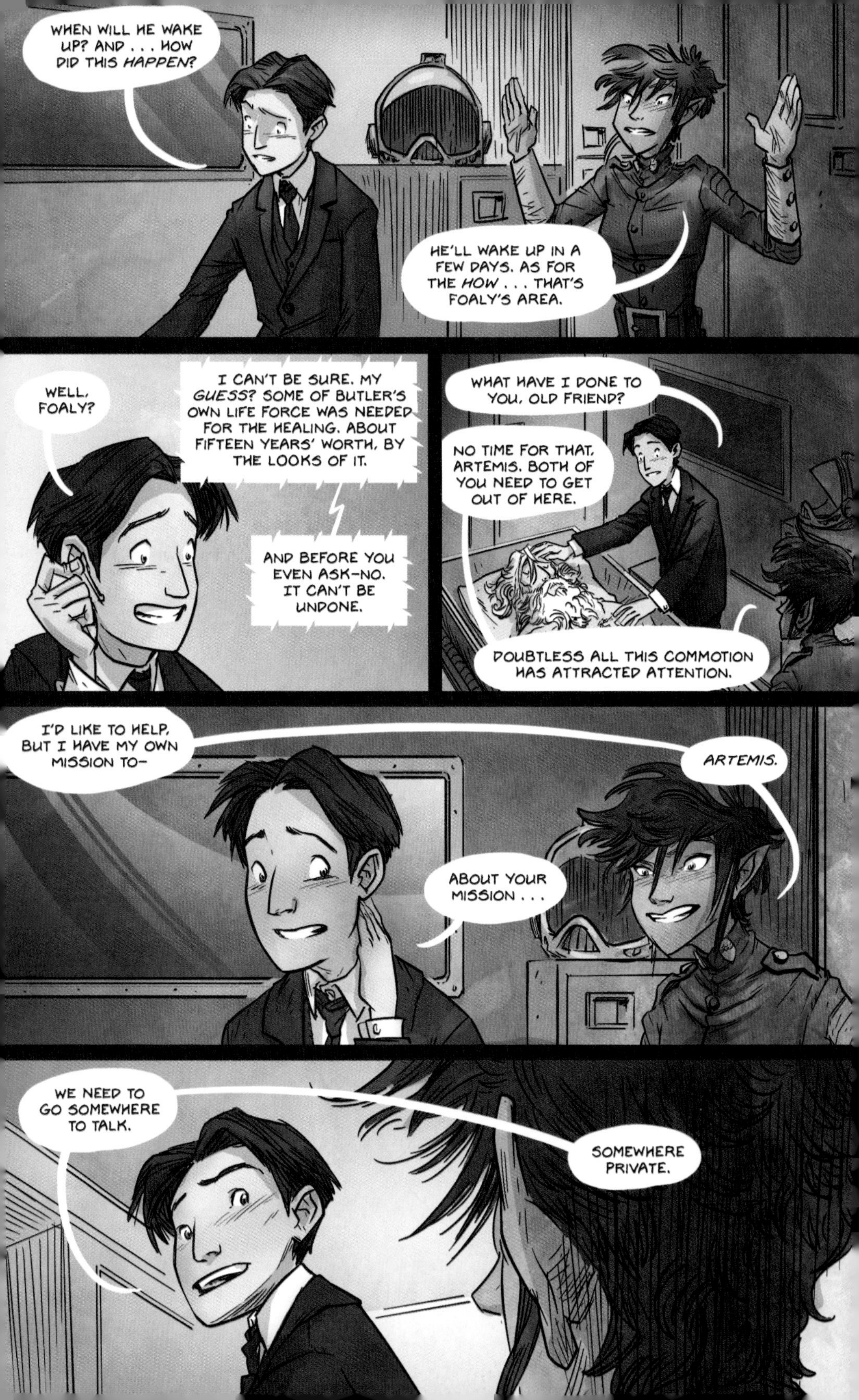
WHEN WILL HE WAKE UP? AND . . . HOW DID THIS *HAPPEN*?
HE'LL WAKE UP IN A FEW DAYS. AS FOR THE *HOW* . . . THAT'S FOALY'S AREA.
WELL, FOALY?
I CAN'T BE SURE. MY *GUESS*? SOME OF BUTLER'S OWN LIFE FORCE WAS NEEDED FOR THE HEALING. ABOUT FIFTEEN YEARS' WORTH, BY THE LOOKS OF IT.
AND BEFORE YOU EVEN ASK—NO. IT CAN'T BE UNDONE.
WHAT HAVE I DONE TO YOU, OLD FRIEND?
NO TIME FOR THAT, ARTEMIS. BOTH OF YOU NEED TO GET OUT OF HERE.
DOUBTLESS ALL THIS COMMOTION HAS ATTRACTED ATTENTION.
I'D LIKE TO HELP, BUT I HAVE MY OWN MISSION TO—
ARTEMIS.
ABOUT YOUR MISSION . . .
WE NEED TO GO SOMEWHERE TO TALK.
SOMEWHERE PRIVATE.

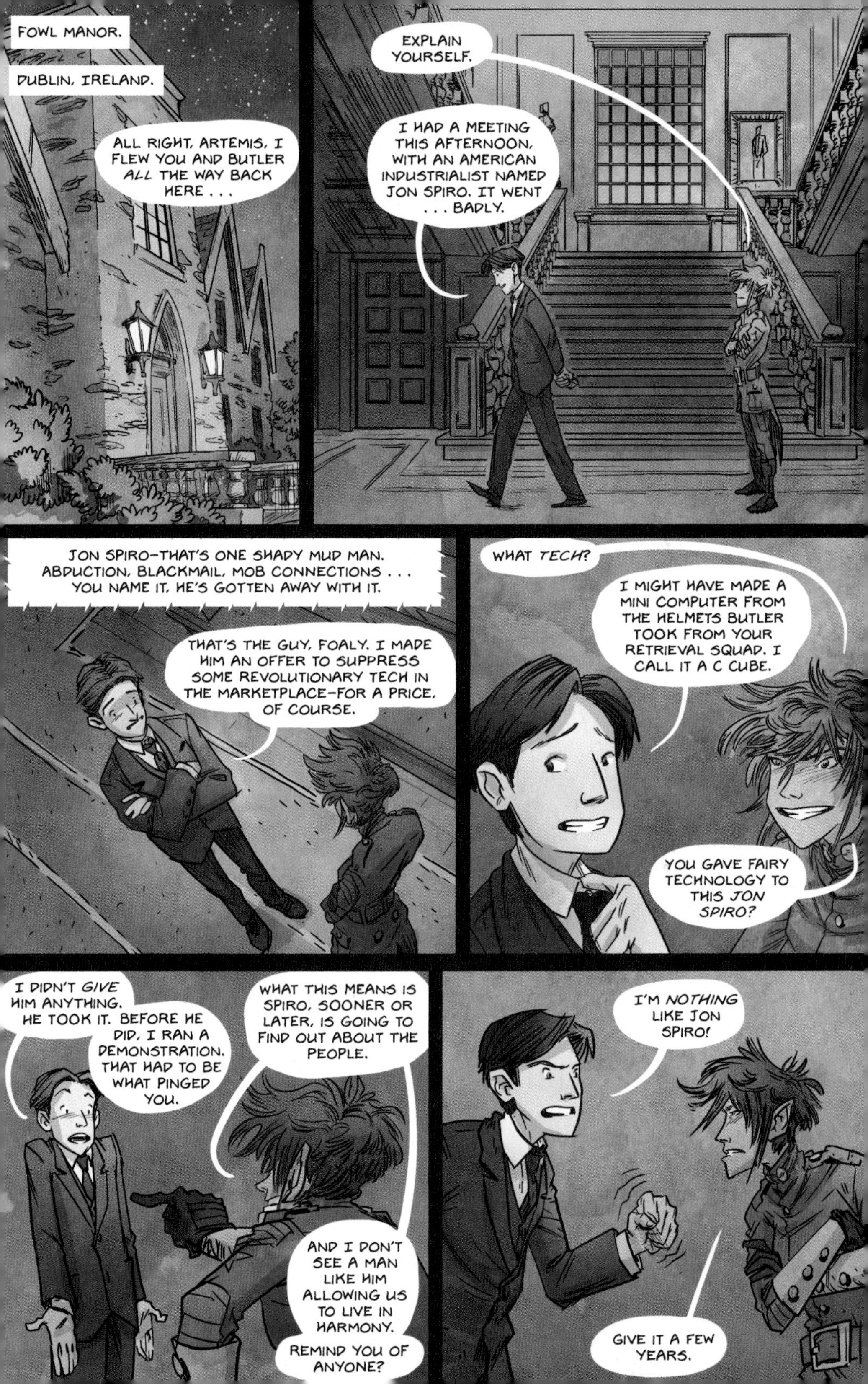
FOWL MANOR.
DUBLIN, IRELAND.
ALL RIGHT, ARTEMIS, I FLEW YOU AND BUTLER *ALL* THE WAY BACK HERE . . .
EXPLAIN YOURSELF.
I HAD A MEETING THIS AFTERNOON, WITH AN AMERICAN INDUSTRIALIST NAMED JON SPIRO. IT WENT . . . BADLY.
JON SPIRO—THAT'S ONE SHADY MUD MAN. ABDUCTION, BLACKMAIL, MOB CONNECTIONS . . . YOU NAME IT, HE'S GOTTEN AWAY WITH IT.
THAT'S THE GUY, FOALY. I MADE HIM AN OFFER TO SUPPRESS SOME REVOLUTIONARY TECH IN THE MARKETPLACE—FOR A PRICE, OF COURSE.
WHAT *TECH*?
I MIGHT HAVE MADE A MINI COMPUTER FROM THE HELMETS BUTLER TOOK FROM YOUR RETRIEVAL SQUAD. I CALL IT A C CUBE.
YOU GAVE FAIRY TECHNOLOGY TO THIS *JON SPIRO*?
I DIDN'T *GIVE* HIM ANYTHING. HE TOOK IT. BEFORE HE DID, I RAN A DEMONSTRATION. THAT HAD TO BE WHAT PINGED YOU.
WHAT THIS MEANS IS SPIRO, SOONER OR LATER, IS GOING TO FIND OUT ABOUT THE PEOPLE.
AND I DON'T SEE A MAN LIKE HIM ALLOWING US TO LIVE IN HARMONY.
REMIND YOU OF ANYONE?
I'M *NOTHING* LIKE JON SPIRO!
GIVE IT A FEW YEARS.

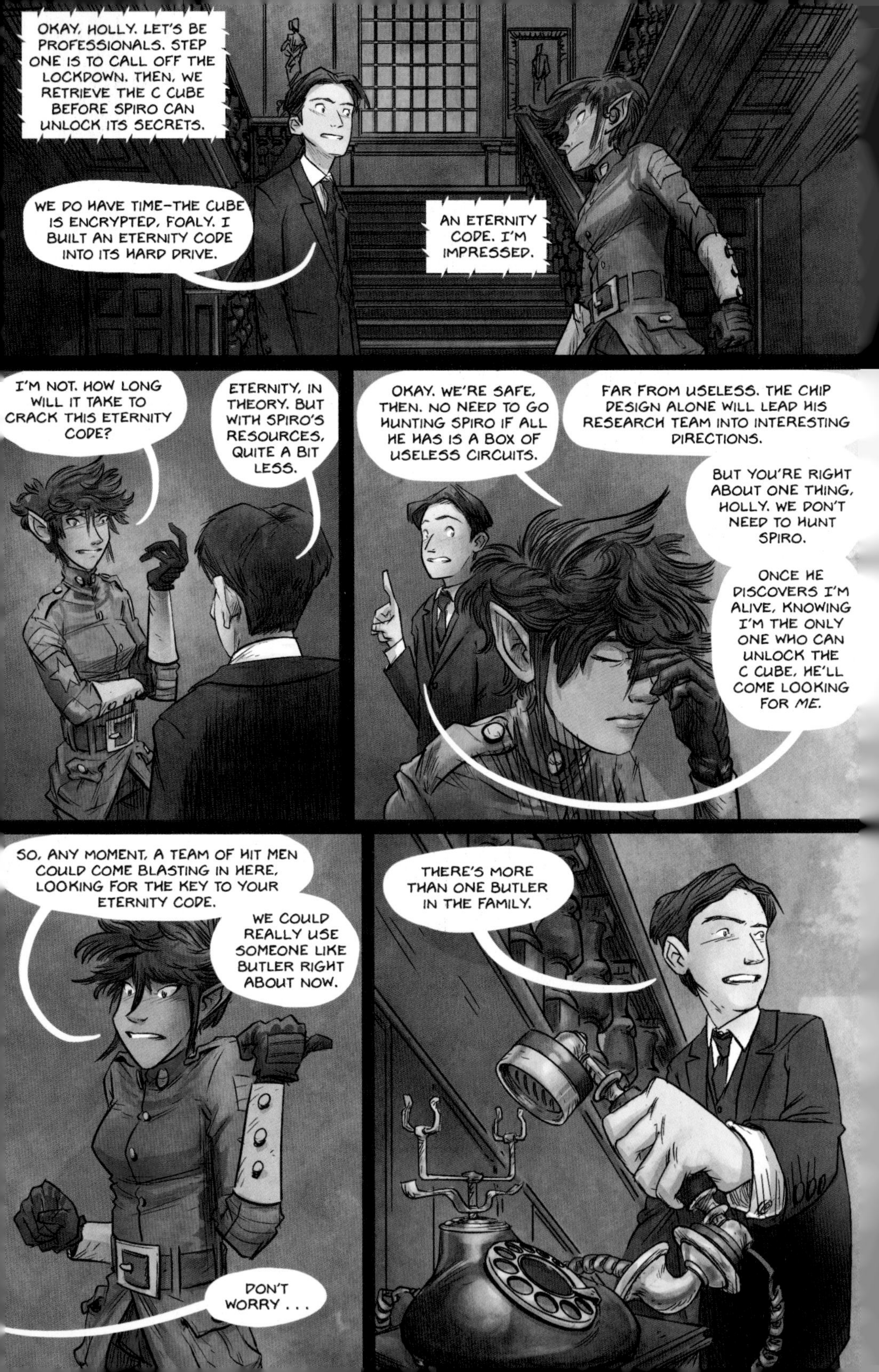
OKAY, HOLLY. LET'S BE PROFESSIONALS. STEP ONE IS TO CALL OFF THE LOCKDOWN. THEN, WE RETRIEVE THE C CUBE BEFORE SPIRO CAN UNLOCK ITS SECRETS.
WE DO HAVE TIME—THE CUBE IS ENCRYPTED, FOALY. I BUILT AN ETERNITY CODE INTO ITS HARD DRIVE.
AN ETERNITY CODE. I'M IMPRESSED.
I'M NOT. HOW LONG WILL IT TAKE TO CRACK THIS ETERNITY CODE?
ETERNITY, IN THEORY. BUT WITH SPIRO'S RESOURCES, QUITE A BIT LESS.
OKAY. WE'RE SAFE, THEN. NO NEED TO GO HUNTING SPIRO IF ALL HE HAS IS A BOX OF USELESS CIRCUITS.
FAR FROM USELESS. THE CHIP DESIGN ALONE WILL LEAD HIS RESEARCH TEAM INTO INTERESTING DIRECTIONS.
BUT YOU'RE RIGHT ABOUT ONE THING, HOLLY. WE DON'T NEED TO HUNT SPIRO.
ONCE HE DISCOVERS I'M ALIVE, KNOWING I'M THE ONLY ONE WHO CAN UNLOCK THE C CUBE, HE'LL COME LOOKING FOR *ME*.
SO, ANY MOMENT, A TEAM OF HIT MEN COULD COME BLASTING IN HERE, LOOKING FOR THE KEY TO YOUR ETERNITY CODE.
WE COULD REALLY USE SOMEONE LIKE BUTLER RIGHT ABOUT NOW.
DON'T WORRY . . .
THERE'S MORE THAN ONE BUTLER IN THE FAMILY.

CHAPTER FOUR

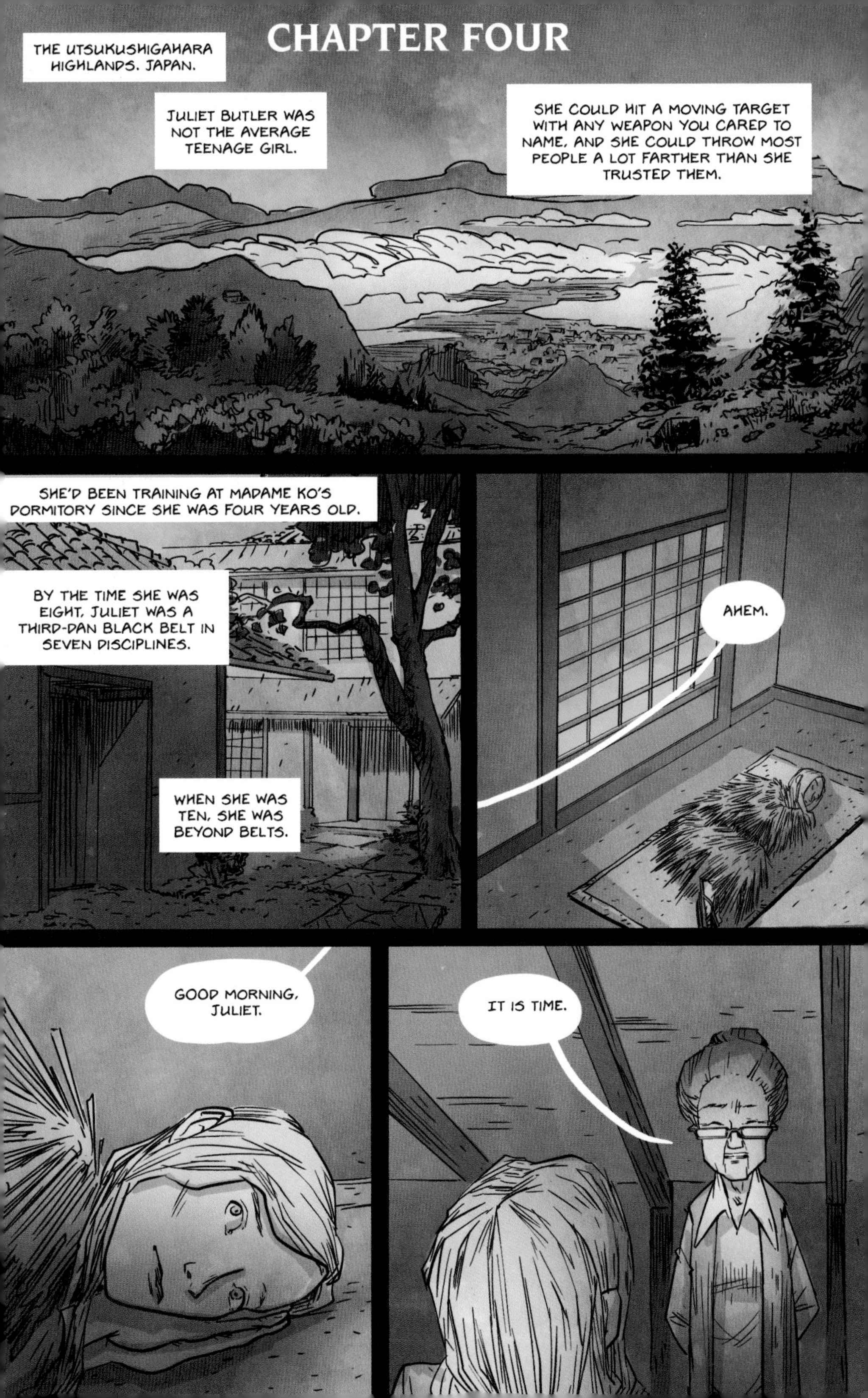
THE UTSUKUSHIGAHARA HIGHLANDS. JAPAN.
JULIET BUTLER WAS NOT THE AVERAGE TEENAGE GIRL.
SHE COULD HIT A MOVING TARGET WITH ANY WEAPON YOU CARED TO NAME, AND SHE COULD THROW MOST PEOPLE A LOT FARTHER THAN SHE TRUSTED THEM.
SHE'D BEEN TRAINING AT MADAME KO'S DORMITORY SINCE SHE WAS FOUR YEARS OLD.
BY THE TIME SHE WAS EIGHT, JULIET WAS A THIRD-DAN BLACK BELT IN SEVEN DISCIPLINES.
WHEN SHE WAS TEN, SHE WAS BEYOND BELTS.
AHEM.
GOOD MORNING, JULIET.
IT IS TIME.

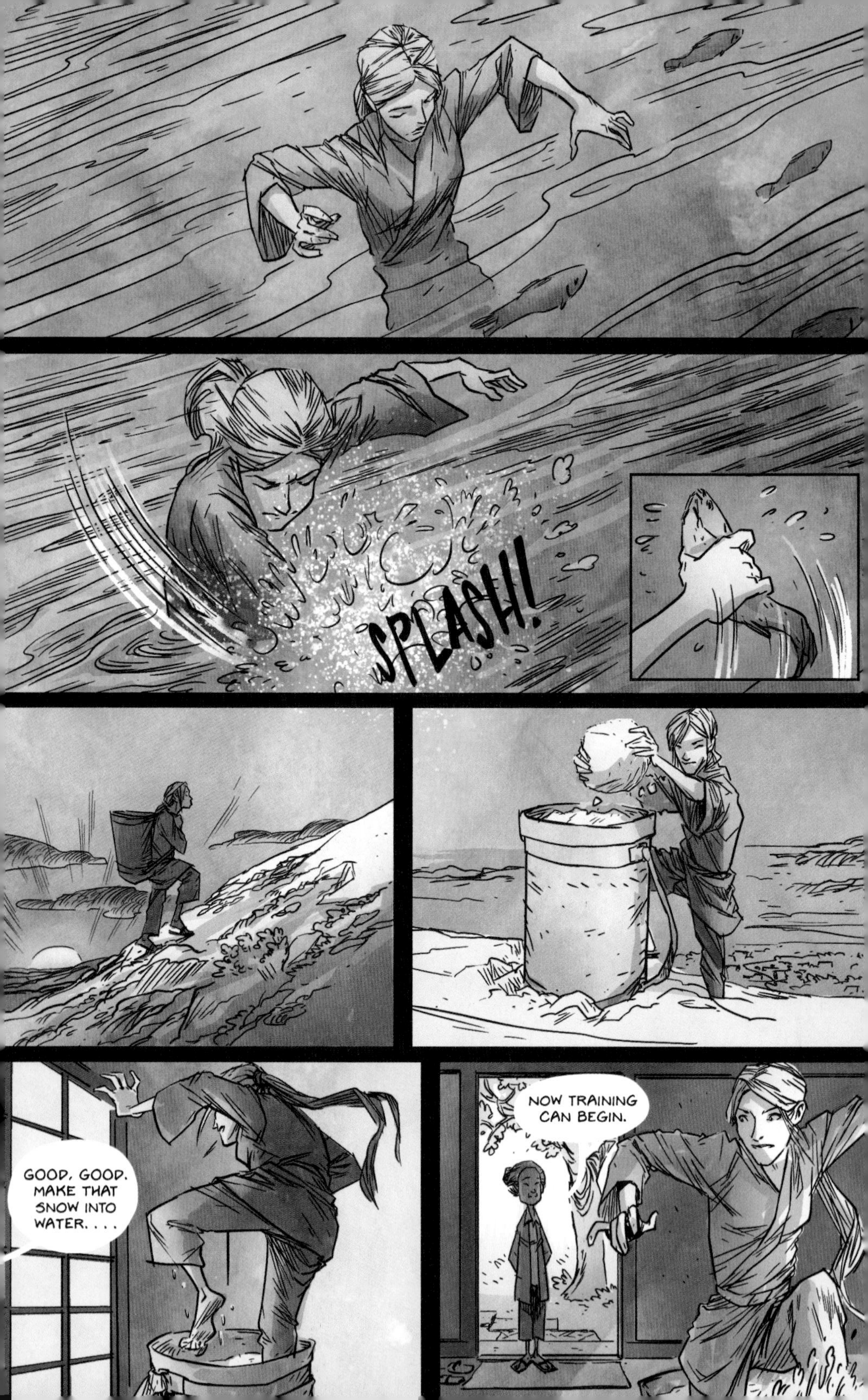
SPLASH!
GOOD, GOOD. MAKE THAT SNOW INTO WATER. . . .
NOW TRAINING CAN BEGIN.

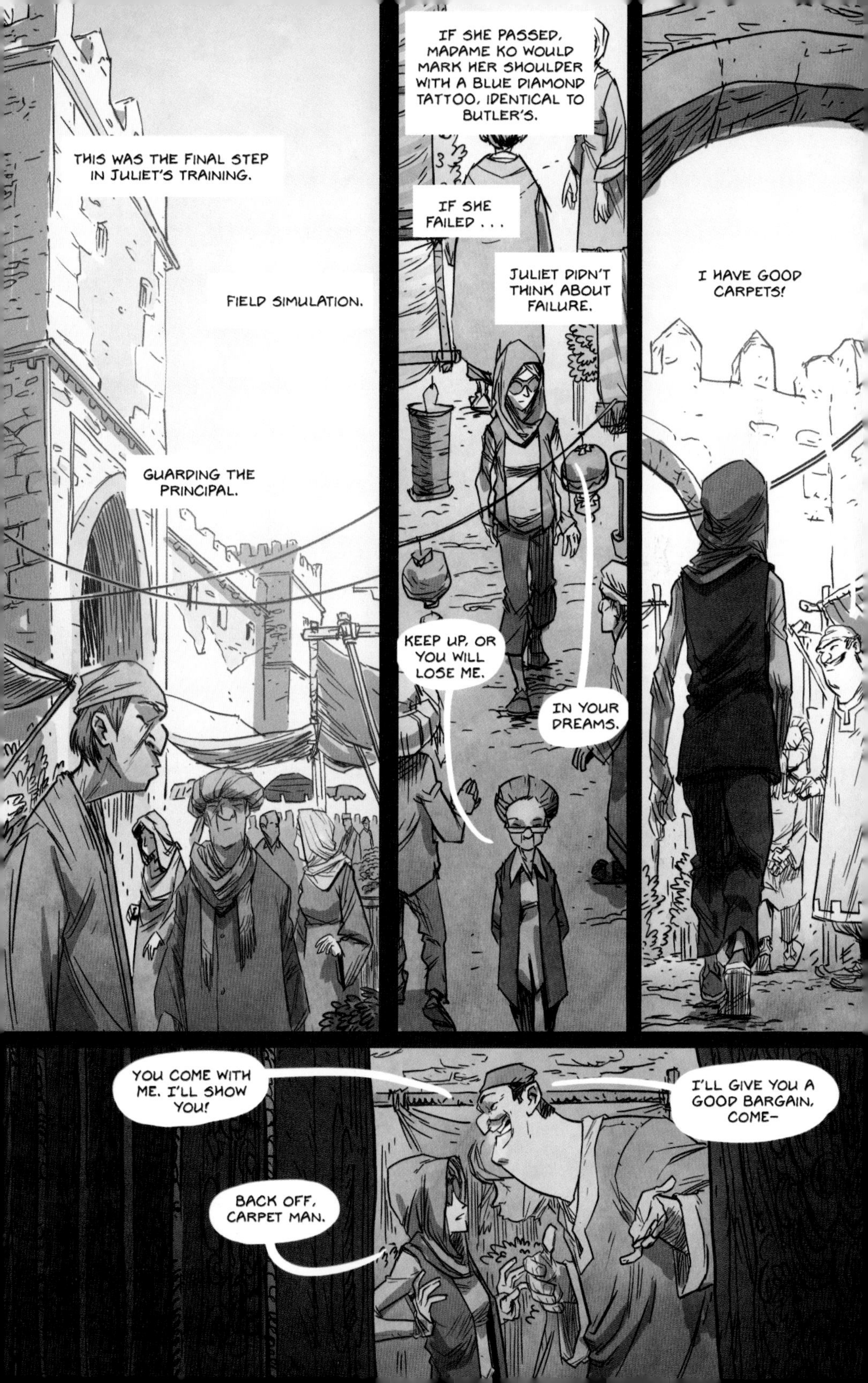

THIS WAS THE FINAL STEP IN JULIET'S TRAINING.
FIELD SIMULATION.
GUARDING THE PRINCIPAL.
IF SHE PASSED, MADAME KO WOULD MARK HER SHOULDER WITH A BLUE DIAMOND TATTOO, IDENTICAL TO BUTLER'S.
IF SHE FAILED . . .
JULIET DIDN'T THINK ABOUT FAILURE.
KEEP UP, OR YOU WILL LOSE ME.
IN YOUR DREAMS.
I HAVE GOOD CARPETS!
YOU COME WITH ME. I'LL SHOW YOU!
I'LL GIVE YOU A GOOD BARGAIN, COME–
BACK OFF, CARPET MAN.

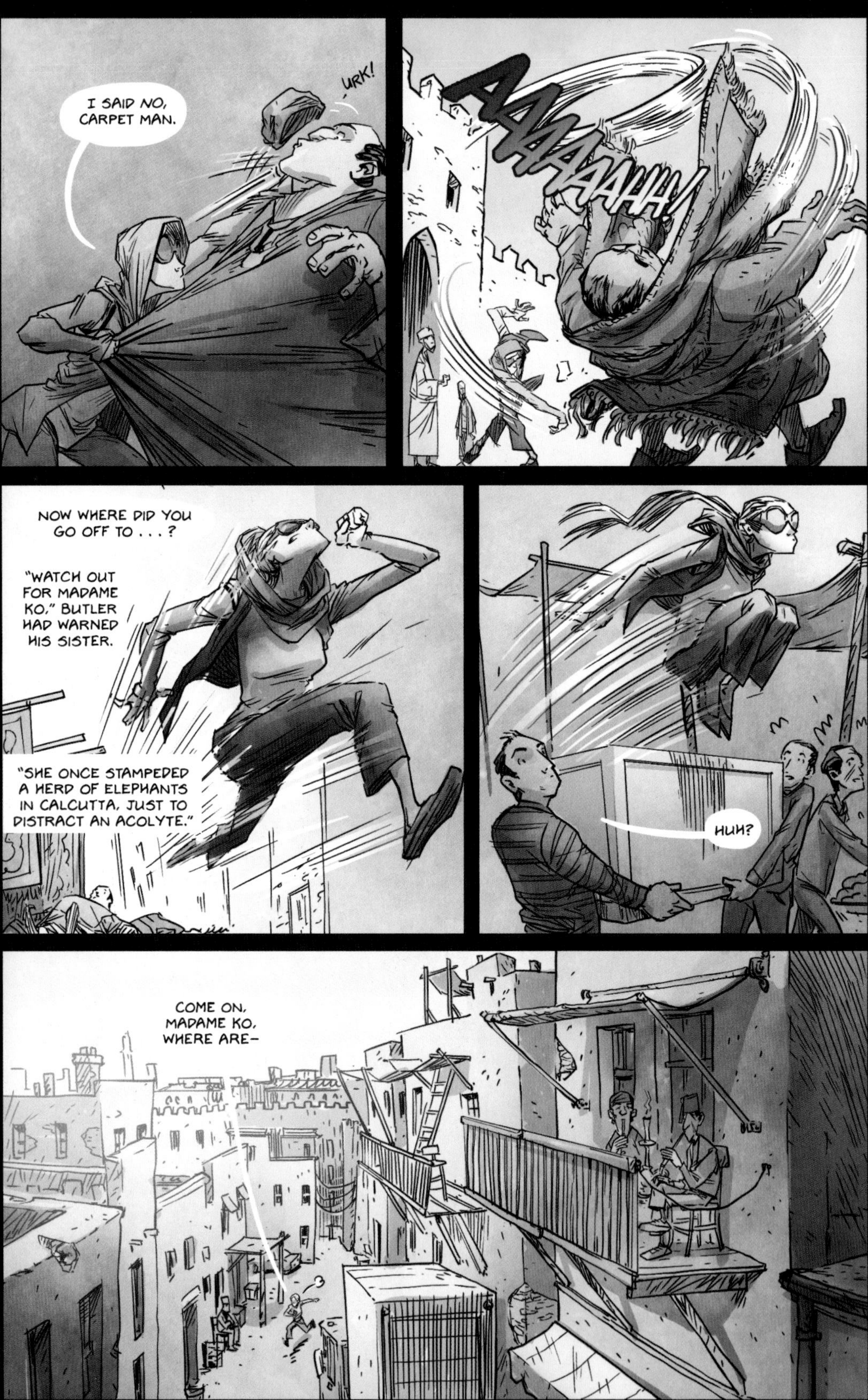
I SAID NO, CARPET MAN.
URK!
AAAAAAAHH!
NOW WHERE DID YOU GO OFF TO . . . ?
"WATCH OUT FOR MADAME KO," BUTLER HAD WARNED HIS SISTER.
"SHE ONCE STAMPEDED A HERD OF ELEPHANTS IN CALCUTTA, JUST TO DISTRACT AN ACOLYTE."
HUH?
COME ON, MADAME KO, WHERE ARE–

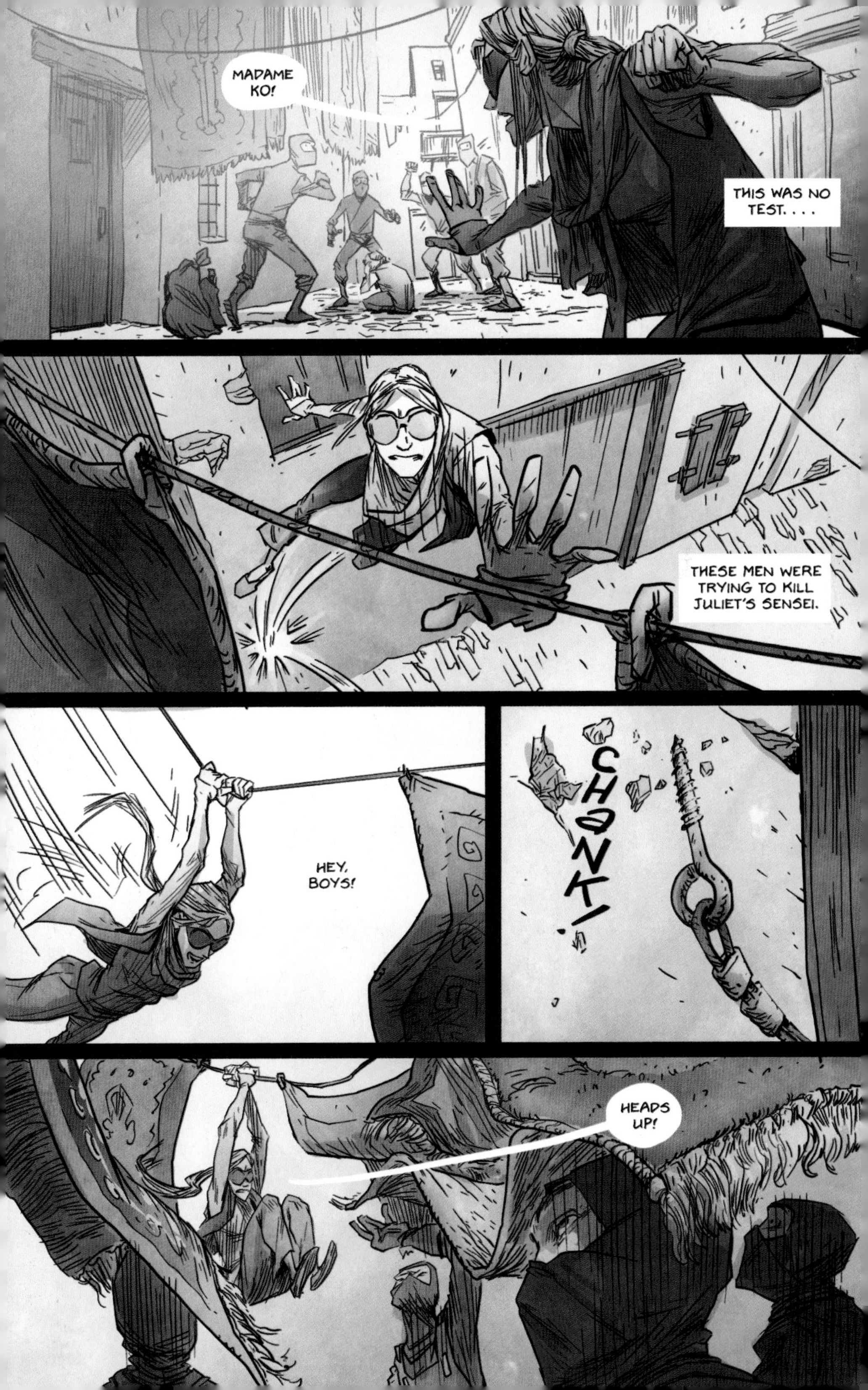
MADAME KO!
THIS WAS NO TEST. . . .
THESE MEN WERE TRYING TO KILL JULIET'S SENSEI.
HEY, BOYS!
CHANK!
HEADS UP!

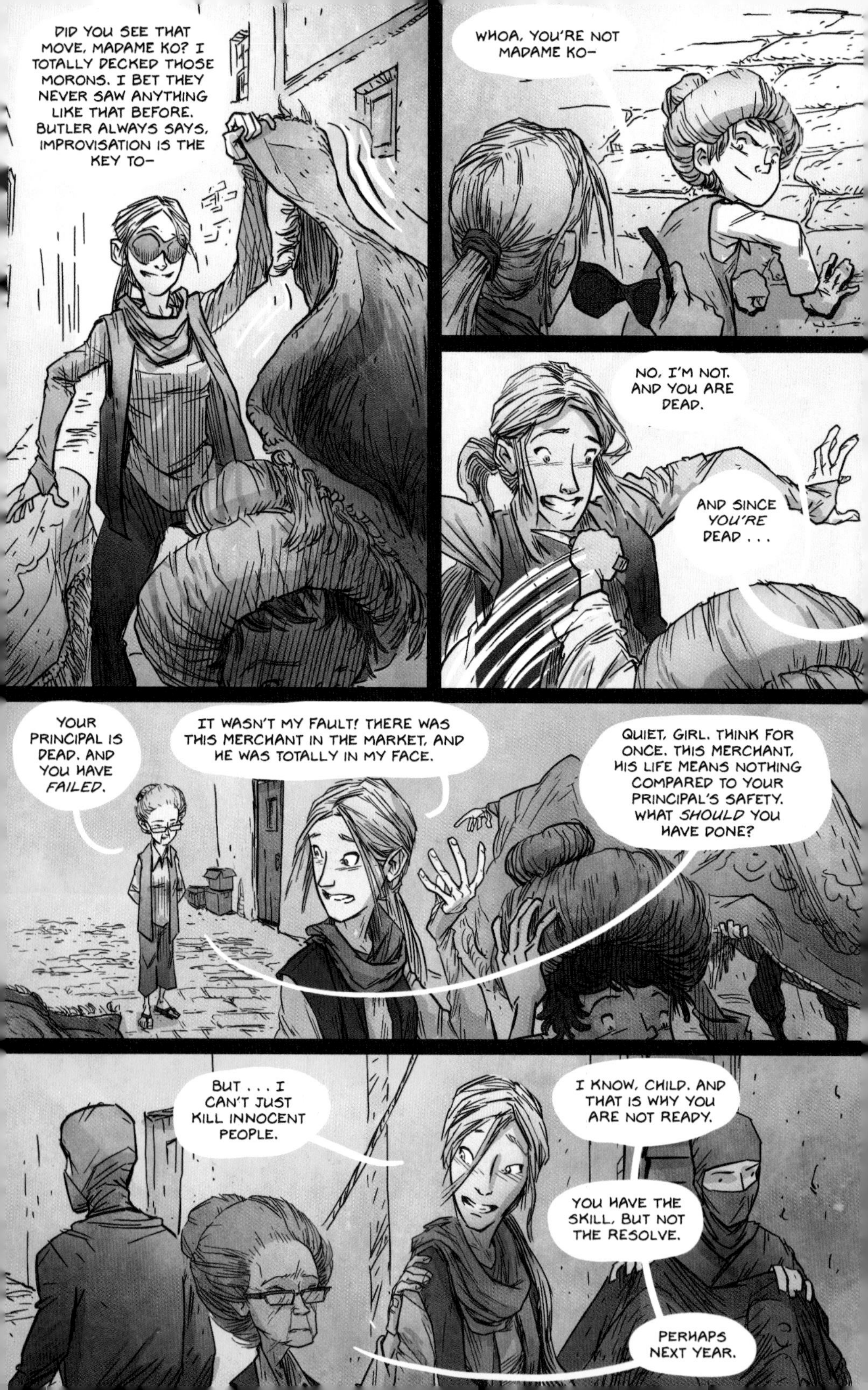
DID YOU SEE THAT MOVE, MADAME KO? I TOTALLY DECKED THOSE MORONS. I BET THEY NEVER SAW ANYTHING LIKE THAT BEFORE. BUTLER ALWAYS SAYS, IMPROVISATION IS THE KEY TO–
WHOA, YOU'RE NOT MADAME KO–
NO, I'M NOT. AND YOU ARE DEAD.
AND SINCE *YOU'RE* DEAD . . .
YOUR PRINCIPAL IS DEAD. AND YOU HAVE *FAILED*.
IT WASN'T MY FAULT! THERE WAS THIS MERCHANT IN THE MARKET, AND HE WAS TOTALLY IN MY FACE.
QUIET, GIRL. THINK FOR ONCE. THIS MERCHANT, HIS LIFE MEANS NOTHING COMPARED TO YOUR PRINCIPAL'S SAFETY. WHAT *SHOULD* YOU HAVE DONE?
BUT . . . I CAN'T JUST KILL INNOCENT PEOPLE.
I KNOW, CHILD. AND THAT IS WHY YOU ARE NOT READY.
YOU HAVE THE SKILL, BUT NOT THE RESOLVE.
PERHAPS NEXT YEAR.

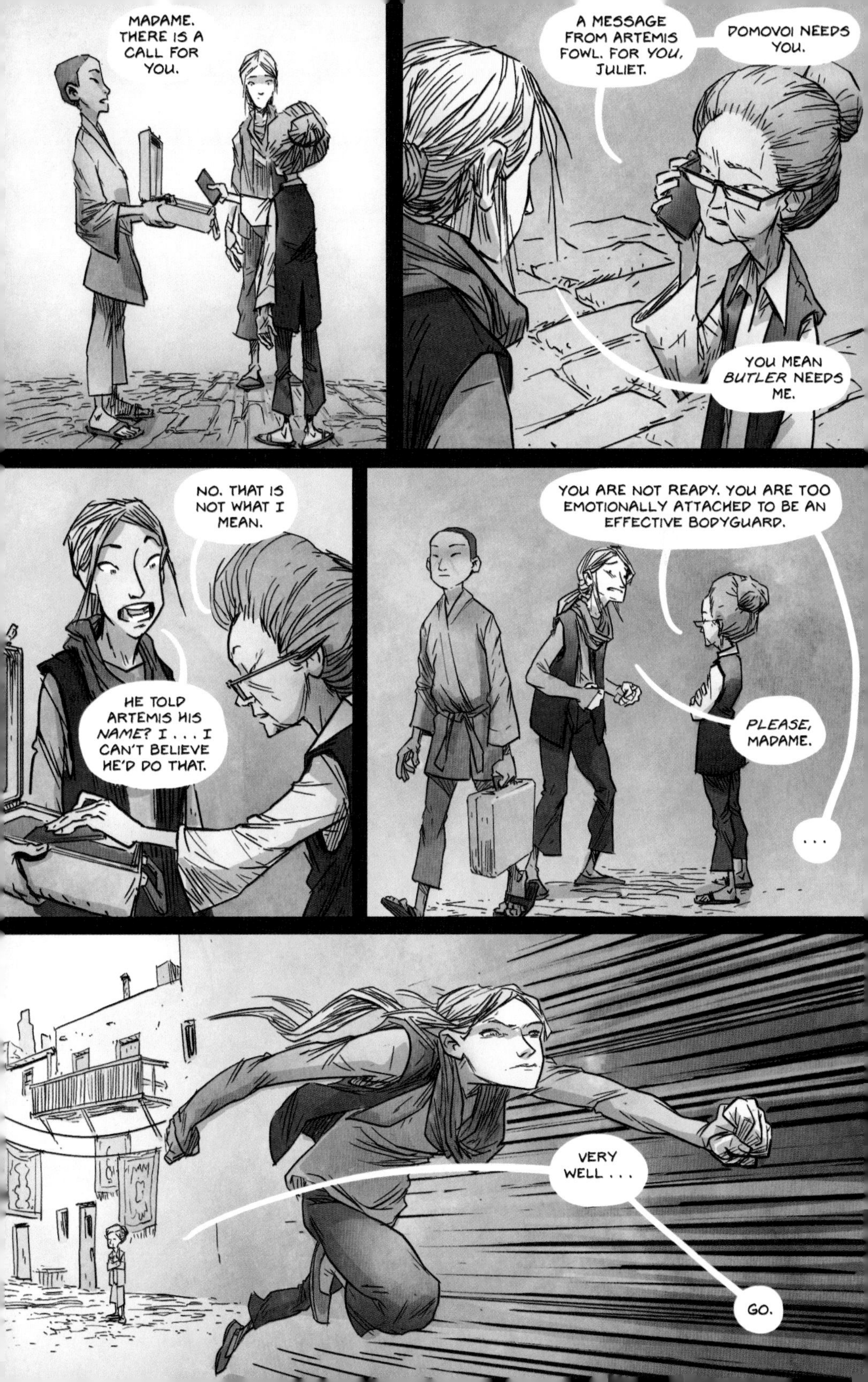
MADAME. THERE IS A CALL FOR YOU.
A MESSAGE FROM ARTEMIS FOWL. FOR *YOU*, JULIET.
DOMOVOI NEEDS YOU.
YOU MEAN *BUTLER* NEEDS ME.
NO. THAT IS NOT WHAT I MEAN.
HE TOLD ARTEMIS HIS *NAME*? I . . . I CAN'T BELIEVE HE'D DO THAT.
YOU ARE NOT READY. YOU ARE TOO EMOTIONALLY ATTACHED TO BE AN EFFECTIVE BODYGUARD.
PLEASE, MADAME.
. . .
VERY WELL . . .
GO.

CHAPTER FIVE

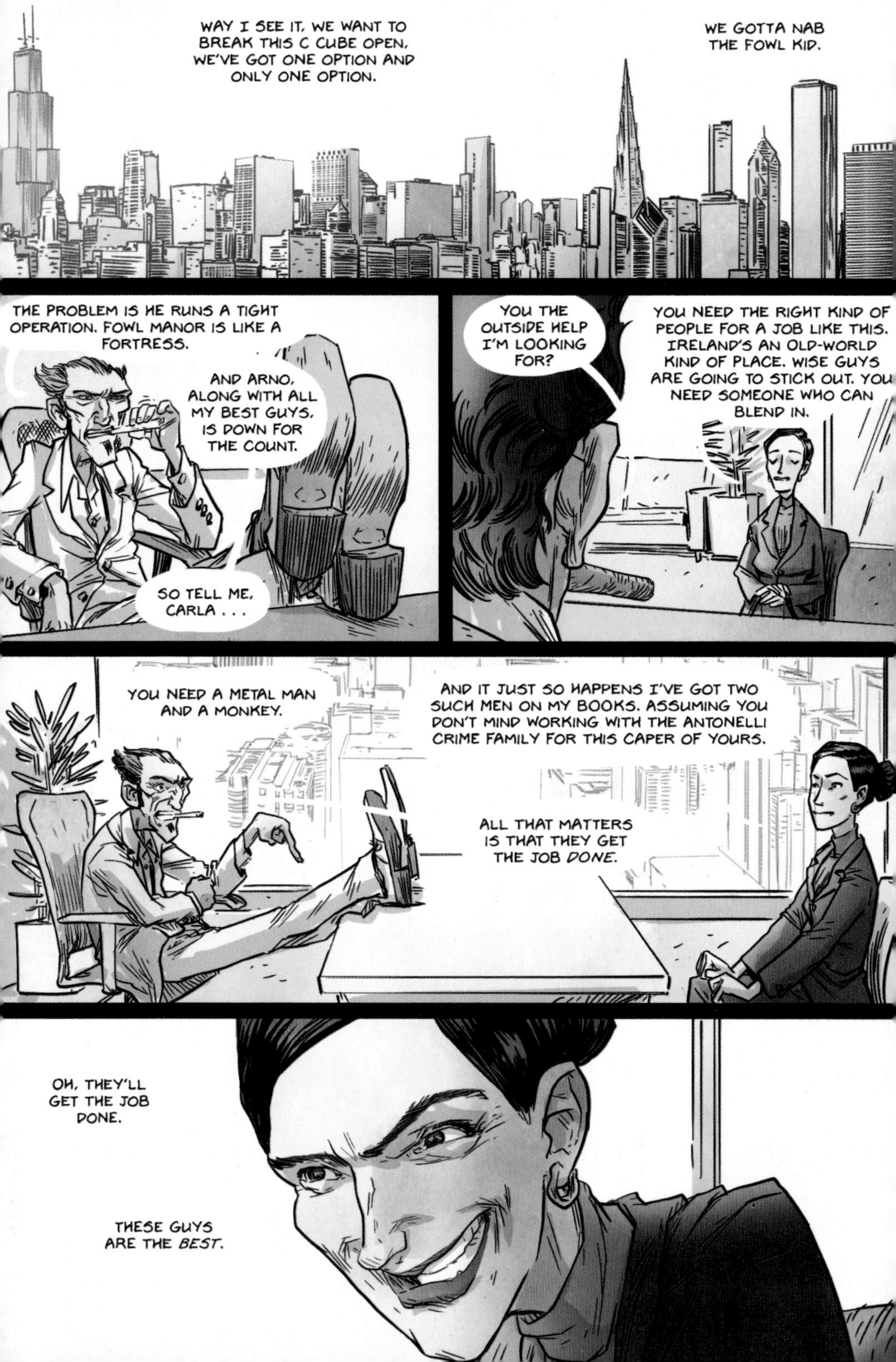

WAY I SEE IT, WE WANT TO BREAK THIS C CUBE OPEN, WE'VE GOT ONE OPTION AND ONLY ONE OPTION.
WE GOTTA NAB THE FOWL KID.
THE PROBLEM IS HE RUNS A TIGHT OPERATION. FOWL MANOR IS LIKE A FORTRESS.
AND ARNO, ALONG WITH ALL MY BEST GUYS, IS DOWN FOR THE COUNT.
SO TELL ME, CARLA . . .
YOU THE OUTSIDE HELP I'M LOOKING FOR?
YOU NEED THE RIGHT KIND OF PEOPLE FOR A JOB LIKE THIS. IRELAND'S AN OLD-WORLD KIND OF PLACE. WISE GUYS ARE GOING TO STICK OUT. YOU NEED SOMEONE WHO CAN BLEND IN.
YOU NEED A METAL MAN AND A MONKEY.
AND IT JUST SO HAPPENS I'VE GOT TWO SUCH MEN ON MY BOOKS. ASSUMING YOU DON'T MIND WORKING WITH THE ANTONELLI CRIME FAMILY FOR THIS CAPER OF YOURS.
ALL THAT MATTERS IS THAT THEY GET THE JOB *DONE*.
OH, THEY'LL GET THE JOB DONE.
THESE GUYS ARE THE *BEST*.

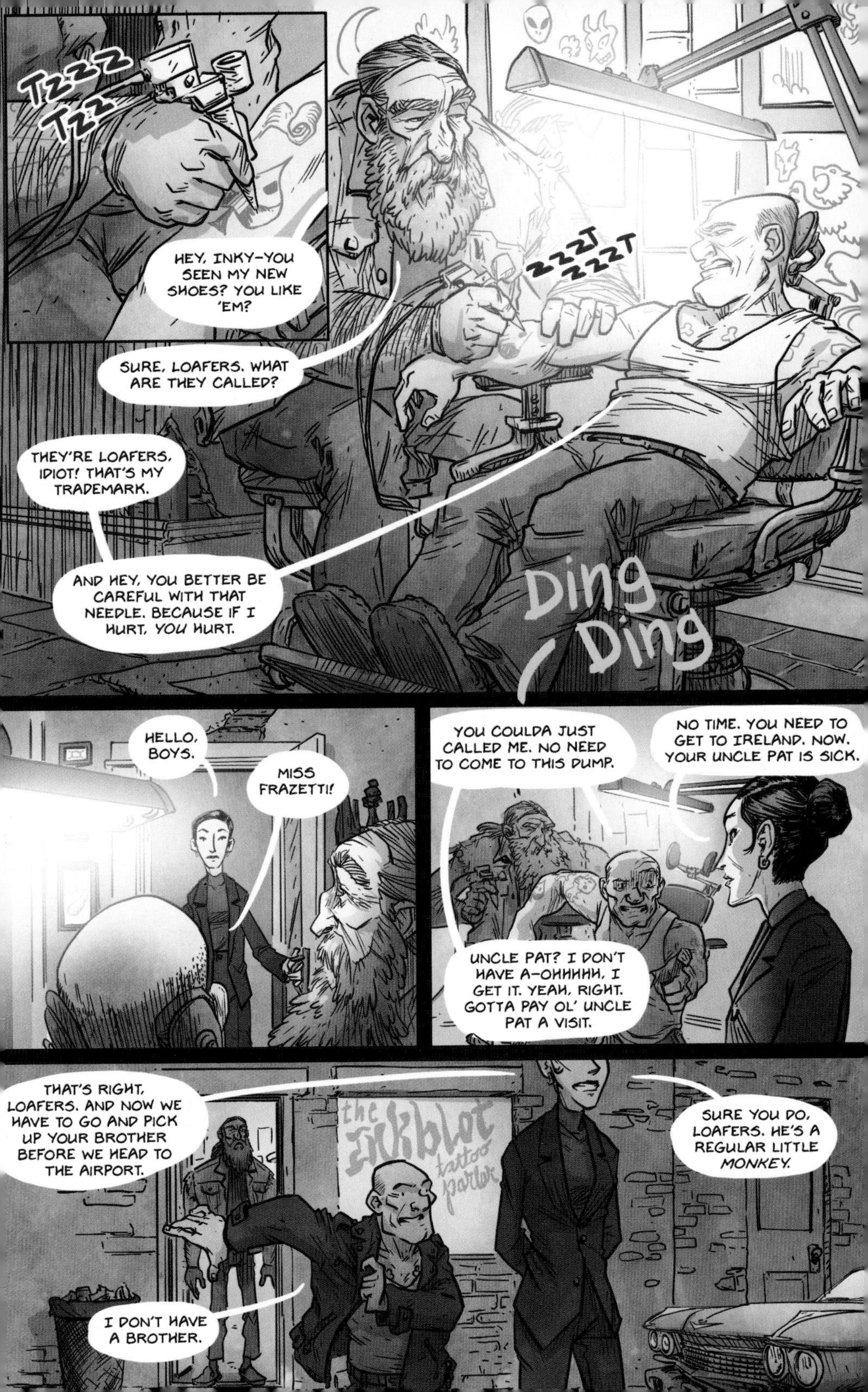
TZZZ
TZZ
HEY, INKY—YOU SEEN MY NEW SHOES? YOU LIKE 'EM?
ZZZT
ZZZT
SURE, LOAFERS. WHAT ARE THEY CALLED?
THEY'RE LOAFERS, IDIOT! THAT'S MY TRADEMARK.
AND HEY, YOU BETTER BE CAREFUL WITH THAT NEEDLE. BECAUSE IF I HURT, *YOU* HURT.
Ding
Ding
HELLO, BOYS.
MISS FRAZETTI!
YOU COULDA JUST CALLED ME. NO NEED TO COME TO THIS DUMP.
NO TIME. YOU NEED TO GET TO IRELAND. NOW. YOUR UNCLE PAT IS SICK.
UNCLE PAT? I DON'T HAVE A—OHHHHH, I GET IT. YEAH, RIGHT. GOTTA PAY OL' UNCLE PAT A VISIT.
THAT'S RIGHT, LOAFERS. AND NOW WE HAVE TO GO AND PICK UP YOUR BROTHER BEFORE WE HEAD TO THE AIRPORT.
the Inkblot tattoo parlor
SURE YOU DO, LOAFERS. HE'S A REGULAR LITTLE *MONKEY*.
I DON'T HAVE A BROTHER.

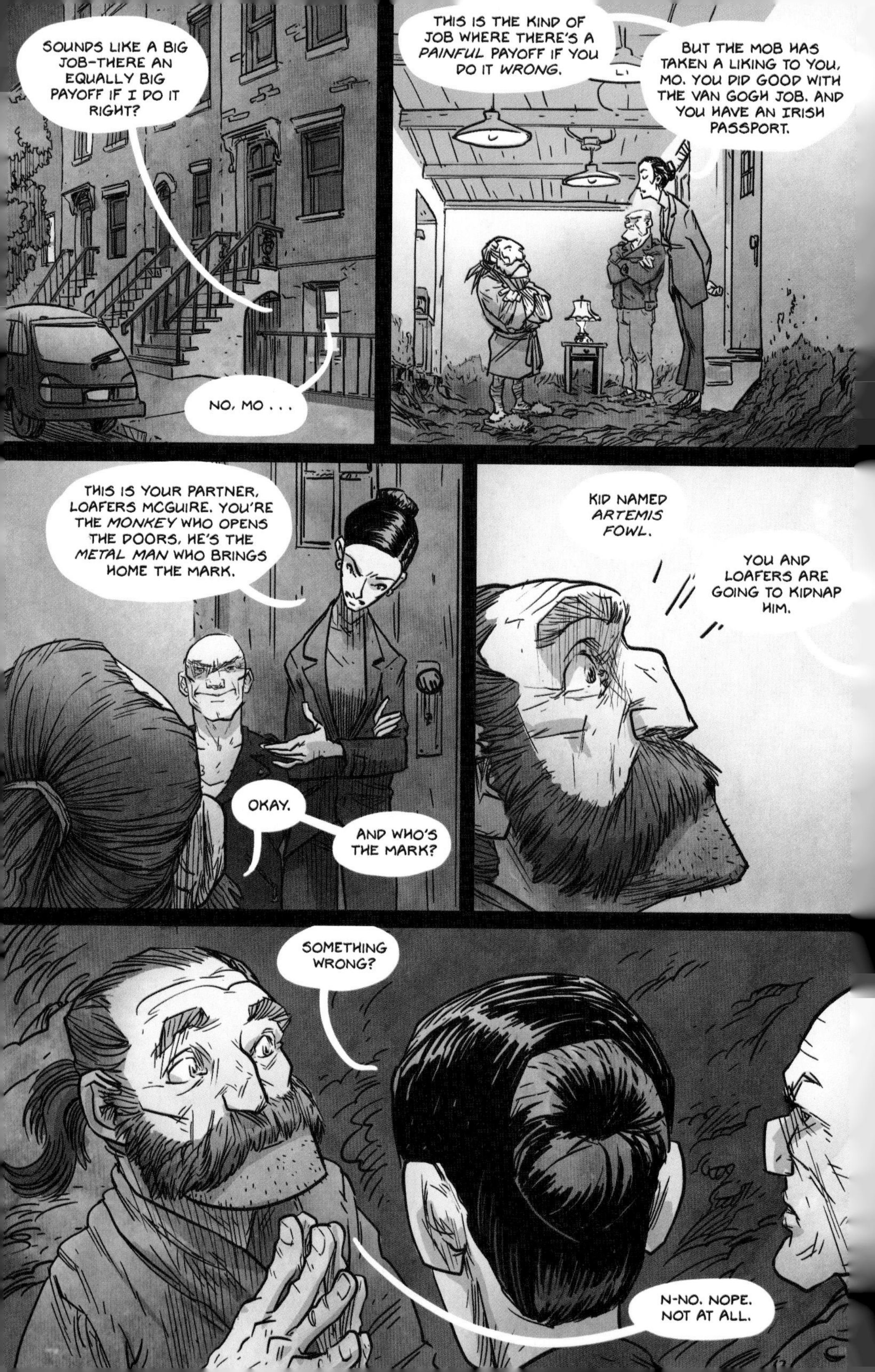
SOUNDS LIKE A BIG JOB—THERE AN EQUALLY BIG PAYOFF IF I DO IT RIGHT?
NO, MO . . .
THIS IS THE KIND OF JOB WHERE THERE'S A *PAINFUL* PAYOFF IF YOU DO IT *WRONG*.
BUT THE MOB HAS TAKEN A LIKING TO YOU, MO. YOU DID GOOD WITH THE VAN GOGH JOB. AND YOU HAVE AN IRISH PASSPORT.
THIS IS YOUR PARTNER, LOAFERS MCGUIRE. YOU'RE THE *MONKEY* WHO OPENS THE DOORS, HE'S THE *METAL MAN* WHO BRINGS HOME THE MARK.
OKAY.
AND WHO'S THE MARK?
KID NAMED *ARTEMIS FOWL*.
YOU AND LOAFERS ARE GOING TO KIDNAP HIM.
SOMETHING WRONG?
N-NO. NOPE. NOT AT ALL.

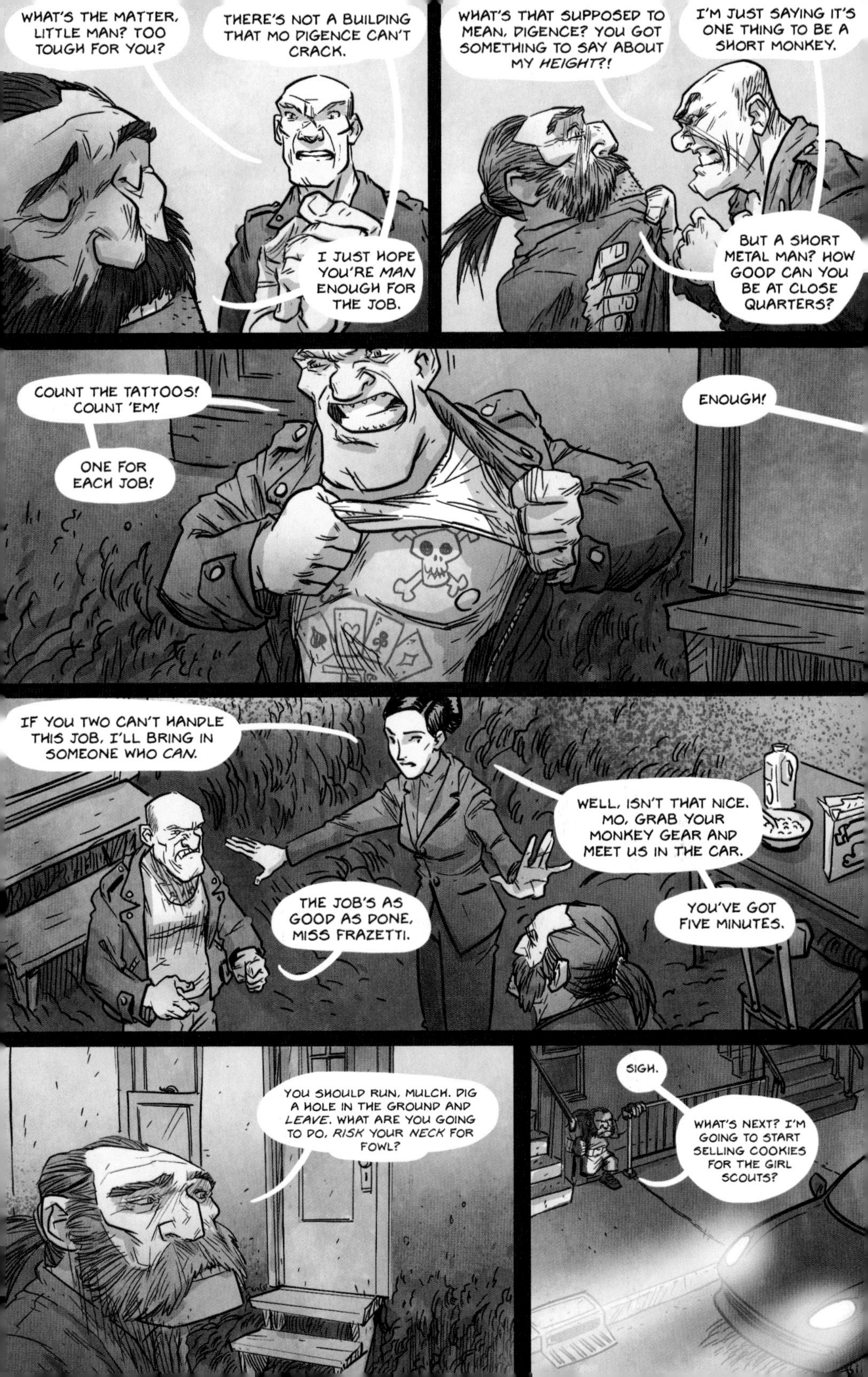
WHAT'S THE MATTER, LITTLE MAN? TOO TOUGH FOR YOU?
THERE'S NOT A BUILDING THAT MO DIGENCE CAN'T CRACK.
I JUST HOPE YOU'RE *MAN* ENOUGH FOR THE JOB.
WHAT'S THAT SUPPOSED TO MEAN, DIGENCE? YOU GOT SOMETHING TO SAY ABOUT MY *HEIGHT*?!
I'M JUST SAYING IT'S ONE THING TO BE A SHORT MONKEY.
BUT A SHORT METAL MAN? HOW GOOD CAN YOU BE AT CLOSE QUARTERS?
COUNT THE TATTOOS! COUNT 'EM!
ONE FOR EACH JOB!
ENOUGH!
IF YOU TWO CAN'T HANDLE THIS JOB, I'LL BRING IN SOMEONE WHO *CAN*.
WELL, ISN'T THAT NICE. MO, GRAB YOUR MONKEY GEAR AND MEET US IN THE CAR.
THE JOB'S AS GOOD AS DONE, MISS FRAZETTI.
YOU'VE GOT FIVE MINUTES.
YOU SHOULD RUN, MULCH. DIG A HOLE IN THE GROUND AND *LEAVE*. WHAT ARE YOU GOING TO DO, *RISK* YOUR *NECK* FOR FOWL?
SIGH.
WHAT'S NEXT? I'M GOING TO START SELLING COOKIES FOR THE GIRL SCOUTS?

CHAPTER SIX

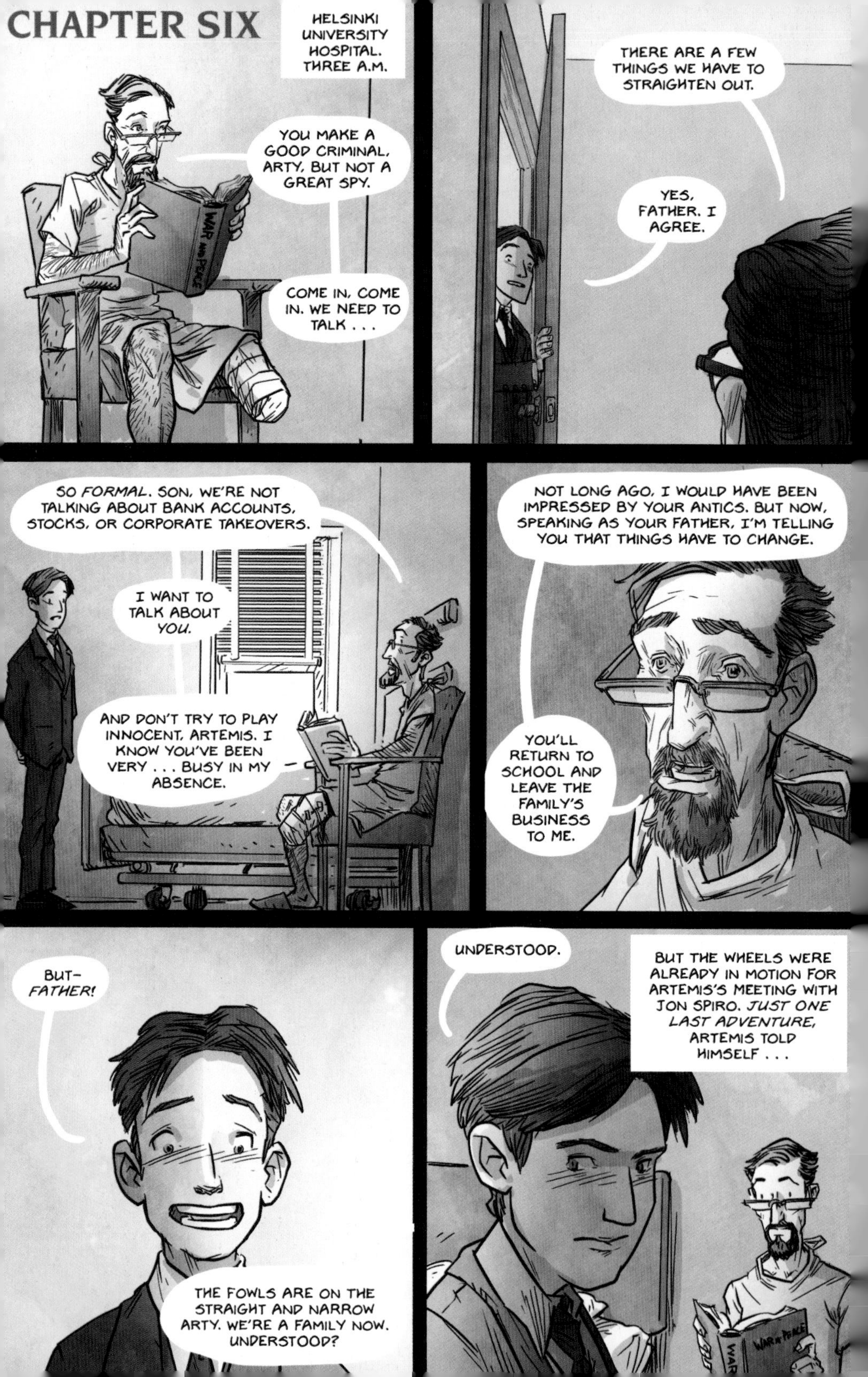
HELSINKI UNIVERSITY HOSPITAL. THREE A.M.
YOU MAKE A GOOD CRIMINAL, ARTY, BUT NOT A GREAT SPY.
COME IN, COME IN. WE NEED TO TALK . . .
WAR AND PEACE
THERE ARE A FEW THINGS WE HAVE TO STRAIGHTEN OUT.
YES, FATHER. I AGREE.
SO *FORMAL*. SON, WE'RE NOT TALKING ABOUT BANK ACCOUNTS, STOCKS, OR CORPORATE TAKEOVERS.
I WANT TO TALK ABOUT *YOU*.
AND DON'T TRY TO PLAY INNOCENT, ARTEMIS. I KNOW YOU'VE BEEN VERY . . . BUSY IN MY ABSENCE.
NOT LONG AGO, I WOULD HAVE BEEN IMPRESSED BY YOUR ANTICS. BUT NOW, SPEAKING AS YOUR FATHER, I'M TELLING YOU THAT THINGS HAVE TO CHANGE.
YOU'LL RETURN TO SCHOOL AND LEAVE THE FAMILY'S BUSINESS TO ME.
BUT- *FATHER!*
THE FOWLS ARE ON THE STRAIGHT AND NARROW ARTY. WE'RE A FAMILY NOW. UNDERSTOOD?
UNDERSTOOD.
BUT THE WHEELS WERE ALREADY IN MOTION FOR ARTEMIS'S MEETING WITH JON SPIRO. *JUST ONE LAST ADVENTURE*, ARTEMIS TOLD HIMSELF . . .
WAR AND PEACE

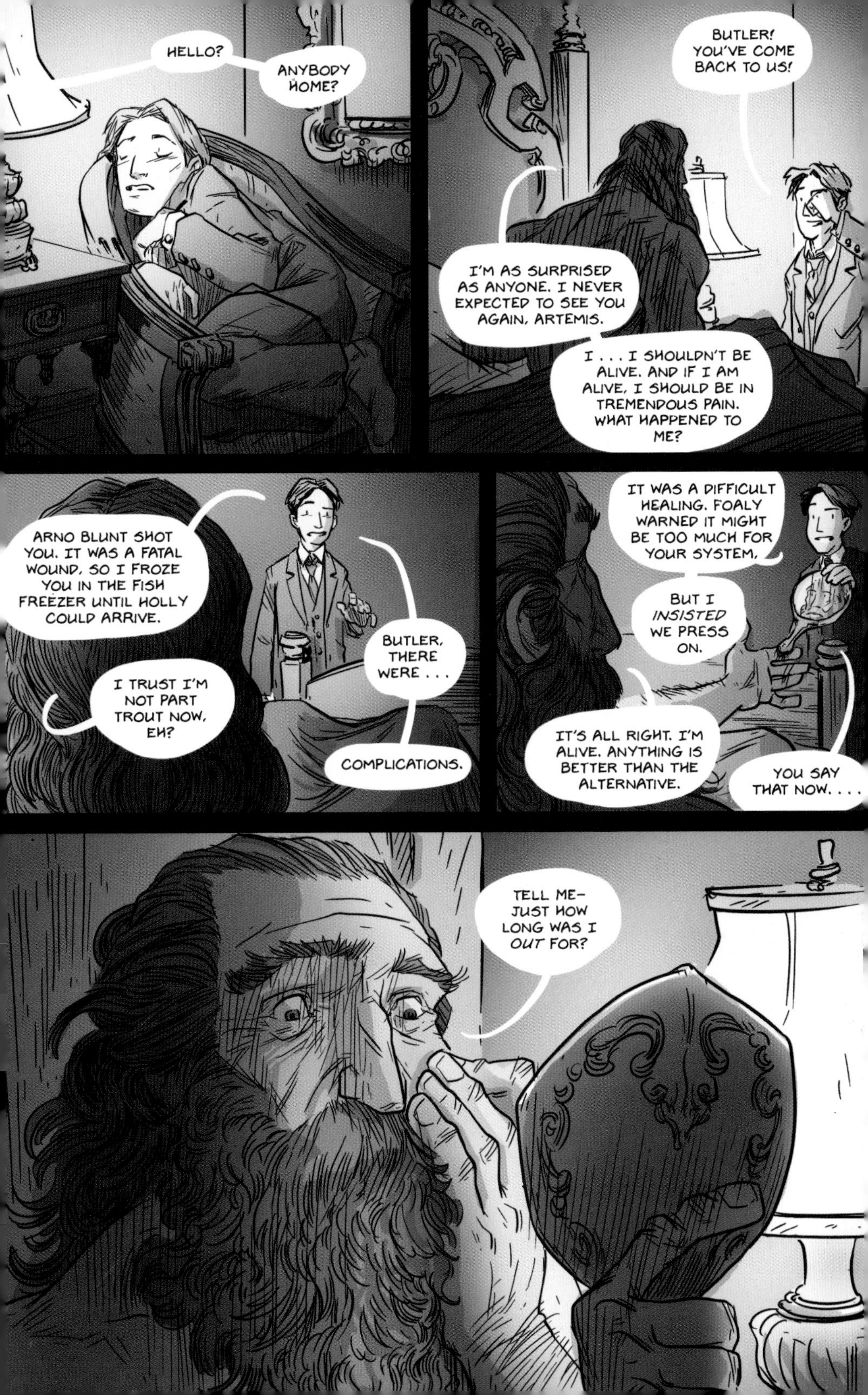

HELLO?
ANYBODY HOME?
BUTLER! YOU'VE COME BACK TO US!
I'M AS SURPRISED AS ANYONE. I NEVER EXPECTED TO SEE YOU AGAIN, ARTEMIS.
I . . . I SHOULDN'T BE ALIVE. AND IF I AM ALIVE, I SHOULD BE IN TREMENDOUS PAIN. WHAT HAPPENED TO ME?
ARNO BLUNT SHOT YOU. IT WAS A FATAL WOUND, SO I FROZE YOU IN THE FISH FREEZER UNTIL HOLLY COULD ARRIVE.
I TRUST I'M NOT PART TROUT NOW, EH?
BUTLER, THERE WERE . . .
COMPLICATIONS.
IT WAS A DIFFICULT HEALING. FOALY WARNED IT MIGHT BE TOO MUCH FOR YOUR SYSTEM.
BUT I *INSISTED* WE PRESS ON.
IT'S ALL RIGHT. I'M ALIVE. ANYTHING IS BETTER THAN THE ALTERNATIVE.
YOU SAY THAT NOW. . . .
TELL ME— JUST HOW LONG WAS I *OUT* FOR?

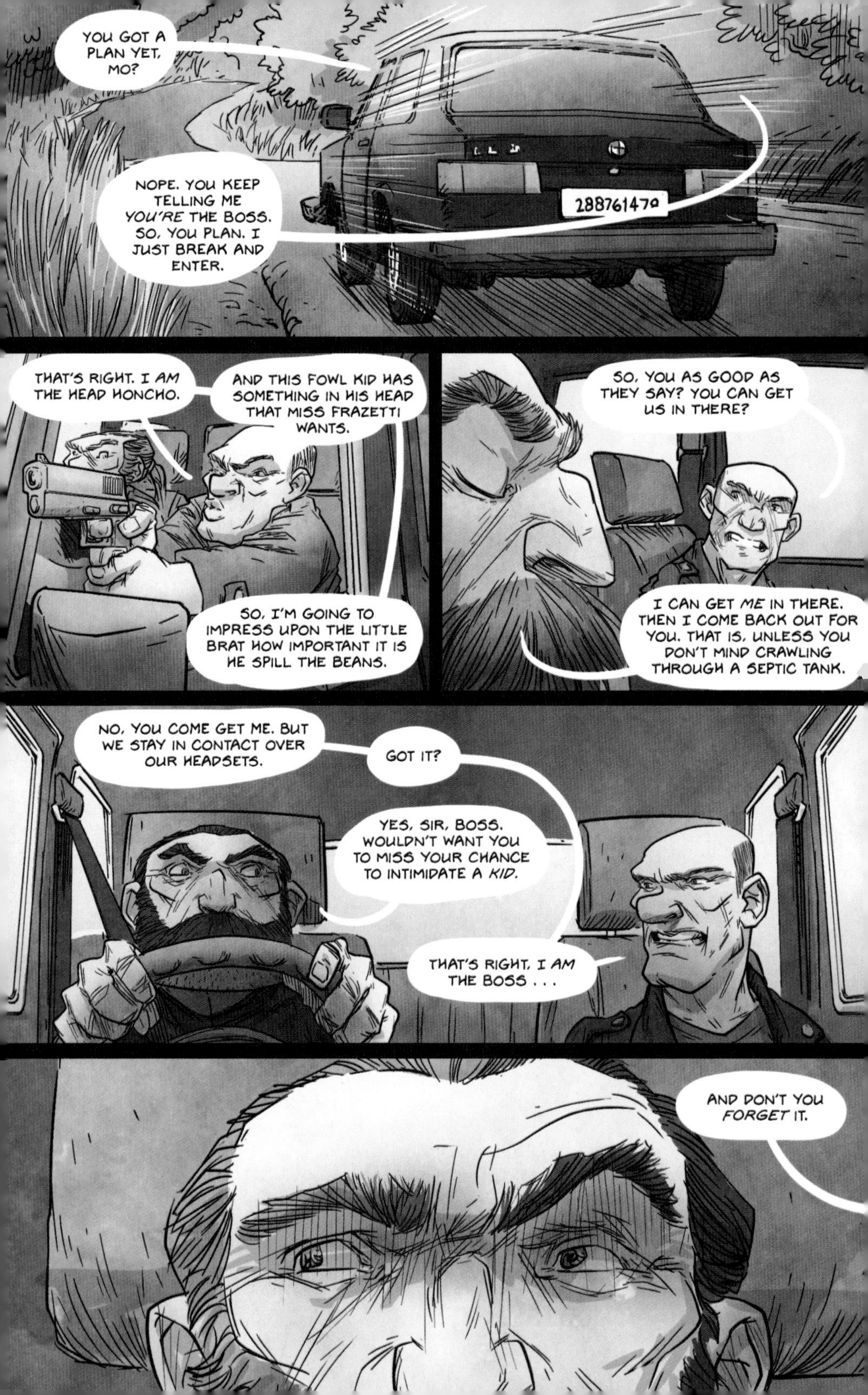
YOU GOT A PLAN YET, MO?
NOPE. YOU KEEP TELLING ME *YOU'RE* THE BOSS. SO, YOU PLAN. I JUST BREAK AND ENTER.
THAT'S RIGHT. I *AM* THE HEAD HONCHO.
AND THIS FOWL KID HAS SOMETHING IN HIS HEAD THAT MISS FRAZETTI WANTS.
SO, I'M GOING TO IMPRESS UPON THE LITTLE BRAT HOW IMPORTANT IT IS HE SPILL THE BEANS.
SO, YOU AS GOOD AS THEY SAY? YOU CAN GET US IN THERE?
I CAN GET *ME* IN THERE. THEN I COME BACK OUT FOR YOU. THAT IS, UNLESS YOU DON'T MIND CRAWLING THROUGH A SEPTIC TANK.
NO, YOU COME GET ME. BUT WE STAY IN CONTACT OVER OUR HEADSETS.
GOT IT?
YES, SIR, BOSS. WOULDN'T WANT YOU TO MISS YOUR CHANCE TO INTIMIDATE A *KID*.
THAT'S RIGHT, I *AM* THE BOSS . . .
AND DON'T YOU *FORGET* IT.

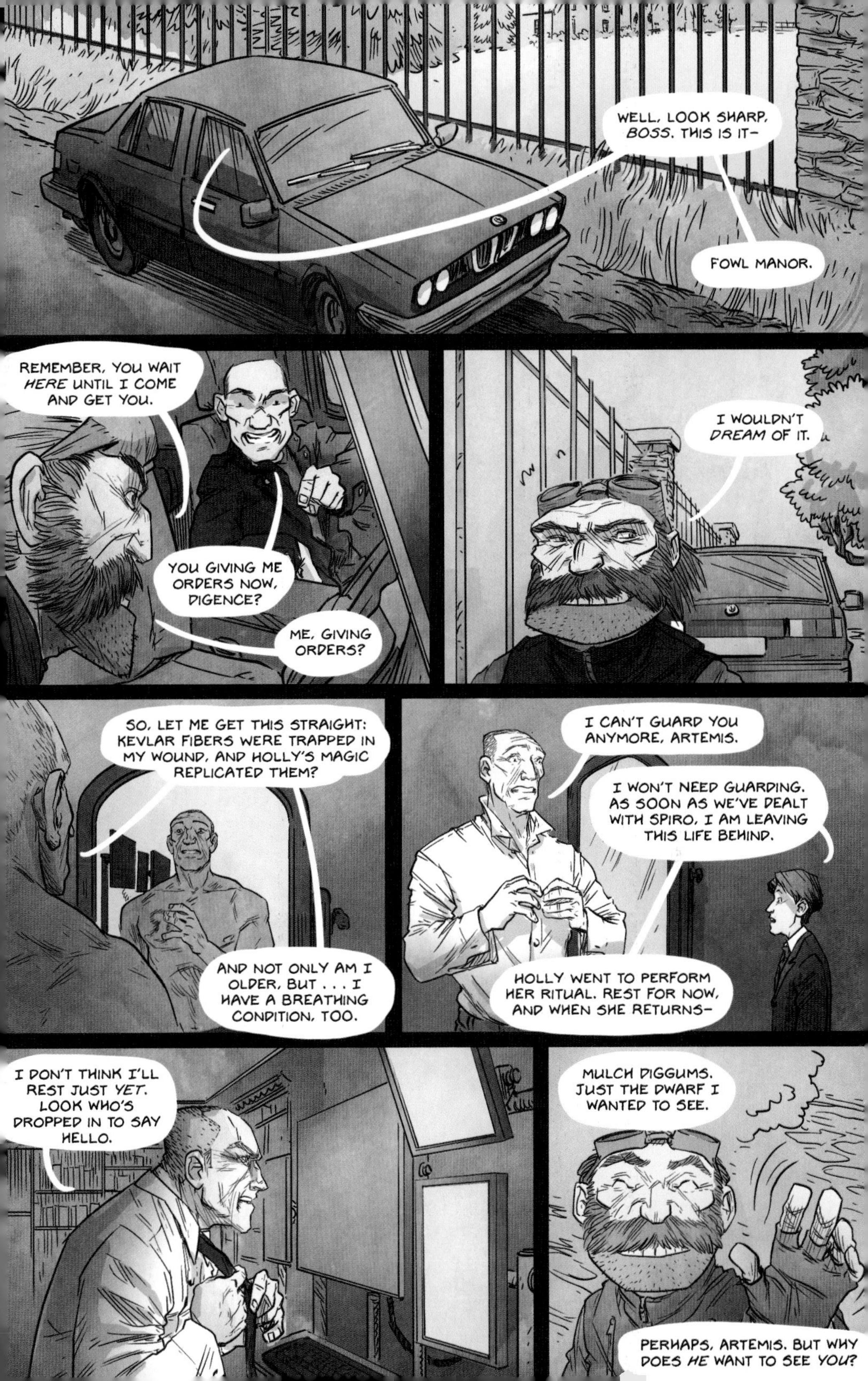
WELL, LOOK SHARP, *BOSS*. THIS IS IT–
FOWL MANOR.
REMEMBER, YOU WAIT *HERE* UNTIL I COME AND GET YOU.
YOU GIVING ME ORDERS NOW, DIGENCE?
ME, GIVING ORDERS?
I WOULDN'T *DREAM* OF IT.
SO, LET ME GET THIS STRAIGHT: KEVLAR FIBERS WERE TRAPPED IN MY WOUND, AND HOLLY'S MAGIC REPLICATED THEM?
AND NOT ONLY AM I OLDER, BUT . . . I HAVE A BREATHING CONDITION, TOO.
I CAN'T GUARD YOU ANYMORE, ARTEMIS.
I WON'T NEED GUARDING. AS SOON AS WE'VE DEALT WITH SPIRO, I AM LEAVING THIS LIFE BEHIND.
HOLLY WENT TO PERFORM HER RITUAL. REST FOR NOW, AND WHEN SHE RETURNS–
I DON'T THINK I'LL REST JUST *YET*. LOOK WHO'S DROPPED IN TO SAY HELLO.
MULCH DIGGUMS. JUST THE DWARF I WANTED TO SEE.
PERHAPS, ARTEMIS. BUT WHY DOES *HE* WANT TO SEE *YOU*?

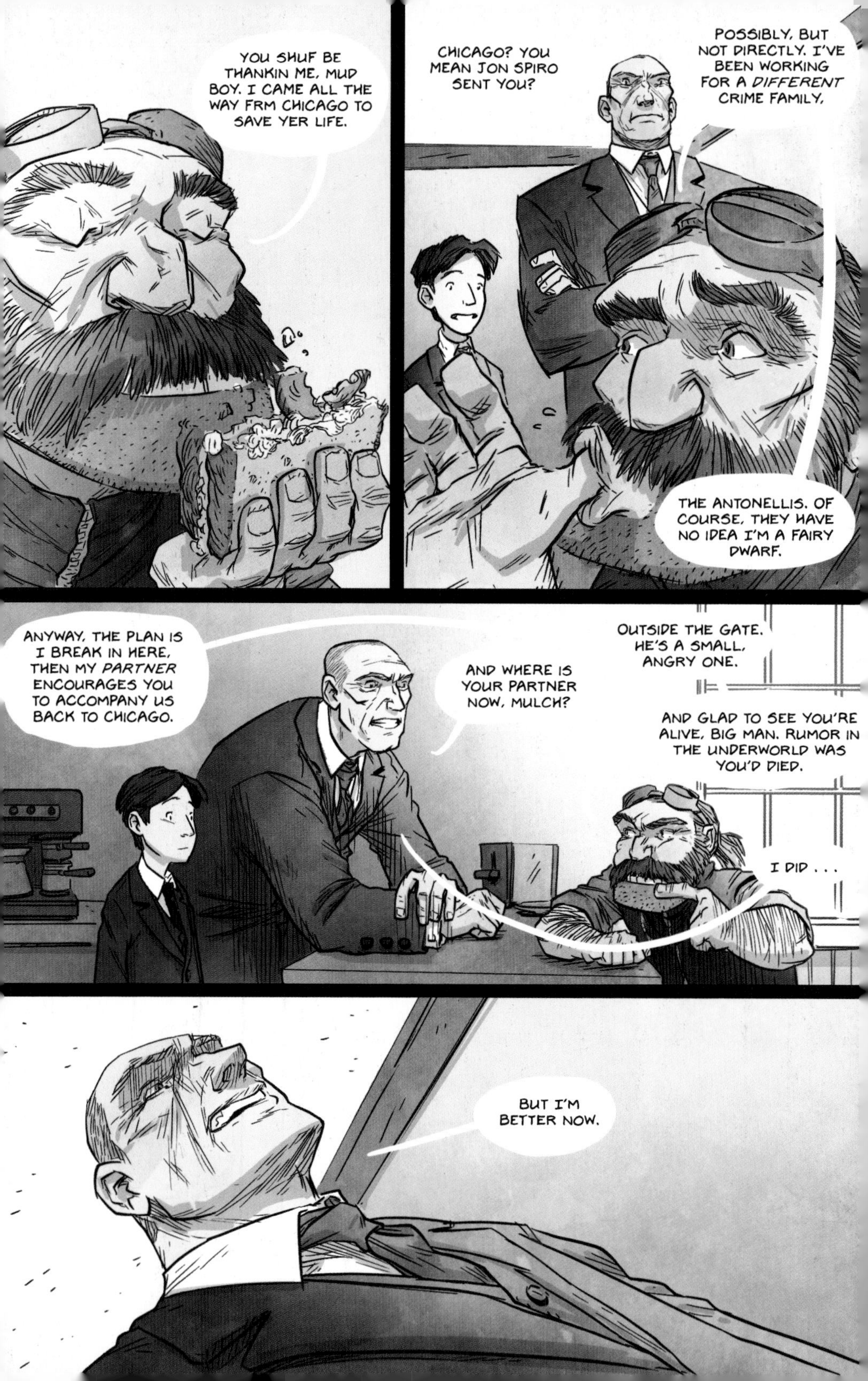
YOU SHUF BE THANKIN ME, MUD BOY. I CAME ALL THE WAY FRM CHICAGO TO SAVE YER LIFE.
CHICAGO? YOU MEAN JON SPIRO SENT YOU?
POSSIBLY, BUT NOT DIRECTLY. I'VE BEEN WORKING FOR A *DIFFERENT* CRIME FAMILY,
THE ANTONELLIS. OF COURSE, THEY HAVE NO IDEA I'M A FAIRY DWARF.
ANYWAY, THE PLAN IS I BREAK IN HERE, THEN MY *PARTNER* ENCOURAGES YOU TO ACCOMPANY US BACK TO CHICAGO.
AND WHERE IS YOUR PARTNER NOW, MULCH?
OUTSIDE THE GATE. HE'S A SMALL, ANGRY ONE.
AND GLAD TO SEE YOU'RE ALIVE, BIG MAN. RUMOR IN THE UNDERWORLD WAS YOU'D DIED.
I DID . . .
BUT I'M BETTER NOW.

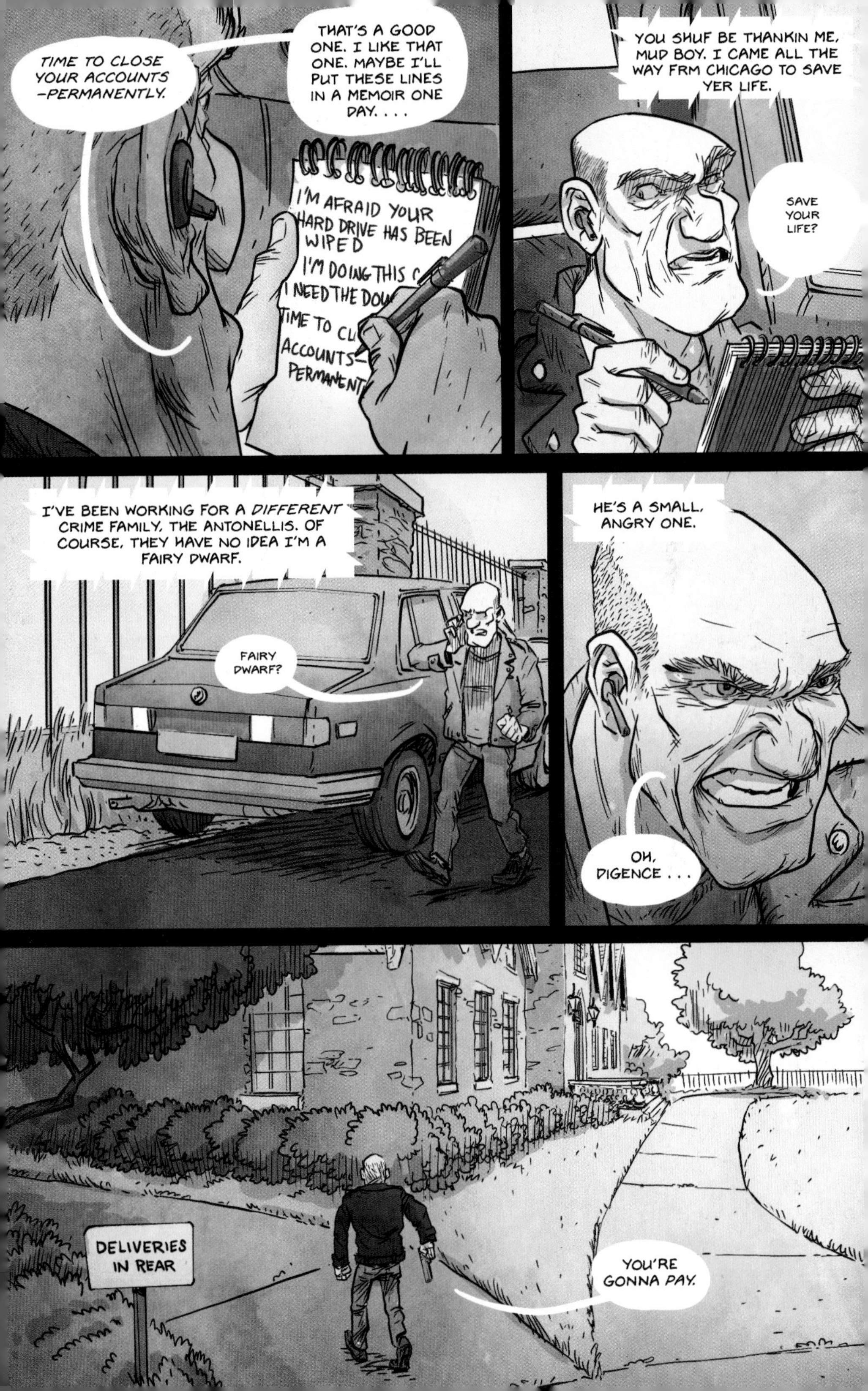
TIME TO CLOSE YOUR ACCOUNTS —PERMANENTLY.
THAT'S A GOOD ONE. I LIKE THAT ONE. MAYBE I'LL PUT THESE LINES IN A MEMOIR ONE DAY. . . .
I'M AFRAID YOUR HARD DRIVE HAS BEEN WIPED
I'M DOING THIS
I NEED THE DOU
TIME TO CL
ACCOUNTS—
PERMANENT
YOU SHUF BE THANKIN ME, MUD BOY. I CAME ALL THE WAY FRM CHICAGO TO SAVE YER LIFE.
SAVE YOUR LIFE?
I'VE BEEN WORKING FOR A DIFFERENT CRIME FAMILY, THE ANTONELLIS. OF COURSE, THEY HAVE NO IDEA I'M A FAIRY DWARF.
FAIRY DWARF?
HE'S A SMALL, ANGRY ONE.
OH, DIGENCE . . .
DELIVERIES IN REAR
YOU'RE GONNA PAY.

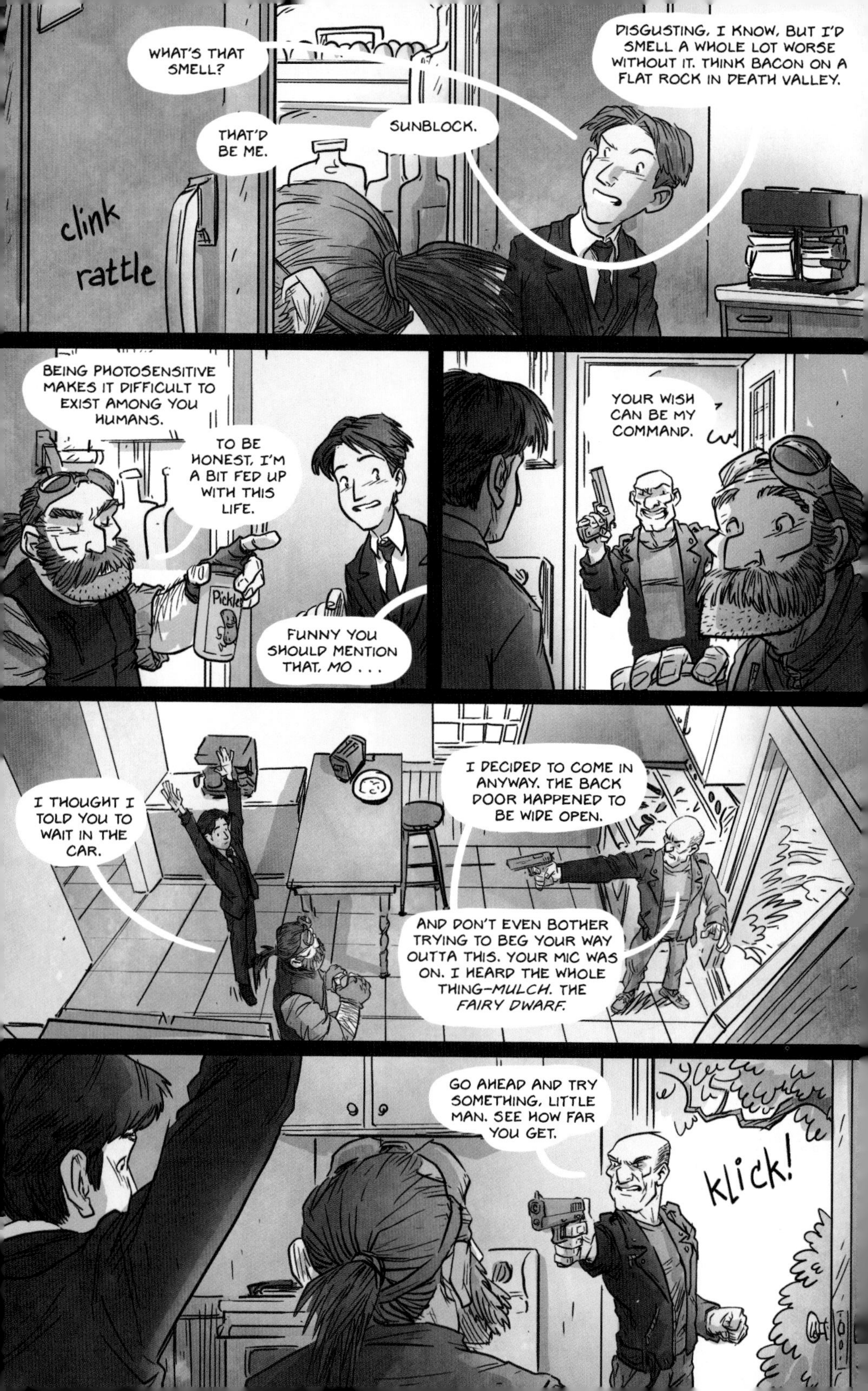
WHAT'S THAT SMELL?
THAT'D BE ME.
SUNBLOCK.
DISGUSTING, I KNOW, BUT I'D SMELL A WHOLE LOT WORSE WITHOUT IT. THINK BACON ON A FLAT ROCK IN DEATH VALLEY.
clink
rattle
BEING PHOTOSENSITIVE MAKES IT DIFFICULT TO EXIST AMONG YOU HUMANS.
TO BE HONEST, I'M A BIT FED UP WITH THIS LIFE.
Pickles
FUNNY YOU SHOULD MENTION THAT, MO . . .
YOUR WISH CAN BE MY COMMAND.
I THOUGHT I TOLD YOU TO WAIT IN THE CAR.
I DECIDED TO COME IN ANYWAY. THE BACK DOOR HAPPENED TO BE WIDE OPEN.
AND DON'T EVEN BOTHER TRYING TO BEG YOUR WAY OUTTA THIS. YOUR MIC WAS ON. I HEARD THE WHOLE THING—*MULCH*. THE *FAIRY DWARF*.
GO AHEAD AND TRY SOMETHING, LITTLE MAN. SEE HOW FAR YOU GET.
KLICK!

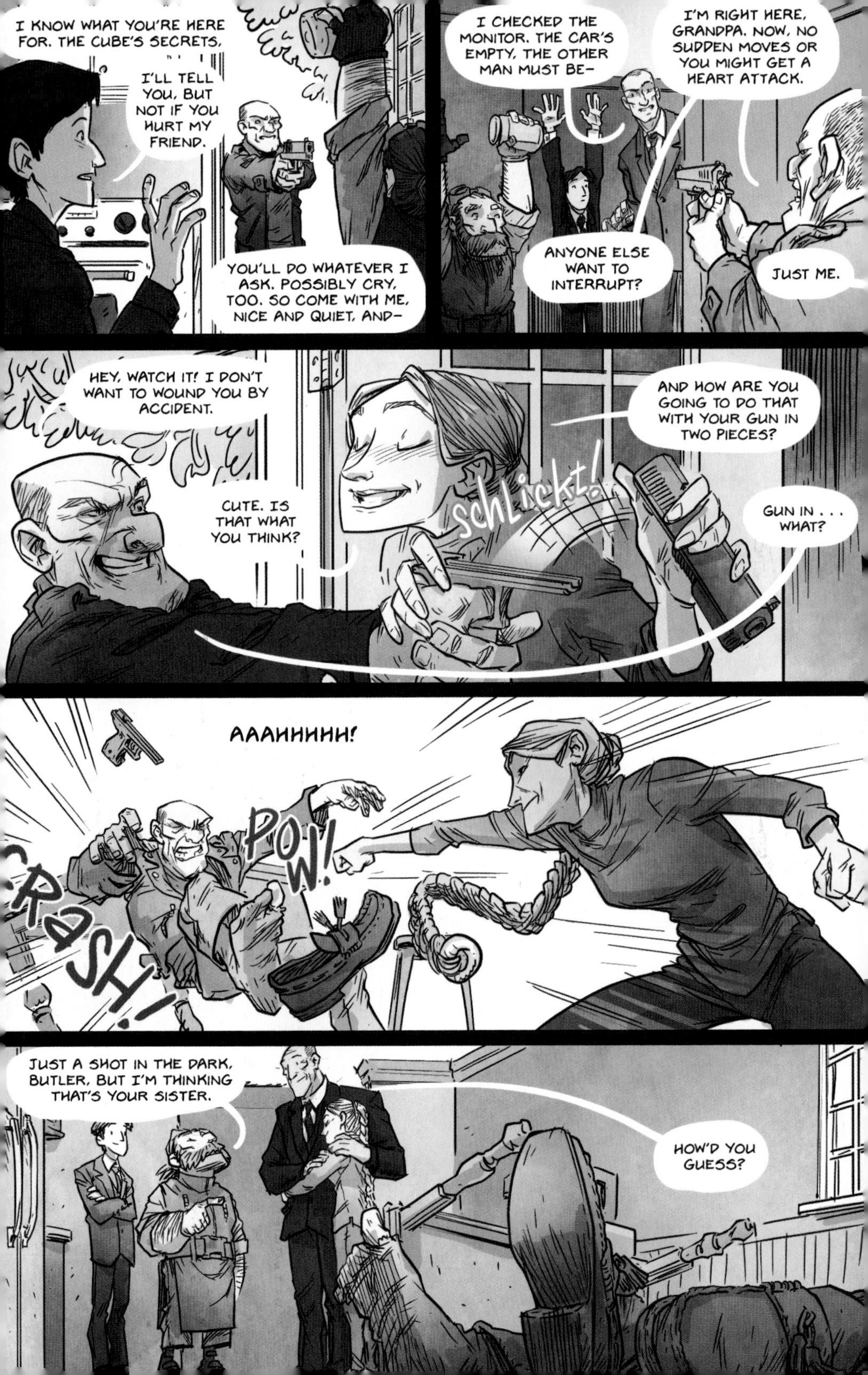
I KNOW WHAT YOU'RE HERE FOR. THE CUBE'S SECRETS.
I'LL TELL YOU, BUT NOT IF YOU HURT MY FRIEND.
YOU'LL DO WHATEVER I ASK. POSSIBLY CRY, TOO. SO COME WITH ME, NICE AND QUIET, AND—
I CHECKED THE MONITOR. THE CAR'S EMPTY. THE OTHER MAN MUST BE—
I'M RIGHT HERE, GRANDPA. NOW, NO SUDDEN MOVES OR YOU MIGHT GET A HEART ATTACK.
ANYONE ELSE WANT TO INTERRUPT?
JUST ME.
HEY, WATCH IT! I DON'T WANT TO WOUND YOU BY ACCIDENT.
AND HOW ARE YOU GOING TO DO THAT WITH YOUR GUN IN TWO PIECES?
SCHLICKT!
CUTE. IS THAT WHAT YOU THINK?
GUN IN . . . WHAT?
AAAHHHHH!
POW!
CRASH!
JUST A SHOT IN THE DARK, BUTLER, BUT I'M THINKING THAT'S YOUR SISTER.
HOW'D YOU GUESS?

CHAPTER SEVEN

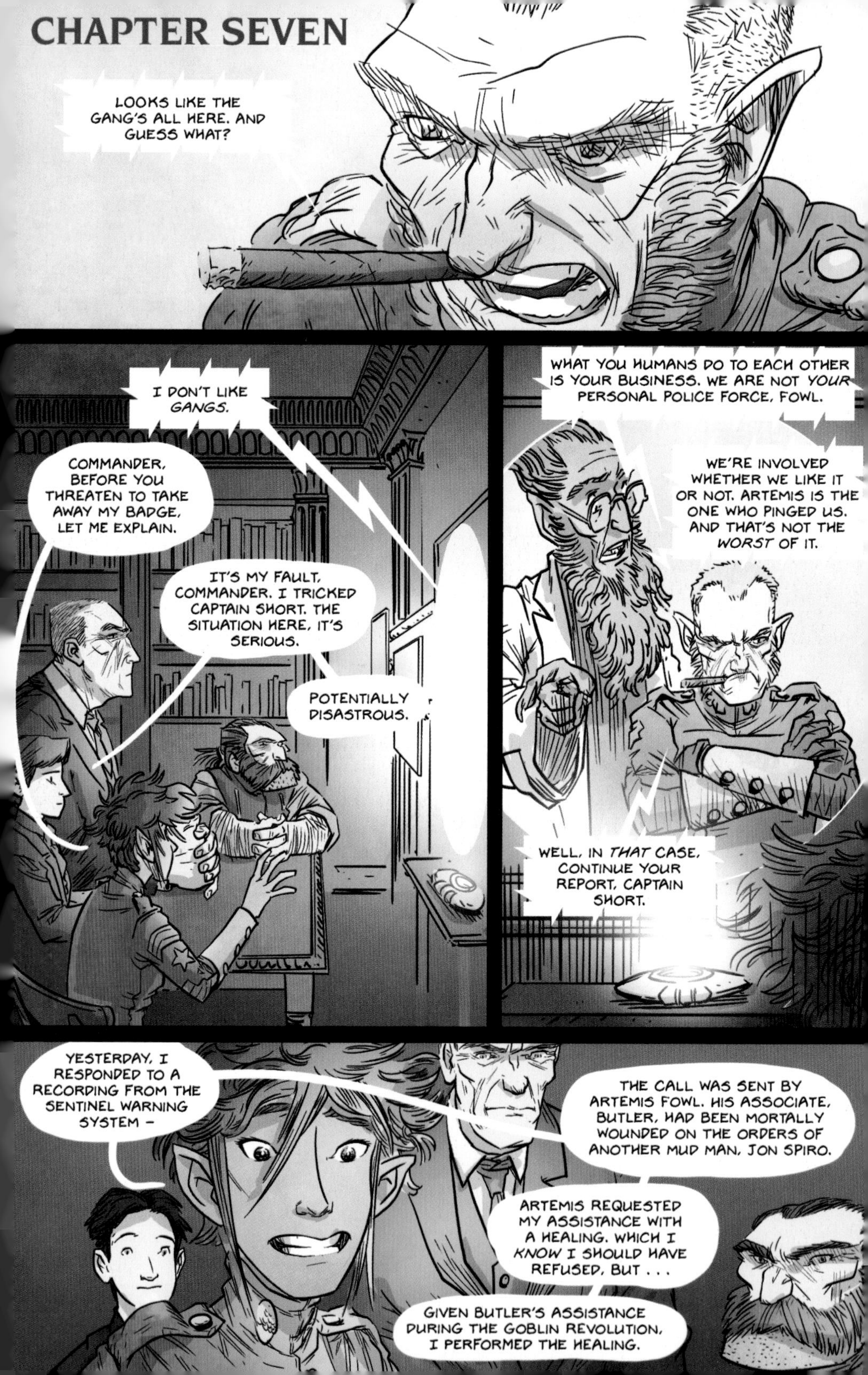

LOOKS LIKE THE GANG'S ALL HERE. AND GUESS WHAT?
I DON'T LIKE *GANGS.*
COMMANDER, BEFORE YOU THREATEN TO TAKE AWAY MY BADGE, LET ME EXPLAIN.
IT'S MY FAULT, COMMANDER. I TRICKED CAPTAIN SHORT. THE SITUATION HERE, IT'S SERIOUS.
POTENTIALLY DISASTROUS.
WHAT YOU HUMANS DO TO EACH OTHER IS YOUR BUSINESS. WE ARE NOT *YOUR* PERSONAL POLICE FORCE, FOWL.
WE'RE INVOLVED WHETHER WE LIKE IT OR NOT. ARTEMIS IS THE ONE WHO PINGED US. AND THAT'S NOT THE *WORST* OF IT.
WELL, IN *THAT* CASE, CONTINUE YOUR REPORT, CAPTAIN SHORT.
YESTERDAY, I RESPONDED TO A RECORDING FROM THE SENTINEL WARNING SYSTEM –
THE CALL WAS SENT BY ARTEMIS FOWL. HIS ASSOCIATE, BUTLER, HAD BEEN MORTALLY WOUNDED ON THE ORDERS OF ANOTHER MUD MAN, JON SPIRO.
ARTEMIS REQUESTED MY ASSISTANCE WITH A HEALING. WHICH I *KNOW* I SHOULD HAVE REFUSED, BUT . . .
GIVEN BUTLER'S ASSISTANCE DURING THE GOBLIN REVOLUTION, I PERFORMED THE HEALING.

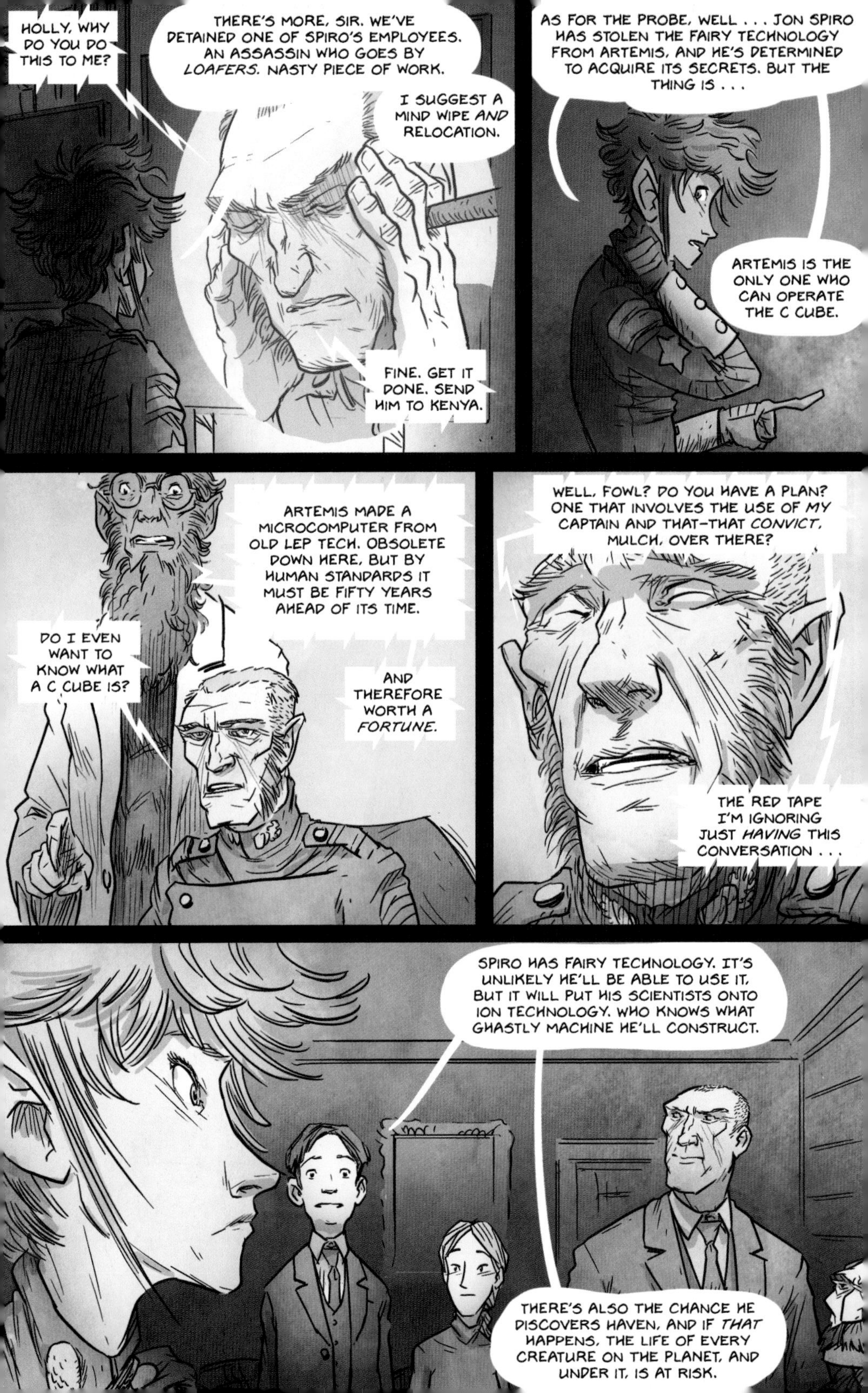
HOLLY, WHY DO YOU DO THIS TO ME?
THERE'S MORE, SIR. WE'VE DETAINED ONE OF SPIRO'S EMPLOYEES. AN ASSASSIN WHO GOES BY *LOAFERS*. NASTY PIECE OF WORK.
I SUGGEST A MIND WIPE *AND* RELOCATION.
FINE. GET IT DONE. SEND HIM TO KENYA.
AS FOR THE PROBE, WELL . . . JON SPIRO HAS STOLEN THE FAIRY TECHNOLOGY FROM ARTEMIS, AND HE'S DETERMINED TO ACQUIRE ITS SECRETS. BUT THE THING IS . . .
ARTEMIS IS THE ONLY ONE WHO CAN OPERATE THE C CUBE.
ARTEMIS MADE A MICROCOMPUTER FROM OLD LEP TECH. OBSOLETE DOWN HERE, BUT BY HUMAN STANDARDS IT MUST BE FIFTY YEARS AHEAD OF ITS TIME.
DO I EVEN WANT TO KNOW WHAT A C CUBE IS?
AND THEREFORE WORTH A *FORTUNE*.
WELL, FOWL? DO YOU HAVE A PLAN? ONE THAT INVOLVES THE USE OF *MY* CAPTAIN AND THAT—THAT *CONVICT*, MULCH, OVER THERE?
THE RED TAPE I'M IGNORING JUST *HAVING* THIS CONVERSATION . . .
SPIRO HAS FAIRY TECHNOLOGY. IT'S UNLIKELY HE'LL BE ABLE TO USE IT, BUT IT WILL PUT HIS SCIENTISTS ONTO ION TECHNOLOGY. WHO KNOWS WHAT GHASTLY MACHINE HE'LL CONSTRUCT.
THERE'S ALSO THE CHANCE HE DISCOVERS HAVEN, AND IF *THAT* HAPPENS, THE LIFE OF EVERY CREATURE ON THE PLANET, AND UNDER IT, IS AT RISK.

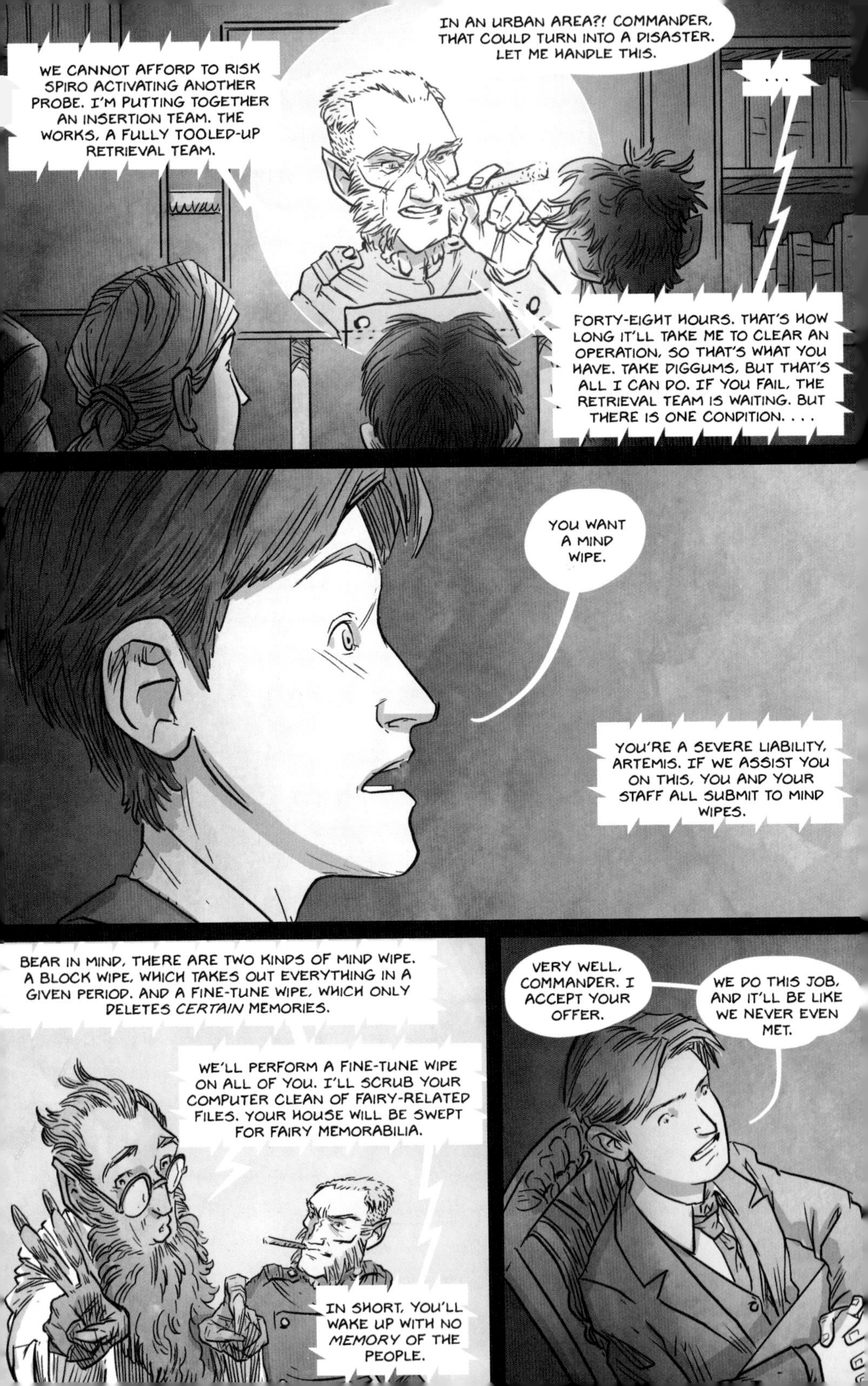
WE CANNOT AFFORD TO RISK SPIRO ACTIVATING ANOTHER PROBE. I'M PUTTING TOGETHER AN INSERTION TEAM. THE WORKS, A FULLY TOOLED-UP RETRIEVAL TEAM.
IN AN URBAN AREA?! COMMANDER, THAT COULD TURN INTO A DISASTER. LET ME HANDLE THIS.
. . .
FORTY-EIGHT HOURS. THAT'S HOW LONG IT'LL TAKE ME TO CLEAR AN OPERATION, SO THAT'S WHAT YOU HAVE. TAKE DIGGUMS, BUT THAT'S ALL I CAN DO. IF YOU FAIL, THE RETRIEVAL TEAM IS WAITING. BUT THERE IS ONE CONDITION. . . .
YOU WANT A MIND WIPE.
YOU'RE A SEVERE LIABILITY, ARTEMIS. IF WE ASSIST YOU ON THIS, YOU AND YOUR STAFF ALL SUBMIT TO MIND WIPES.
BEAR IN MIND, THERE ARE TWO KINDS OF MIND WIPE. A BLOCK WIPE, WHICH TAKES OUT EVERYTHING IN A GIVEN PERIOD. AND A FINE-TUNE WIPE, WHICH ONLY DELETES *CERTAIN* MEMORIES.
WE'LL PERFORM A FINE-TUNE WIPE ON ALL OF YOU. I'LL SCRUB YOUR COMPUTER CLEAN OF FAIRY-RELATED FILES. YOUR HOUSE WILL BE SWEPT FOR FAIRY MEMORABILIA.
IN SHORT, YOU'LL WAKE UP WITH NO *MEMORY* OF THE PEOPLE.
VERY WELL, COMMANDER. I ACCEPT YOUR OFFER.
WE DO THIS JOB, AND IT'LL BE LIKE WE NEVER EVEN MET.

CHAPTER EIGHT

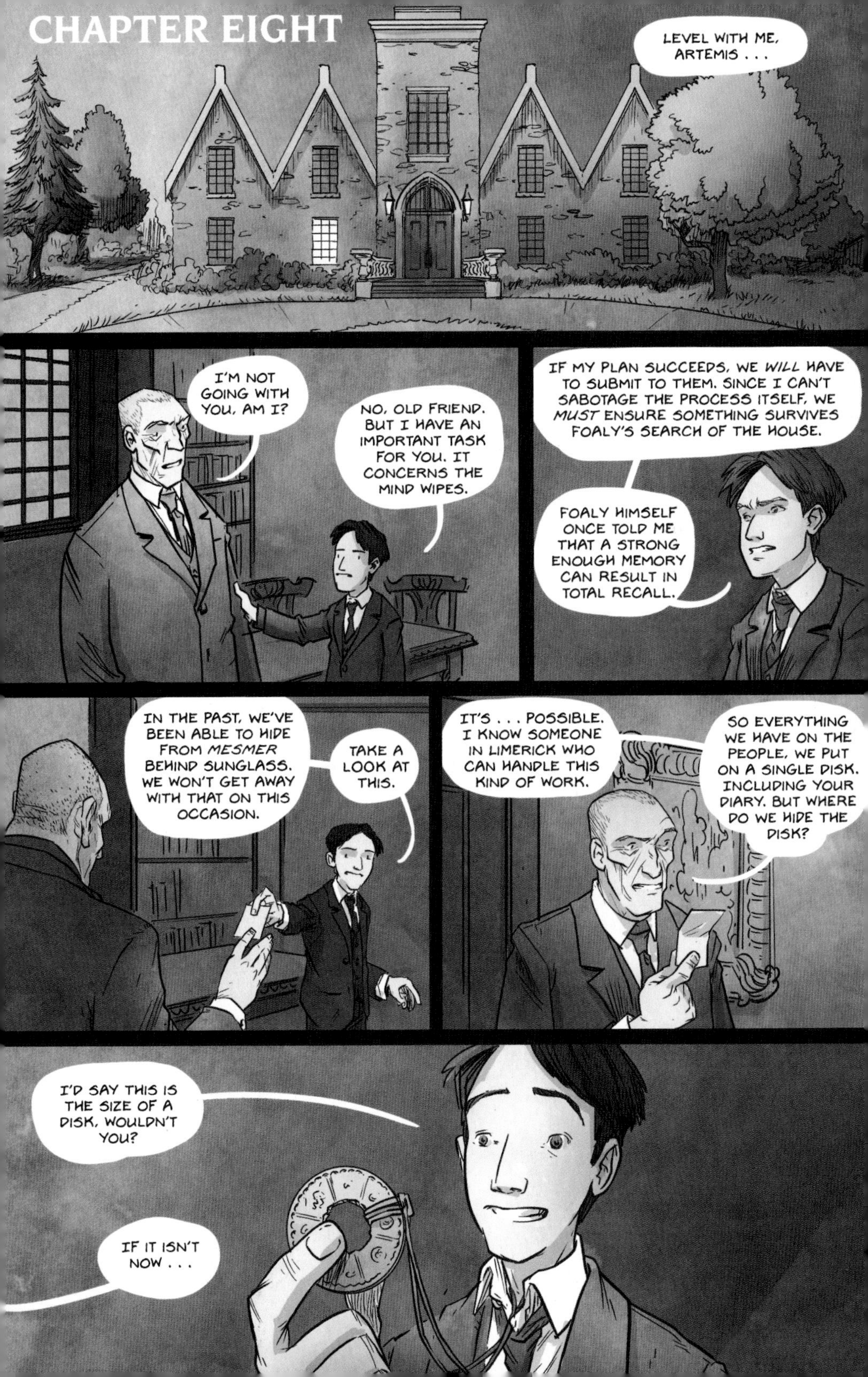
LEVEL WITH ME, ARTEMIS . . .
I'M NOT GOING WITH YOU, AM I?
NO, OLD FRIEND. BUT I HAVE AN IMPORTANT TASK FOR YOU. IT CONCERNS THE MIND WIPES.
IF MY PLAN SUCCEEDS, WE *WILL* HAVE TO SUBMIT TO THEM. SINCE I CAN'T SABOTAGE THE PROCESS ITSELF, WE *MUST* ENSURE SOMETHING SURVIVES FOALY'S SEARCH OF THE HOUSE.
FOALY HIMSELF ONCE TOLD ME THAT A STRONG ENOUGH MEMORY CAN RESULT IN TOTAL RECALL.
IN THE PAST, WE'VE BEEN ABLE TO HIDE FROM *MESMER* BEHIND SUNGLASS. WE WON'T GET AWAY WITH THAT ON THIS OCCASION.
TAKE A LOOK AT THIS.
IT'S . . . POSSIBLE. I KNOW SOMEONE IN LIMERICK WHO CAN HANDLE THIS KIND OF WORK.
SO EVERYTHING WE HAVE ON THE PEOPLE, WE PUT ON A SINGLE DISK. INCLUDING YOUR DIARY. BUT WHERE DO WE HIDE THE DISK?
I'D SAY THIS IS THE SIZE OF A DISK, WOULDN'T YOU?
IF IT ISN'T NOW . . .

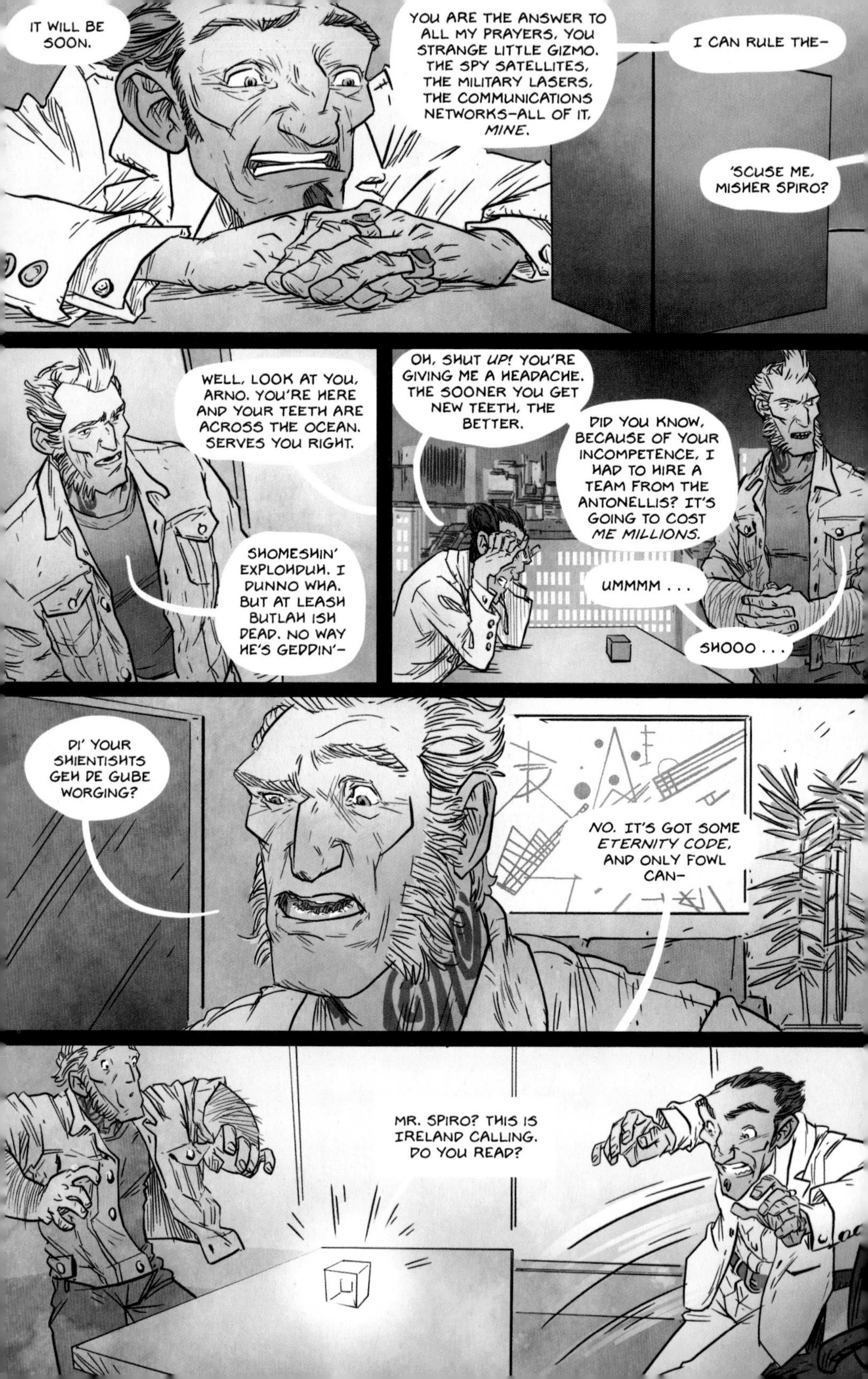
IT WILL BE SOON.
YOU ARE THE ANSWER TO ALL MY PRAYERS, YOU STRANGE LITTLE GIZMO. THE SPY SATELLITES, THE MILITARY LASERS, THE COMMUNICATIONS NETWORKS—ALL OF IT, *MINE*.
I CAN RULE THE—
'SCUSE ME, MISHER SPIRO?
WELL, LOOK AT YOU, ARNO. YOU'RE HERE AND YOUR TEETH ARE ACROSS THE OCEAN. SERVES YOU RIGHT.
SHOMESHIN' EXPLOHDUH. I DUNNO WHA. BUT AT LEASH BUTLAH ISH DEAD. NO WAY HE'S GEDDIN'—
OH, SHUT *UP!* YOU'RE GIVING ME A HEADACHE. THE SOONER YOU GET NEW TEETH, THE BETTER.
DID YOU KNOW, BECAUSE OF YOUR INCOMPETENCE, I HAD TO HIRE A TEAM FROM THE ANTONELLIS? IT'S GOING TO COST *ME MILLIONS*.
UMMMM . . .
SHOOO . . .
DI' YOUR SHIENTISHTS GEH DE GUBE WORGING?
NO. IT'S GOT SOME *ETERNITY CODE*, AND ONLY FOWL CAN—
MR. SPIRO? THIS IS IRELAND CALLING. DO YOU READ?

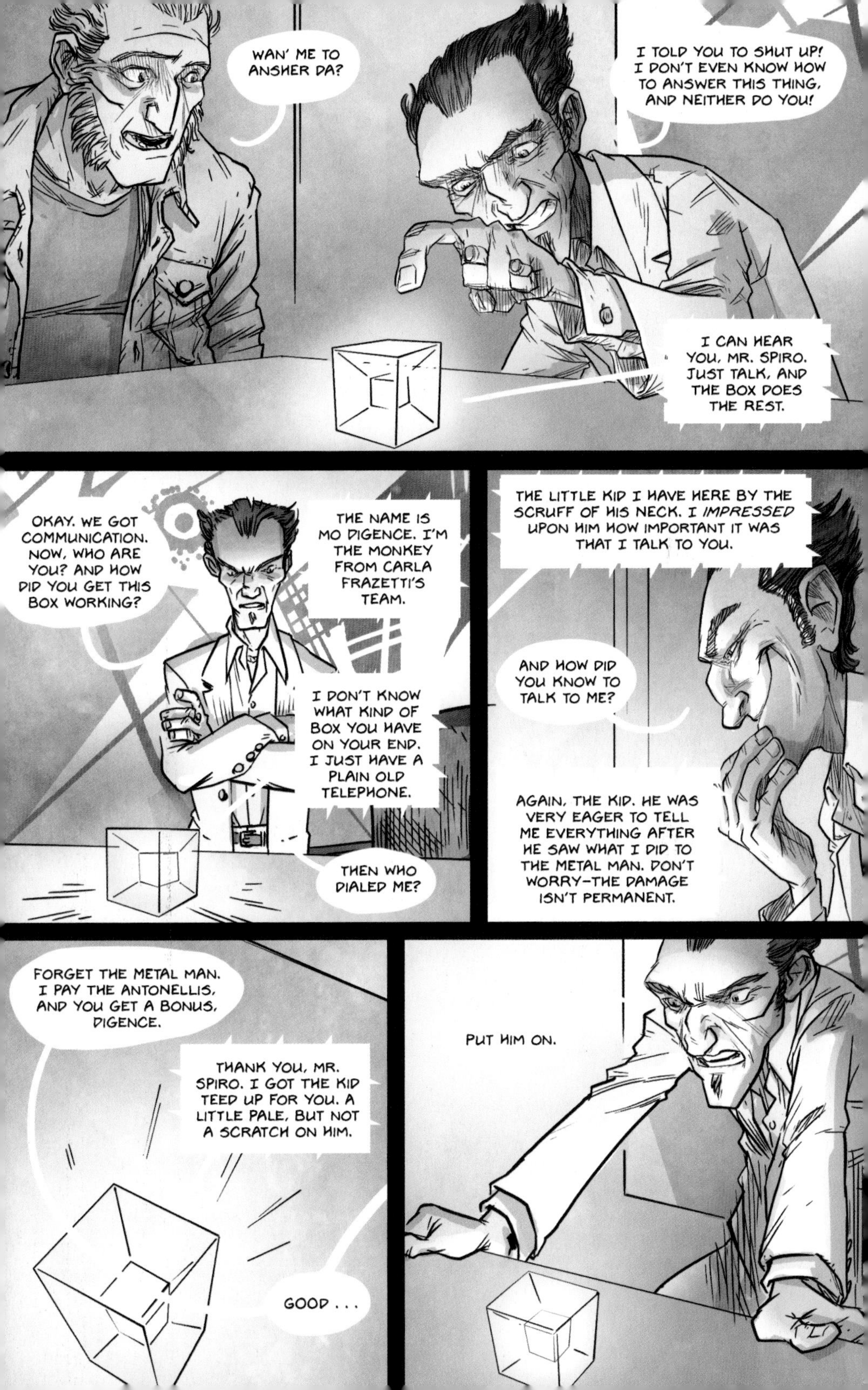
WAN' ME TO ANSHER DA?
I TOLD YOU TO SHUT UP! I DON'T EVEN KNOW HOW TO ANSWER THIS THING, AND NEITHER DO YOU!
I CAN HEAR YOU, MR. SPIRO. JUST TALK, AND THE BOX DOES THE REST.
OKAY. WE GOT COMMUNICATION. NOW, WHO ARE YOU? AND HOW DID YOU GET THIS BOX WORKING?
THE NAME IS MO DIGENCE. I'M THE MONKEY FROM CARLA FRAZETTI'S TEAM.
I DON'T KNOW WHAT KIND OF BOX YOU HAVE ON YOUR END. I JUST HAVE A PLAIN OLD TELEPHONE.
THEN WHO DIALED ME?
THE LITTLE KID I HAVE HERE BY THE SCRUFF OF HIS NECK. I *IMPRESSED* UPON HIM HOW IMPORTANT IT WAS THAT I TALK TO YOU.
AND HOW DID YOU KNOW TO TALK TO ME?
AGAIN, THE KID. HE WAS VERY EAGER TO TELL ME EVERYTHING AFTER HE SAW WHAT I DID TO THE METAL MAN. DON'T WORRY—THE DAMAGE ISN'T PERMANENT.
FORGET THE METAL MAN. I PAY THE ANTONELLIS, AND YOU GET A BONUS, DIGENCE.
THANK YOU, MR. SPIRO. I GOT THE KID TEED UP FOR YOU. A LITTLE PALE, BUT NOT A SCRATCH ON HIM.
GOOD . . .
PUT HIM ON.

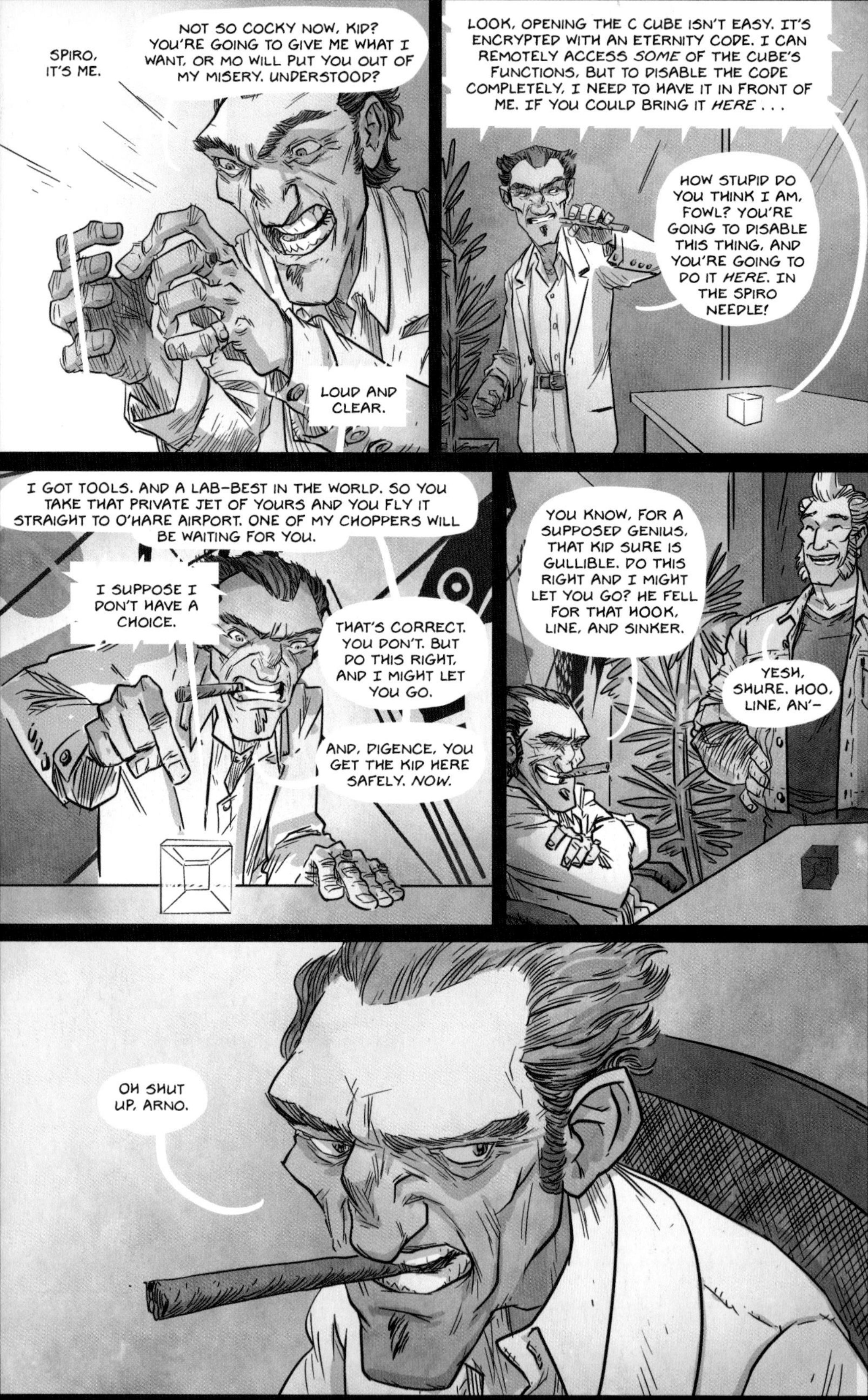
SPIRO, IT'S ME.
NOT SO COCKY NOW, KID? YOU'RE GOING TO GIVE ME WHAT I WANT, OR MO WILL PUT YOU OUT OF MY MISERY. UNDERSTOOD?
LOUD AND CLEAR.
LOOK, OPENING THE C CUBE ISN'T EASY. IT'S ENCRYPTED WITH AN ETERNITY CODE. I CAN REMOTELY ACCESS *SOME* OF THE CUBE'S FUNCTIONS, BUT TO DISABLE THE CODE COMPLETELY, I NEED TO HAVE IT IN FRONT OF ME. IF YOU COULD BRING IT *HERE* . . .
HOW STUPID DO YOU THINK I AM, FOWL? YOU'RE GOING TO DISABLE THIS THING, AND YOU'RE GOING TO DO IT *HERE*. IN THE SPIRO NEEDLE!
I GOT TOOLS. AND A LAB—BEST IN THE WORLD. SO YOU TAKE THAT PRIVATE JET OF YOURS AND YOU FLY IT STRAIGHT TO O'HARE AIRPORT. ONE OF MY CHOPPERS WILL BE WAITING FOR YOU.
I SUPPOSE I DON'T HAVE A CHOICE.
THAT'S CORRECT. YOU DON'T. BUT DO THIS RIGHT, AND I MIGHT LET YOU GO.
AND, DIGENCE, YOU GET THE KID HERE SAFELY. *NOW.*
YOU KNOW, FOR A SUPPOSED GENIUS, THAT KID SURE IS GULLIBLE. DO THIS RIGHT AND I MIGHT LET YOU GO? HE FELL FOR THAT HOOK, LINE, AND SINKER.
YESH, SHURE. HOO, LINE, AN'—
OH SHUT UP, ARNO.

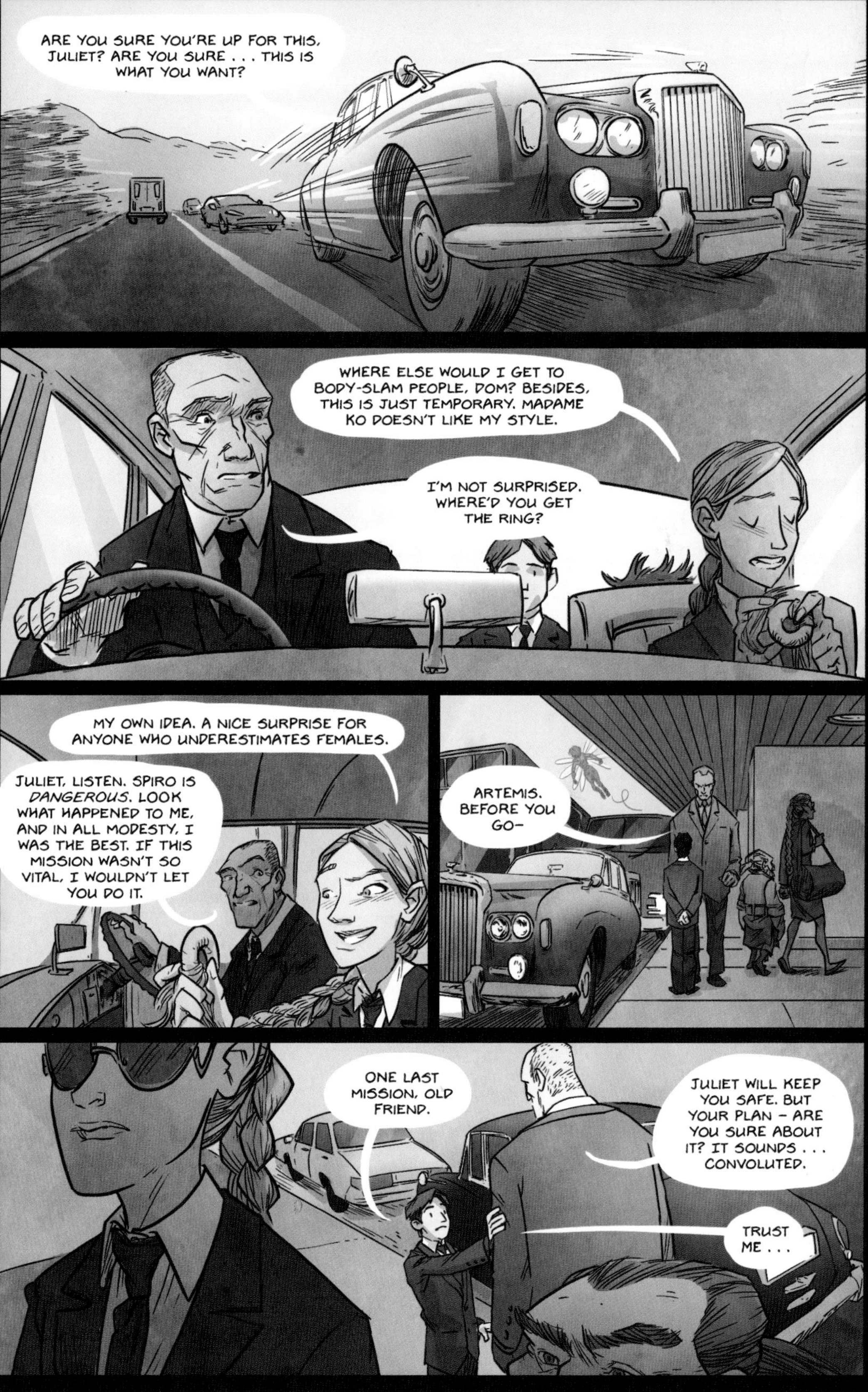
ARE YOU SURE YOU'RE UP FOR THIS, JULIET? ARE YOU SURE . . . THIS IS WHAT YOU WANT?
WHERE ELSE WOULD I GET TO BODY-SLAM PEOPLE, DOM? BESIDES, THIS IS JUST TEMPORARY. MADAME KO DOESN'T LIKE MY STYLE.
I'M NOT SURPRISED. WHERE'D YOU GET THE RING?
MY OWN IDEA. A NICE SURPRISE FOR ANYONE WHO UNDERESTIMATES FEMALES.
JULIET, LISTEN. SPIRO IS *DANGEROUS*. LOOK WHAT HAPPENED TO ME, AND IN ALL MODESTY, I WAS THE BEST. IF THIS MISSION WASN'T SO VITAL, I WOULDN'T LET YOU DO IT.
ARTEMIS. BEFORE YOU GO–
ONE LAST MISSION, OLD FRIEND.
JULIET WILL KEEP YOU SAFE. BUT YOUR PLAN – ARE YOU SURE ABOUT IT? IT SOUNDS . . . CONVOLUTED.
TRUST ME . . .

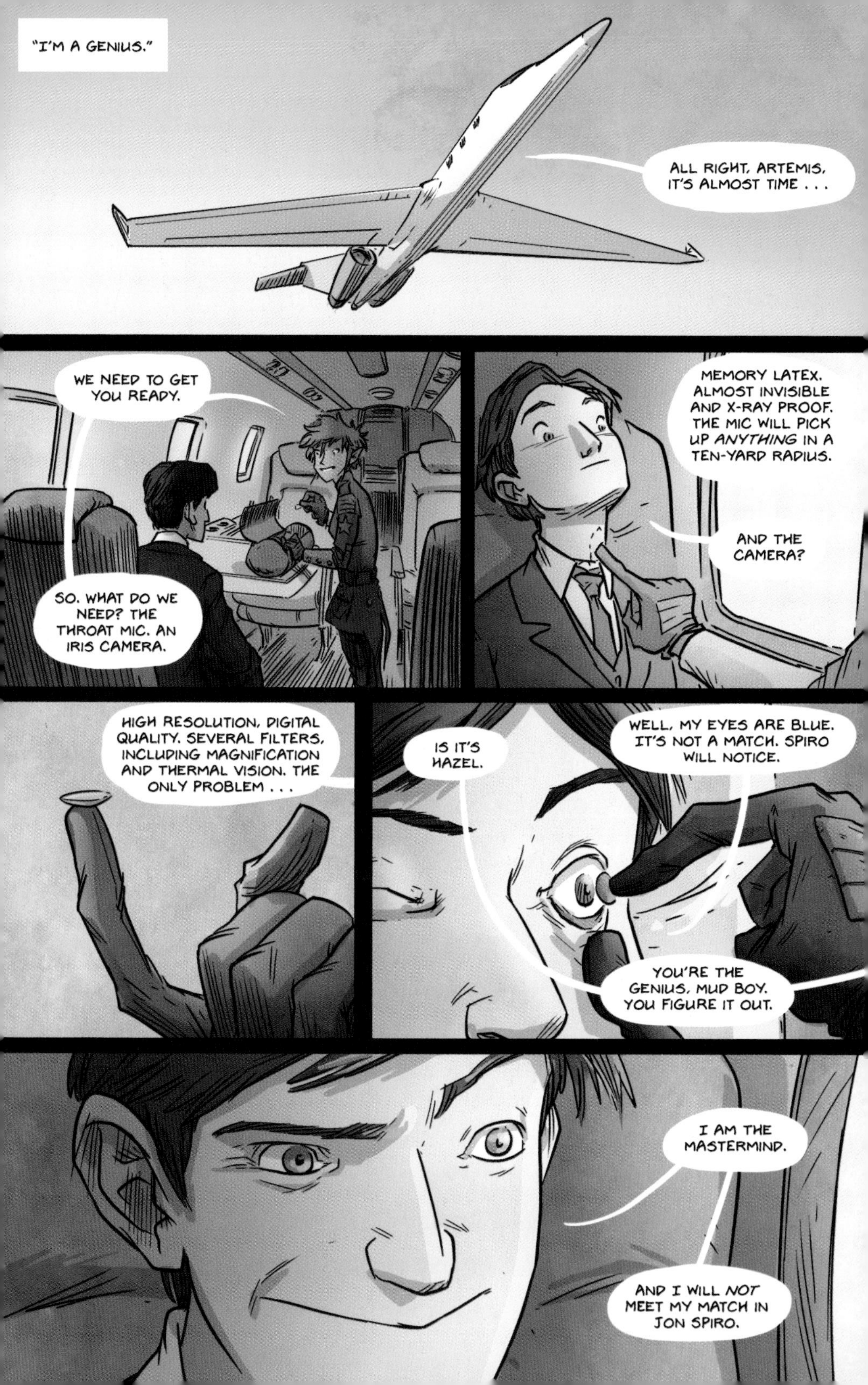
"I'M A GENIUS."
ALL RIGHT, ARTEMIS, IT'S ALMOST TIME . . .
WE NEED TO GET YOU READY.
SO. WHAT DO WE NEED? THE THROAT MIC. AN IRIS CAMERA.
MEMORY LATEX. ALMOST INVISIBLE AND X-RAY PROOF. THE MIC WILL PICK UP *ANYTHING* IN A TEN-YARD RADIUS.
AND THE CAMERA?
HIGH RESOLUTION, DIGITAL QUALITY. SEVERAL FILTERS, INCLUDING MAGNIFICATION AND THERMAL VISION. THE ONLY PROBLEM . . .
IS IT'S HAZEL.
WELL, MY EYES ARE BLUE. IT'S NOT A MATCH. SPIRO WILL NOTICE.
YOU'RE THE GENIUS, MUD BOY. YOU FIGURE IT OUT.
I AM THE MASTERMIND.
AND I WILL *NOT* MEET MY MATCH IN JON SPIRO.

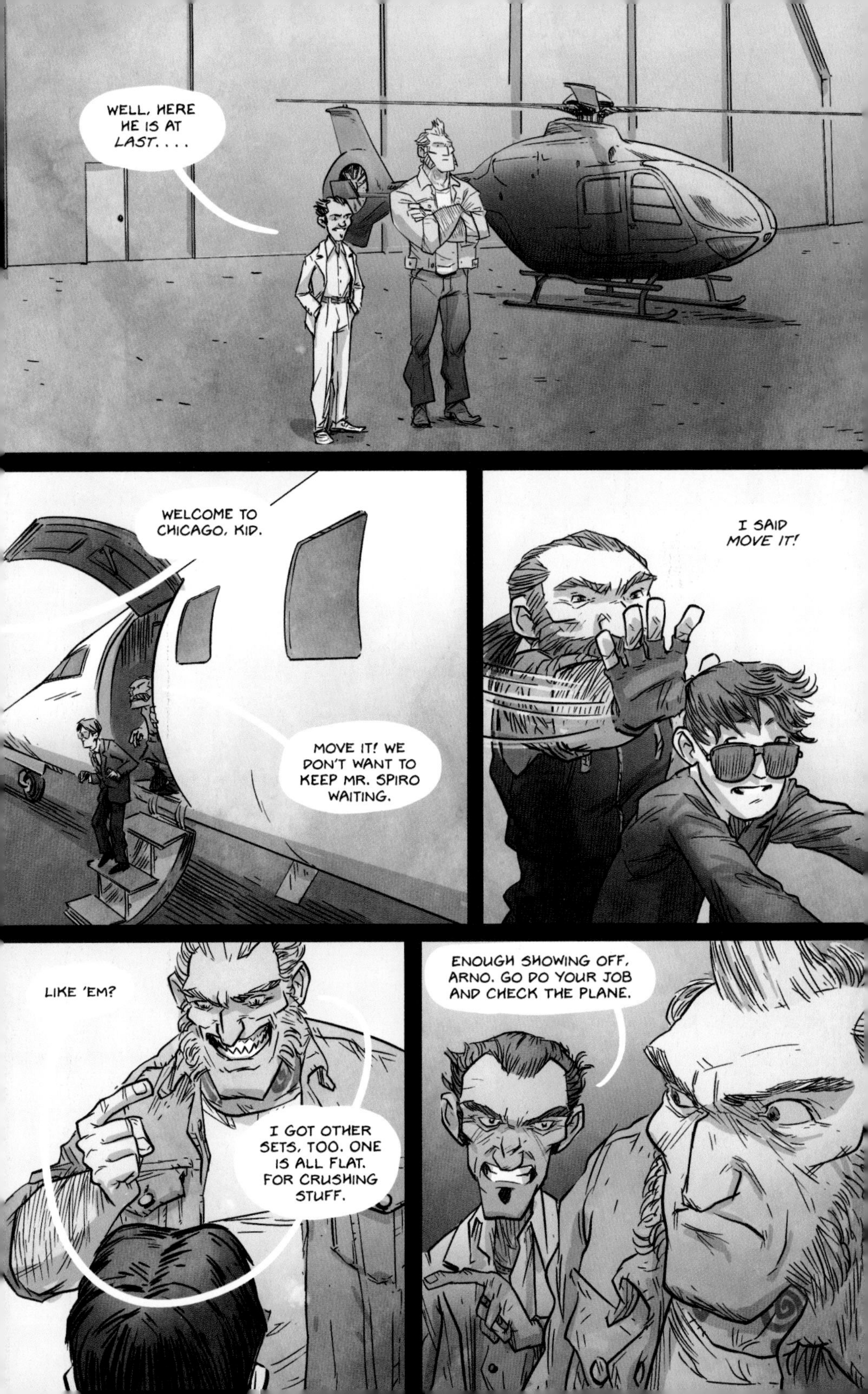
WELL, HERE HE IS AT LAST. . . .
WELCOME TO CHICAGO, KID.
MOVE IT! WE DON'T WANT TO KEEP MR. SPIRO WAITING.
I SAID MOVE IT!
LIKE 'EM?
I GOT OTHER SETS, TOO. ONE IS ALL FLAT. FOR CRUSHING STUFF.
ENOUGH SHOWING OFF, ARNO. GO DO YOUR JOB AND CHECK THE PLANE.

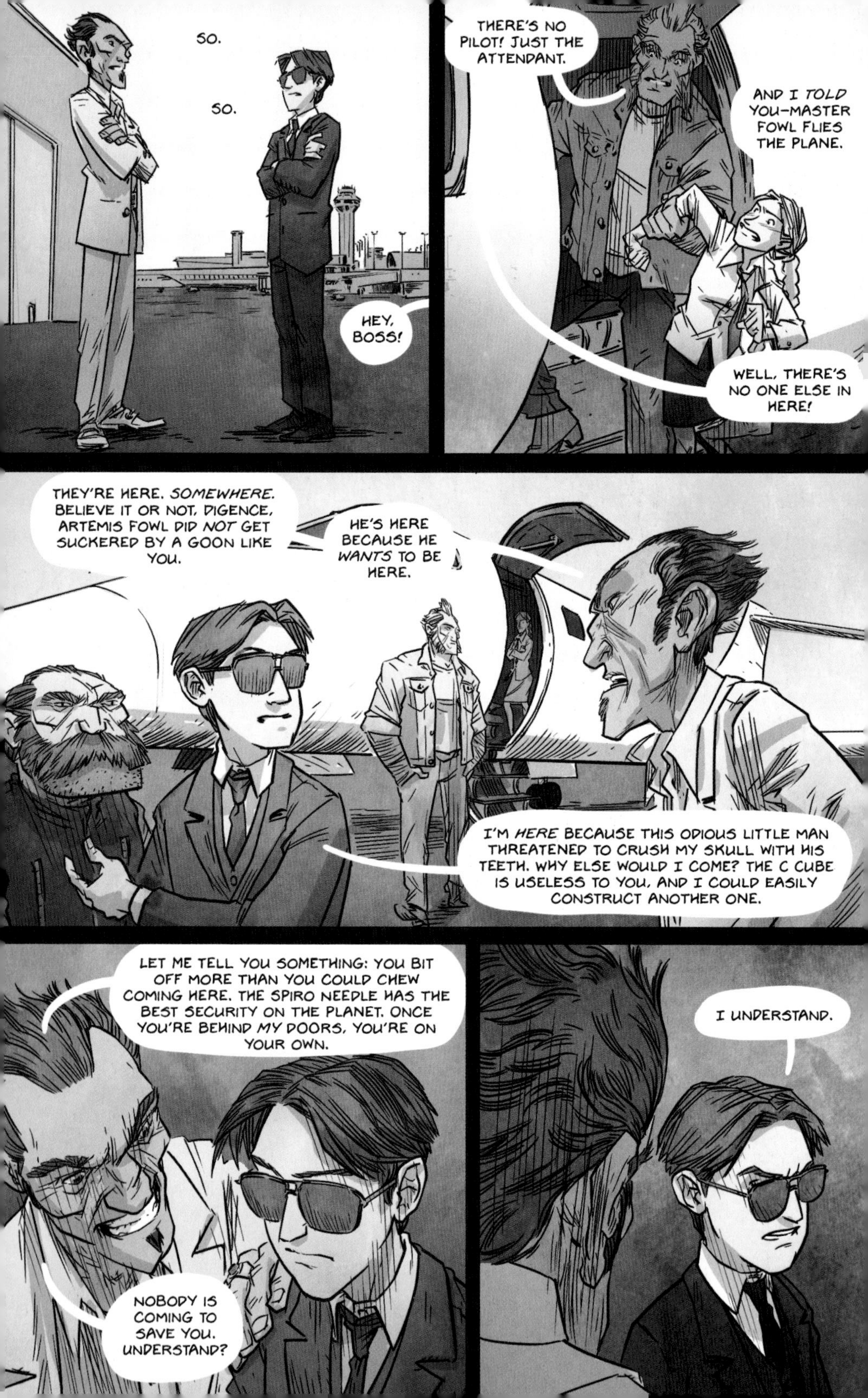
SO.
SO.
HEY, BOSS!
THERE'S NO PILOT! JUST THE ATTENDANT.
AND I TOLD YOU—MASTER FOWL FLIES THE PLANE.
WELL, THERE'S NO ONE ELSE IN HERE!
THEY'RE HERE. SOMEWHERE. BELIEVE IT OR NOT, DIGENCE, ARTEMIS FOWL DID NOT GET SUCKERED BY A GOON LIKE YOU.
HE'S HERE BECAUSE HE WANTS TO BE HERE.
I'M HERE BECAUSE THIS ODIOUS LITTLE MAN THREATENED TO CRUSH MY SKULL WITH HIS TEETH. WHY ELSE WOULD I COME? THE C CUBE IS USELESS TO YOU, AND I COULD EASILY CONSTRUCT ANOTHER ONE.
LET ME TELL YOU SOMETHING: YOU BIT OFF MORE THAN YOU COULD CHEW COMING HERE. THE SPIRO NEEDLE HAS THE BEST SECURITY ON THE PLANET. ONCE YOU'RE BEHIND MY DOORS, YOU'RE ON YOUR OWN.
NOBODY IS COMING TO SAVE YOU. UNDERSTAND?
I UNDERSTAND.

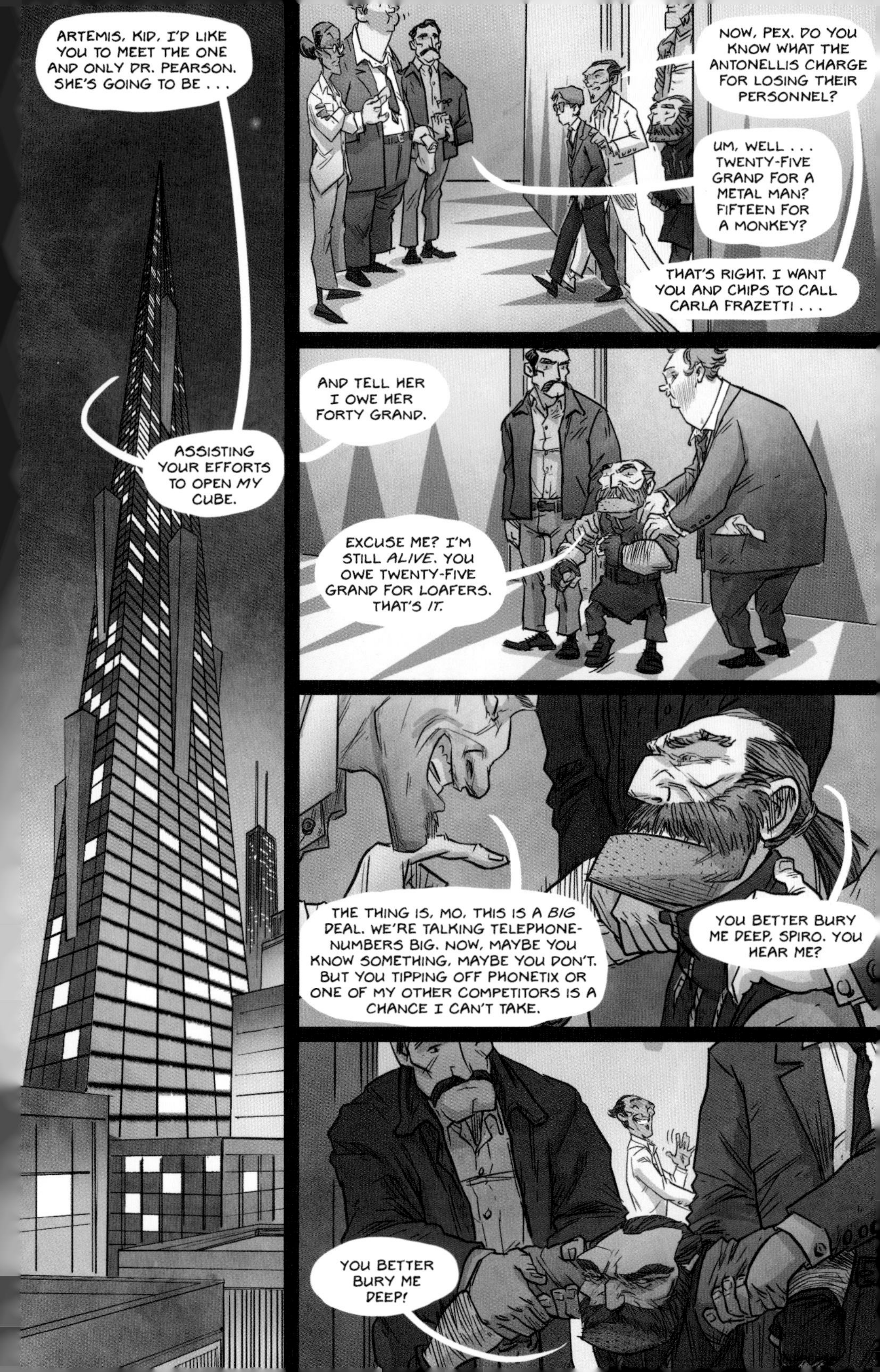
ARTEMIS, KID. I'D LIKE YOU TO MEET THE ONE AND ONLY DR. PEARSON. SHE'S GOING TO BE . . .
ASSISTING YOUR EFFORTS TO OPEN MY CUBE.
NOW, PEX. DO YOU KNOW WHAT THE ANTONELLIS CHARGE FOR LOSING THEIR PERSONNEL?
UM, WELL . . . TWENTY-FIVE GRAND FOR A METAL MAN? FIFTEEN FOR A MONKEY?
THAT'S RIGHT. I WANT YOU AND CHIPS TO CALL CARLA FRAZETTI . . .
AND TELL HER I OWE HER FORTY GRAND.
EXCUSE ME? I'M STILL *ALIVE*. YOU OWE TWENTY-FIVE GRAND FOR LOAFERS. THAT'S *IT*.
THE THING IS, MO, THIS IS A *BIG* DEAL. WE'RE TALKING TELEPHONE-NUMBERS BIG. NOW, MAYBE YOU KNOW SOMETHING, MAYBE YOU DON'T. BUT YOU TIPPING OFF PHONETIX OR ONE OF MY OTHER COMPETITORS IS A CHANCE I CAN'T TAKE.
YOU BETTER BURY ME DEEP, SPIRO. YOU HEAR ME?
YOU BETTER BURY ME DEEP!

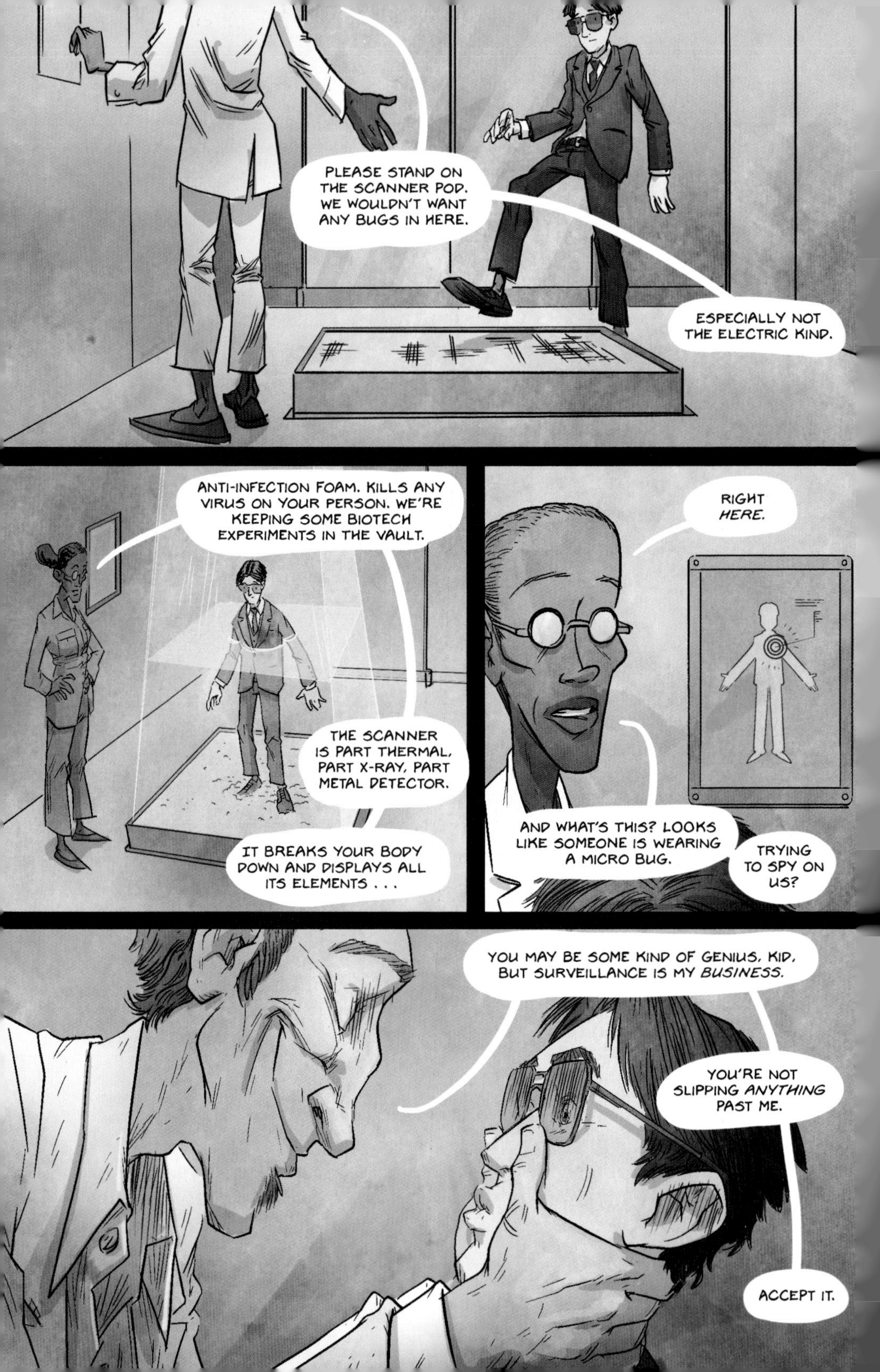
PLEASE STAND ON THE SCANNER POD. WE WOULDN'T WANT ANY BUGS IN HERE.
ESPECIALLY NOT THE ELECTRIC KIND.
ANTI-INFECTION FOAM. KILLS ANY VIRUS ON YOUR PERSON. WE'RE KEEPING SOME BIOTECH EXPERIMENTS IN THE VAULT.
THE SCANNER IS PART THERMAL, PART X-RAY, PART METAL DETECTOR.
IT BREAKS YOUR BODY DOWN AND DISPLAYS ALL ITS ELEMENTS . . .
RIGHT *HERE.*
AND WHAT'S THIS? LOOKS LIKE SOMEONE IS WEARING A MICRO BUG.
TRYING TO SPY ON US?
YOU MAY BE SOME KIND OF GENIUS, KID, BUT SURVEILLANCE IS MY *BUSINESS.*
YOU'RE NOT SLIPPING *ANYTHING* PAST ME.
ACCEPT IT.

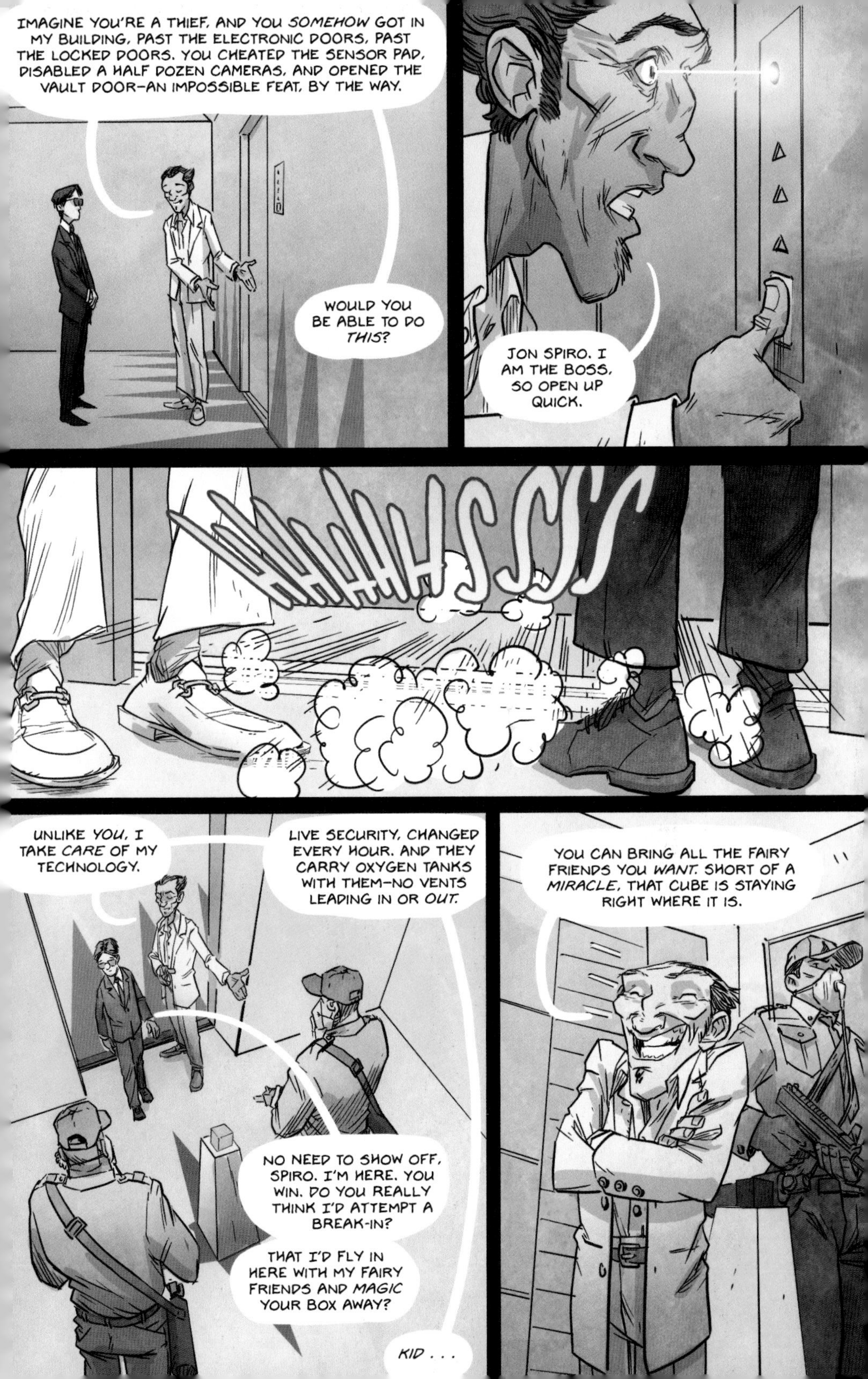
IMAGINE YOU'RE A THIEF, AND YOU *SOMEHOW* GOT IN MY BUILDING, PAST THE ELECTRONIC DOORS, PAST THE LOCKED DOORS. YOU CHEATED THE SENSOR PAD, DISABLED A HALF DOZEN CAMERAS, AND OPENED THE VAULT DOOR—AN IMPOSSIBLE FEAT, BY THE WAY.
WOULD YOU BE ABLE TO DO *THIS*?
JON SPIRO. I AM THE BOSS, SO OPEN UP QUICK.
UNLIKE *YOU*, I TAKE *CARE* OF MY TECHNOLOGY.
LIVE SECURITY, CHANGED EVERY HOUR. AND THEY CARRY OXYGEN TANKS WITH THEM—NO VENTS LEADING IN OR *OUT*.
NO NEED TO SHOW OFF, SPIRO. I'M HERE. YOU WIN. DO YOU REALLY THINK I'D ATTEMPT A BREAK-IN?
THAT I'D FLY IN HERE WITH MY FAIRY FRIENDS AND *MAGIC* YOUR BOX AWAY?
KID . . .
YOU CAN BRING ALL THE FAIRY FRIENDS YOU *WANT*. SHORT OF A *MIRACLE*, THAT CUBE IS STAYING RIGHT WHERE IT IS.

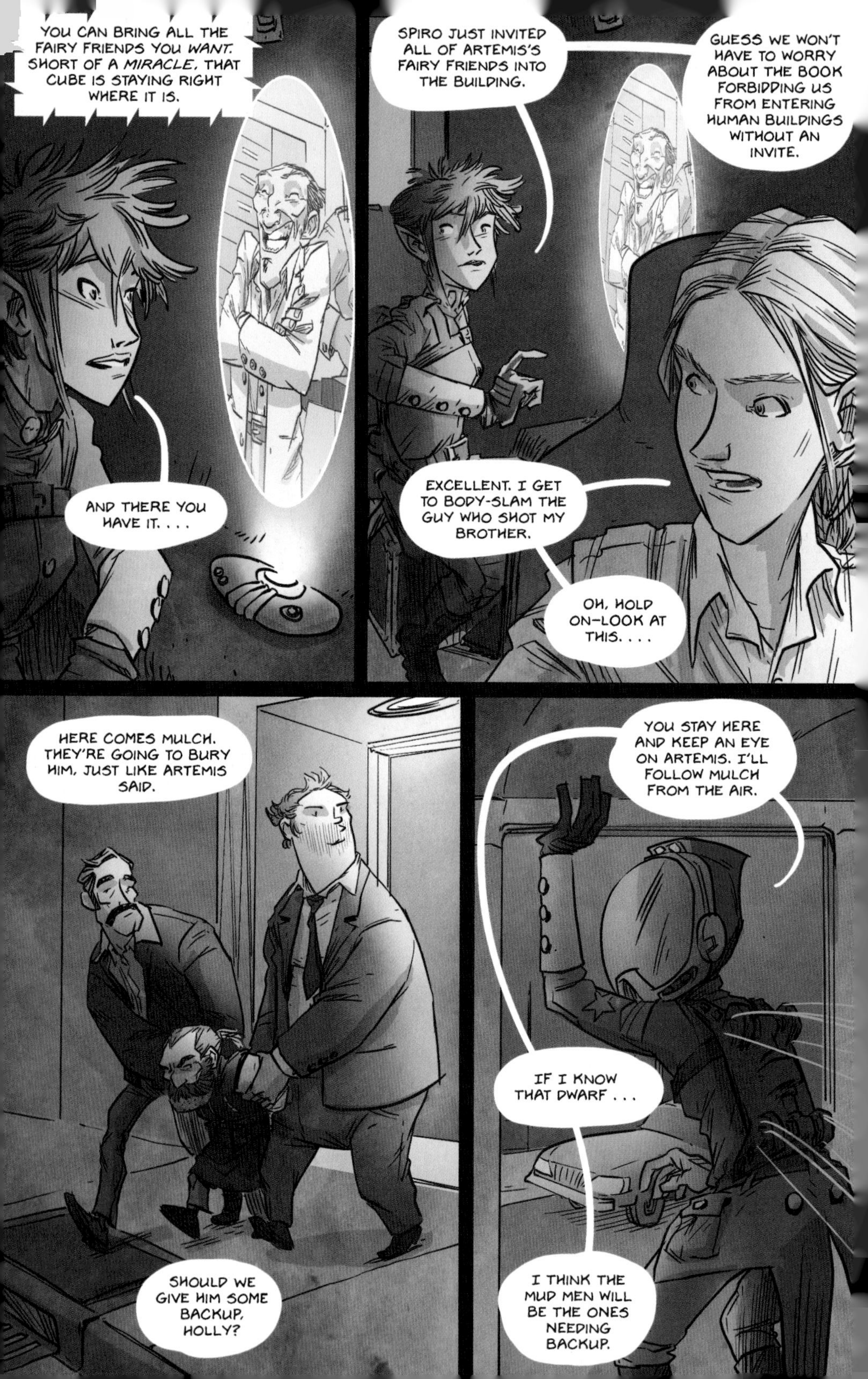
YOU CAN BRING ALL THE FAIRY FRIENDS YOU *WANT.* SHORT OF A *MIRACLE,* THAT CUBE IS STAYING RIGHT WHERE IT IS.
AND THERE YOU HAVE IT. . . .
SPIRO JUST INVITED ALL OF ARTEMIS'S FAIRY FRIENDS INTO THE BUILDING.
GUESS WE WON'T HAVE TO WORRY ABOUT THE BOOK FORBIDDING US FROM ENTERING HUMAN BUILDINGS WITHOUT AN INVITE.
EXCELLENT. I GET TO BODY-SLAM THE GUY WHO SHOT MY BROTHER.
OH, HOLD ON—LOOK AT THIS. . . .
HERE COMES MULCH. THEY'RE GOING TO BURY HIM, JUST LIKE ARTEMIS SAID.
SHOULD WE GIVE HIM SOME BACKUP, HOLLY?
YOU STAY HERE AND KEEP AN EYE ON ARTEMIS. I'LL FOLLOW MULCH FROM THE AIR.
IF I KNOW THAT DWARF . . .
I THINK THE MUD MEN WILL BE THE ONES NEEDING BACKUP.

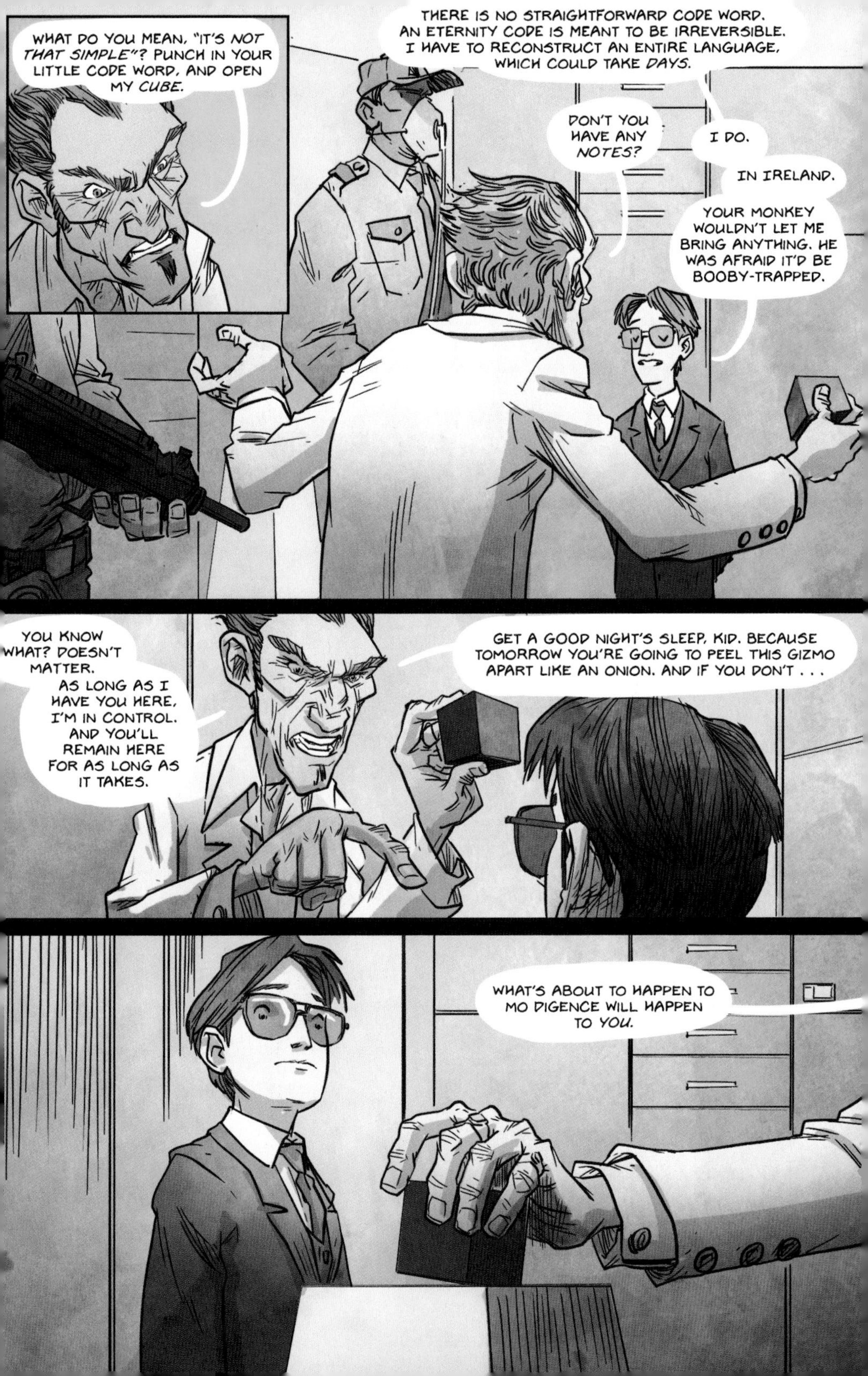
WHAT DO YOU MEAN, "IT'S *NOT THAT SIMPLE*"? PUNCH IN YOUR LITTLE CODE WORD, AND OPEN MY *CUBE*.
THERE IS NO STRAIGHTFORWARD CODE WORD. AN ETERNITY CODE IS MEANT TO BE IRREVERSIBLE. I HAVE TO RECONSTRUCT AN ENTIRE LANGUAGE, WHICH COULD TAKE *DAYS*.
DON'T YOU HAVE ANY *NOTES*?
I DO.
IN IRELAND.
YOUR MONKEY WOULDN'T LET ME BRING ANYTHING. HE WAS AFRAID IT'D BE BOOBY-TRAPPED.
YOU KNOW WHAT? DOESN'T MATTER.
AS LONG AS I HAVE YOU HERE, I'M IN CONTROL. AND YOU'LL REMAIN HERE FOR AS LONG AS IT TAKES.
GET A GOOD NIGHT'S SLEEP, KID. BECAUSE TOMORROW YOU'RE GOING TO PEEL THIS GIZMO APART LIKE AN ONION. AND IF YOU DON'T . . .
WHAT'S ABOUT TO HAPPEN TO MO DIGENCE WILL HAPPEN TO *YOU*.

CHAPTER NINE

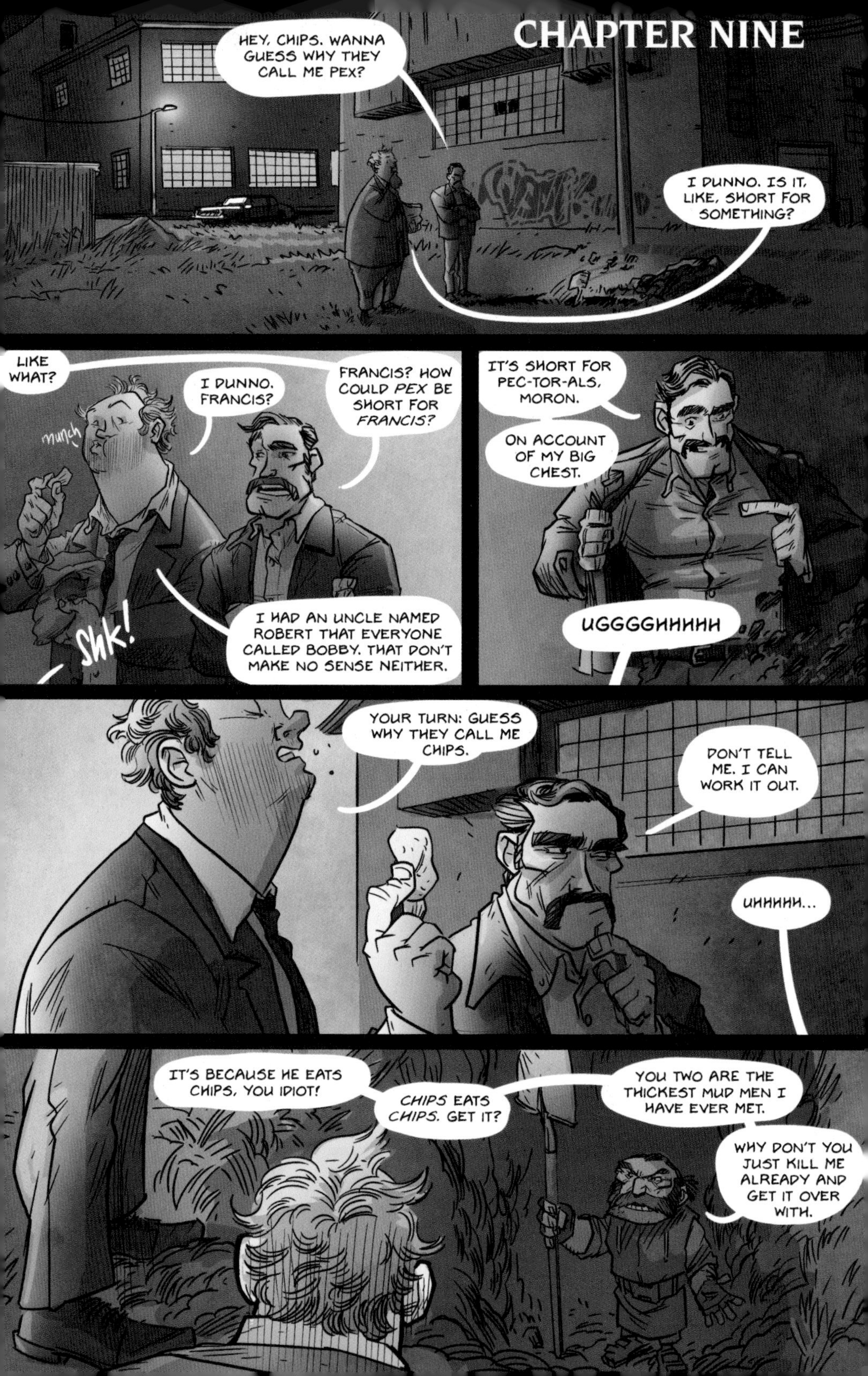
HEY, CHIPS. WANNA GUESS WHY THEY CALL ME PEX?
I DUNNO. IS IT, LIKE, SHORT FOR SOMETHING?
LIKE WHAT?
I DUNNO. FRANCIS?
FRANCIS? HOW COULD *PEX* BE SHORT FOR *FRANCIS?*
munch
I HAD AN UNCLE NAMED ROBERT THAT EVERYONE CALLED BOBBY. THAT DON'T MAKE NO SENSE NEITHER.
SHK!
IT'S SHORT FOR PEC-TOR-ALS, MORON.
ON ACCOUNT OF MY BIG CHEST.
UGGGGHHHHH
YOUR TURN: GUESS WHY THEY CALL ME CHIPS.
DON'T TELL ME. I CAN WORK IT OUT.
UHHHHH...
IT'S BECAUSE HE EATS CHIPS, YOU IDIOT!
CHIPS EATS *CHIPS.* GET IT?
YOU TWO ARE THE THICKEST MUD MEN I HAVE EVER MET.
WHY DON'T YOU JUST KILL ME ALREADY AND GET IT OVER WITH.

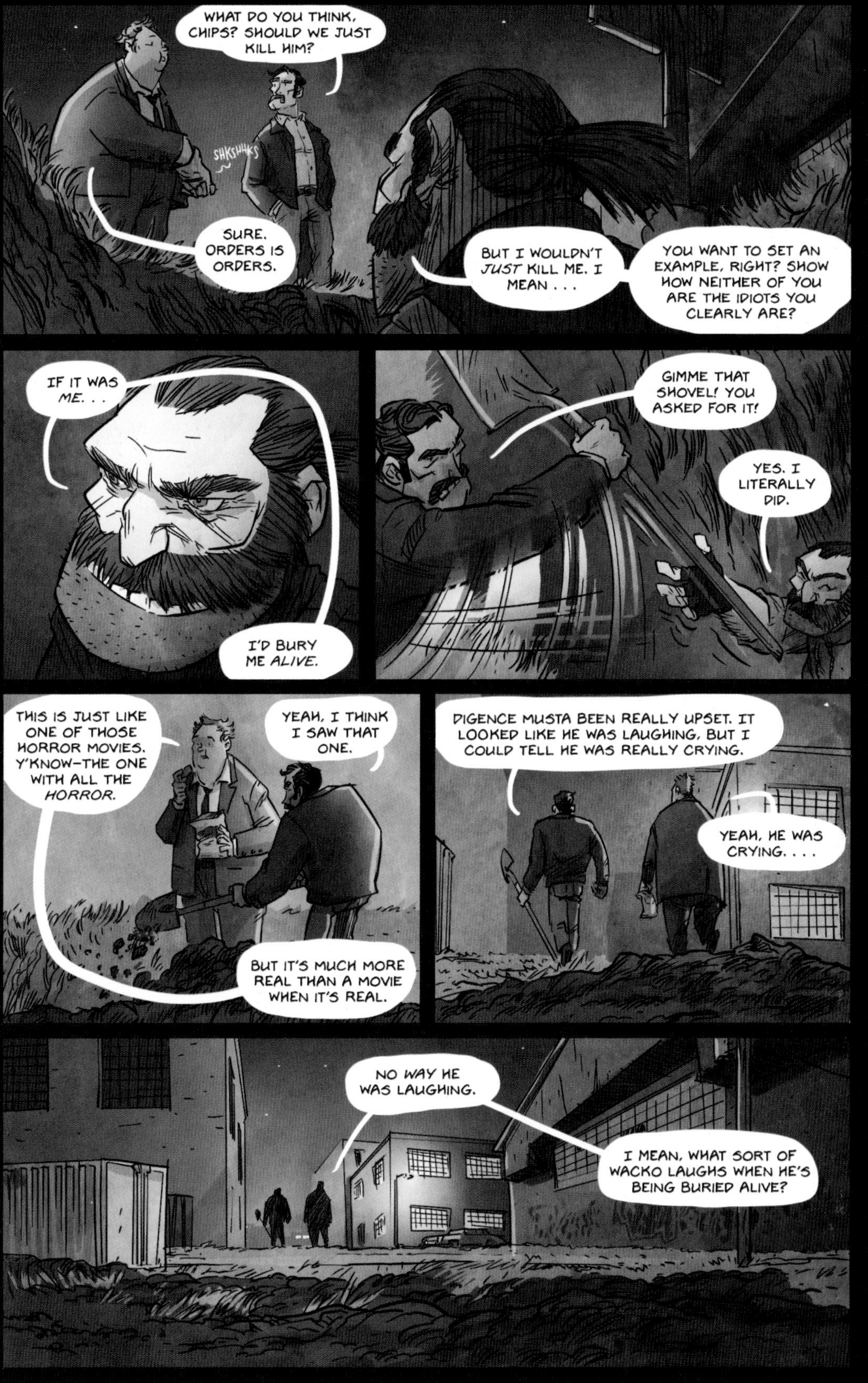
WHAT DO YOU THINK, CHIPS? SHOULD WE JUST KILL HIM?
SHKSHKS
SURE. ORDERS IS ORDERS.
BUT I WOULDN'T *JUST* KILL ME. I MEAN . . .
YOU WANT TO SET AN EXAMPLE, RIGHT? SHOW HOW NEITHER OF YOU ARE THE IDIOTS YOU CLEARLY ARE?
IF IT WAS *ME*. . .
I'D BURY ME *ALIVE*.
GIMME THAT SHOVEL! YOU ASKED FOR IT!
YES. I LITERALLY DID.
THIS IS JUST LIKE ONE OF THOSE HORROR MOVIES. Y'KNOW—THE ONE WITH ALL THE *HORROR*.
YEAH, I THINK I SAW THAT ONE.
BUT IT'S MUCH MORE REAL THAN A MOVIE WHEN IT'S REAL.
DIGENCE MUSTA BEEN REALLY UPSET. IT LOOKED LIKE HE WAS LAUGHING, BUT I COULD TELL HE WAS REALLY CRYING.
YEAH, HE WAS CRYING. . . .
NO WAY HE WAS LAUGHING.
I MEAN, WHAT SORT OF WACKO LAUGHS WHEN HE'S BEING BURIED ALIVE?

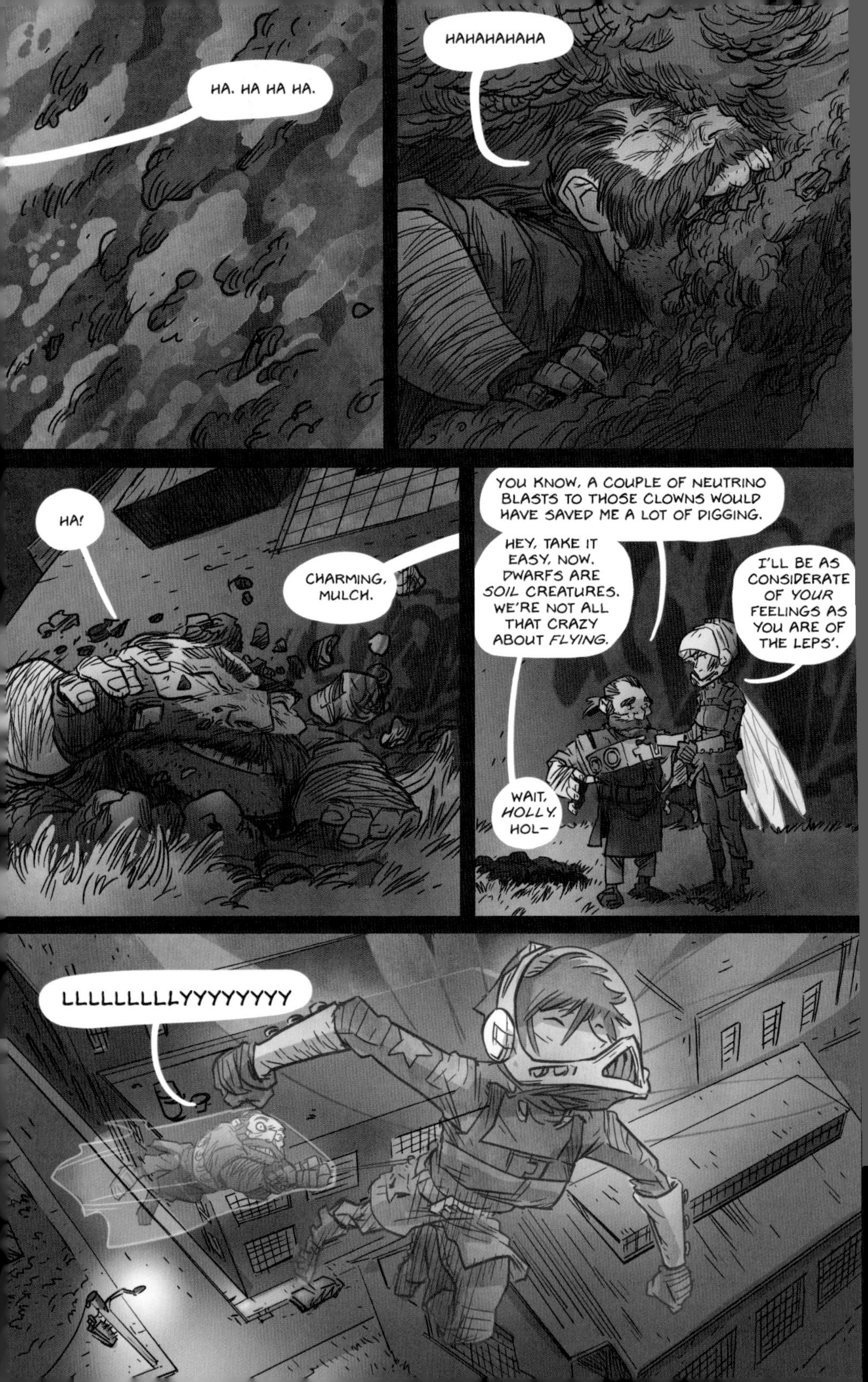
HA. HA HA HA.
HAHAHAHAHA
HA!
CHARMING, MULCH.
YOU KNOW, A COUPLE OF NEUTRINO BLASTS TO THOSE CLOWNS WOULD HAVE SAVED ME A LOT OF DIGGING.
HEY, TAKE IT EASY, NOW. DWARFS ARE SOIL CREATURES. WE'RE NOT ALL THAT CRAZY ABOUT FLYING.
I'LL BE AS CONSIDERATE OF YOUR FEELINGS AS YOU ARE OF THE LEPS'.
WAIT, HOLLY. HOL–
LLLLLLLLLYYYYYYYY

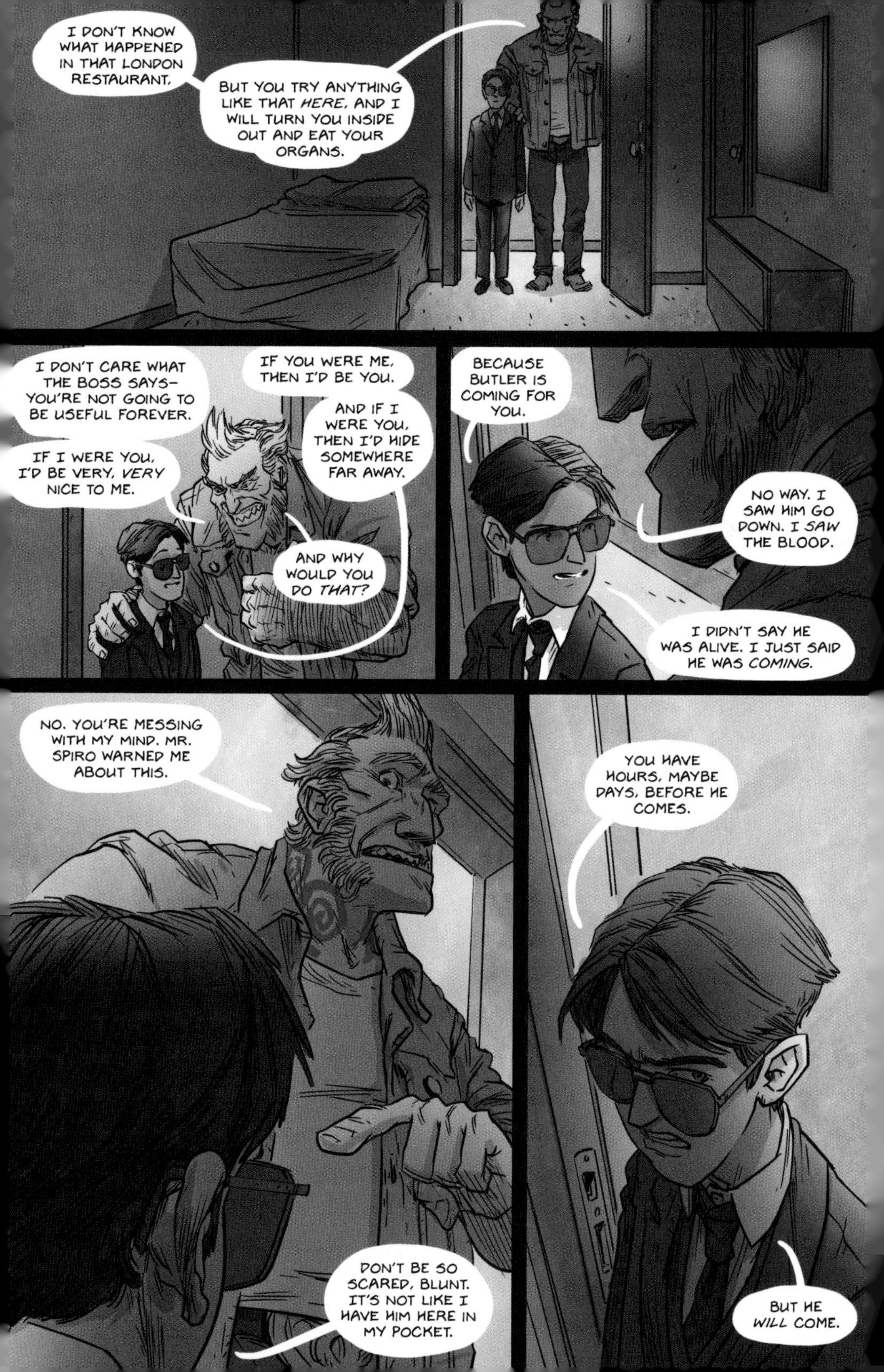
I DON'T KNOW WHAT HAPPENED IN THAT LONDON RESTAURANT,
BUT YOU TRY ANYTHING LIKE THAT *HERE*, AND I WILL TURN YOU INSIDE OUT AND EAT YOUR ORGANS.
I DON'T CARE WHAT THE BOSS SAYS— YOU'RE NOT GOING TO BE USEFUL FOREVER.
IF YOU WERE ME, THEN I'D BE YOU.
AND IF I WERE YOU, THEN I'D HIDE SOMEWHERE FAR AWAY.
IF I WERE YOU, I'D BE VERY, *VERY* NICE TO ME.
AND WHY WOULD YOU DO *THAT*?
BECAUSE BUTLER IS COMING FOR YOU.
NO WAY. I SAW HIM GO DOWN. I *SAW* THE BLOOD.
I DIDN'T SAY HE WAS ALIVE. I JUST SAID HE WAS *COMING*.
NO. YOU'RE MESSING WITH MY MIND. MR. SPIRO WARNED ME ABOUT THIS.
YOU HAVE HOURS, MAYBE DAYS, BEFORE HE COMES.
DON'T BE SO SCARED, BLUNT. IT'S NOT LIKE I HAVE HIM HERE IN MY POCKET.
BUT HE *WILL* COME.

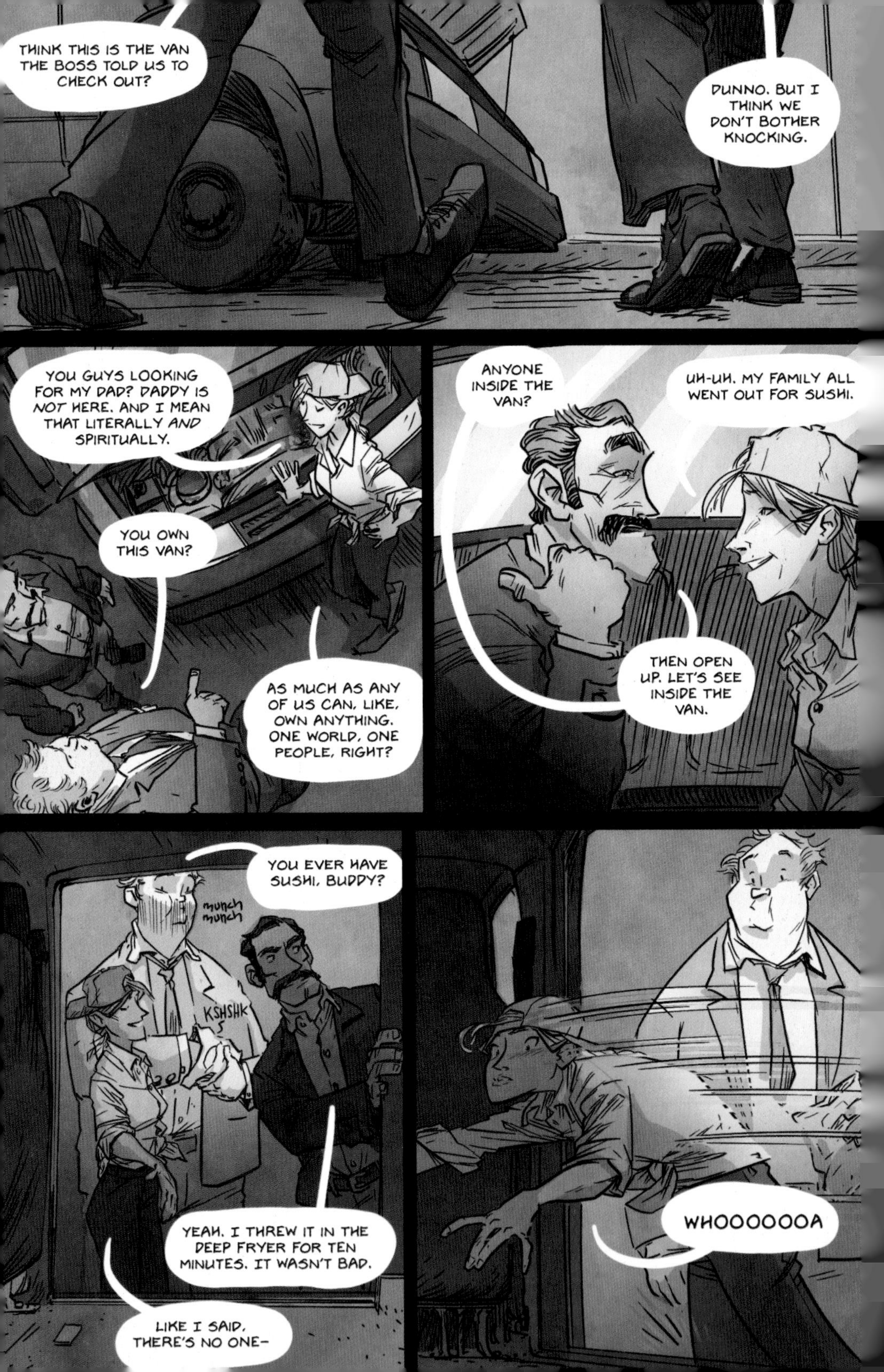
THINK THIS IS THE VAN THE BOSS TOLD US TO CHECK OUT?
DUNNO. BUT I THINK WE DON'T BOTHER KNOCKING.
YOU GUYS LOOKING FOR MY DAD? DADDY IS *NOT* HERE. AND I MEAN THAT LITERALLY *AND* SPIRITUALLY.
YOU OWN THIS VAN?
AS MUCH AS ANY OF US CAN, LIKE, OWN ANYTHING. ONE WORLD, ONE PEOPLE, RIGHT?
ANYONE INSIDE THE VAN?
UH-UH. MY FAMILY ALL WENT OUT FOR SUSHI.
THEN OPEN UP. LET'S SEE INSIDE THE VAN.
YOU EVER HAVE SUSHI, BUDDY?
munch munch
KSHSHK
YEAH. I THREW IT IN THE DEEP FRYER FOR TEN MINUTES. IT WASN'T BAD.
LIKE I SAID, THERE'S NO ONE-
WHOOOOOOA

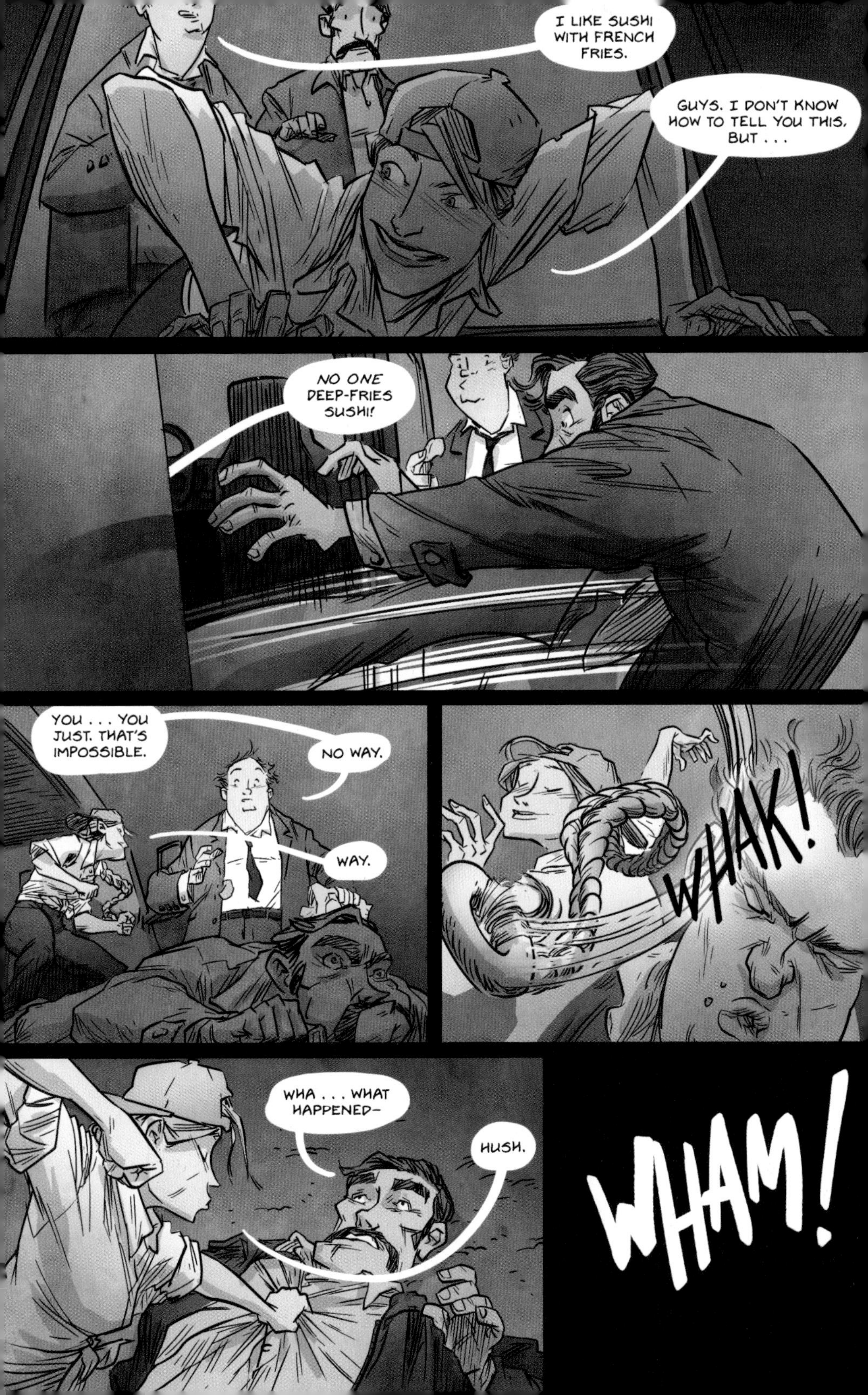
I LIKE SUSHI WITH FRENCH FRIES.
GUYS. I DON'T KNOW HOW TO TELL YOU THIS, BUT . . .
NO ONE DEEP-FRIES SUSHI!
YOU . . . YOU JUST. THAT'S IMPOSSIBLE.
NO WAY.
WAY.
WHAK!
WHA . . . WHAT HAPPENED–
HUSH.
WHAM!

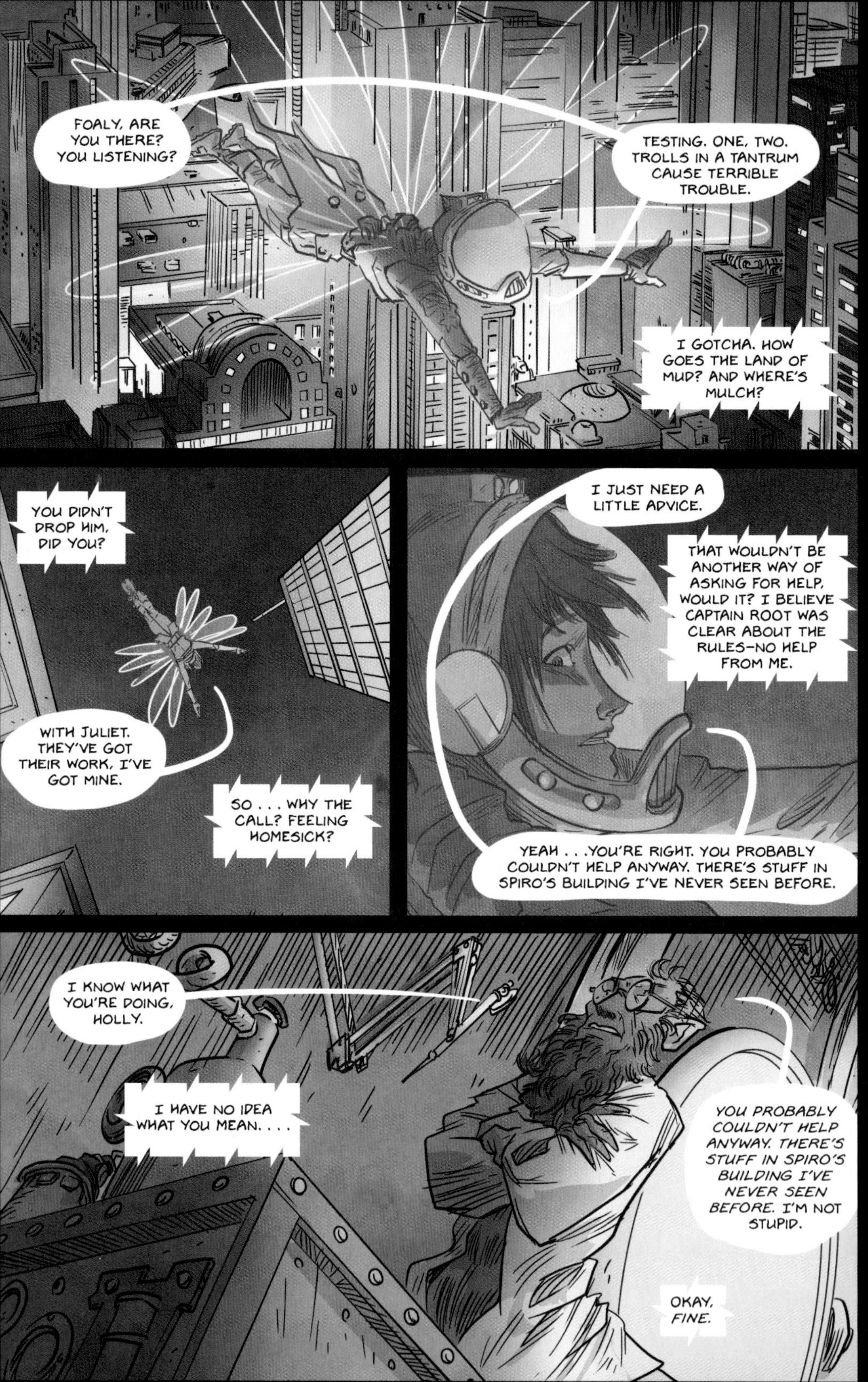
FOALY, ARE YOU THERE? YOU LISTENING?
TESTING. ONE, TWO. TROLLS IN A TANTRUM CAUSE TERRIBLE TROUBLE.
I GOTCHA. HOW GOES THE LAND OF MUD? AND WHERE'S MULCH?
YOU DIDN'T DROP HIM, DID YOU?
WITH JULIET. THEY'VE GOT THEIR WORK, I'VE GOT MINE.
SO . . . WHY THE CALL? FEELING HOMESICK?
I JUST NEED A LITTLE ADVICE.
THAT WOULDN'T BE ANOTHER WAY OF ASKING FOR HELP, WOULD IT? I BELIEVE CAPTAIN ROOT WAS CLEAR ABOUT THE RULES—NO HELP FROM ME.
YEAH . . . YOU'RE RIGHT. YOU PROBABLY COULDN'T HELP ANYWAY. THERE'S STUFF IN SPIRO'S BUILDING I'VE NEVER SEEN BEFORE.
I KNOW WHAT YOU'RE DOING, HOLLY.
I HAVE NO IDEA WHAT YOU MEAN. . . .
YOU PROBABLY COULDN'T HELP ANYWAY. THERE'S STUFF IN SPIRO'S BUILDING I'VE NEVER SEEN BEFORE. I'M NOT STUPID.
OKAY, FINE.

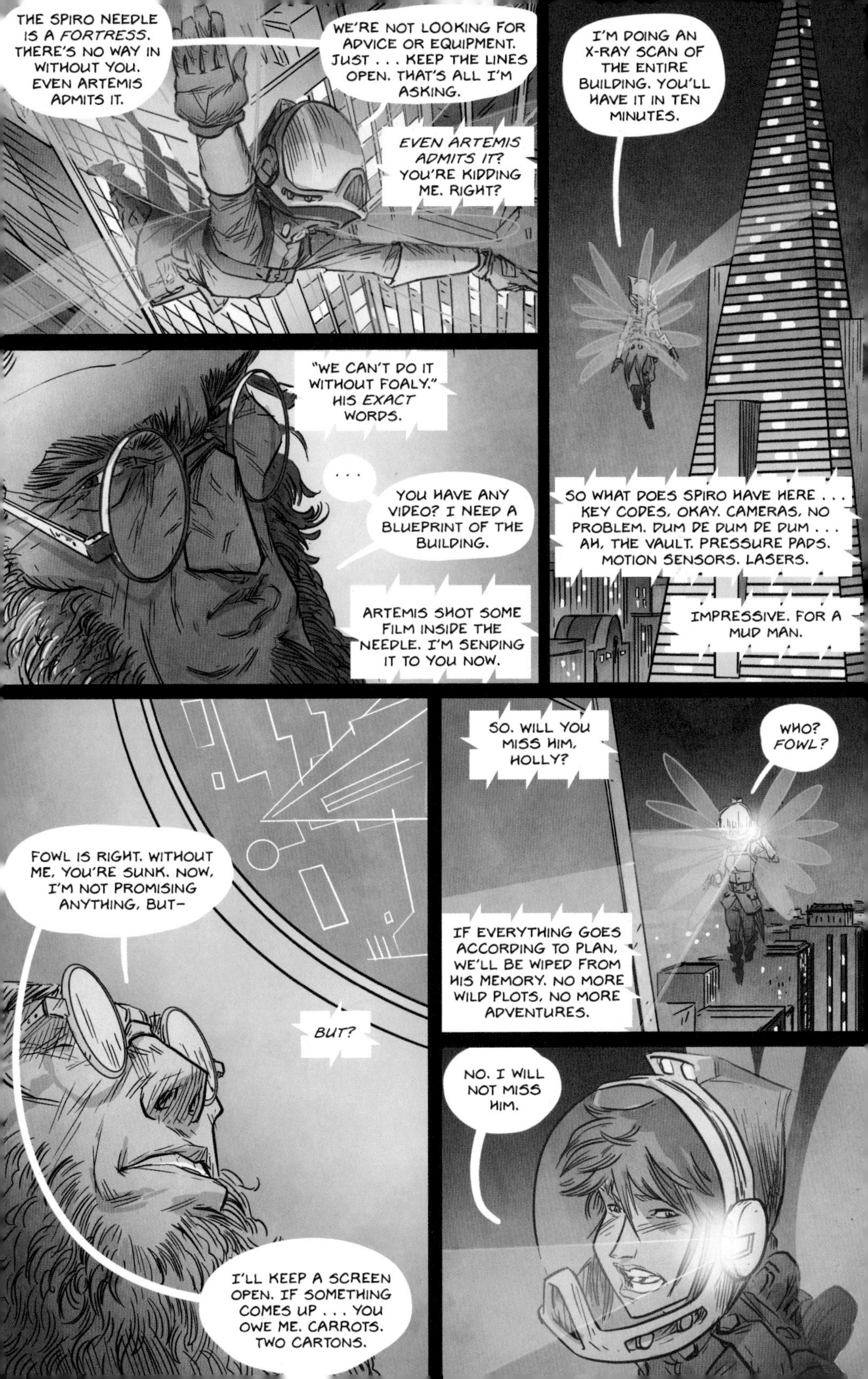
THE SPIRO NEEDLE IS A *FORTRESS*. THERE'S NO WAY IN WITHOUT YOU. EVEN ARTEMIS ADMITS IT.
WE'RE NOT LOOKING FOR ADVICE OR EQUIPMENT. JUST . . . KEEP THE LINES OPEN. THAT'S ALL I'M ASKING.
EVEN ARTEMIS ADMITS IT? YOU'RE KIDDING ME. RIGHT?
I'M DOING AN X-RAY SCAN OF THE ENTIRE BUILDING. YOU'LL HAVE IT IN TEN MINUTES.
"WE CAN'T DO IT WITHOUT FOALY." HIS *EXACT* WORDS.
. . .
YOU HAVE ANY VIDEO? I NEED A BLUEPRINT OF THE BUILDING.
ARTEMIS SHOT SOME FILM INSIDE THE NEEDLE. I'M SENDING IT TO YOU NOW.
SO WHAT DOES SPIRO HAVE HERE . . . KEY CODES, OKAY. CAMERAS, NO PROBLEM. DUM DE DUM DE DUM . . . AH, THE VAULT. PRESSURE PADS. MOTION SENSORS. LASERS.
IMPRESSIVE. FOR A MUD MAN.
FOWL IS RIGHT. WITHOUT ME, YOU'RE SUNK. NOW, I'M NOT PROMISING ANYTHING, BUT–
BUT?
I'LL KEEP A SCREEN OPEN. IF SOMETHING COMES UP . . . YOU OWE ME. CARROTS. TWO CARTONS.
SO. WILL YOU MISS HIM, HOLLY?
WHO? *FOWL?*
IF EVERYTHING GOES ACCORDING TO PLAN, WE'LL BE WIPED FROM HIS MEMORY. NO MORE WILD PLOTS, NO MORE ADVENTURES.
NO. I WILL NOT MISS HIM.

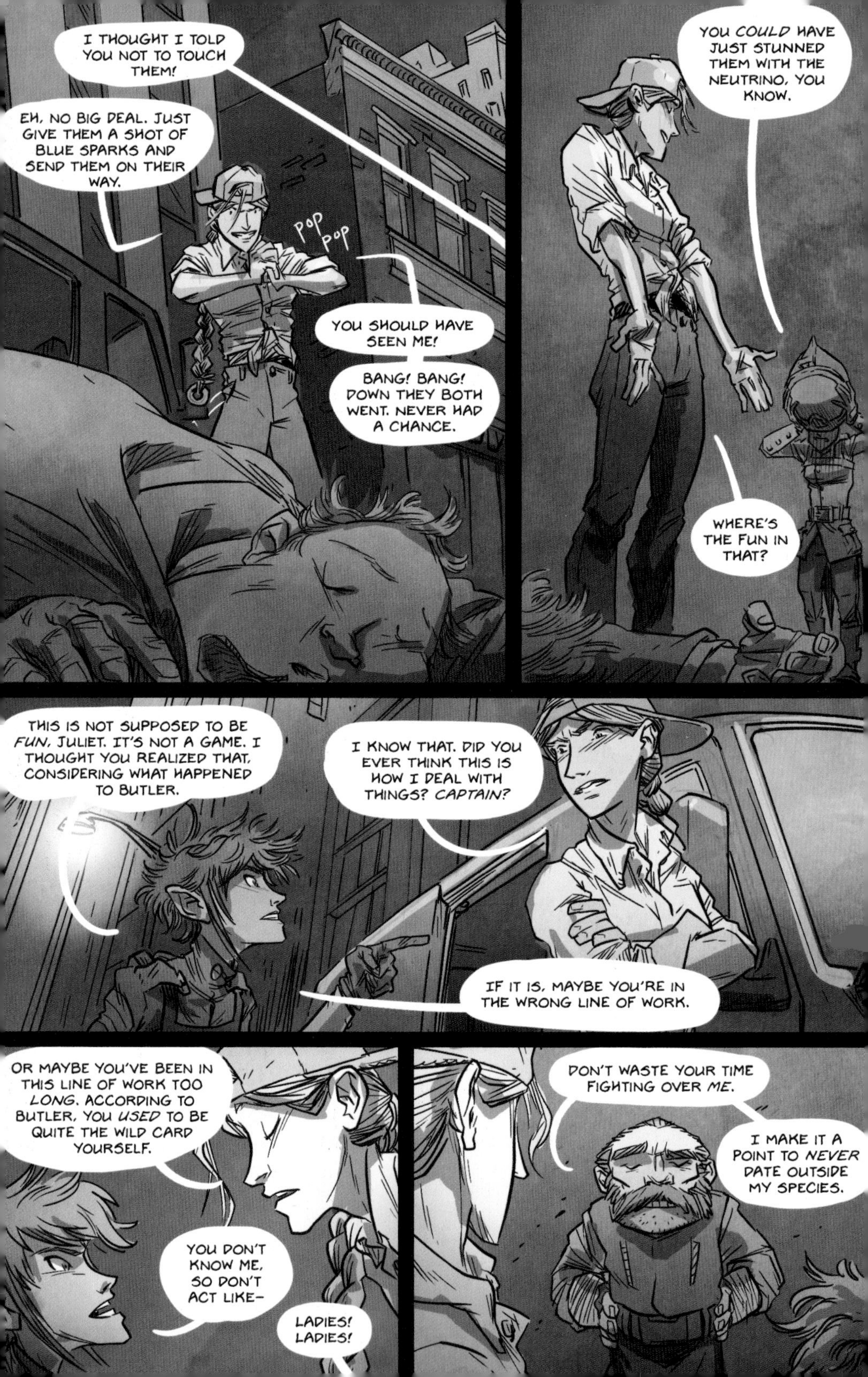
I THOUGHT I TOLD YOU NOT TO TOUCH THEM!
EH, NO BIG DEAL. JUST GIVE THEM A SHOT OF BLUE SPARKS AND SEND THEM ON THEIR WAY.
POP POP
YOU SHOULD HAVE SEEN ME!
BANG! BANG! DOWN THEY BOTH WENT. NEVER HAD A CHANCE.
YOU *COULD* HAVE JUST STUNNED THEM WITH THE NEUTRINO, YOU KNOW.
WHERE'S THE FUN IN THAT?
THIS IS NOT SUPPOSED TO BE *FUN*, JULIET. IT'S NOT A GAME. I THOUGHT YOU REALIZED THAT, CONSIDERING WHAT HAPPENED TO BUTLER.
I KNOW THAT. DID YOU EVER THINK THIS IS HOW I DEAL WITH THINGS? *CAPTAIN?*
IF IT IS, MAYBE YOU'RE IN THE WRONG LINE OF WORK.
OR MAYBE YOU'VE BEEN IN THIS LINE OF WORK TOO *LONG*. ACCORDING TO BUTLER, YOU *USED* TO BE QUITE THE WILD CARD YOURSELF.
YOU DON'T KNOW ME, SO DON'T ACT LIKE–
LADIES! LADIES!
DON'T WASTE YOUR TIME FIGHTING OVER *ME*.
I MAKE IT A POINT TO *NEVER* DATE OUTSIDE MY SPECIES.

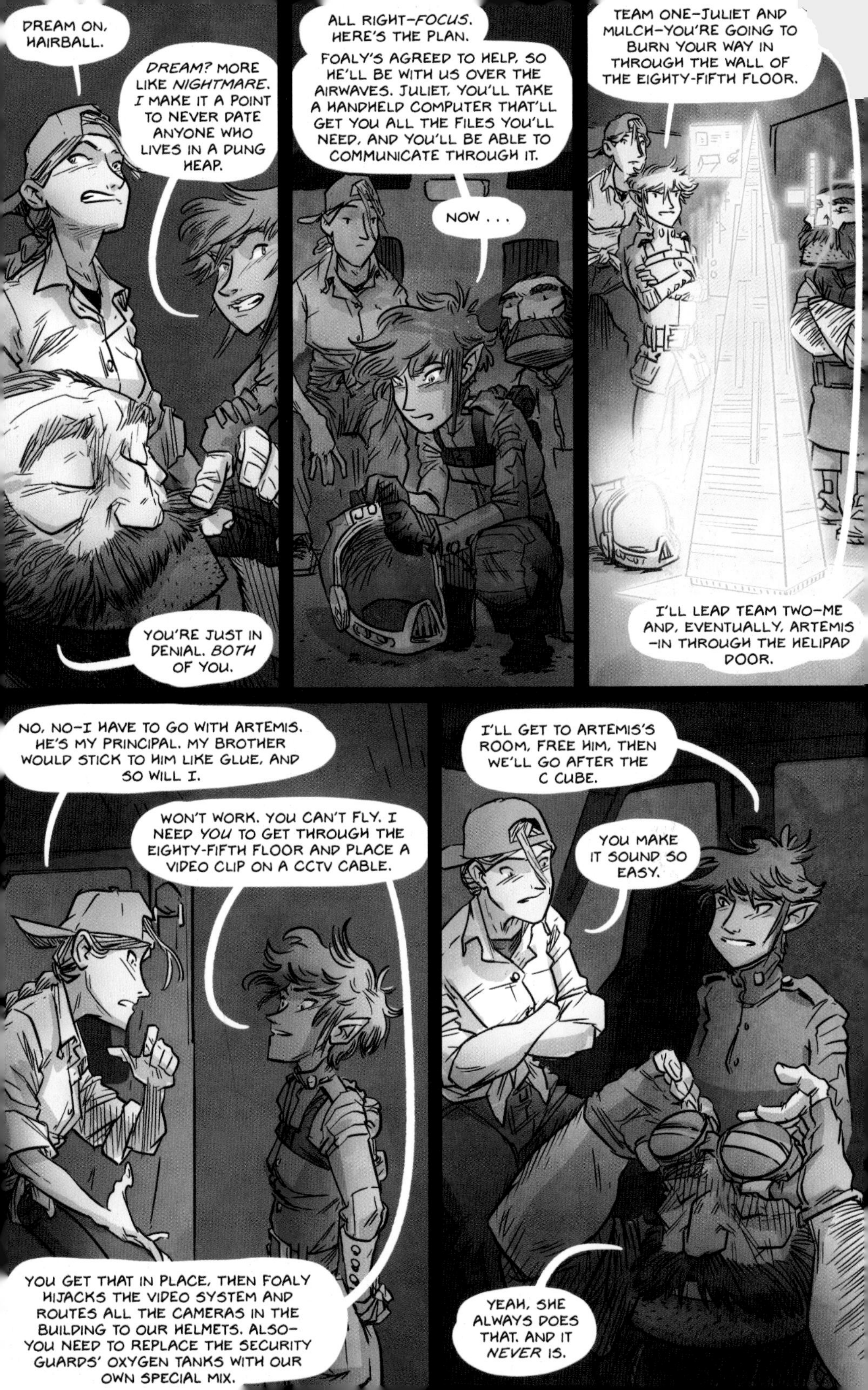

DREAM ON, HAIRBALL.
DREAM? MORE LIKE *NIGHTMARE*. I MAKE IT A POINT TO NEVER DATE ANYONE WHO LIVES IN A DUNG HEAP.
YOU'RE JUST IN DENIAL. *BOTH* OF YOU.
ALL RIGHT—*FOCUS*. HERE'S THE PLAN.
FOALY'S AGREED TO HELP, SO HE'LL BE WITH US OVER THE AIRWAVES. JULIET, YOU'LL TAKE A HANDHELD COMPUTER THAT'LL GET YOU ALL THE FILES YOU'LL NEED, AND YOU'LL BE ABLE TO COMMUNICATE THROUGH IT.
NOW . . .
TEAM ONE—JULIET AND MULCH—YOU'RE GOING TO BURN YOUR WAY IN THROUGH THE WALL OF THE EIGHTY-FIFTH FLOOR.
I'LL LEAD TEAM TWO—ME AND, EVENTUALLY, ARTEMIS—IN THROUGH THE HELIPAD DOOR.
NO, NO—I HAVE TO GO WITH ARTEMIS. HE'S MY PRINCIPAL. MY BROTHER WOULD STICK TO HIM LIKE GLUE, AND SO WILL I.
WON'T WORK. YOU CAN'T FLY. I NEED *YOU* TO GET THROUGH THE EIGHTY-FIFTH FLOOR AND PLACE A VIDEO CLIP ON A CCTV CABLE.
YOU GET THAT IN PLACE, THEN FOALY HIJACKS THE VIDEO SYSTEM AND ROUTES ALL THE CAMERAS IN THE BUILDING TO OUR HELMETS. ALSO—YOU NEED TO REPLACE THE SECURITY GUARDS' OXYGEN TANKS WITH OUR OWN SPECIAL MIX.
I'LL GET TO ARTEMIS'S ROOM, FREE HIM, THEN WE'LL GO AFTER THE C CUBE.
YOU MAKE IT SOUND SO EASY.
YEAH, SHE ALWAYS DOES THAT. AND IT *NEVER* IS.

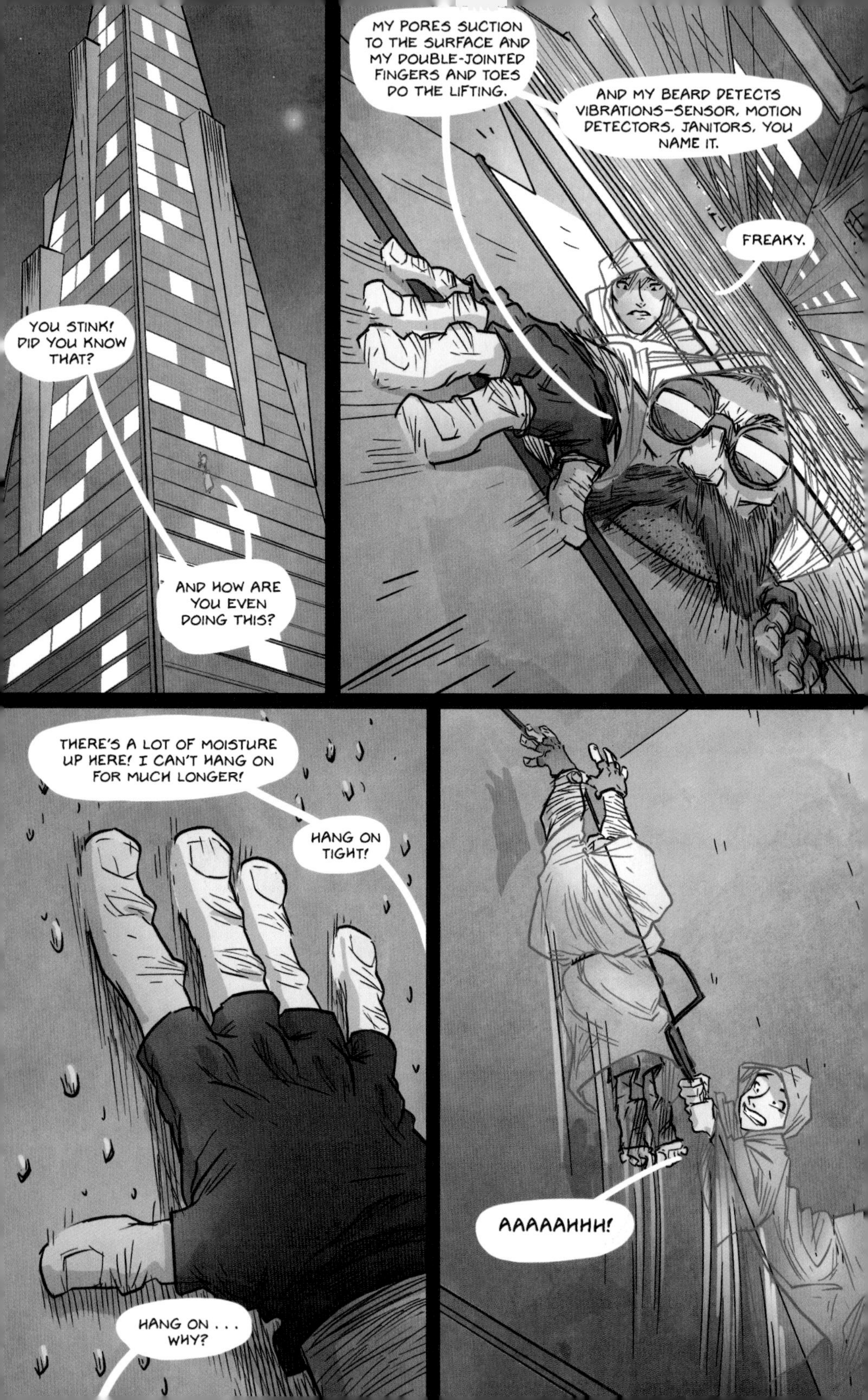
YOU STINK! DID YOU KNOW THAT?
AND HOW ARE YOU EVEN DOING THIS?
MY PORES SUCTION TO THE SURFACE AND MY DOUBLE-JOINTED FINGERS AND TOES DO THE LIFTING.
AND MY BEARD DETECTS VIBRATIONS—SENSOR, MOTION DETECTORS, JANITORS, YOU NAME IT.
FREAKY.
THERE'S A LOT OF MOISTURE UP HERE! I CAN'T HANG ON FOR MUCH LONGER!
HANG ON TIGHT!
HANG ON . . . WHY?
AAAAAHHH!

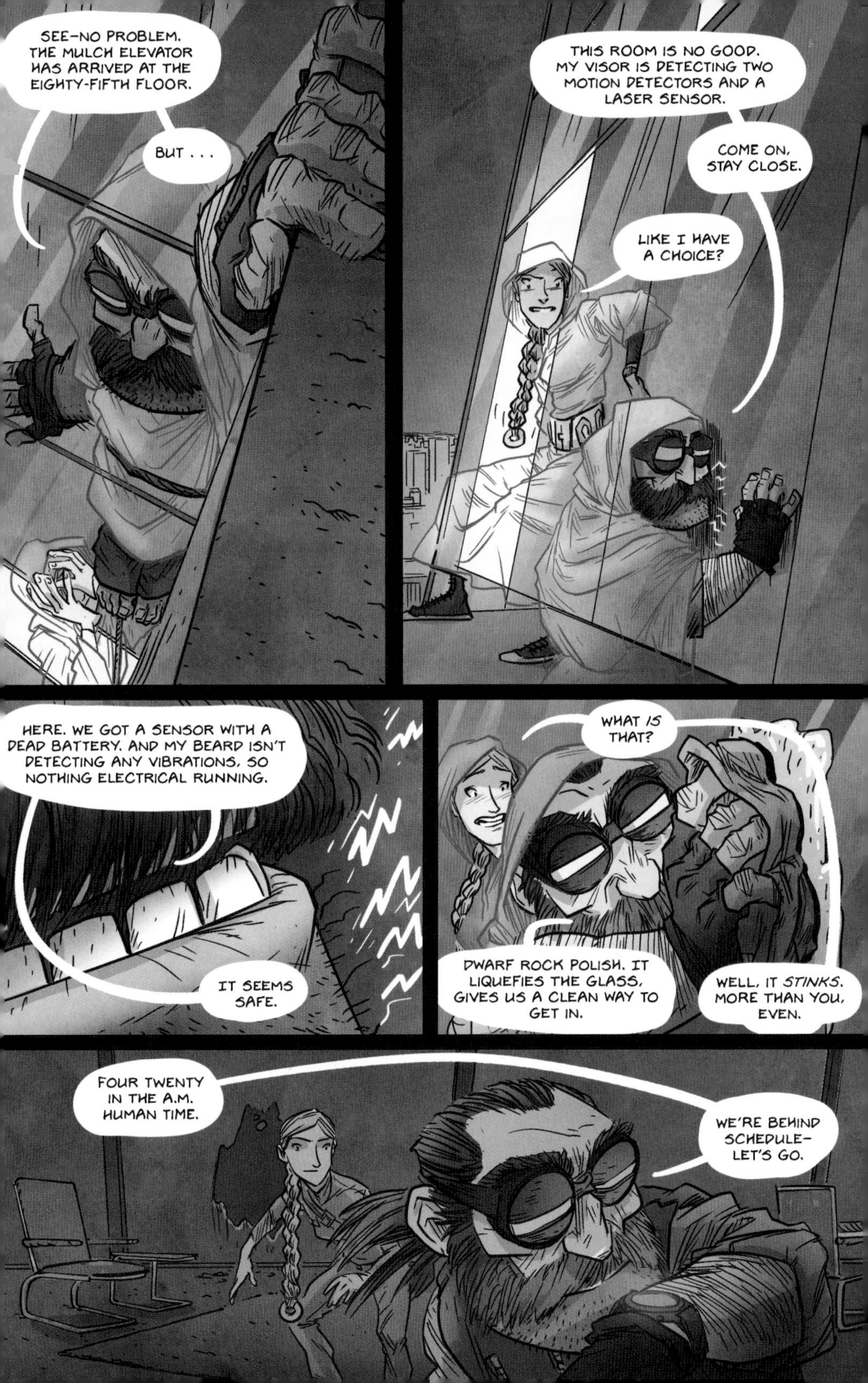
SEE—NO PROBLEM. THE MULCH ELEVATOR HAS ARRIVED AT THE EIGHTY-FIFTH FLOOR.
BUT . . .
THIS ROOM IS NO GOOD. MY VISOR IS DETECTING TWO MOTION DETECTORS AND A LASER SENSOR.
COME ON, STAY CLOSE.
LIKE I HAVE A CHOICE?
HERE. WE GOT A SENSOR WITH A DEAD BATTERY. AND MY BEARD ISN'T DETECTING ANY VIBRATIONS, SO NOTHING ELECTRICAL RUNNING.
IT SEEMS SAFE.
WHAT *IS* THAT?
DWARF ROCK POLISH. IT LIQUEFIES THE GLASS, GIVES US A CLEAN WAY TO GET IN.
WELL, IT *STINKS*. MORE THAN YOU, EVEN.
FOUR TWENTY IN THE A.M. HUMAN TIME.
WE'RE BEHIND SCHEDULE—LET'S GO.

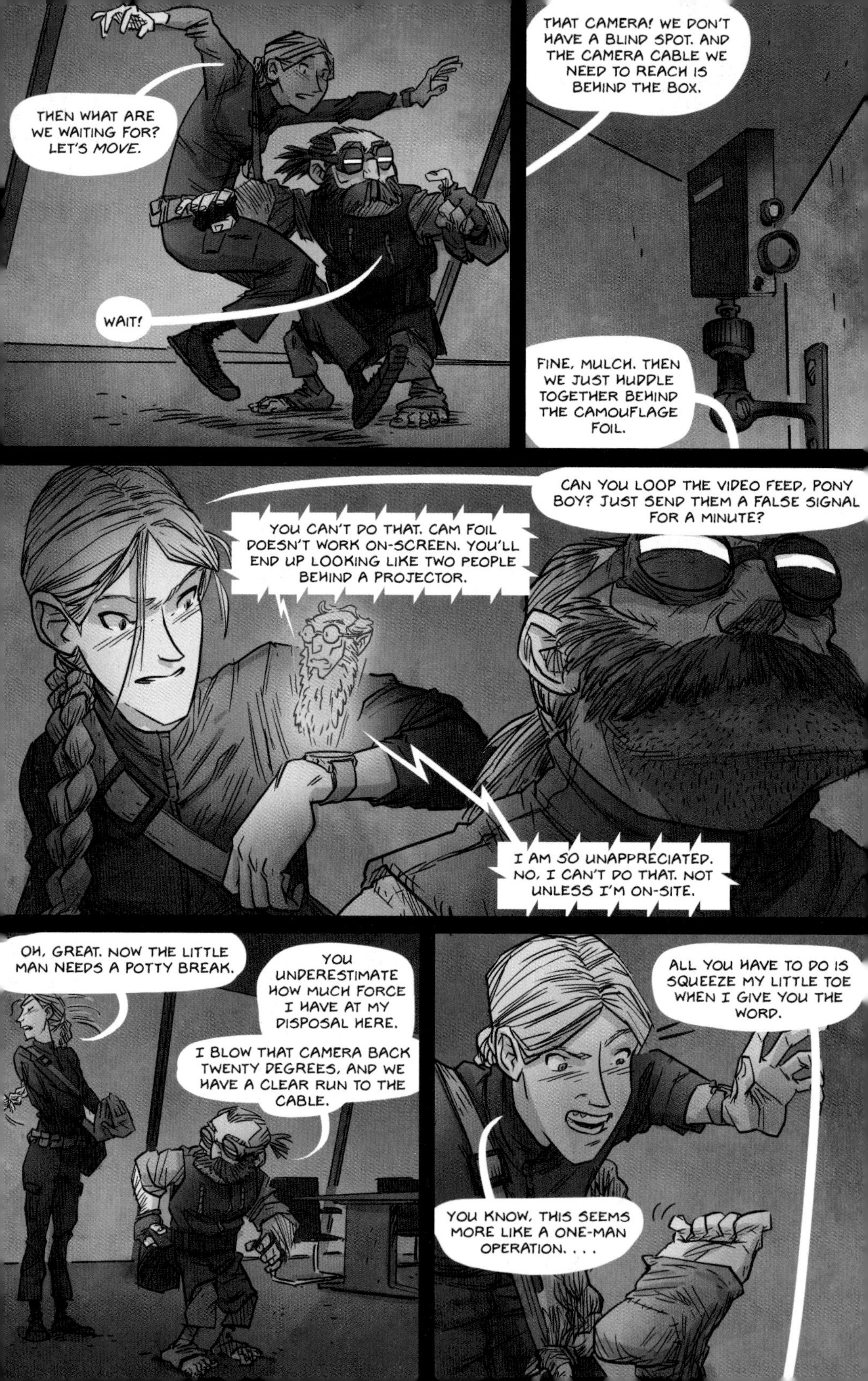
THEN WHAT ARE WE WAITING FOR? LET'S *MOVE*.
WAIT!
THAT CAMERA! WE DON'T HAVE A BLIND SPOT. AND THE CAMERA CABLE WE NEED TO REACH IS BEHIND THE BOX.
FINE, MULCH. THEN WE JUST HUDDLE TOGETHER BEHIND THE CAMOUFLAGE FOIL.
CAN YOU LOOP THE VIDEO FEED, PONY BOY? JUST SEND THEM A FALSE SIGNAL FOR A MINUTE?
YOU CAN'T DO THAT. CAM FOIL DOESN'T WORK ON-SCREEN. YOU'LL END UP LOOKING LIKE TWO PEOPLE BEHIND A PROJECTOR.
I AM SO UNAPPRECIATED. NO, I CAN'T DO THAT. NOT UNLESS I'M ON-SITE.
OH, GREAT. NOW THE LITTLE MAN NEEDS A POTTY BREAK.
YOU UNDERESTIMATE HOW MUCH FORCE I HAVE AT MY DISPOSAL HERE.
I BLOW THAT CAMERA BACK TWENTY DEGREES, AND WE HAVE A CLEAR RUN TO THE CABLE.
ALL YOU HAVE TO DO IS SQUEEZE MY LITTLE TOE WHEN I GIVE YOU THE WORD.
YOU KNOW, THIS SEEMS MORE LIKE A ONE-MAN OPERATION. . . .

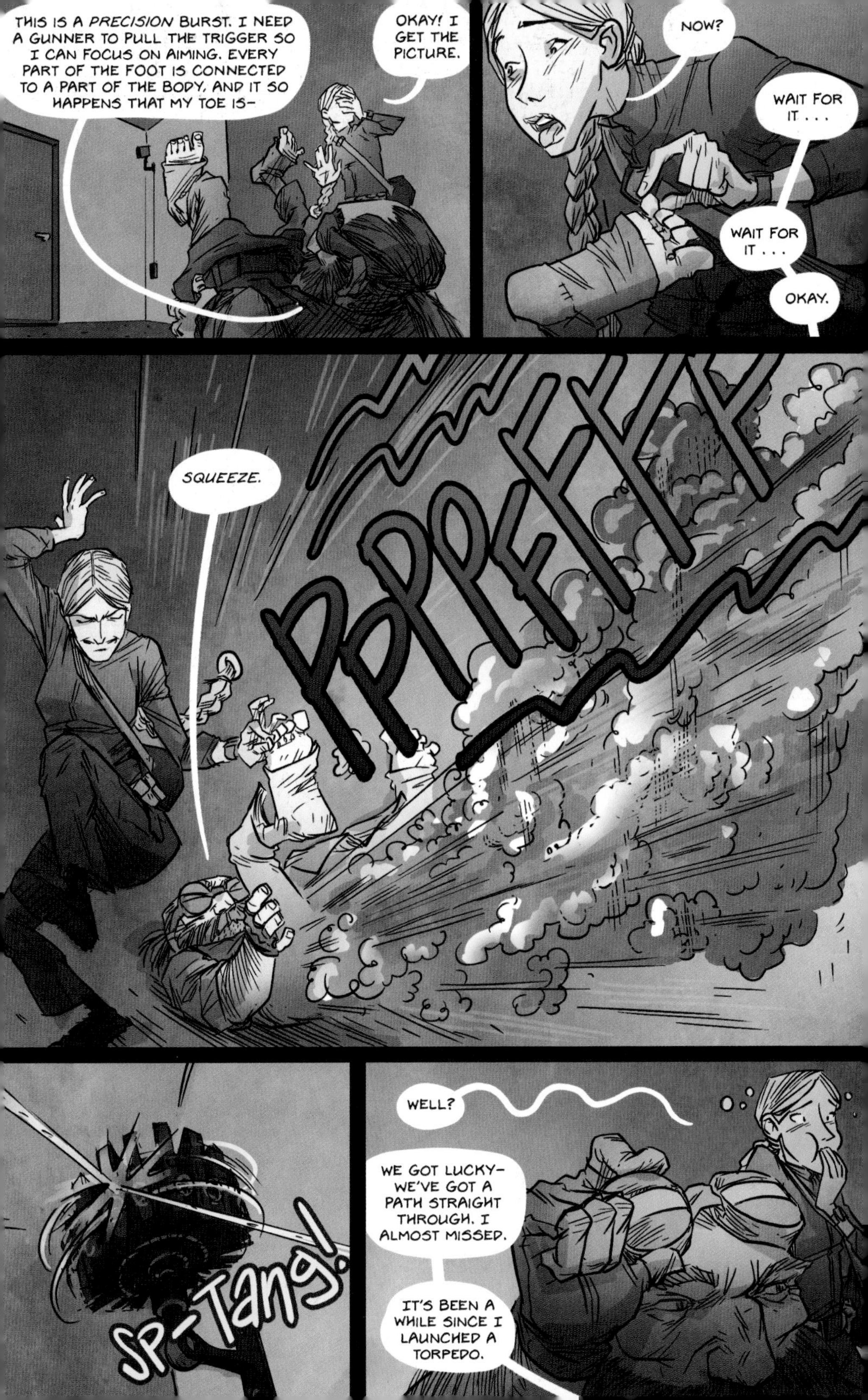
THIS IS A *PRECISION* BURST. I NEED A GUNNER TO PULL THE TRIGGER SO I CAN FOCUS ON AIMING. EVERY PART OF THE FOOT IS CONNECTED TO A PART OF THE BODY, AND IT SO HAPPENS THAT MY TOE IS—
OKAY! I GET THE PICTURE.
NOW?
WAIT FOR IT . . .
WAIT FOR IT . . .
OKAY.
SQUEEZE.
PPPFFFFF
SP-Tang!
WELL?
WE GOT LUCKY—WE'VE GOT A PATH STRAIGHT THROUGH. I ALMOST MISSED.
IT'S BEEN A WHILE SINCE I LAUNCHED A TORPEDO.

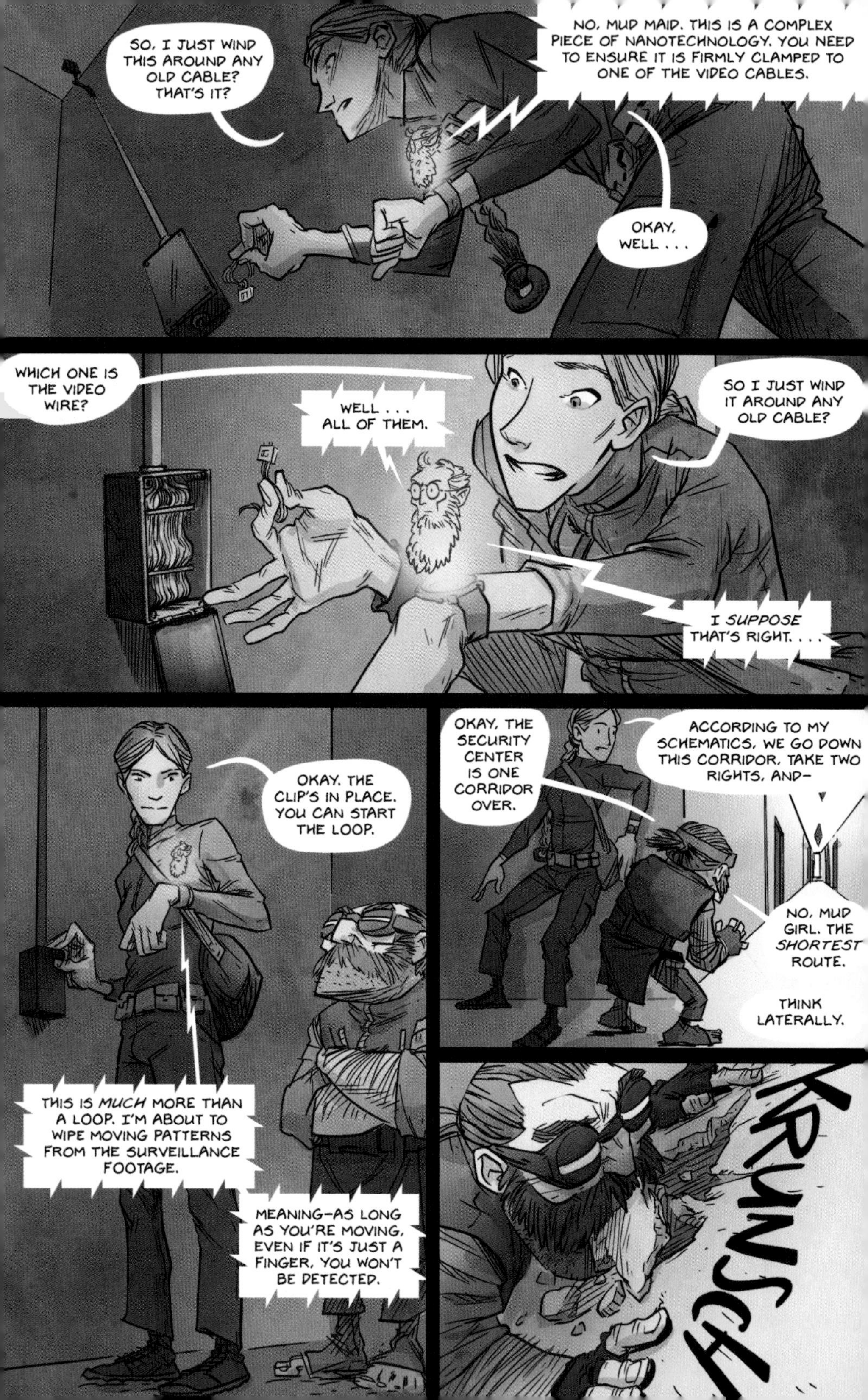
SO, I JUST WIND THIS AROUND ANY OLD CABLE? THAT'S IT?
NO, MUD MAID. THIS IS A COMPLEX PIECE OF NANOTECHNOLOGY. YOU NEED TO ENSURE IT IS FIRMLY CLAMPED TO ONE OF THE VIDEO CABLES.
OKAY, WELL . . .
WHICH ONE IS THE VIDEO WIRE?
WELL . . . ALL OF THEM.
SO I JUST WIND IT AROUND ANY OLD CABLE?
I *SUPPOSE* THAT'S RIGHT. . . .
OKAY. THE CLIP'S IN PLACE. YOU CAN START THE LOOP.
THIS IS *MUCH* MORE THAN A LOOP. I'M ABOUT TO WIPE MOVING PATTERNS FROM THE SURVEILLANCE FOOTAGE.
MEANING—AS LONG AS YOU'RE MOVING, EVEN IF IT'S JUST A FINGER, YOU WON'T BE DETECTED.
OKAY, THE SECURITY CENTER IS ONE CORRIDOR OVER.
ACCORDING TO MY SCHEMATICS, WE GO DOWN THIS CORRIDOR, TAKE TWO RIGHTS, AND—
NO, MUD GIRL. THE *SHORTEST* ROUTE.
THINK LATERALLY.
KRUNSCH

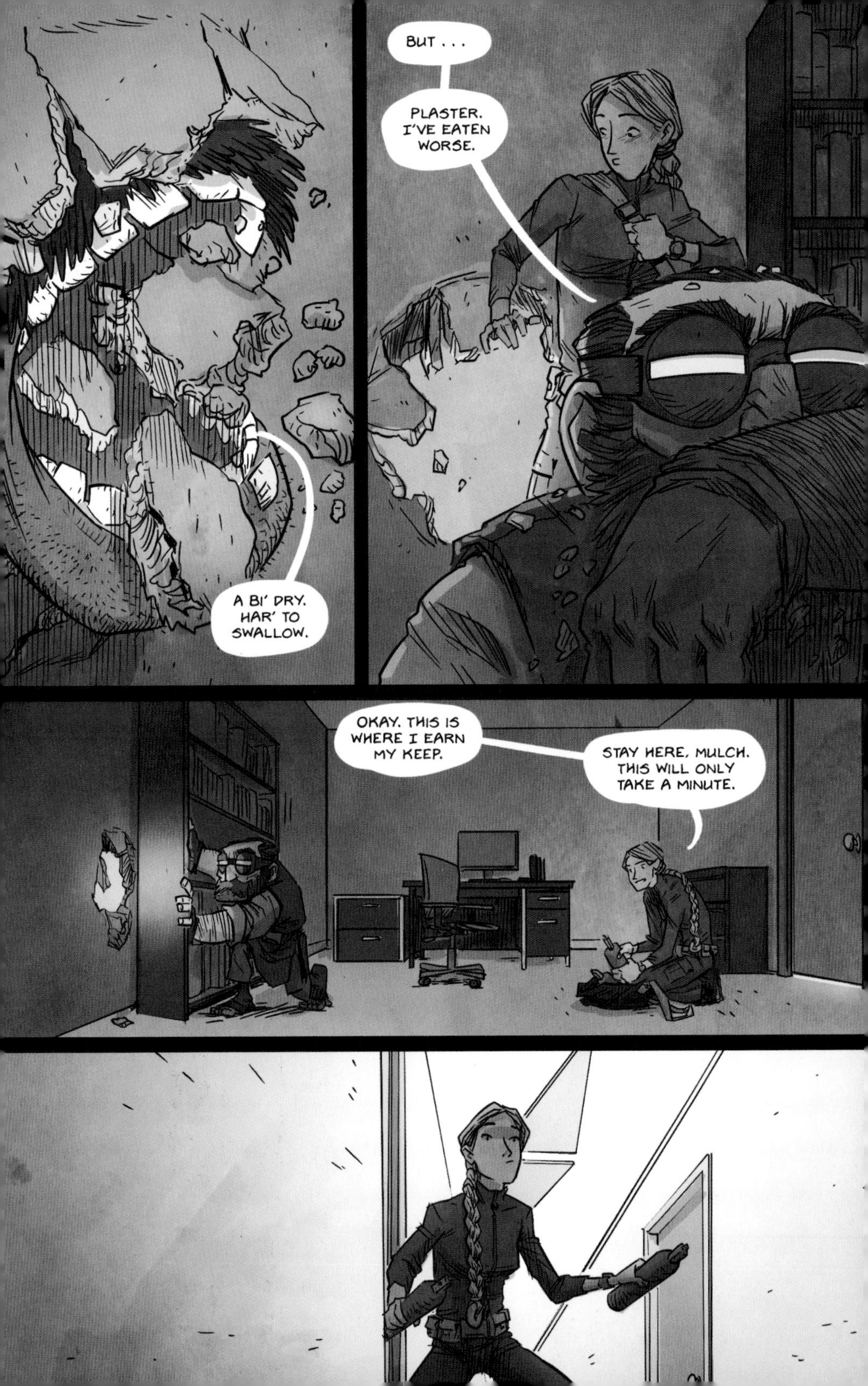
A BI' DRY. HAR' TO SWALLOW.
BUT . . .
PLASTER. I'VE EATEN WORSE.
OKAY. THIS IS WHERE I EARN MY KEEP.
STAY HERE, MULCH. THIS WILL ONLY TAKE A MINUTE.

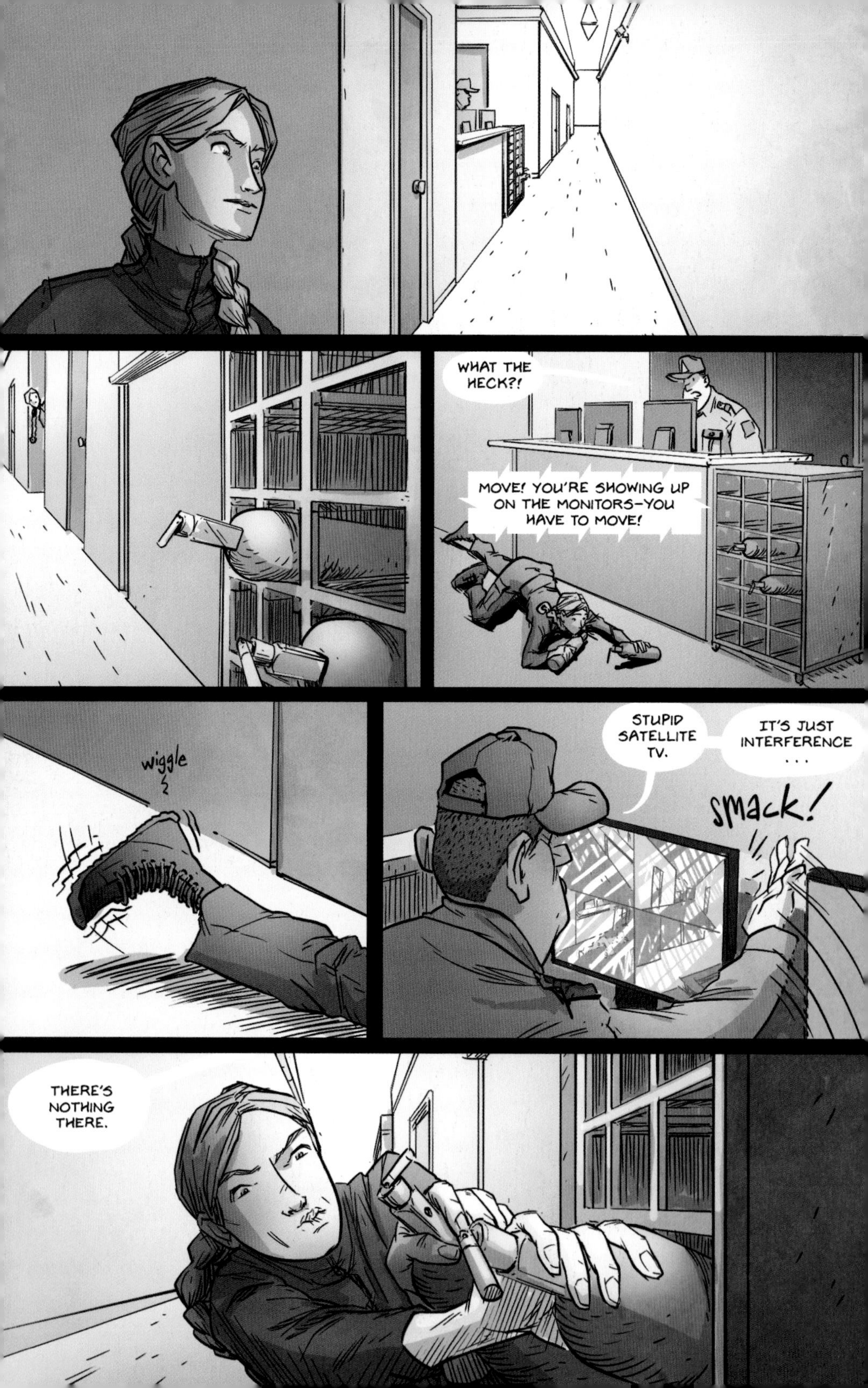
WHAT THE HECK?!
MOVE! YOU'RE SHOWING UP ON THE MONITORS—YOU HAVE TO MOVE!
wiggle
STUPID SATELLITE TV.
IT'S JUST INTERFERENCE . . .
SMACK!
THERE'S NOTHING THERE.

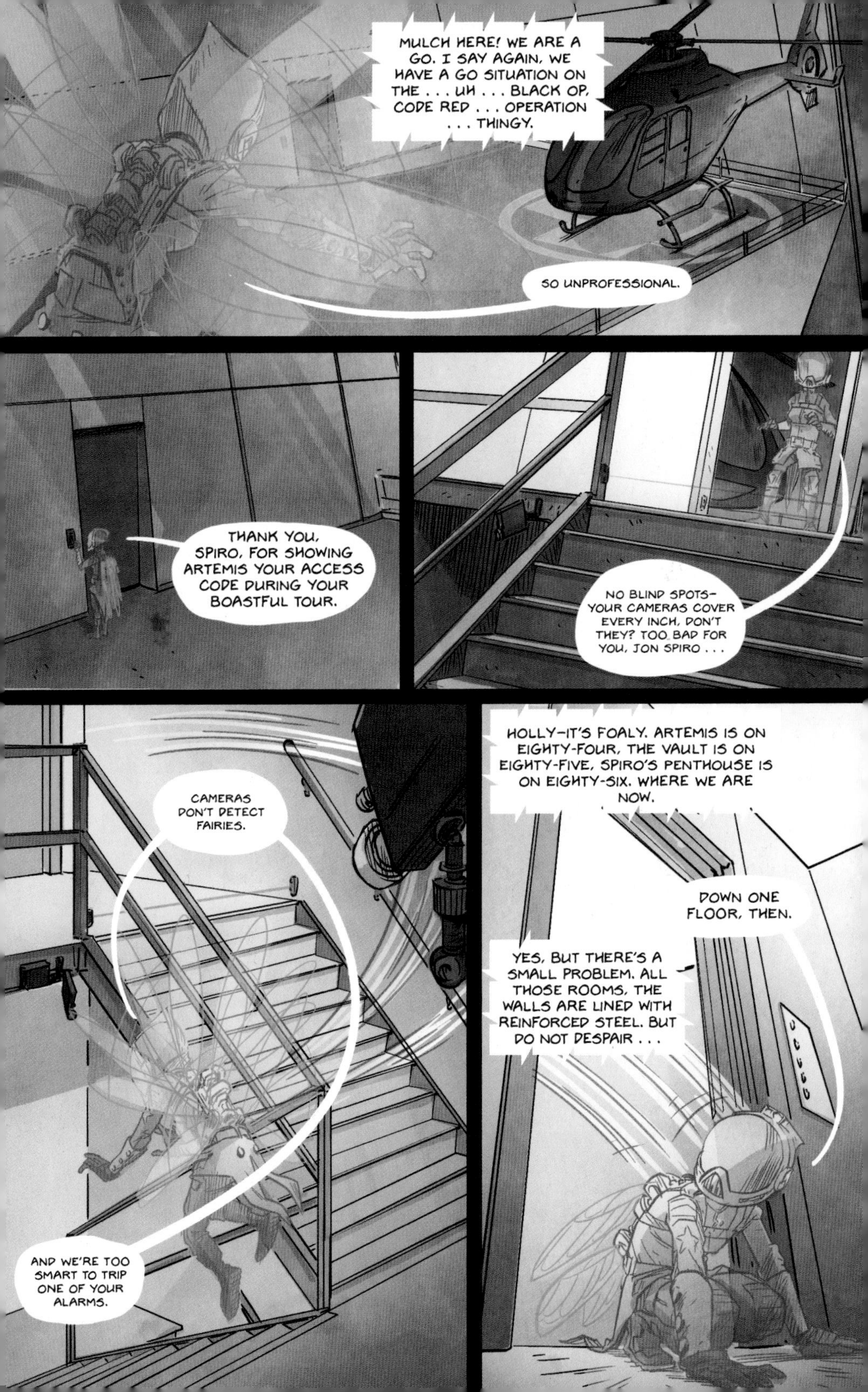
MULCH HERE! WE ARE A GO. I SAY AGAIN, WE HAVE A GO SITUATION ON THE . . . UH . . . BLACK OP, CODE RED . . . OPERATION . . . THINGY.
SO UNPROFESSIONAL.
THANK YOU, SPIRO, FOR SHOWING ARTEMIS YOUR ACCESS CODE DURING YOUR BOASTFUL TOUR.
NO BLIND SPOTS—YOUR CAMERAS COVER EVERY INCH, DON'T THEY? TOO BAD FOR YOU, JON SPIRO . . .
CAMERAS DON'T DETECT FAIRIES.
AND WE'RE TOO SMART TO TRIP ONE OF YOUR ALARMS.
HOLLY—IT'S FOALY. ARTEMIS IS ON EIGHTY-FOUR, THE VAULT IS ON EIGHTY-FIVE, SPIRO'S PENTHOUSE IS ON EIGHTY-SIX. WHERE WE ARE NOW.
DOWN ONE FLOOR, THEN.
YES, BUT THERE'S A SMALL PROBLEM. ALL THOSE ROOMS, THE WALLS ARE LINED WITH REINFORCED STEEL. BUT DO NOT DESPAIR . . .

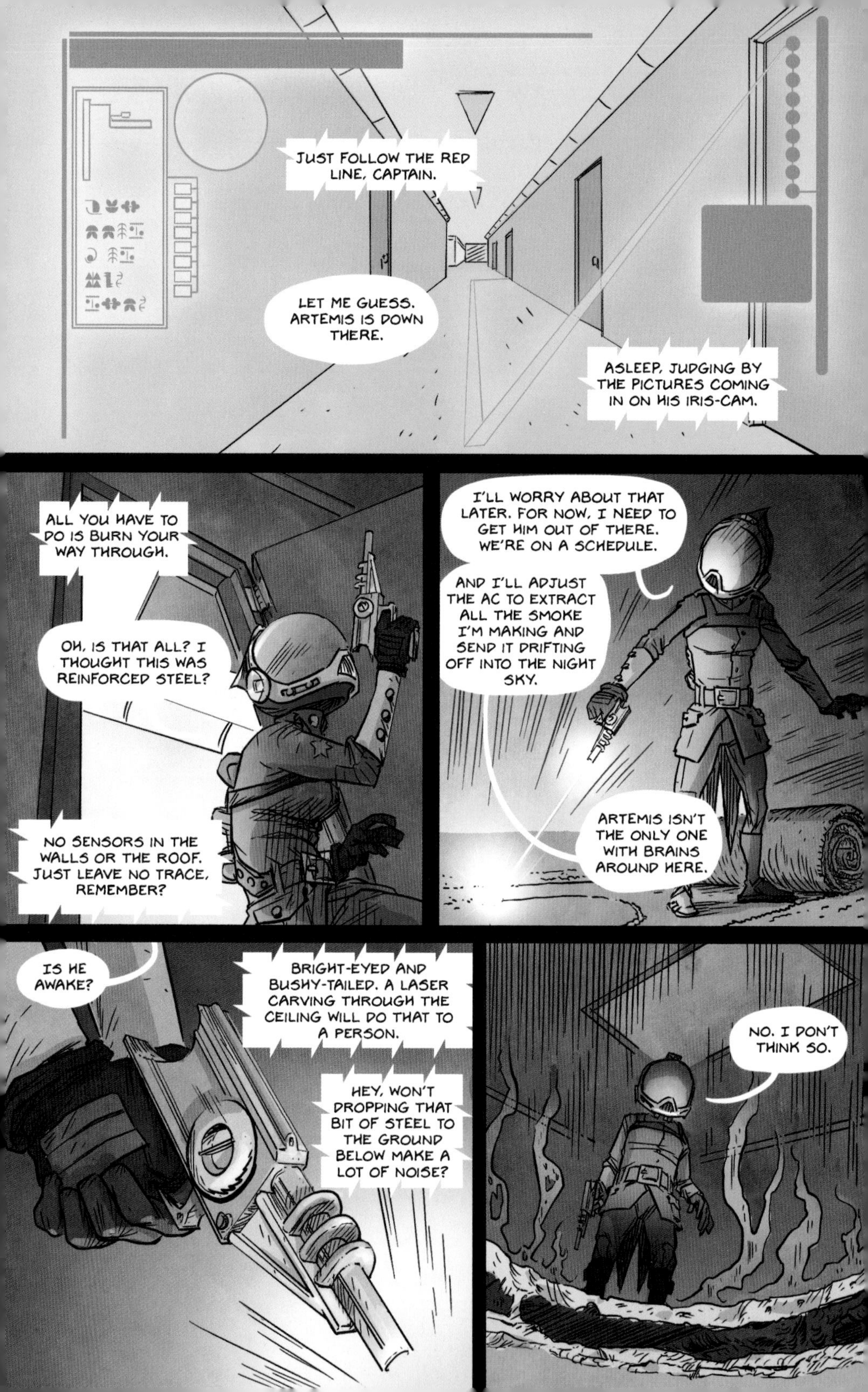
JUST FOLLOW THE RED LINE, CAPTAIN.
LET ME GUESS. ARTEMIS IS DOWN THERE.
ASLEEP, JUDGING BY THE PICTURES COMING IN ON HIS IRIS-CAM.
ALL YOU HAVE TO DO IS BURN YOUR WAY THROUGH.
OH, IS THAT ALL? I THOUGHT THIS WAS REINFORCED STEEL?
NO SENSORS IN THE WALLS OR THE ROOF. JUST LEAVE NO TRACE, REMEMBER?
I'LL WORRY ABOUT THAT LATER. FOR NOW, I NEED TO GET HIM OUT OF THERE. WE'RE ON A SCHEDULE.
AND I'LL ADJUST THE AC TO EXTRACT ALL THE SMOKE I'M MAKING AND SEND IT DRIFTING OFF INTO THE NIGHT SKY.
ARTEMIS ISN'T THE ONLY ONE WITH BRAINS AROUND HERE.
IS HE AWAKE?
BRIGHT-EYED AND BUSHY-TAILED. A LASER CARVING THROUGH THE CEILING WILL DO THAT TO A PERSON.
HEY, WON'T DROPPING THAT BIT OF STEEL TO THE GROUND BELOW MAKE A LOT OF NOISE?
NO. I DON'T THINK SO.

CHAPTER TEN

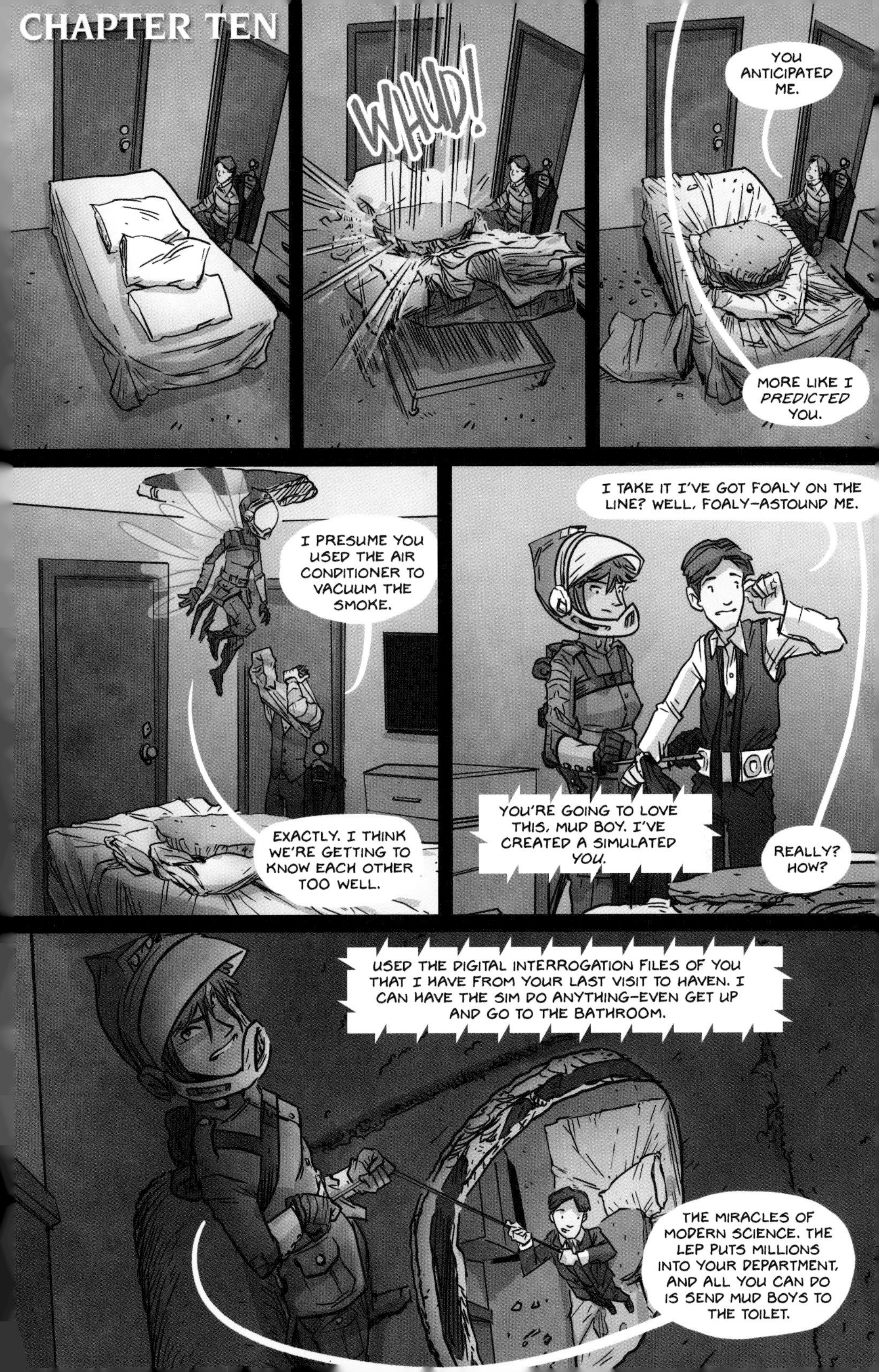
WHUD!
YOU ANTICIPATED ME.
MORE LIKE I *PREDICTED* YOU.
I PRESUME YOU USED THE AIR CONDITIONER TO VACUUM THE SMOKE.
EXACTLY. I THINK WE'RE GETTING TO KNOW EACH OTHER TOO WELL.
I TAKE IT I'VE GOT FOALY ON THE LINE? WELL, FOALY—ASTOUND ME.
YOU'RE GOING TO LOVE THIS, MUD BOY. I'VE CREATED A SIMULATED *YOU*.
REALLY? HOW?
USED THE DIGITAL INTERROGATION FILES OF YOU THAT I HAVE FROM YOUR LAST VISIT TO HAVEN. I CAN HAVE THE SIM DO ANYTHING—EVEN GET UP AND GO TO THE BATHROOM.
THE MIRACLES OF MODERN SCIENCE. THE LEP PUTS MILLIONS INTO YOUR DEPARTMENT, AND ALL YOU CAN DO IS SEND MUD BOYS TO THE TOILET.

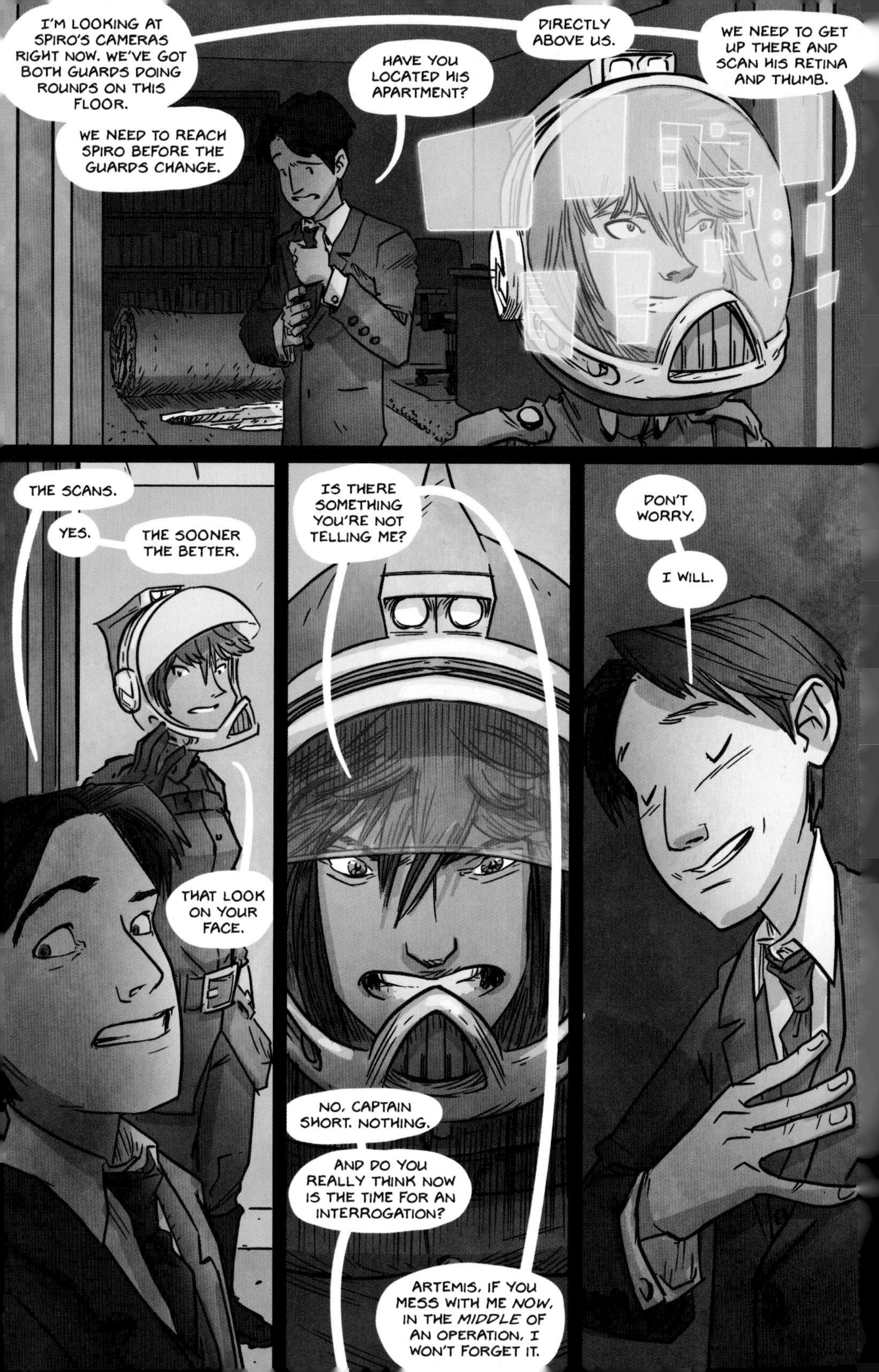
I'M LOOKING AT SPIRO'S CAMERAS RIGHT NOW. WE'VE GOT BOTH GUARDS DOING ROUNDS ON THIS FLOOR.
WE NEED TO REACH SPIRO BEFORE THE GUARDS CHANGE.
HAVE YOU LOCATED HIS APARTMENT?
DIRECTLY ABOVE US.
WE NEED TO GET UP THERE AND SCAN HIS RETINA AND THUMB.
THE SCANS.
YES.
THE SOONER THE BETTER.
THAT LOOK ON YOUR FACE.
IS THERE SOMETHING YOU'RE NOT TELLING ME?
NO, CAPTAIN SHORT. NOTHING.
AND DO YOU REALLY THINK NOW IS THE TIME FOR AN INTERROGATION?
ARTEMIS, IF YOU MESS WITH ME *NOW*, IN THE *MIDDLE* OF AN OPERATION, I WON'T FORGET IT.
DON'T WORRY.
I WILL.

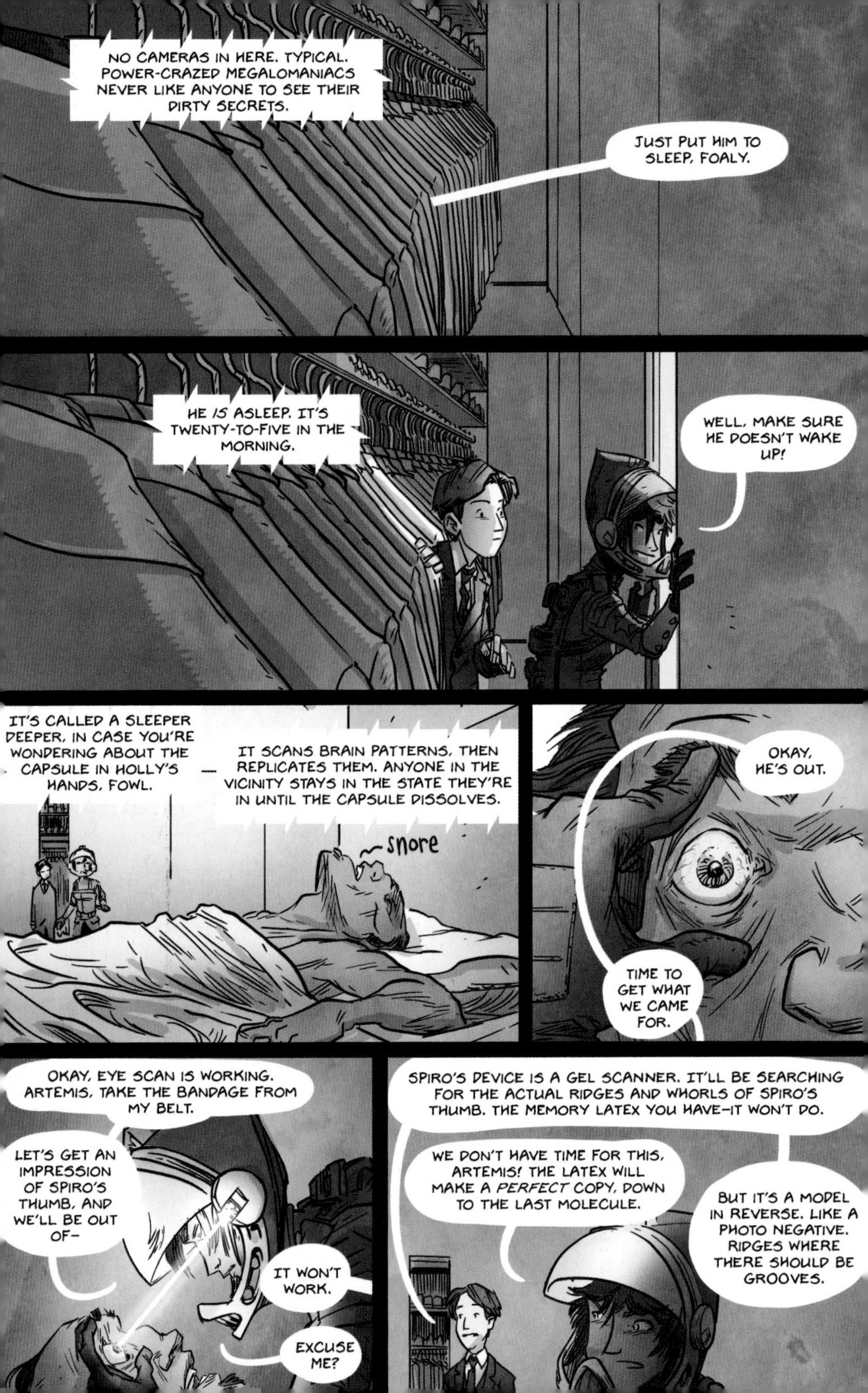
NO CAMERAS IN HERE. TYPICAL. POWER-CRAZED MEGALOMANIACS NEVER LIKE ANYONE TO SEE THEIR DIRTY SECRETS.
JUST PUT HIM TO SLEEP, FOALY.
HE *IS* ASLEEP. IT'S TWENTY-TO-FIVE IN THE MORNING.
WELL, MAKE SURE HE DOESN'T WAKE UP!
IT'S CALLED A SLEEPER DEEPER, IN CASE YOU'RE WONDERING ABOUT THE CAPSULE IN HOLLY'S HANDS, FOWL.
IT SCANS BRAIN PATTERNS, THEN REPLICATES THEM. ANYONE IN THE VICINITY STAYS IN THE STATE THEY'RE IN UNTIL THE CAPSULE DISSOLVES.
~SNORE
OKAY, HE'S OUT.
TIME TO GET WHAT WE CAME FOR.
OKAY, EYE SCAN IS WORKING. ARTEMIS, TAKE THE BANDAGE FROM MY BELT.
LET'S GET AN IMPRESSION OF SPIRO'S THUMB, AND WE'LL BE OUT OF–
IT WON'T WORK.
EXCUSE ME?
SPIRO'S DEVICE IS A GEL SCANNER. IT'LL BE SEARCHING FOR THE ACTUAL RIDGES AND WHORLS OF SPIRO'S THUMB. THE MEMORY LATEX YOU HAVE–IT WON'T DO.
WE DON'T HAVE TIME FOR THIS, ARTEMIS! THE LATEX WILL MAKE A *PERFECT* COPY, DOWN TO THE LAST MOLECULE.
BUT IT'S A MODEL IN REVERSE. LIKE A PHOTO NEGATIVE. RIDGES WHERE THERE SHOULD BE GROOVES.

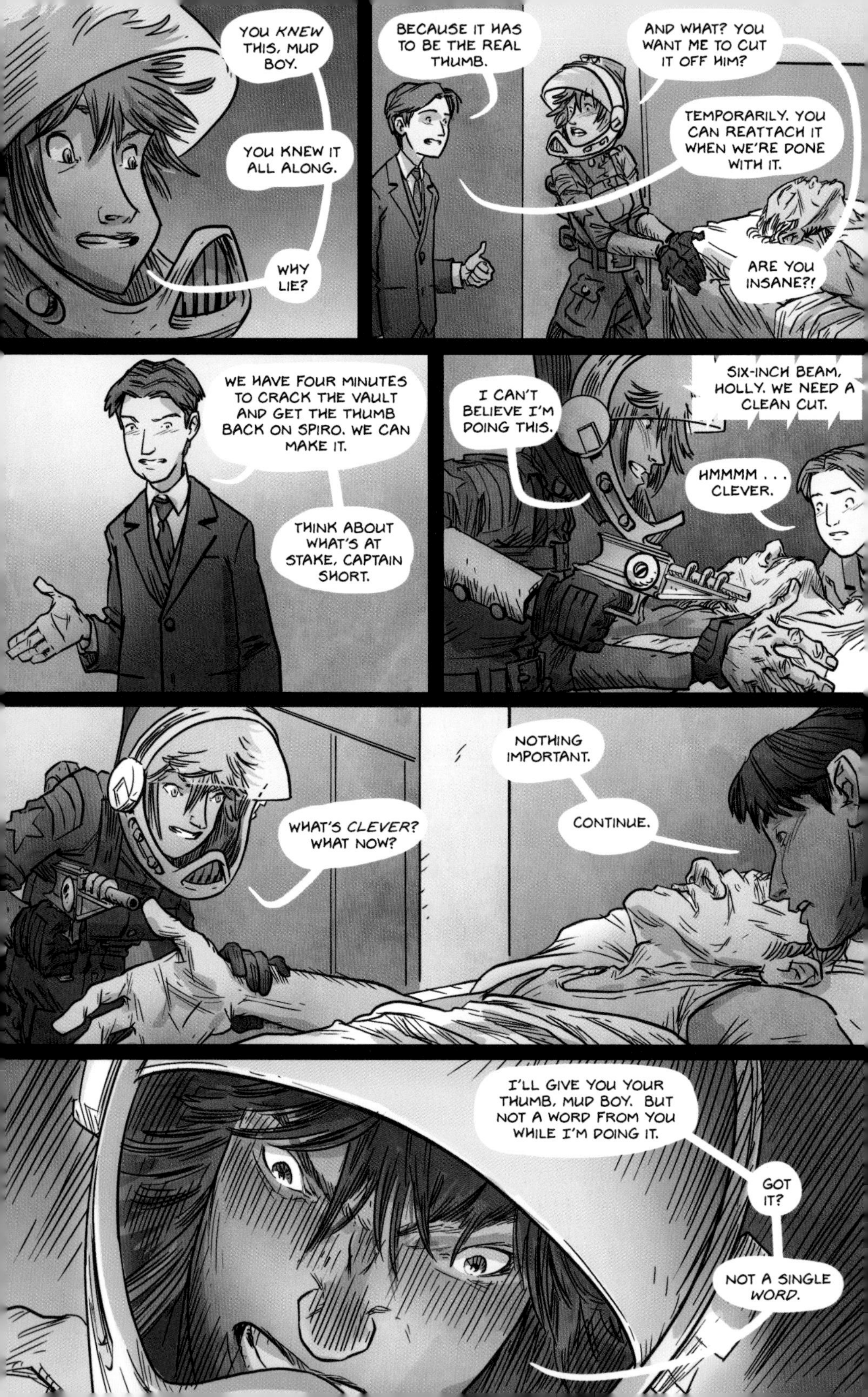
YOU KNEW THIS, MUD BOY.
YOU KNEW IT ALL ALONG.
WHY LIE?
BECAUSE IT HAS TO BE THE REAL THUMB.
AND WHAT? YOU WANT ME TO CUT IT OFF HIM?
TEMPORARILY. YOU CAN REATTACH IT WHEN WE'RE DONE WITH IT.
ARE YOU INSANE?!
WE HAVE FOUR MINUTES TO CRACK THE VAULT AND GET THE THUMB BACK ON SPIRO. WE CAN MAKE IT.
THINK ABOUT WHAT'S AT STAKE, CAPTAIN SHORT.
I CAN'T BELIEVE I'M DOING THIS.
SIX-INCH BEAM, HOLLY. WE NEED A CLEAN CUT.
HMMMM . . . CLEVER.
WHAT'S CLEVER? WHAT NOW?
NOTHING IMPORTANT.
CONTINUE.
I'LL GIVE YOU YOUR THUMB, MUD BOY. BUT NOT A WORD FROM YOU WHILE I'M DOING IT.
GOT IT?
NOT A SINGLE WORD.

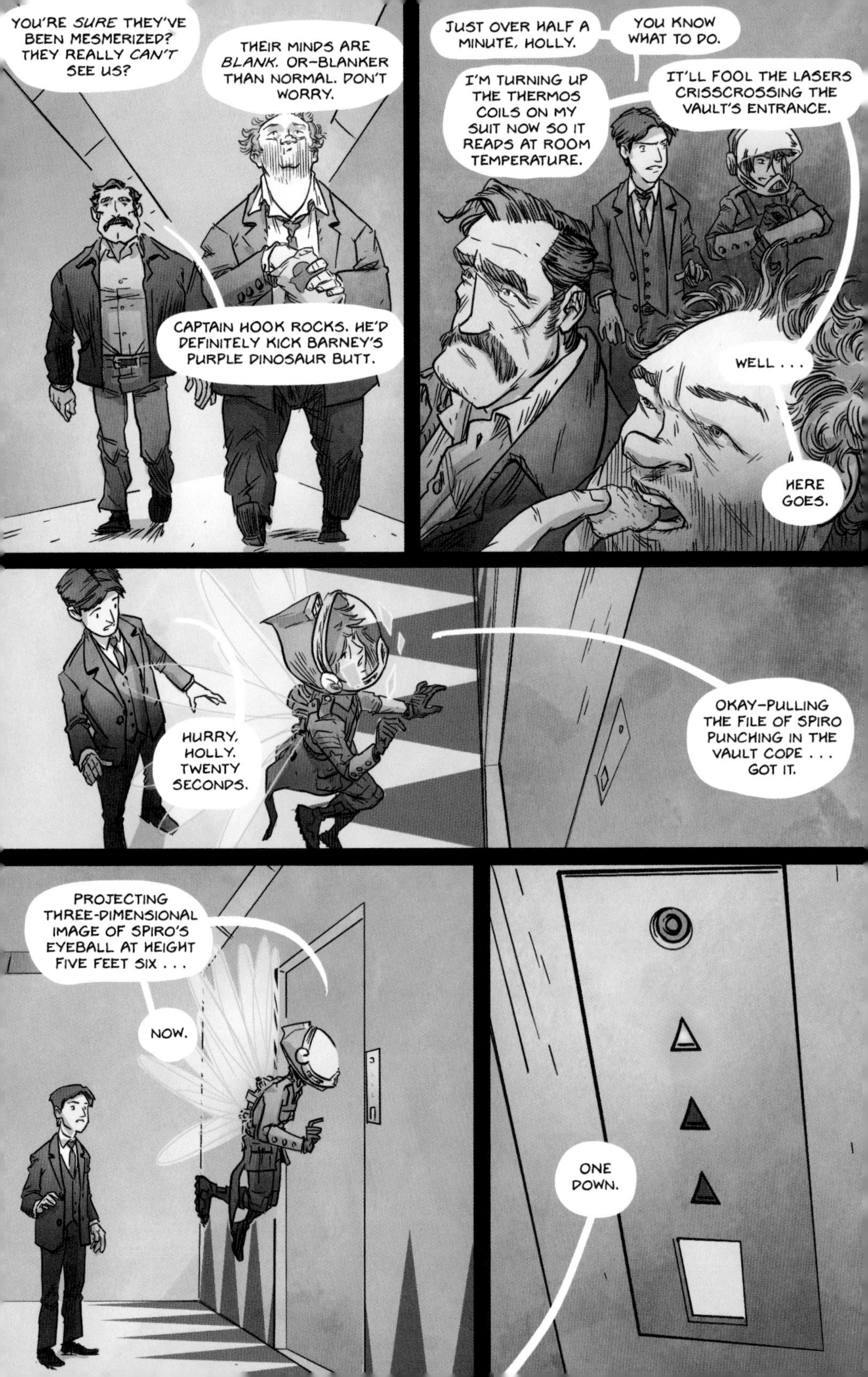
YOU'RE *SURE* THEY'VE BEEN MESMERIZED? THEY REALLY *CAN'T* SEE US?
THEIR MINDS ARE *BLANK.* OR—BLANKER THAN NORMAL. DON'T WORRY.
CAPTAIN HOOK ROCKS. HE'D DEFINITELY KICK BARNEY'S PURPLE DINOSAUR BUTT.
JUST OVER HALF A MINUTE, HOLLY.
YOU KNOW WHAT TO DO.
I'M TURNING UP THE THERMOS COILS ON MY SUIT NOW SO IT READS AT ROOM TEMPERATURE.
IT'LL FOOL THE LASERS CRISSCROSSING THE VAULT'S ENTRANCE.
WELL . . .
HERE GOES.
OKAY—PULLING THE FILE OF SPIRO PUNCHING IN THE VAULT CODE . . . GOT IT.
HURRY, HOLLY. TWENTY SECONDS.
PROJECTING THREE-DIMENSIONAL IMAGE OF SPIRO'S EYEBALL AT HEIGHT FIVE FEET SIX . . .
NOW.
ONE DOWN.

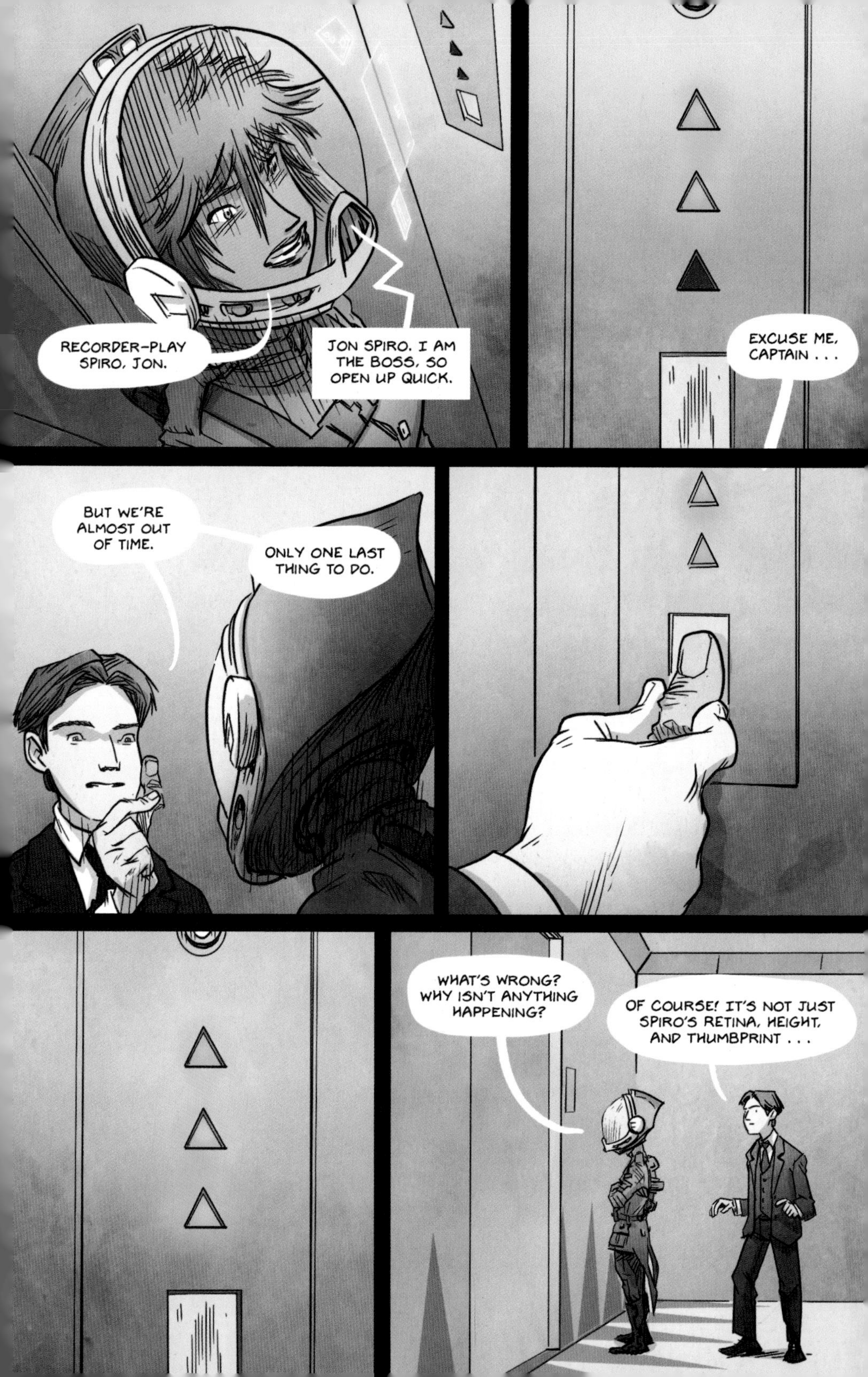
RECORDER-PLAY SPIRO, JON.
JON SPIRO. I AM THE BOSS, SO OPEN UP QUICK.
EXCUSE ME, CAPTAIN . . .
BUT WE'RE ALMOST OUT OF TIME.
ONLY ONE LAST THING TO DO.
WHAT'S WRONG? WHY ISN'T ANYTHING HAPPENING?
OF COURSE! IT'S NOT JUST SPIRO'S RETINA, HEIGHT, AND THUMBPRINT . . .

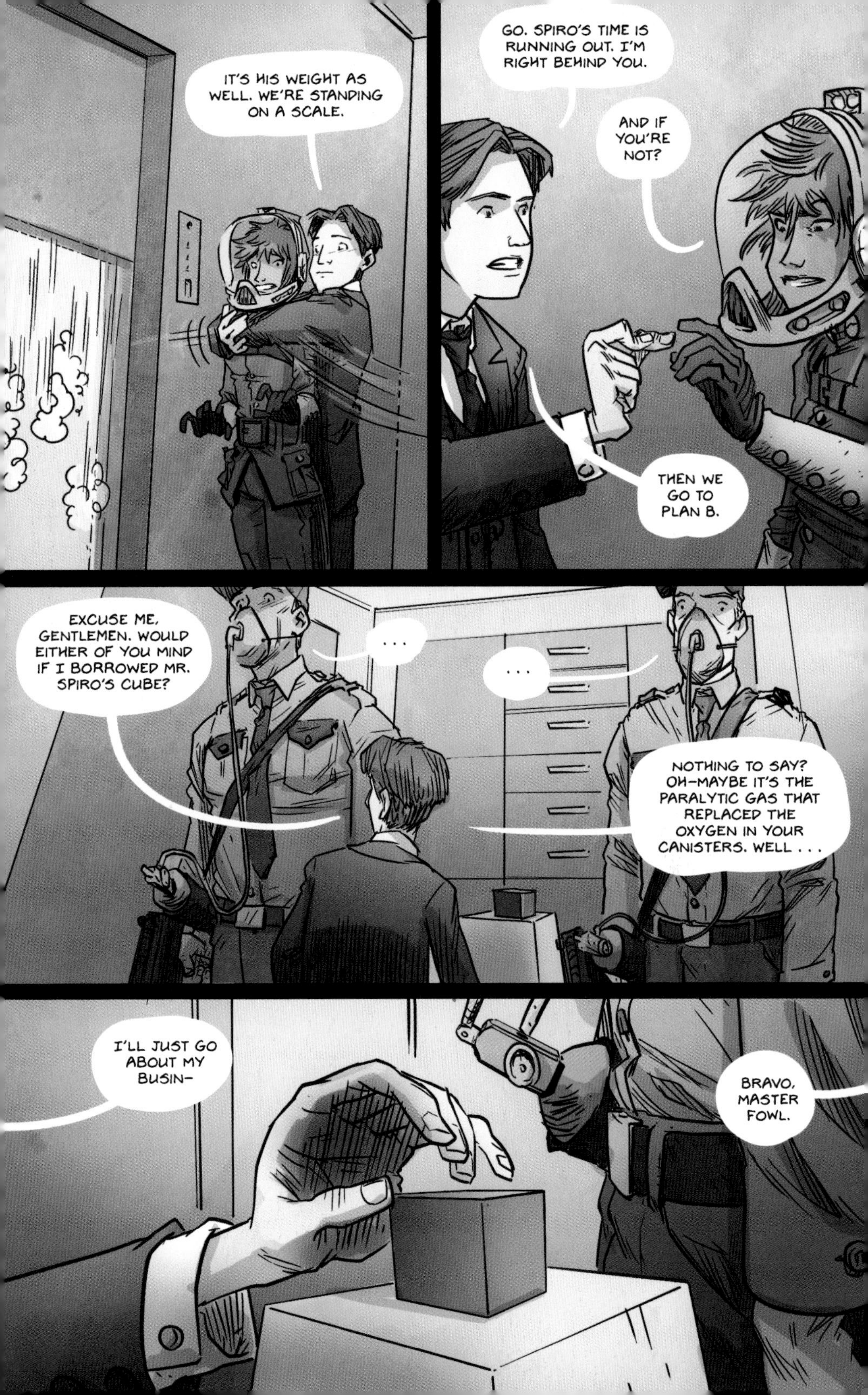
IT'S HIS WEIGHT AS WELL. WE'RE STANDING ON A SCALE.
GO. SPIRO'S TIME IS RUNNING OUT. I'M RIGHT BEHIND YOU.
AND IF YOU'RE NOT?
THEN WE GO TO PLAN B.
EXCUSE ME, GENTLEMEN. WOULD EITHER OF YOU MIND IF I BORROWED MR. SPIRO'S CUBE?
. . .
. . .
NOTHING TO SAY? OH–MAYBE IT'S THE PARALYTIC GAS THAT REPLACED THE OXYGEN IN YOUR CANISTERS. WELL . . .
I'LL JUST GO ABOUT MY BUSIN–
BRAVO, MASTER FOWL.

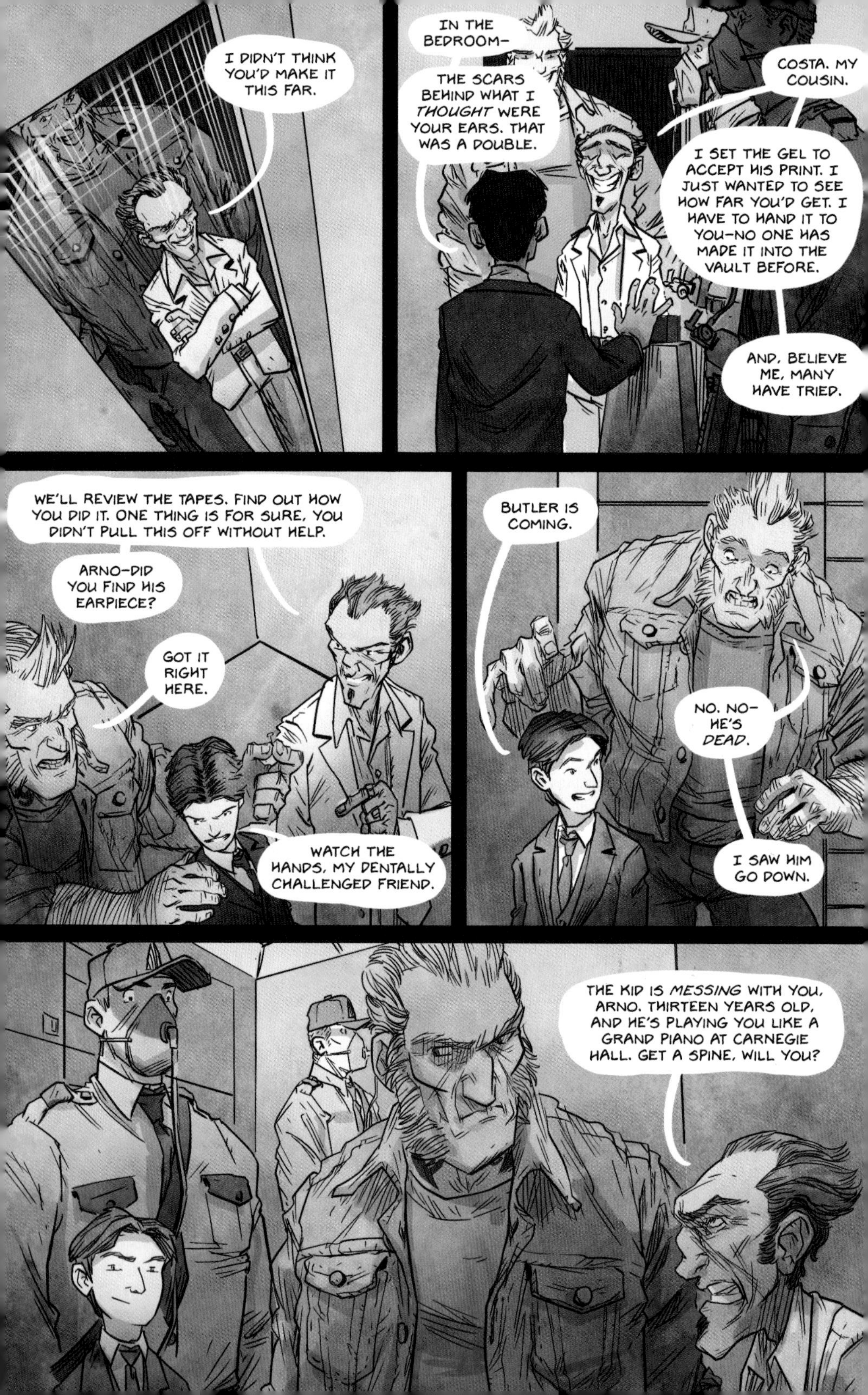
I DIDN'T THINK YOU'D MAKE IT THIS FAR.
IN THE BEDROOM—
THE SCARS BEHIND WHAT I *THOUGHT* WERE YOUR EARS. THAT WAS A DOUBLE.
COSTA. MY COUSIN.
I SET THE GEL TO ACCEPT HIS PRINT. I JUST WANTED TO SEE HOW FAR YOU'D GET. I HAVE TO HAND IT TO YOU—NO ONE HAS MADE IT INTO THE VAULT BEFORE.
AND, BELIEVE ME, MANY HAVE TRIED.
WE'LL REVIEW THE TAPES. FIND OUT HOW YOU DID IT. ONE THING IS FOR SURE, YOU DIDN'T PULL THIS OFF WITHOUT HELP.
ARNO—DID YOU FIND HIS EARPIECE?
GOT IT RIGHT HERE.
WATCH THE HANDS, MY DENTALLY CHALLENGED FRIEND.
BUTLER IS COMING.
NO. NO— HE'S *DEAD*.
I SAW HIM GO DOWN.
THE KID IS *MESSING* WITH YOU, ARNO. THIRTEEN YEARS OLD, AND HE'S PLAYING YOU LIKE A GRAND PIANO AT CARNEGIE HALL. GET A SPINE, WILL YOU?

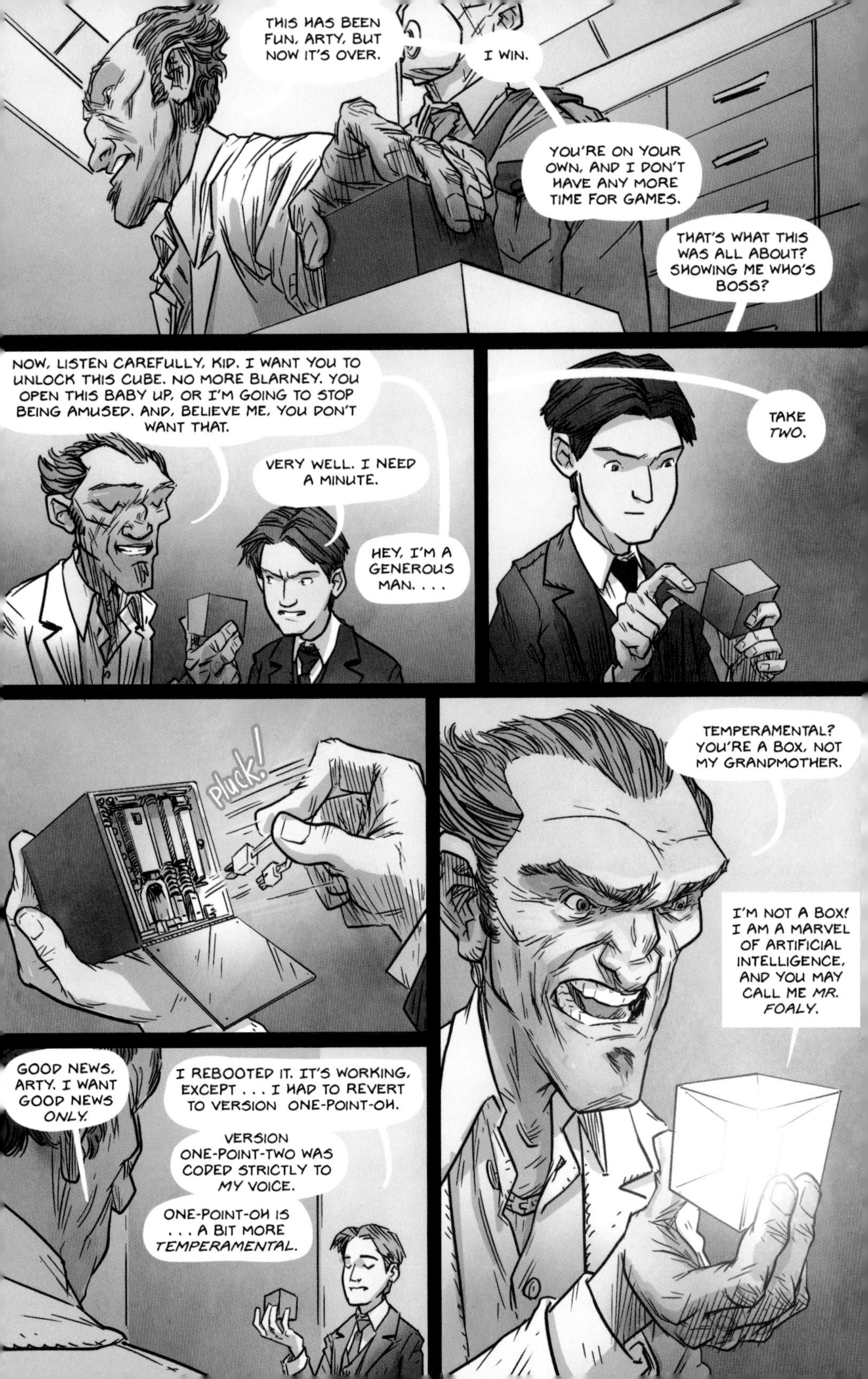
THIS HAS BEEN FUN, ARTY, BUT NOW IT'S OVER.
I WIN.
YOU'RE ON YOUR OWN, AND I DON'T HAVE ANY MORE TIME FOR GAMES.
THAT'S WHAT THIS WAS ALL ABOUT? SHOWING ME WHO'S BOSS?
NOW, LISTEN CAREFULLY, KID. I WANT YOU TO UNLOCK THIS CUBE. NO MORE BLARNEY. YOU OPEN THIS BABY UP, OR I'M GOING TO STOP BEING AMUSED. AND, BELIEVE ME, YOU DON'T WANT THAT.
VERY WELL. I NEED A MINUTE.
HEY, I'M A GENEROUS MAN. . . .
TAKE *TWO*.
pluck!
GOOD NEWS, ARTY. I WANT GOOD NEWS *ONLY*.
I REBOOTED IT. IT'S WORKING, EXCEPT . . . I HAD TO REVERT TO VERSION ONE-POINT-OH.
VERSION ONE-POINT-TWO WAS CODED STRICTLY TO *MY* VOICE.
ONE-POINT-OH IS . . . A BIT MORE *TEMPERAMENTAL*.
TEMPERAMENTAL? YOU'RE A BOX, NOT MY GRANDMOTHER.
I'M NOT A BOX! I AM A MARVEL OF ARTIFICIAL INTELLIGENCE, AND YOU MAY CALL ME *MR. FOALY*.

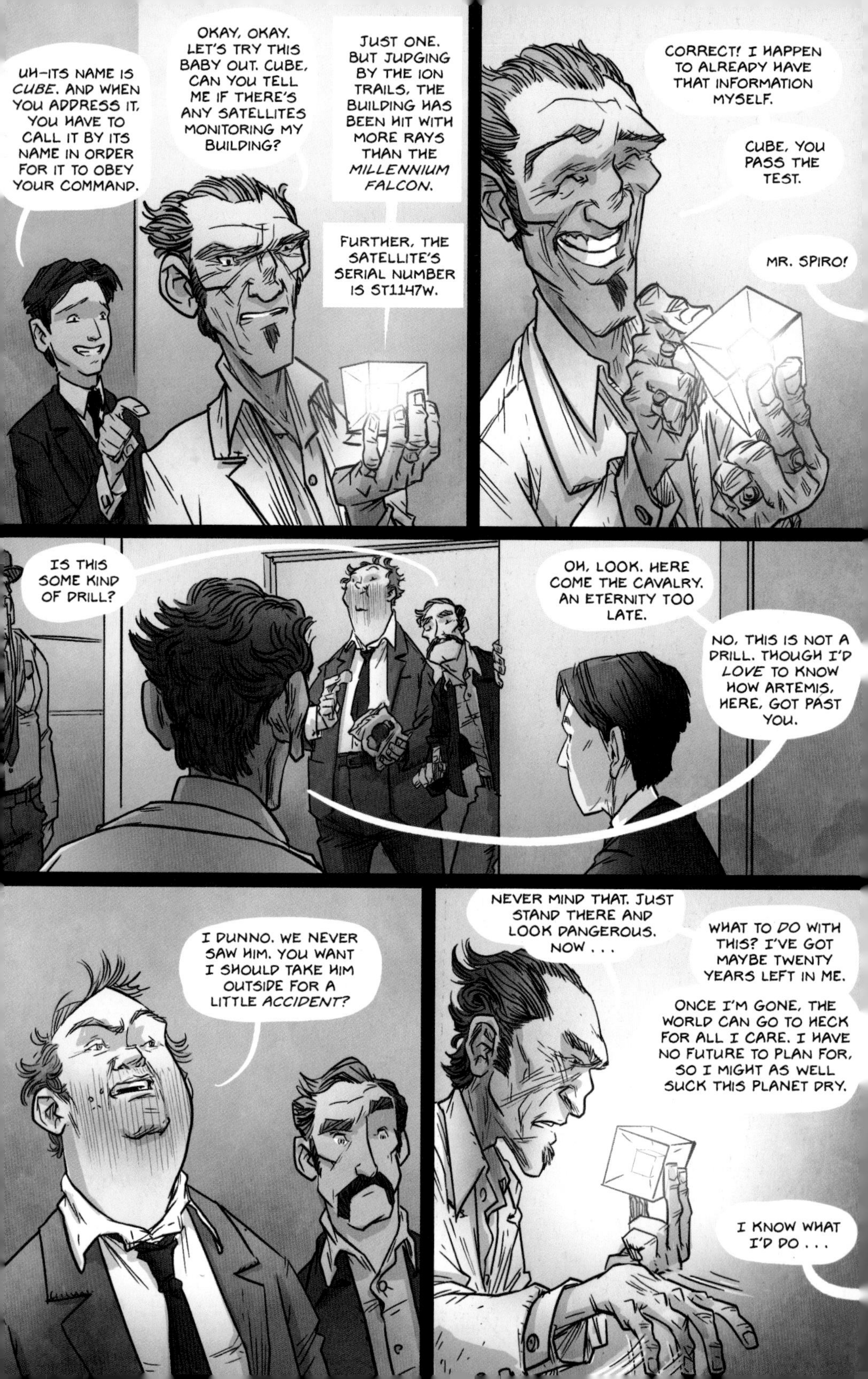
UH—ITS NAME IS *CUBE*. AND WHEN YOU ADDRESS IT, YOU HAVE TO CALL IT BY ITS NAME IN ORDER FOR IT TO OBEY YOUR COMMAND.
OKAY, OKAY. LET'S TRY THIS BABY OUT. CUBE, CAN YOU TELL ME IF THERE'S ANY SATELLITES MONITORING MY BUILDING?
JUST ONE. BUT JUDGING BY THE ION TRAILS, THE BUILDING HAS BEEN HIT WITH MORE RAYS THAN THE *MILLENNIUM FALCON*.
FURTHER, THE SATELLITE'S SERIAL NUMBER IS ST1147W.
CORRECT! I HAPPEN TO ALREADY HAVE THAT INFORMATION MYSELF.
CUBE, YOU PASS THE TEST.
MR. SPIRO!
IS THIS SOME KIND OF DRILL?
OH, LOOK. HERE COME THE CAVALRY. AN ETERNITY TOO LATE.
NO, THIS IS NOT A DRILL. THOUGH I'D *LOVE* TO KNOW HOW ARTEMIS, HERE, GOT PAST YOU.
I DUNNO. WE NEVER SAW HIM. YOU WANT I SHOULD TAKE HIM OUTSIDE FOR A LITTLE *ACCIDENT*?
NEVER MIND THAT. JUST STAND THERE AND LOOK DANGEROUS. NOW . . .
WHAT TO *DO* WITH THIS? I'VE GOT MAYBE TWENTY YEARS LEFT IN ME.
ONCE I'M GONE, THE WORLD CAN GO TO HECK FOR ALL I CARE. I HAVE NO FUTURE TO PLAN FOR, SO I MIGHT AS WELL SUCK THIS PLANET DRY.
I KNOW WHAT I'D DO . . .

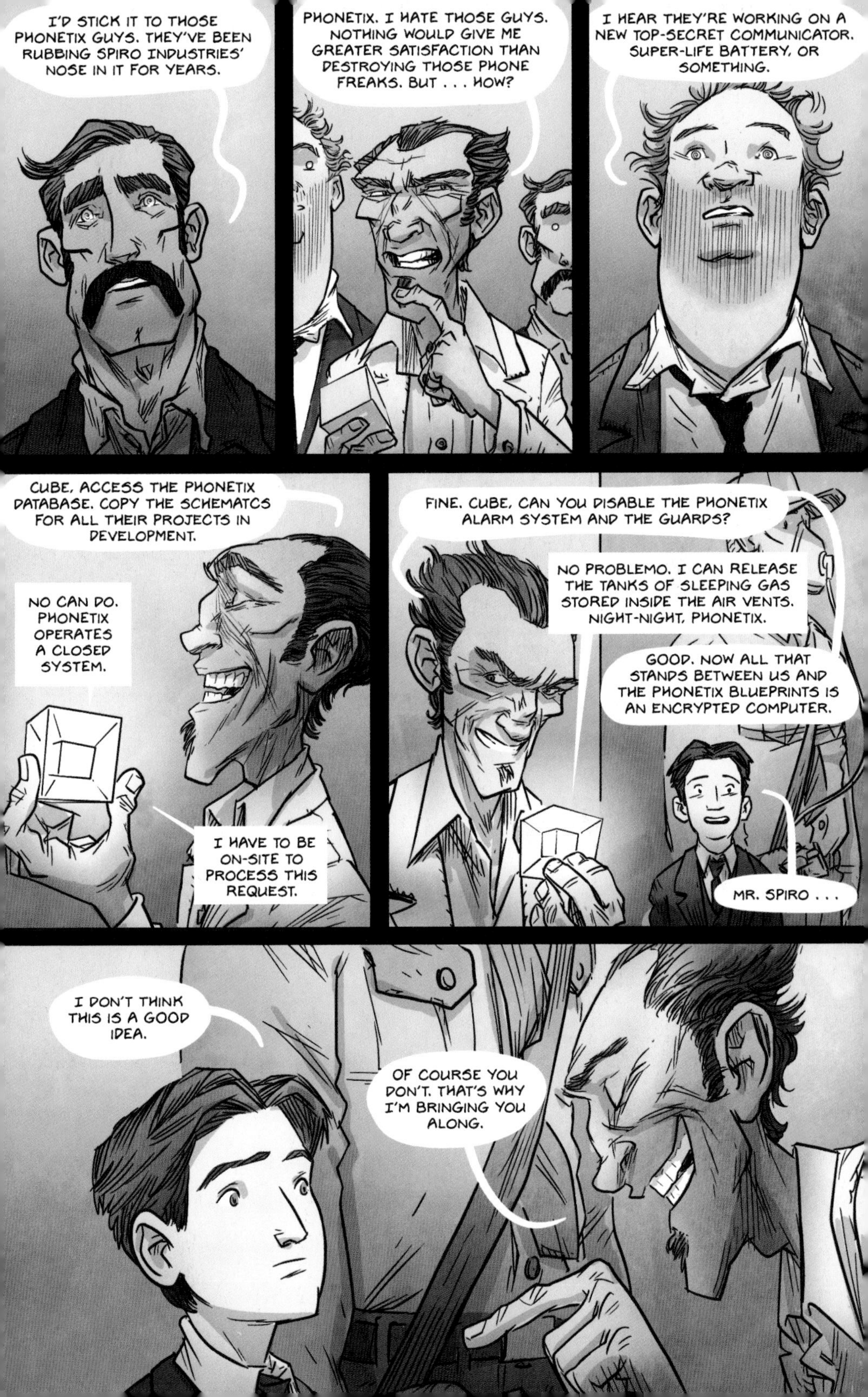
I'D STICK IT TO THOSE PHONETIX GUYS. THEY'VE BEEN RUBBING SPIRO INDUSTRIES' NOSE IN IT FOR YEARS.
PHONETIX. I HATE THOSE GUYS. NOTHING WOULD GIVE ME GREATER SATISFACTION THAN DESTROYING THOSE PHONE FREAKS. BUT . . . HOW?
I HEAR THEY'RE WORKING ON A NEW TOP-SECRET COMMUNICATOR. SUPER-LIFE BATTERY, OR SOMETHING.
CUBE, ACCESS THE PHONETIX DATABASE. COPY THE SCHEMATCS FOR ALL THEIR PROJECTS IN DEVELOPMENT.
NO CAN DO. PHONETIX OPERATES A CLOSED SYSTEM.
I HAVE TO BE ON-SITE TO PROCESS THIS REQUEST.
FINE. CUBE, CAN YOU DISABLE THE PHONETIX ALARM SYSTEM AND THE GUARDS?
NO PROBLEMO. I CAN RELEASE THE TANKS OF SLEEPING GAS STORED INSIDE THE AIR VENTS. NIGHT-NIGHT, PHONETIX.
GOOD. NOW ALL THAT STANDS BETWEEN US AND THE PHONETIX BLUEPRINTS IS AN ENCRYPTED COMPUTER.
MR. SPIRO . . .
I DON'T THINK THIS IS A GOOD IDEA.
OF COURSE YOU DON'T. THAT'S WHY I'M BRINGING YOU ALONG.

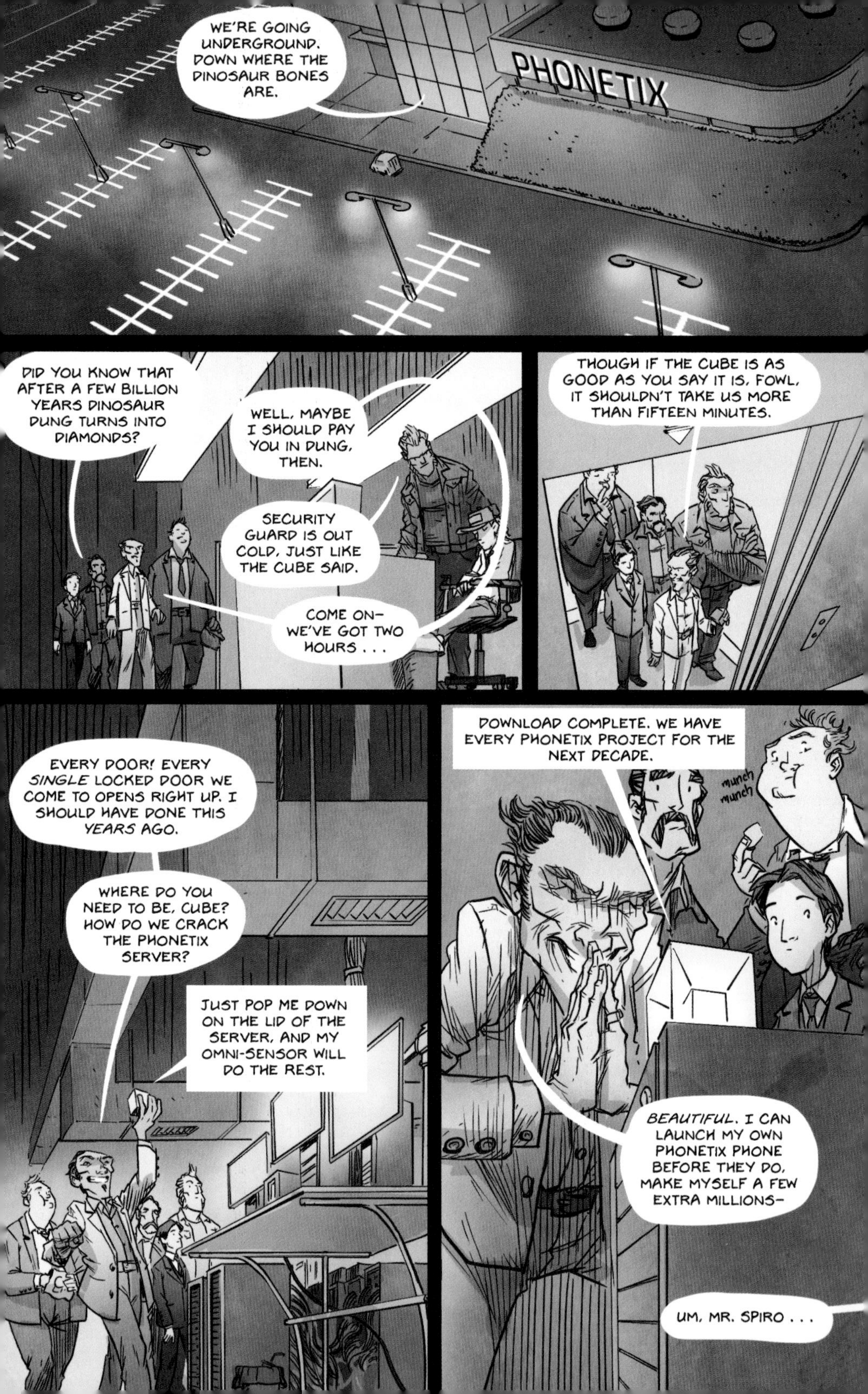
WE'RE GOING UNDERGROUND. DOWN WHERE THE DINOSAUR BONES ARE.
PHONETIX
DID YOU KNOW THAT AFTER A FEW BILLION YEARS DINOSAUR DUNG TURNS INTO DIAMONDS?
WELL, MAYBE I SHOULD PAY YOU IN DUNG, THEN.
SECURITY GUARD IS OUT COLD, JUST LIKE THE CUBE SAID.
COME ON— WE'VE GOT TWO HOURS . . .
THOUGH IF THE CUBE IS AS GOOD AS YOU SAY IT IS, FOWL, IT SHOULDN'T TAKE US MORE THAN FIFTEEN MINUTES.
EVERY DOOR! EVERY *SINGLE* LOCKED DOOR WE COME TO OPENS RIGHT UP. I SHOULD HAVE DONE THIS *YEARS* AGO.
WHERE DO YOU NEED TO BE, CUBE? HOW DO WE CRACK THE PHONETIX SERVER?
JUST POP ME DOWN ON THE LID OF THE SERVER, AND MY OMNI-SENSOR WILL DO THE REST.
DOWNLOAD COMPLETE. WE HAVE EVERY PHONETIX PROJECT FOR THE NEXT DECADE.
munch munch
BEAUTIFUL. I CAN LAUNCH MY OWN PHONETIX PHONE BEFORE THEY DO, MAKE MYSELF A FEW EXTRA MILLIONS—
UM, MR. SPIRO . . .

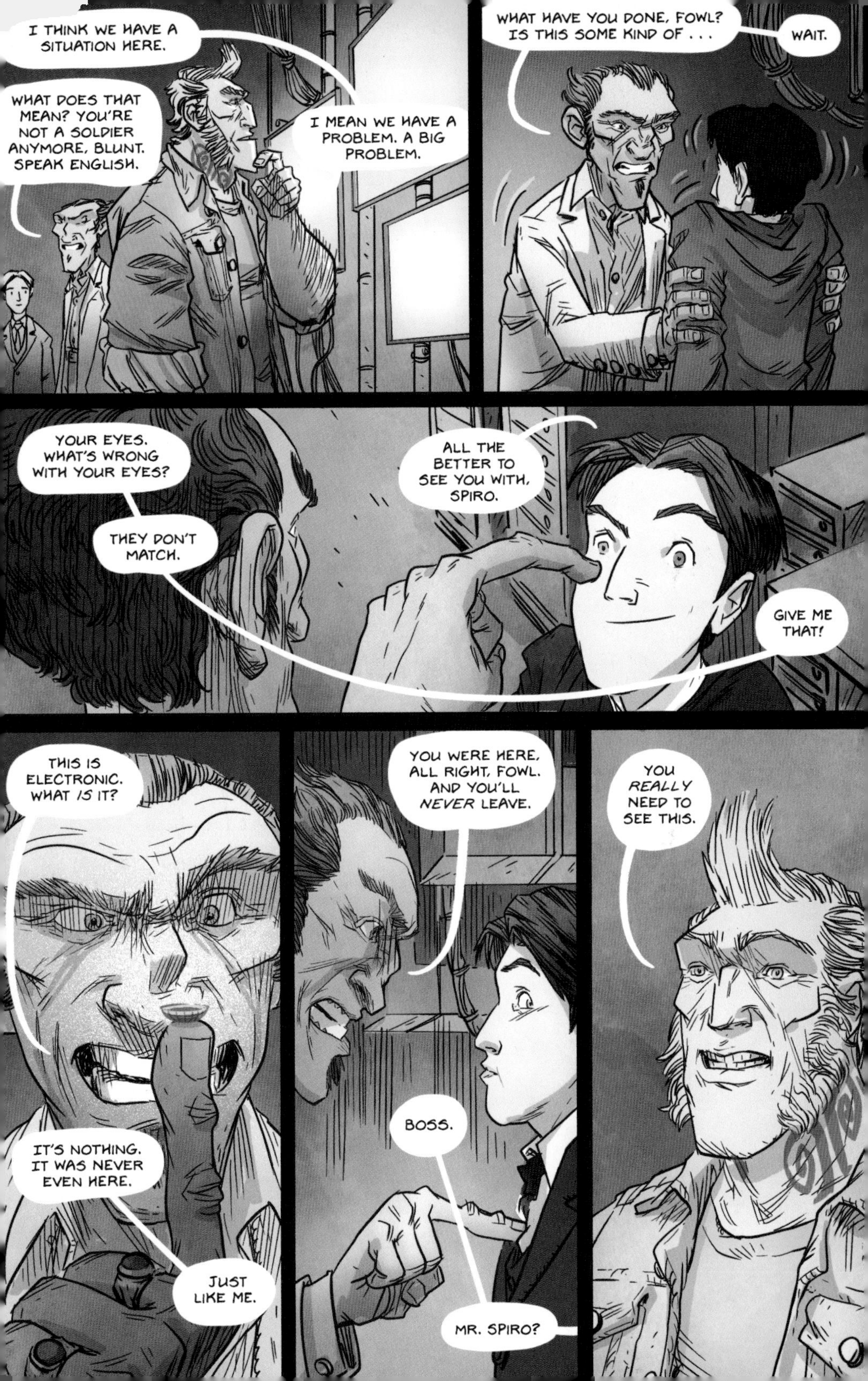
I THINK WE HAVE A SITUATION HERE.
WHAT DOES THAT MEAN? YOU'RE NOT A SOLDIER ANYMORE, BLUNT. SPEAK ENGLISH.
I MEAN WE HAVE A PROBLEM. A BIG PROBLEM.
WHAT HAVE YOU DONE, FOWL? IS THIS SOME KIND OF . . .
WAIT.
YOUR EYES. WHAT'S WRONG WITH YOUR EYES?
THEY DON'T MATCH.
ALL THE BETTER TO SEE YOU WITH, SPIRO.
GIVE ME THAT!
THIS IS ELECTRONIC. WHAT *IS* IT?
IT'S NOTHING. IT WAS NEVER EVEN HERE.
JUST LIKE ME.
YOU WERE HERE, ALL RIGHT, FOWL. AND YOU'LL *NEVER* LEAVE.
BOSS.
MR. SPIRO?
YOU *REALLY* NEED TO SEE THIS.

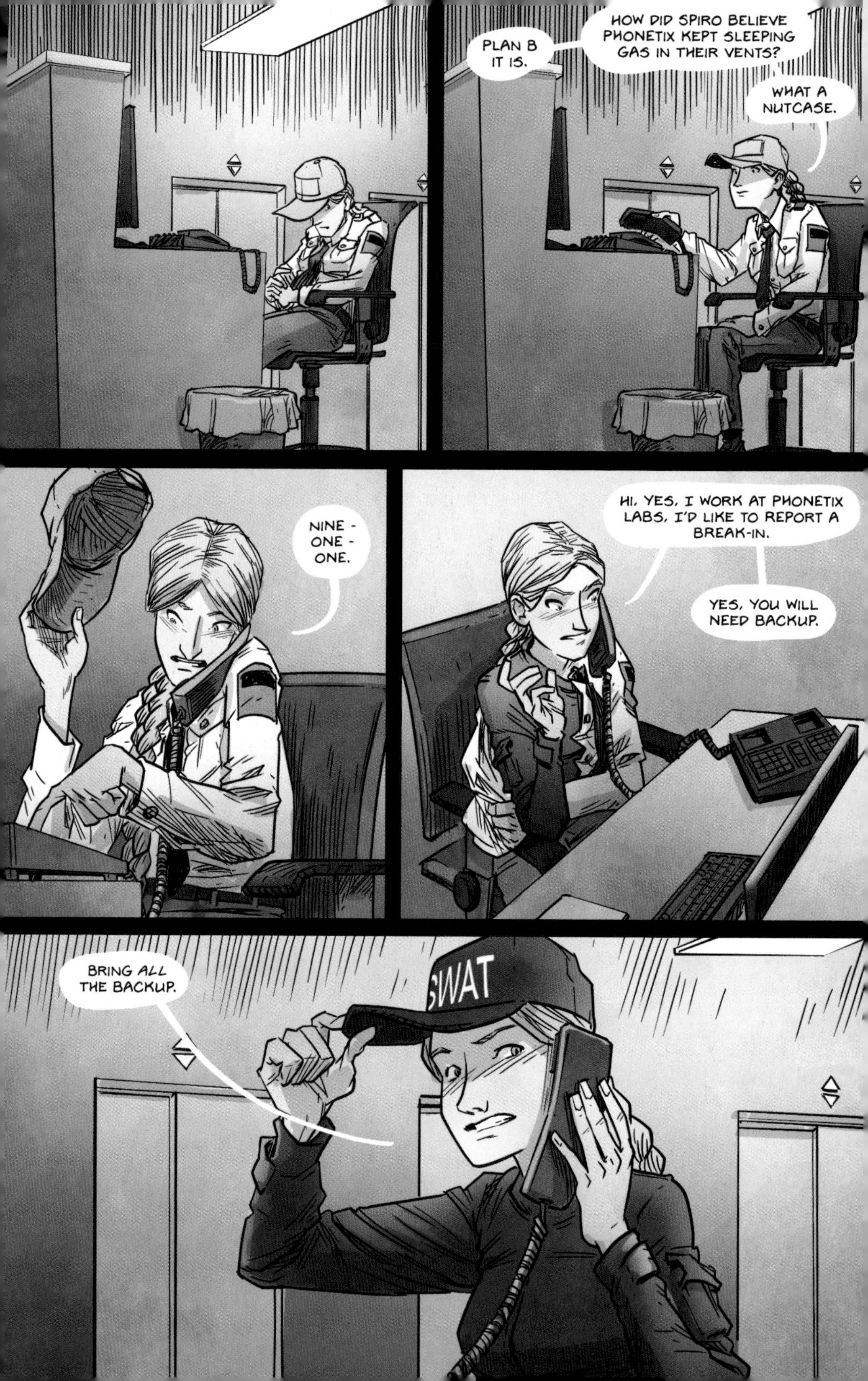
PLAN B IT IS.
HOW DID SPIRO BELIEVE PHONETIX KEPT SLEEPING GAS IN THEIR VENTS?
WHAT A NUTCASE.
NINE - ONE - ONE.
HI, YES, I WORK AT PHONETIX LABS, I'D LIKE TO REPORT A BREAK-IN.
YES, YOU WILL NEED BACKUP.
BRING ALL THE BACKUP.
SWAT

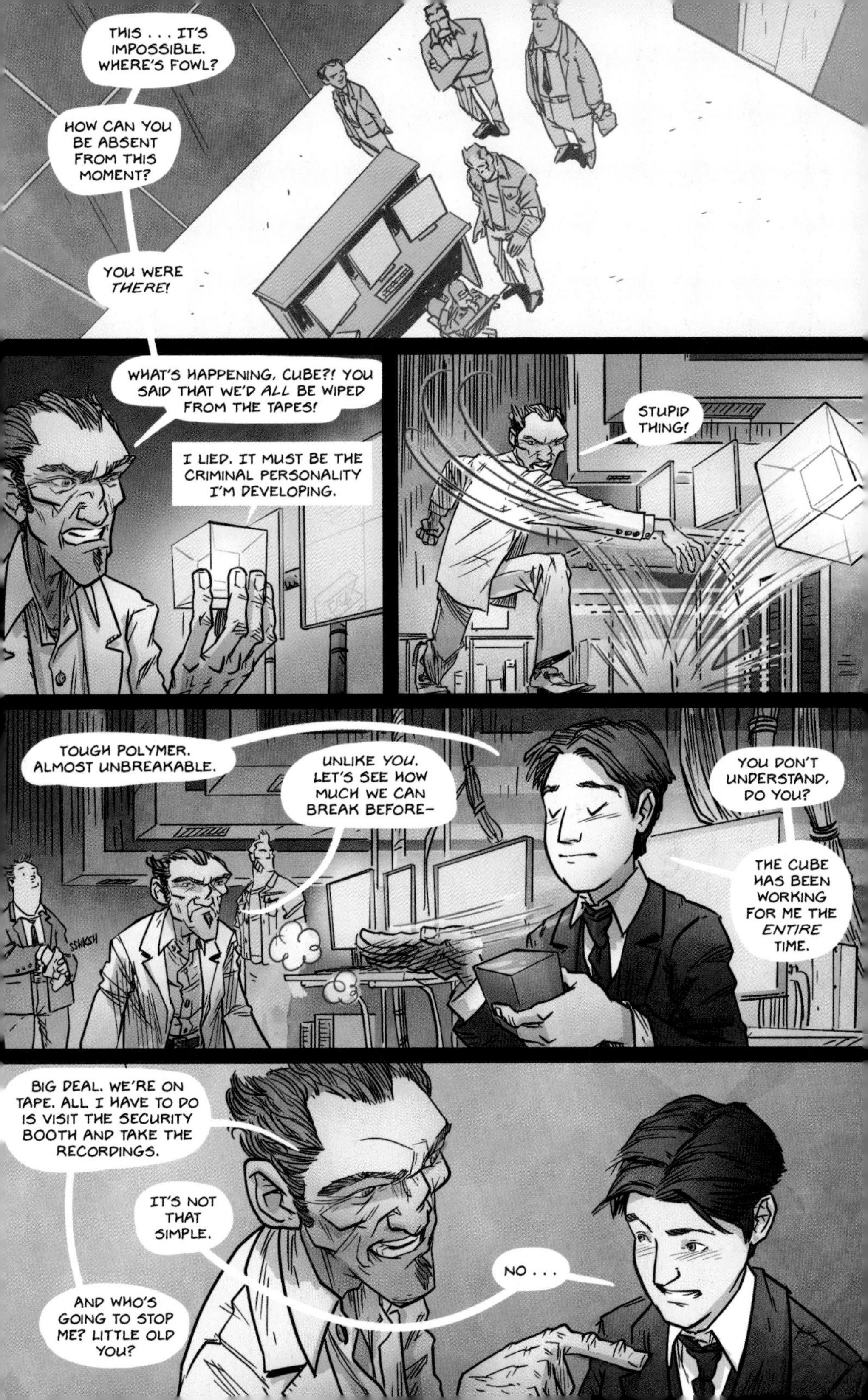
THIS . . . IT'S IMPOSSIBLE. WHERE'S FOWL?
HOW CAN YOU BE ABSENT FROM THIS MOMENT?
YOU WERE *THERE!*
WHAT'S HAPPENING, CUBE?! YOU SAID THAT WE'D *ALL* BE WIPED FROM THE TAPES!
I LIED. IT MUST BE THE CRIMINAL PERSONALITY I'M DEVELOPING.
STUPID THING!
TOUGH POLYMER. ALMOST UNBREAKABLE.
UNLIKE *YOU*. LET'S SEE HOW MUCH WE CAN BREAK BEFORE–
SSHKSH
YOU DON'T UNDERSTAND, DO YOU?
THE CUBE HAS BEEN WORKING FOR ME THE *ENTIRE* TIME.
BIG DEAL. WE'RE ON TAPE. ALL I HAVE TO DO IS VISIT THE SECURITY BOOTH AND TAKE THE RECORDINGS.
IT'S NOT THAT SIMPLE.
AND WHO'S GOING TO STOP ME? LITTLE OLD YOU?
NO . . .

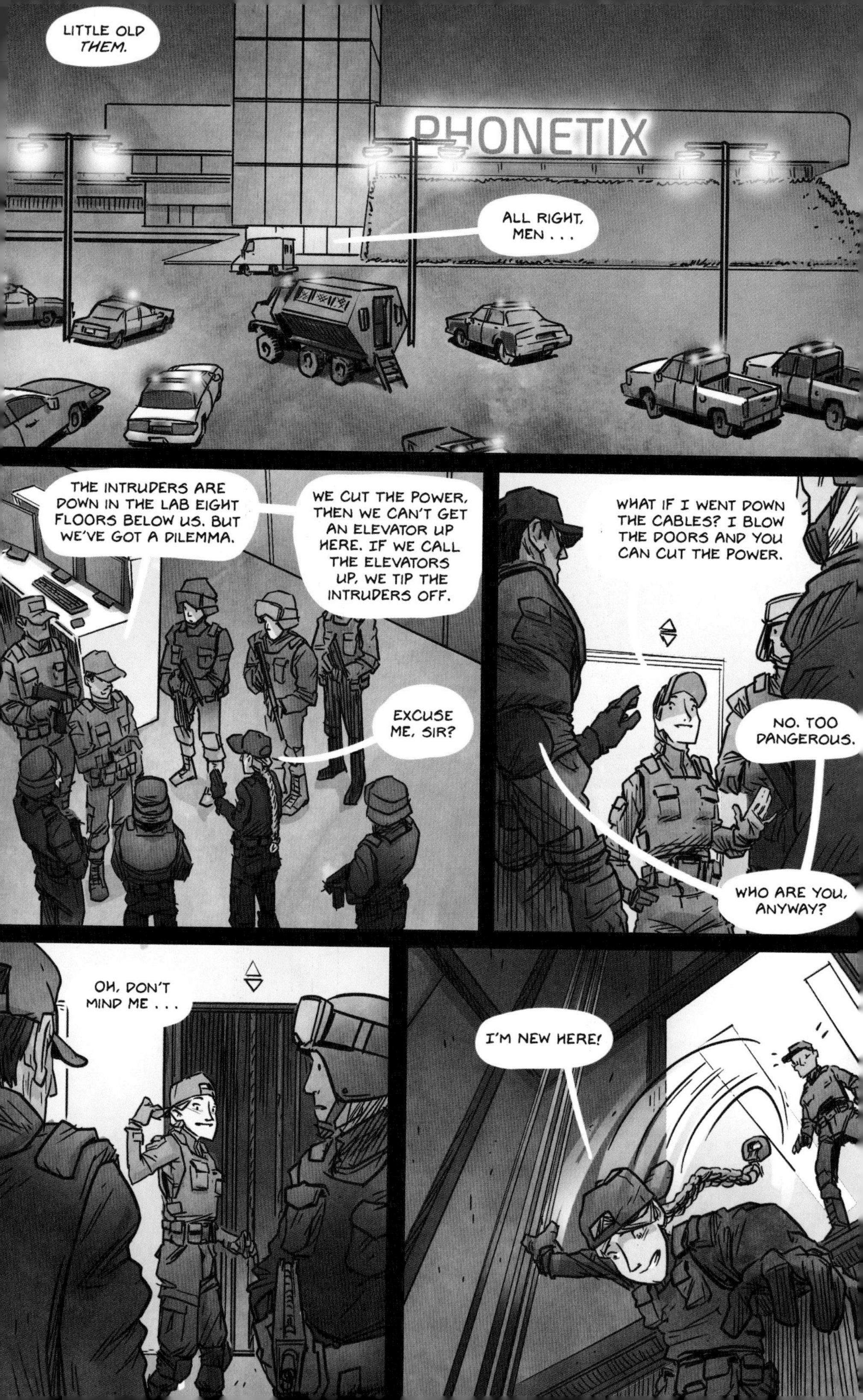
LITTLE OLD *THEM.*
PHONETIX
ALL RIGHT, MEN . . .
THE INTRUDERS ARE DOWN IN THE LAB EIGHT FLOORS BELOW US. BUT WE'VE GOT A DILEMMA.
WE CUT THE POWER, THEN WE CAN'T GET AN ELEVATOR UP HERE. IF WE CALL THE ELEVATORS UP, WE TIP THE INTRUDERS OFF.
EXCUSE ME, SIR?
WHAT IF I WENT DOWN THE CABLES? I BLOW THE DOORS AND YOU CAN CUT THE POWER.
NO. TOO DANGEROUS.
WHO ARE YOU, ANYWAY?
OH, DON'T MIND ME . . .
I'M NEW HERE!

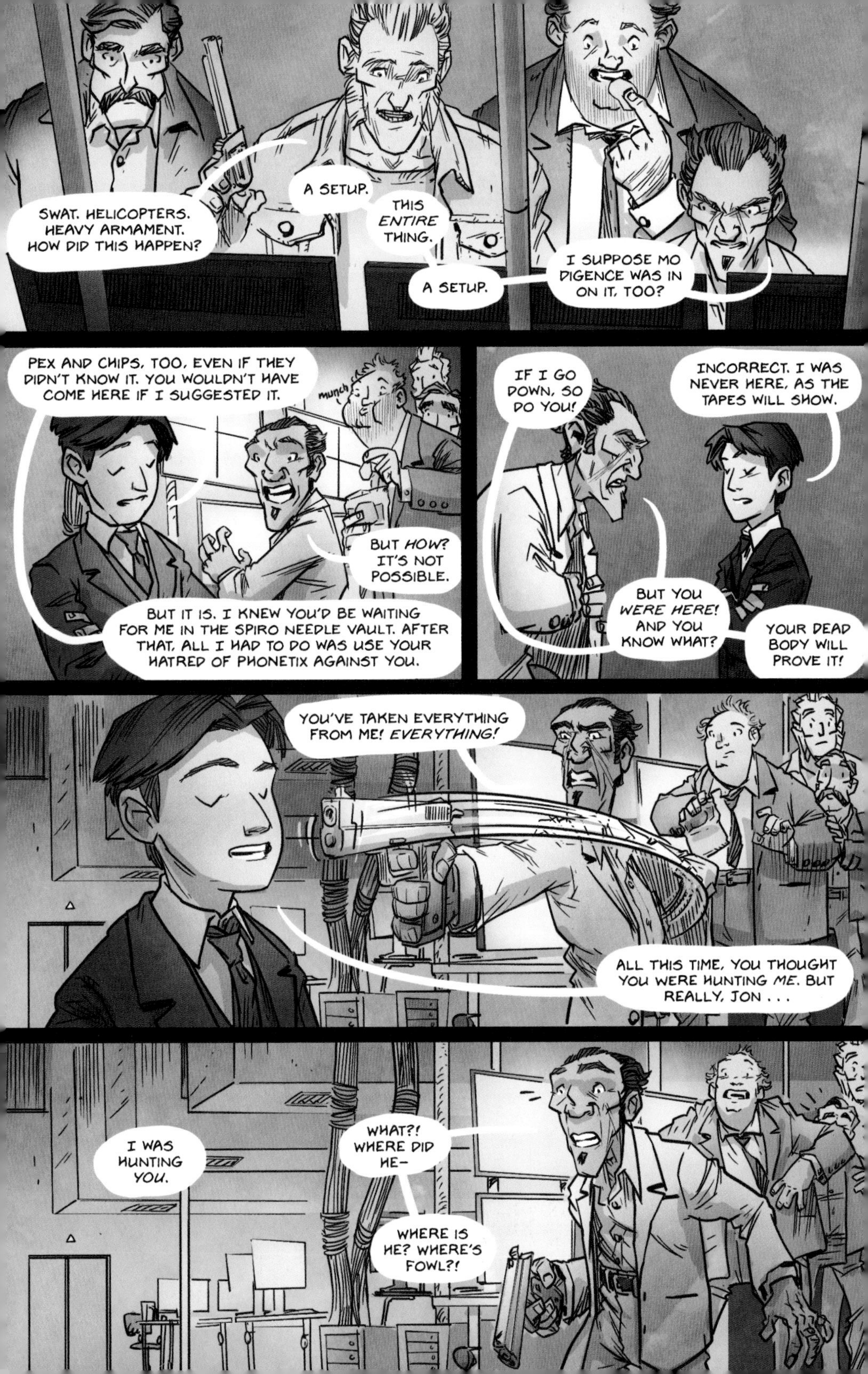
SWAT. HELICOPTERS. HEAVY ARMAMENT. HOW DID THIS HAPPEN?
A SETUP.
THIS *ENTIRE* THING.
A SETUP.
I SUPPOSE MO DIGENCE WAS IN ON IT, TOO?
PEX AND CHIPS, TOO, EVEN IF THEY DIDN'T KNOW IT. YOU WOULDN'T HAVE COME HERE IF I SUGGESTED IT.
munch
BUT *HOW*? IT'S NOT POSSIBLE.
BUT IT IS. I KNEW YOU'D BE WAITING FOR ME IN THE SPIRO NEEDLE VAULT. AFTER THAT, ALL I HAD TO DO WAS USE YOUR HATRED OF PHONETIX AGAINST YOU.
IF I GO DOWN, SO DO YOU!
INCORRECT. I WAS NEVER HERE, AS THE TAPES WILL SHOW.
BUT YOU *WERE HERE*! AND YOU KNOW WHAT?
YOUR DEAD BODY WILL PROVE IT!
YOU'VE TAKEN EVERYTHING FROM ME! *EVERYTHING!*
ALL THIS TIME, YOU THOUGHT YOU WERE HUNTING *ME*. BUT REALLY, JON . . .
I WAS HUNTING *YOU*.
WHAT?! WHERE DID HE–
WHERE IS HE? WHERE'S FOWL?!

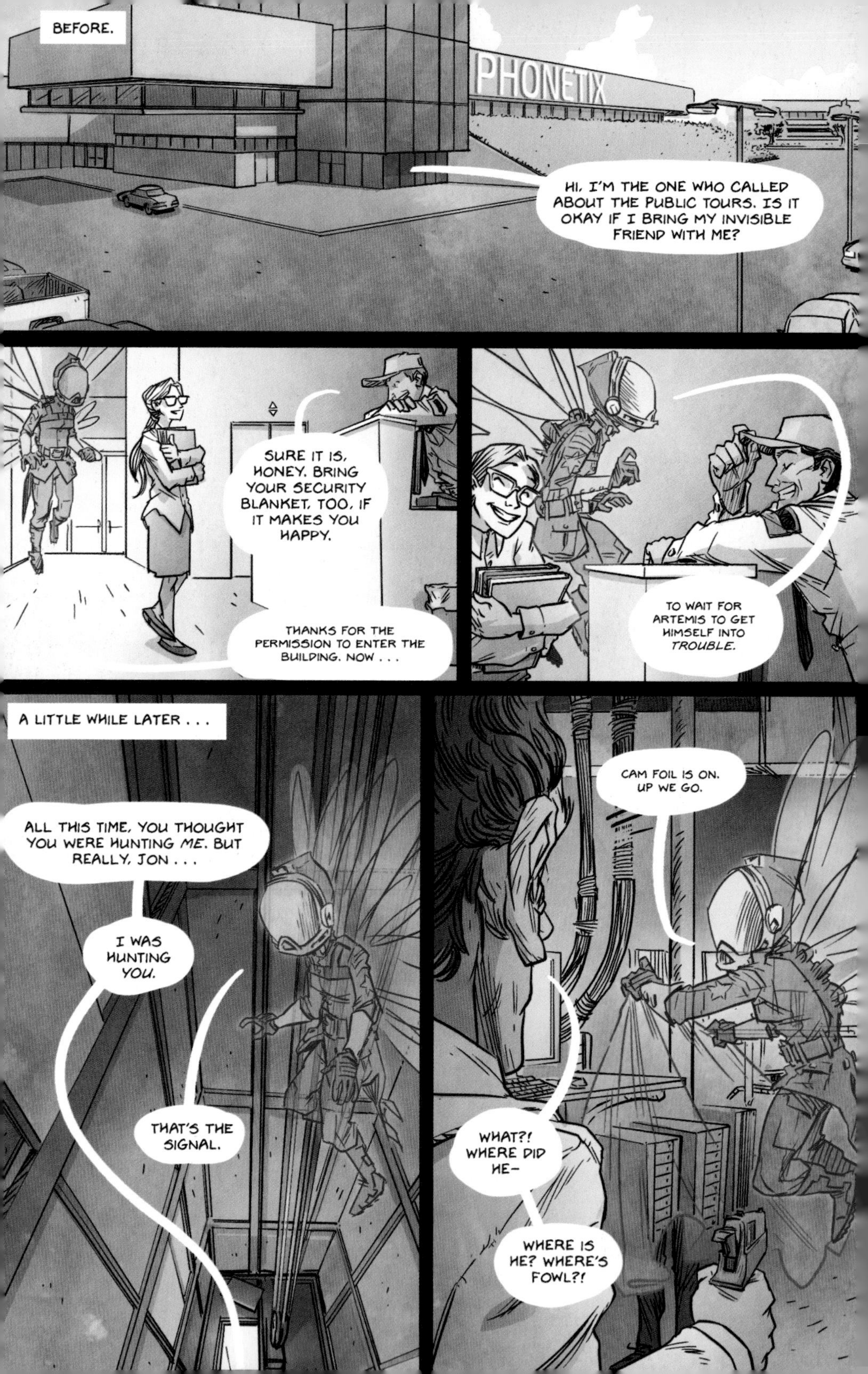
BEFORE.
PHONETIX
HI, I'M THE ONE WHO CALLED ABOUT THE PUBLIC TOURS. IS IT OKAY IF I BRING MY INVISIBLE FRIEND WITH ME?
SURE IT IS, HONEY. BRING YOUR SECURITY BLANKET, TOO, IF IT MAKES YOU HAPPY.
THANKS FOR THE PERMISSION TO ENTER THE BUILDING. NOW . . .
TO WAIT FOR ARTEMIS TO GET HIMSELF INTO *TROUBLE.*
A LITTLE WHILE LATER . . .
ALL THIS TIME, YOU THOUGHT YOU WERE HUNTING *ME*. BUT REALLY, JON . . .
I WAS HUNTING *YOU.*
THAT'S THE SIGNAL.
CAM FOIL IS ON. UP WE GO.
WHAT?! WHERE DID HE–
WHERE IS HE? WHERE'S FOWL?!

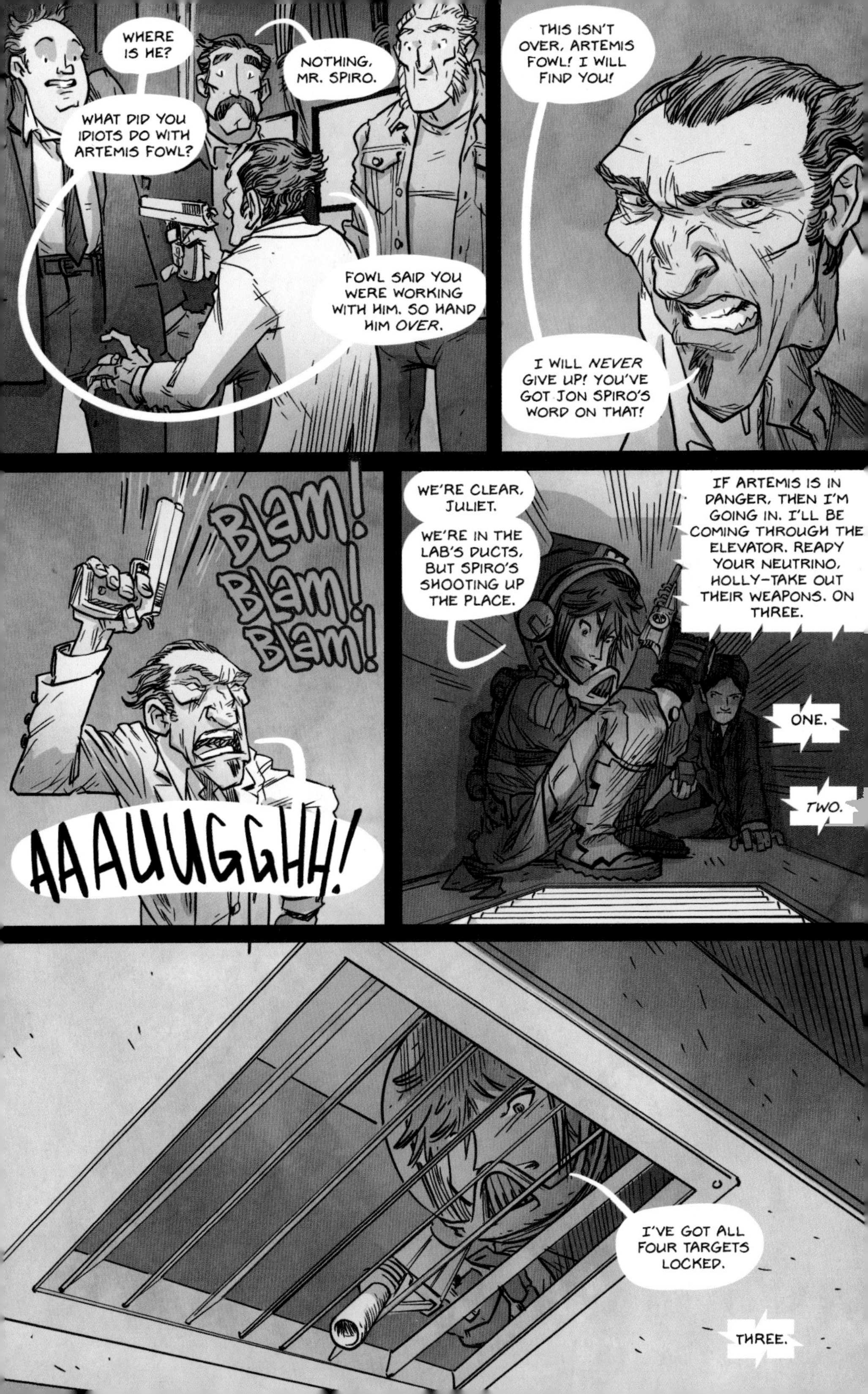
WHERE IS HE?
WHAT DID YOU IDIOTS DO WITH ARTEMIS FOWL?
NOTHING, MR. SPIRO.
FOWL SAID YOU WERE WORKING WITH HIM. SO HAND HIM *OVER*.
THIS ISN'T OVER, ARTEMIS FOWL! I WILL FIND YOU!
I WILL *NEVER* GIVE UP! YOU'VE GOT JON SPIRO'S WORD ON THAT!
BLAM! BLAM! BLAM!
AAAUUGGHH!
WE'RE CLEAR, JULIET.
WE'RE IN THE LAB'S DUCTS, BUT SPIRO'S SHOOTING UP THE PLACE.
IF ARTEMIS IS IN DANGER, THEN I'M GOING IN. I'LL BE COMING THROUGH THE ELEVATOR. READY YOUR NEUTRINO, HOLLY—TAKE OUT THEIR WEAPONS. ON THREE.
ONE.
TWO.
I'VE GOT ALL FOUR TARGETS LOCKED.
THREE.

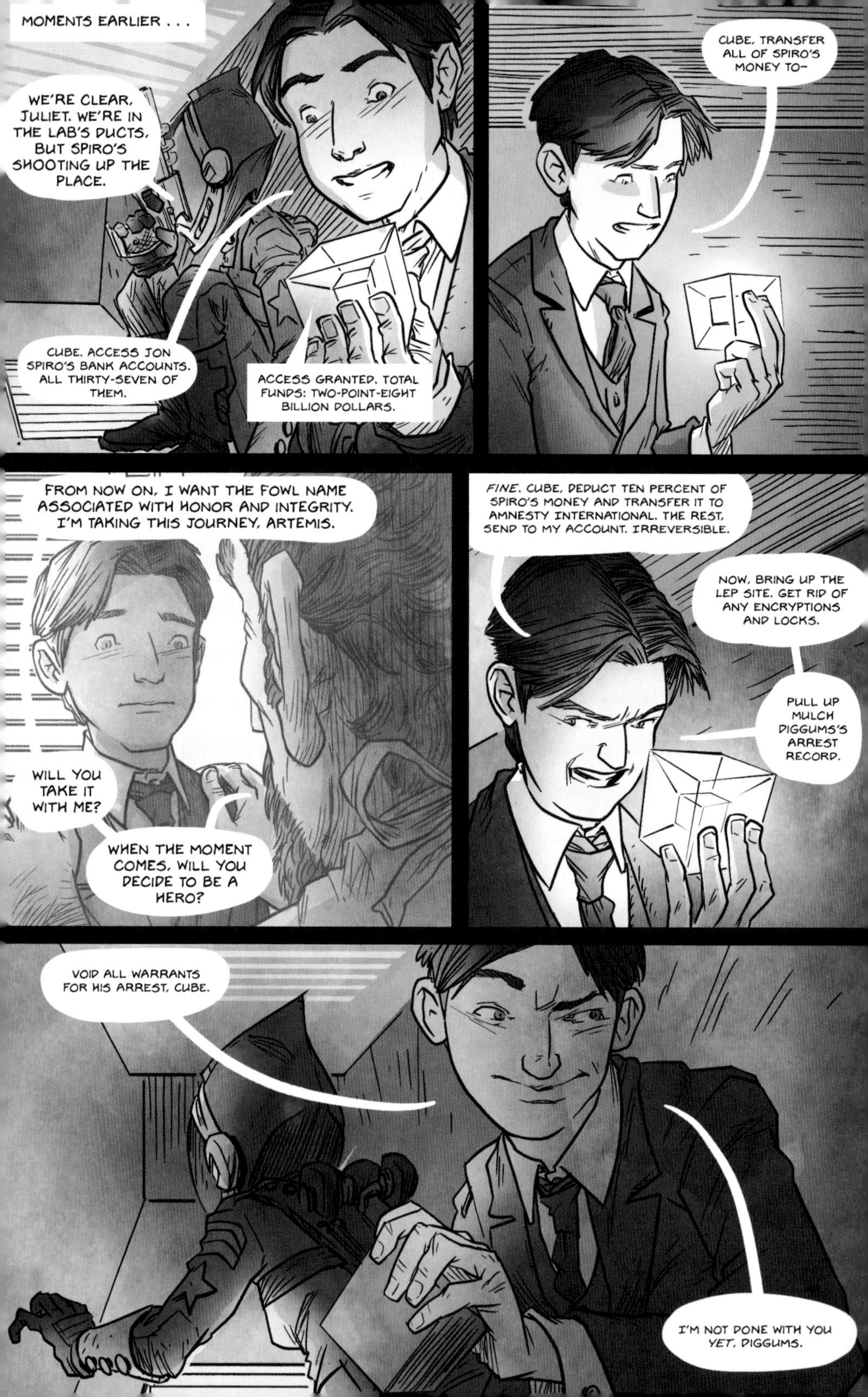
MOMENTS EARLIER . . .
WE'RE CLEAR, JULIET. WE'RE IN THE LAB'S DUCTS, BUT SPIRO'S SHOOTING UP THE PLACE.
CUBE. ACCESS JON SPIRO'S BANK ACCOUNTS. ALL THIRTY-SEVEN OF THEM.
ACCESS GRANTED. TOTAL FUNDS: TWO-POINT-EIGHT BILLION DOLLARS.
CUBE, TRANSFER ALL OF SPIRO'S MONEY TO–
FROM NOW ON, I WANT THE FOWL NAME ASSOCIATED WITH HONOR AND INTEGRITY. I'M TAKING THIS JOURNEY, ARTEMIS.
WILL YOU TAKE IT WITH ME?
WHEN THE MOMENT COMES, WILL YOU DECIDE TO BE A HERO?
FINE. CUBE, DEDUCT TEN PERCENT OF SPIRO'S MONEY AND TRANSFER IT TO AMNESTY INTERNATIONAL. THE REST, SEND TO MY ACCOUNT. IRREVERSIBLE.
NOW, BRING UP THE LEP SITE. GET RID OF ANY ENCRYPTIONS AND LOCKS.
PULL UP MULCH DIGGUMS'S ARREST RECORD.
VOID ALL WARRANTS FOR HIS ARREST, CUBE.
I'M NOT DONE WITH YOU *YET*, DIGGUMS.

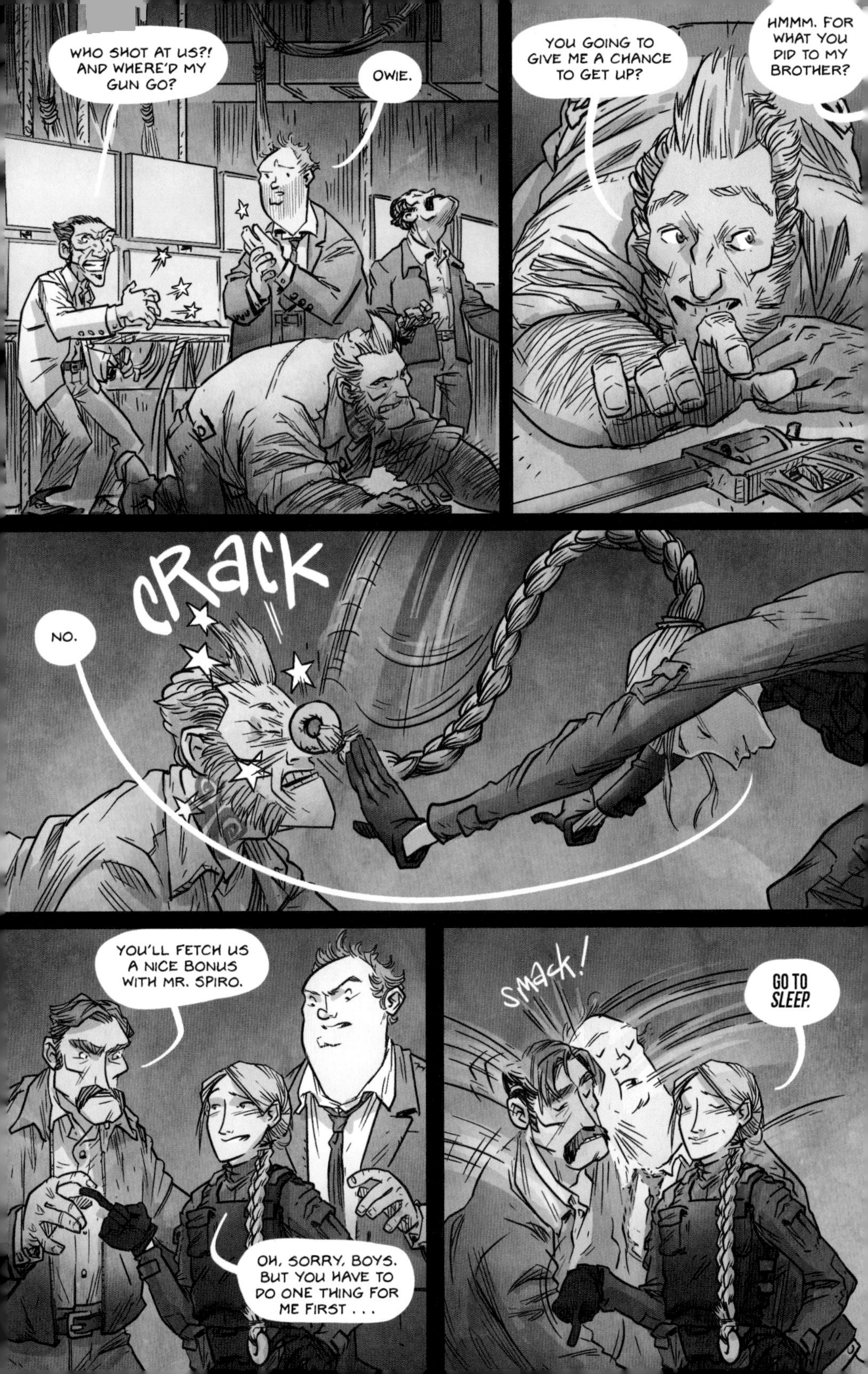
WHO SHOT AT US?! AND WHERE'D MY GUN GO?
OWIE.
YOU GOING TO GIVE ME A CHANCE TO GET UP?
HMMM. FOR WHAT YOU DID TO MY BROTHER?
CRACK
NO.
YOU'LL FETCH US A NICE BONUS WITH MR. SPIRO.
OH, SORRY, BOYS. BUT YOU HAVE TO DO ONE THING FOR ME FIRST . . .
SMACK!
GO TO SLEEP.

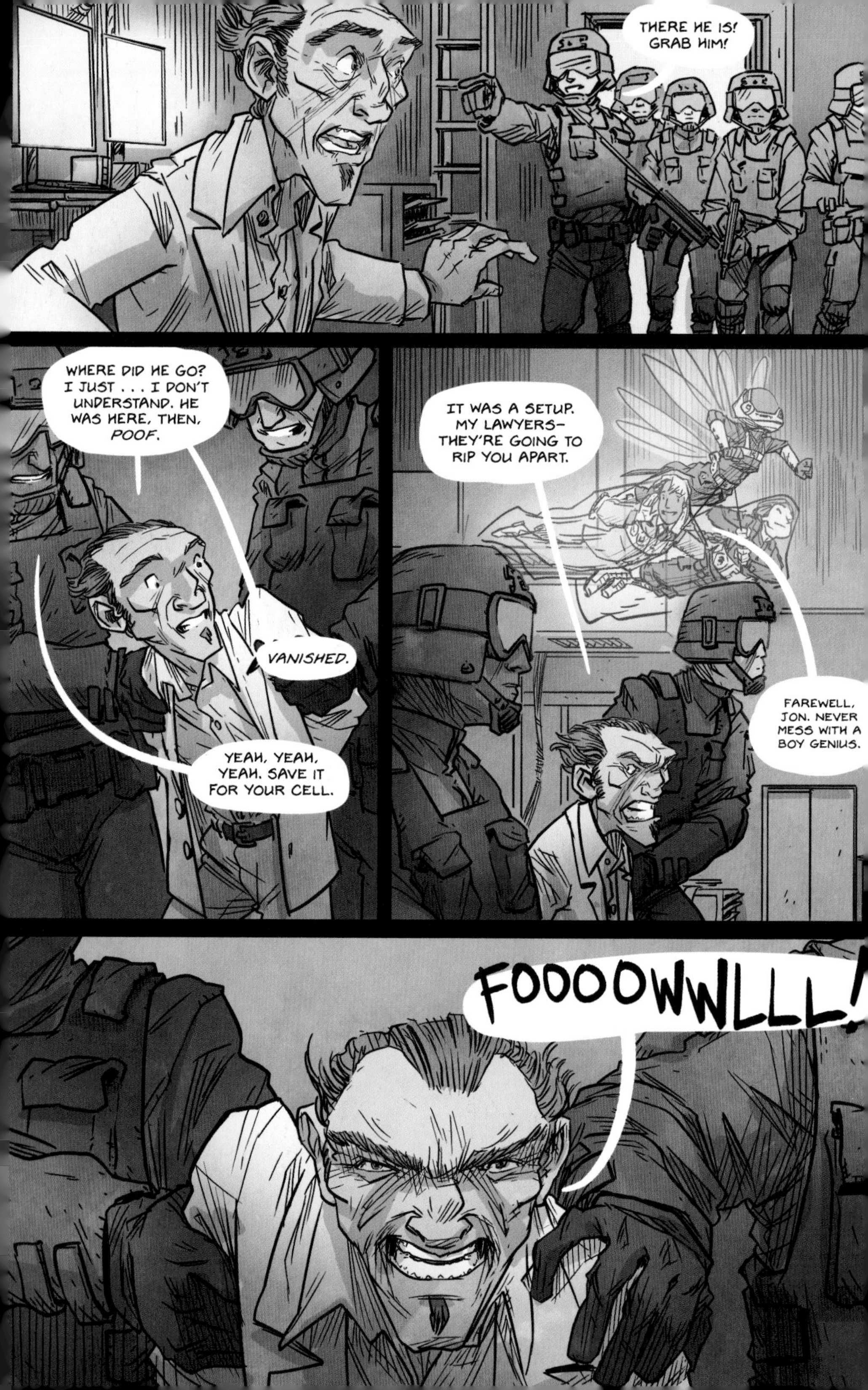
THERE HE IS! GRAB HIM!
WHERE DID HE GO? I JUST . . . I DON'T UNDERSTAND. HE WAS HERE, THEN, *POOF*.
VANISHED.
YEAH, YEAH, YEAH. SAVE IT FOR YOUR CELL.
IT WAS A SETUP. MY LAWYERS— THEY'RE GOING TO RIP YOU APART.
FAREWELL, JON. NEVER MESS WITH A BOY GENIUS.
FOOOOWWLLL!

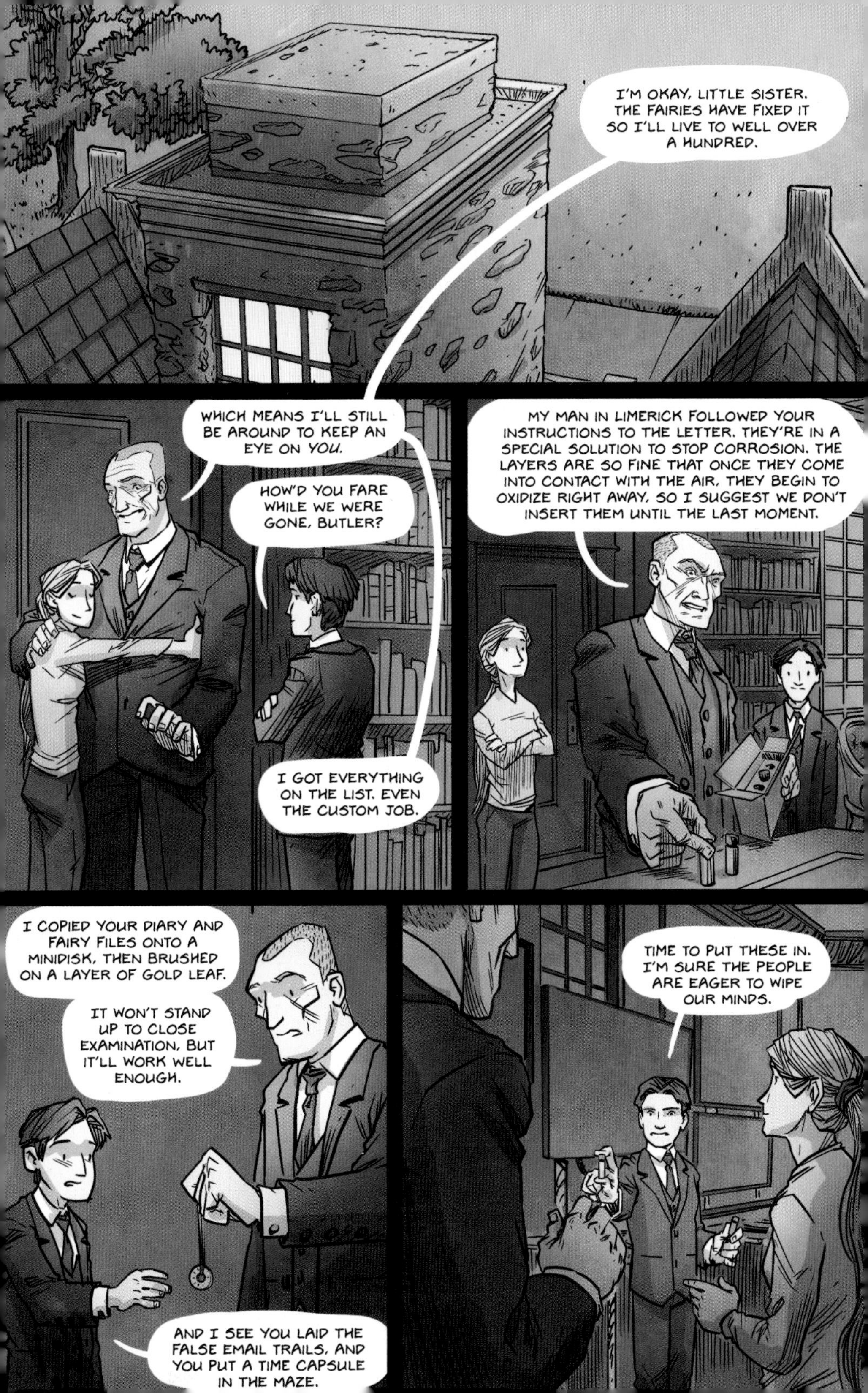

I'M OKAY, LITTLE SISTER. THE FAIRIES HAVE FIXED IT SO I'LL LIVE TO WELL OVER A HUNDRED.
WHICH MEANS I'LL STILL BE AROUND TO KEEP AN EYE ON *YOU*.
HOW'D YOU FARE WHILE WE WERE GONE, BUTLER?
I GOT EVERYTHING ON THE LIST. EVEN THE CUSTOM JOB.
MY MAN IN LIMERICK FOLLOWED YOUR INSTRUCTIONS TO THE LETTER. THEY'RE IN A SPECIAL SOLUTION TO STOP CORROSION. THE LAYERS ARE SO FINE THAT ONCE THEY COME INTO CONTACT WITH THE AIR, THEY BEGIN TO OXIDIZE RIGHT AWAY, SO I SUGGEST WE DON'T INSERT THEM UNTIL THE LAST MOMENT.
I COPIED YOUR DIARY AND FAIRY FILES ONTO A MINIDISK, THEN BRUSHED ON A LAYER OF GOLD LEAF.
IT WON'T STAND UP TO CLOSE EXAMINATION, BUT IT'LL WORK WELL ENOUGH.
AND I SEE YOU LAID THE FALSE EMAIL TRAILS, AND YOU PUT A TIME CAPSULE IN THE MAZE.
TIME TO PUT THESE IN. I'M SURE THE PEOPLE ARE EAGER TO WIPE OUR MINDS.

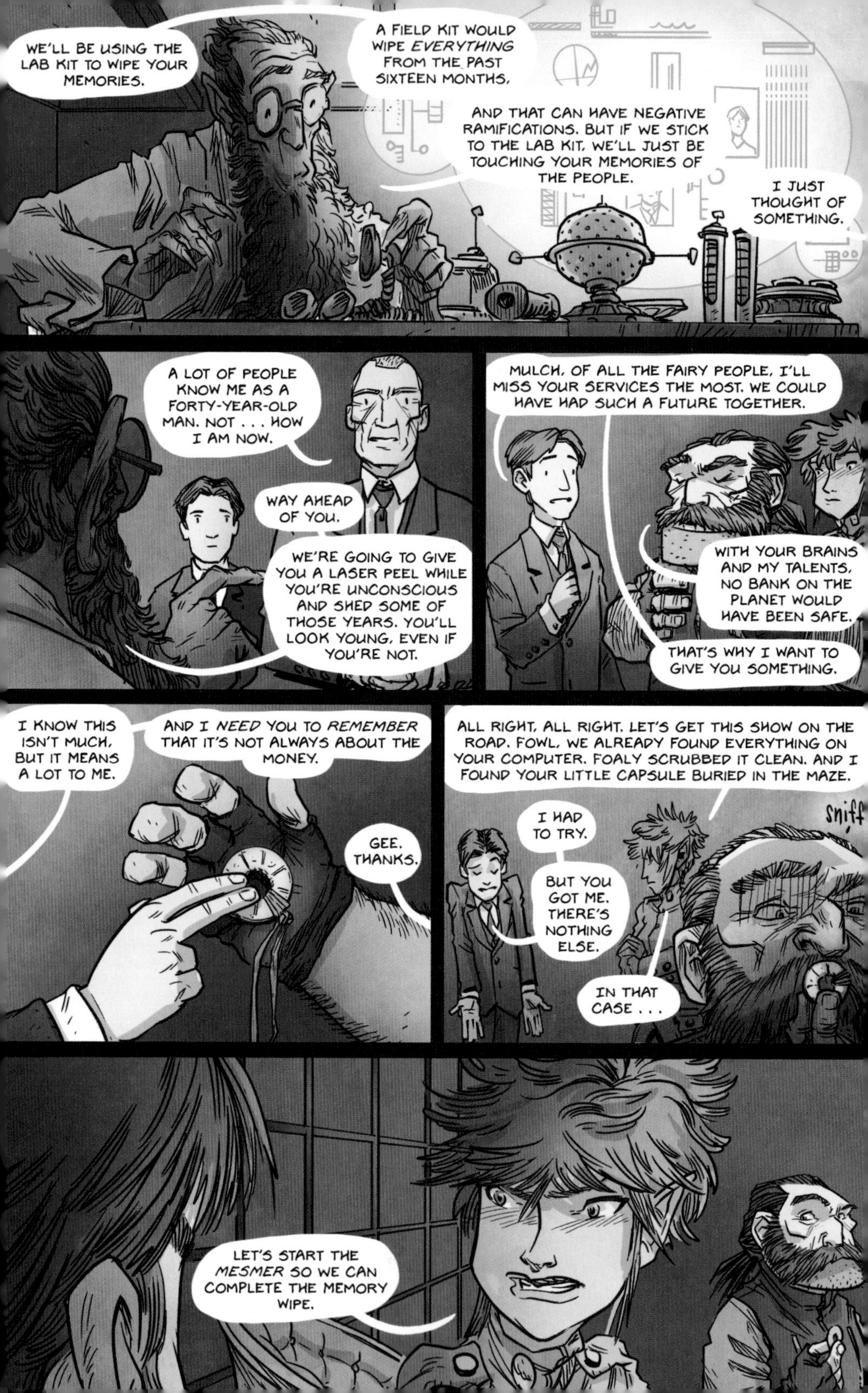

WE'LL BE USING THE LAB KIT TO WIPE YOUR MEMORIES.
A FIELD KIT WOULD WIPE *EVERYTHING* FROM THE PAST SIXTEEN MONTHS,
AND THAT CAN HAVE NEGATIVE RAMIFICATIONS. BUT IF WE STICK TO THE LAB KIT, WE'LL JUST BE TOUCHING YOUR MEMORIES OF THE PEOPLE.
I JUST THOUGHT OF SOMETHING.
A LOT OF PEOPLE KNOW ME AS A FORTY-YEAR-OLD MAN. NOT . . . HOW I AM NOW.
WAY AHEAD OF YOU.
WE'RE GOING TO GIVE YOU A LASER PEEL WHILE YOU'RE UNCONSCIOUS AND SHED SOME OF THOSE YEARS. YOU'LL LOOK YOUNG, EVEN IF YOU'RE NOT.
MULCH, OF ALL THE FAIRY PEOPLE, I'LL MISS YOUR SERVICES THE MOST. WE COULD HAVE HAD SUCH A FUTURE TOGETHER.
WITH YOUR BRAINS AND MY TALENTS, NO BANK ON THE PLANET WOULD HAVE BEEN SAFE.
THAT'S WHY I WANT TO GIVE YOU SOMETHING.
I KNOW THIS ISN'T MUCH, BUT IT MEANS A LOT TO ME.
AND I *NEED* YOU TO *REMEMBER* THAT IT'S NOT ALWAYS ABOUT THE MONEY.
GEE. THANKS.
ALL RIGHT, ALL RIGHT. LET'S GET THIS SHOW ON THE ROAD. FOWL, WE ALREADY FOUND EVERYTHING ON YOUR COMPUTER. FOALY SCRUBBED IT CLEAN. AND I FOUND YOUR LITTLE CAPSULE BURIED IN THE MAZE.
SNIFF
I HAD TO TRY.
BUT YOU GOT ME. THERE'S NOTHING ELSE.
IN THAT CASE . . .
LET'S START THE *MESMER* SO WE CAN COMPLETE THE MEMORY WIPE.

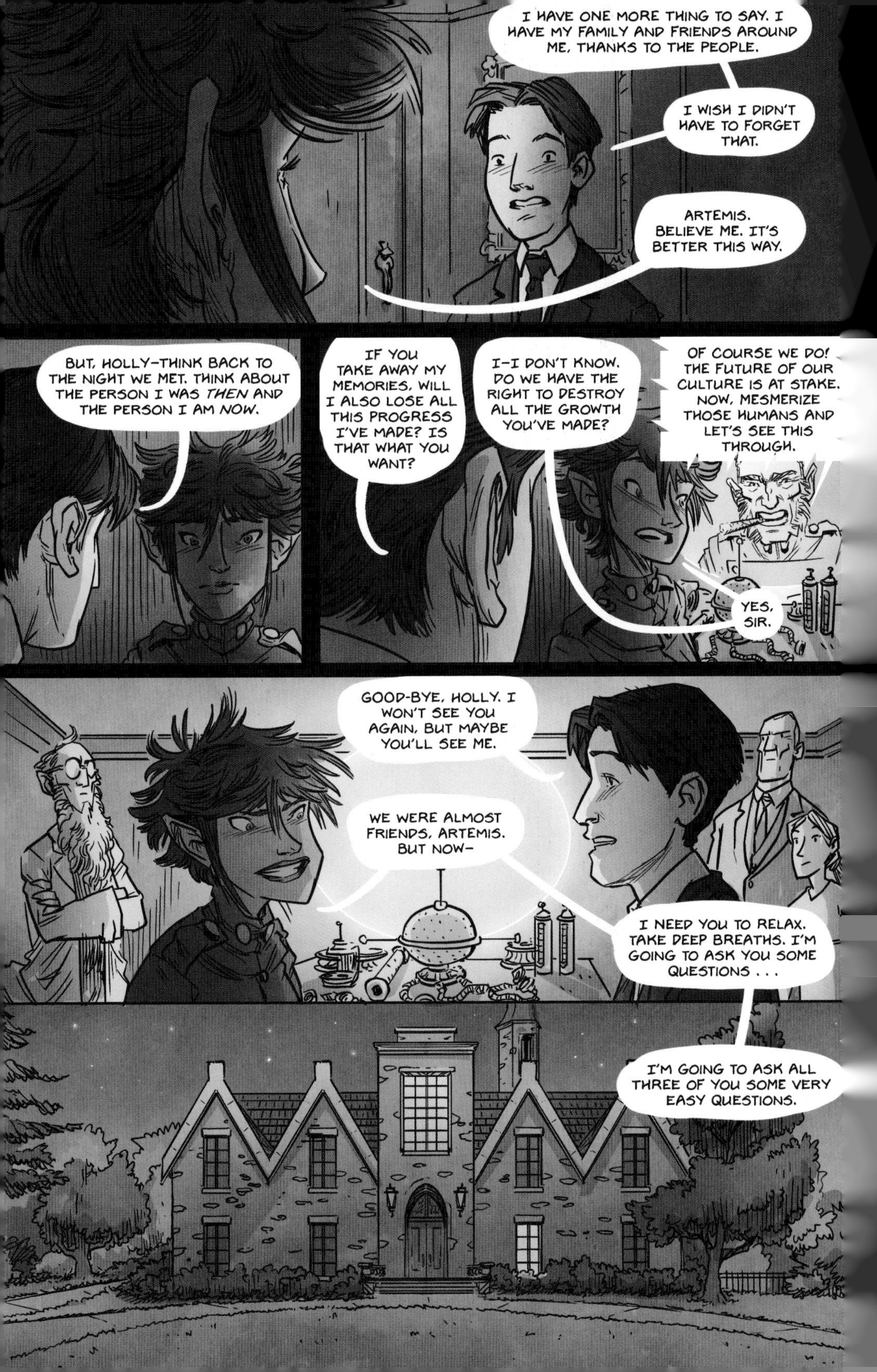
I HAVE ONE MORE THING TO SAY. I HAVE MY FAMILY AND FRIENDS AROUND ME, THANKS TO THE PEOPLE.
I WISH I DIDN'T HAVE TO FORGET THAT.
ARTEMIS. BELIEVE ME. IT'S BETTER THIS WAY.
BUT, HOLLY–THINK BACK TO THE NIGHT WE MET. THINK ABOUT THE PERSON I WAS *THEN* AND THE PERSON I AM *NOW*.
IF YOU TAKE AWAY MY MEMORIES, WILL I ALSO LOSE ALL THIS PROGRESS I'VE MADE? IS THAT WHAT YOU WANT?
I–I DON'T KNOW. DO WE HAVE THE RIGHT TO DESTROY ALL THE GROWTH YOU'VE MADE?
OF COURSE WE DO! THE FUTURE OF OUR CULTURE IS AT STAKE. NOW, MESMERIZE THOSE HUMANS AND LET'S SEE THIS THROUGH.
YES, SIR.
GOOD-BYE, HOLLY. I WON'T SEE YOU AGAIN, BUT MAYBE YOU'LL SEE ME.
WE WERE ALMOST FRIENDS, ARTEMIS. BUT NOW–
I NEED YOU TO RELAX. TAKE DEEP BREATHS. I'M GOING TO ASK YOU SOME QUESTIONS . . .
I'M GOING TO ASK ALL THREE OF YOU SOME VERY EASY QUESTIONS.

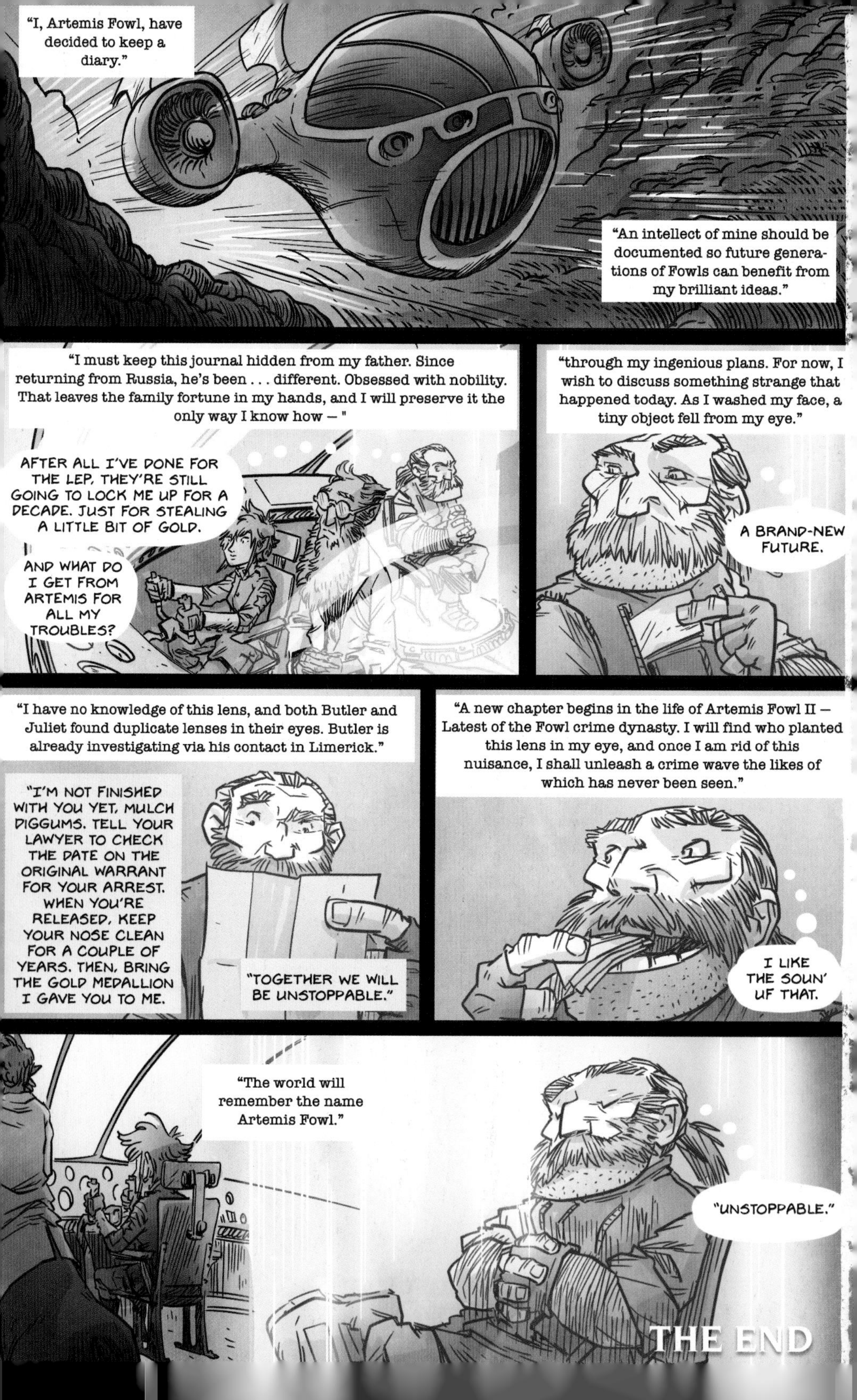
"I, Artemis Fowl, have decided to keep a diary."
"An intellect of mine should be documented so future generations of Fowls can benefit from my brilliant ideas."
"I must keep this journal hidden from my father. Since returning from Russia, he's been . . . different. Obsessed with nobility. That leaves the family fortune in my hands, and I will preserve it the only way I know how — "
AFTER ALL I'VE DONE FOR THE LEP, THEY'RE STILL GOING TO LOCK ME UP FOR A DECADE. JUST FOR STEALING A LITTLE BIT OF GOLD.
AND WHAT DO I GET FROM ARTEMIS FOR ALL MY TROUBLES?
"through my ingenious plans. For now, I wish to discuss something strange that happened today. As I washed my face, a tiny object fell from my eye."
A BRAND-NEW FUTURE.
"I have no knowledge of this lens, and both Butler and Juliet found duplicate lenses in their eyes. Butler is already investigating via his contact in Limerick."
"I'M NOT FINISHED WITH YOU YET, MULCH DIGGUMS. TELL YOUR LAWYER TO CHECK THE DATE ON THE ORIGINAL WARRANT FOR YOUR ARREST. WHEN YOU'RE RELEASED, KEEP YOUR NOSE CLEAN FOR A COUPLE OF YEARS. THEN, BRING THE GOLD MEDALLION I GAVE YOU TO ME.
"TOGETHER WE WILL BE UNSTOPPABLE."
"A new chapter begins in the life of Artemis Fowl II — Latest of the Fowl crime dynasty. I will find who planted this lens in my eye, and once I am rid of this nuisance, I shall unleash a crime wave the likes of which has never been seen."
I LIKE THE SOUN' UF THAT.
"The world will remember the name Artemis Fowl."
"UNSTOPPABLE."
THE END